Summers at the Saint

SUMMERS AT THE SAINT

MARY KAY ANDREWS

ST. MARTIN'S PRESS

New York

First published in the United States by St. Martin's Press, an imprint of St. Martin's Publishing Group

SUMMERS AT THE SAINT. Copyright © 2024 by Whodunnit, Inc. All rights reserved. Printed in the United States of America. For information, address St. Martin's Publishing Group, 120 Broadway, New York, NY 10271.

www.stmartins.com

Designed by Donna Sinisgalli Noetzel

The Library of Congress Cataloging-in-Publication Data is available upon request.

ISBN 978-1-250-27838-8 (hardcover)
ISBN 978-1-250-36115-8 (international, sold outside the U.S., subject to rights availability)
ISBN 978-1-250-27839-5 (ebook)

Our books may be purchased in bulk for promotional, educational, or business use. Please contact your local bookseller or the Macmillan Corporate and Premium Sales Department at 1-800-221-7945, extension 5442, or by email at MacmillanSpecialMarkets@macmillan.com.

First U.S. Edition: 2024
First International Edition: 2024

10 9 8 7 6 5 4 3 2 1

For my starter husband, Tom. We promised to grow old together, and it looks like, by Gawd, we did it.

PROLOGUE

* * *

The first time Traci Eddings saw the Saint she was six or seven. It was an early summer morning, and she was with her grandfather, in his twelve-foot aluminum fishing boat, drifting along in the river, when she glimpsed the improbable pink turrets and crenelated towers rising up from the fog-shrouded marsh, like something out of one of her storybooks.

"Pops, look!" She pointed at the apparition. "It's a fairy castle."

Her grandfather would only have been in his early fifties back then, but he already seemed ancient, bent and beat down from all those years working on the loading dock at the paper bag plant over in Bonaventure.

He'd been studying the red-and-white bobber he'd cast out a few minutes earlier, letting it float along on the river's placid gray-green surface.

Pops looked up now and flicked half an inch of ash from his ever-present Marlboro into the water.

"Why, honey. That's just the Saint. No fairies. Just a whole lot of rich people."

"I want to go there," Traci wheedled, knowing that this was surely a place of enchantment. "Please, Pops, can we?"

His weathered face softened, but only for an instant. "Afraid not. People like us don't belong over there."

He'd quickly changed the subject, pointing at the ripples surrounding the bobber. "Look there, doodlebug," he whispered. "You got a fish on the line." He handed her the slender rod with the Zebco spinning reel. "Now you wait 'til he takes that bobber down a little bit more, then you pull back and reel that bad boy on in here. Can you do that?"

But her eyes were still fixed on the pink wedding-cake-looking building, and by the time she turned her attention back to the bobber, the line had gone slack, and Pops was shaking his head in disappointment.

The first time she actually stepped onto the property came when she was thirteen, and Meredith, a new girl from school, invited just eight girls to join her for a birthday party to be held at the Saint. Traci had been surprised to be included and dismayed that Shannon, her best friend, had not.

"I don't want to go to that rich bitch's party anyway," Shannon had claimed, tossing her long tresses, which she'd recently begun highlighting with a bottle of Miss Clairol that she'd shoplifted from the CVS.

Traci had felt torn between loyalty to her best friend and the excitement of finally experiencing the Saint. In the end, the lure of the pink castle, which is how she still secretly thought of it, won out.

She'd used all her babysitting money to buy a new bikini to wear to the party. When her mother offered to drive her to the Saint, Traci recoiled in horror at the idea of anyone spotting her rolling up to the resort in her mother's battered beige Aerostar minivan. Instead, she'd bribed Shannon's older brother Joe to drop her off in return for doing his English homework.

The big day was a steamy Saturday. After the security guards at the Saint's main gate checked her name off the guest list, Joe pulled up to the hotel's front door to drop her off.

Traci had gaped at the lobby's high ceilings, marble floors, and the grand staircase with its intricate wrought-iron railings rising up to a mezzanine. A man in a tuxedo sat at a gleaming baby grand piano playing soft classical music, and scattered about the vast room were seating areas with plush sofas and chairs, and tables with huge bouquets of fresh flowers. Even the air in the room was rich with a faint floral scent.

When she got home that night she gave Shannon a recap of the party. "You were right, Meredith is a bitch. And her mom is too, but they gave out these amazing goody bags, and her birthday cake had three layers with strawberry filling and I ate so much I barfed in a fountain when nobody was looking and oh, my God, the Saint. Someday you and I are going to live at that place."

Two years later, when they were fifteen, through a friend of a friend, Traci and Shannon got summer jobs working at the Saint's ice-cream parlor, biking across the river on the causeway that led from their working-class Bonaventure neighborhood to the rarefied atmosphere of the Saint Cecelia resort.

Three weeks into that first summer the girls got educated about the two distinct social classes existing in their small coastal community.

It was Gayla, the ice-cream shop's twenty-year-old manager, who set them straight, when she noticed Traci and Shannon lingering near the pool after they'd gotten off work, flirting with two preppy-looking teenaged boys.

"Y'all can't be messing with the hotel guests or the members or the members' kids," she'd counseled when they reported for work the next day.

"Why not?" Traci asked.

"'Cuz the bosses don't like it. And the members don't like their kids hanging out with the townies or the help. Don't you get it? Those rich kids, they're Saints. Y'all are just Ain'ts."

And that's how Traci found out that instead of living on the wrong side of the railroad tracks, she lived on the wrong side of the causeway. And that was pretty much the way things had stayed, until she met Hoke Eddings.

CHAPTER 1

* * *

"Got a minute?" Traci Eddings looked up from the spreadsheet of doom that she'd been studying. Her GM was standing just outside her office doorway, and from the pained expression on his usually sunny countenance she knew the news wasn't good.

Charlie Burroughs had worked at the Saint since the age of fourteen, and he was in his early sixties now. His face, wreathed in wrinkles and sun blotches, was a roadmap of all the disasters he'd witnessed: the 1972 hurricane that had peeled the roof off the main lodge; the food poisoning debacle in the men's grill in 1988; the drought of 1996, when temperatures had hovered in the nineties for thirty-seven days straight and a watering ban had burned every blade of turf on the golf course. He'd seen the Saint through stuff nobody talked about, stuff that still made Traci shudder. Charlie had been there the summer of 2001, when the red tide had caused a massive fish kill resulting in three tons of dead fish washed up on the beach, and of course, the plane crash four years ago that had claimed the life of Hoke Eddings and transformed her into a widow at the age of forty.

Charlie had been a tower of strength to Traci in the years that followed.

Traci pushed her reading glasses into her hair and waved him inside, pointing at the chair across from Hoke's desk. Well, her desk now.

"Do I even want to know?" She rubbed her forehead and closed her eyes.

"Mehdi's leaving us," Charlie said as soon as he was seated. "Accepted an offer at that new resort up the coast."

"Nooo," Traci moaned. "Not Mehdi."

"Afraid so. And of course, Sam is going with her."

"Which means I'm out my guest relations director, as well as a chef who went to culinary school on our dime," Traci said. She looked over at Charlie. "Is it definite? I mean, could we offer them both a raise, some kind of incentive to persuade them to stay on?"

"No. Mehdi showed me their offer. It's stupid money and she'd be stupid not to take it. Hell, I'd take it if they were looking for a washed-up old grouch with a bad knee."

"You're not that old," Traci said. "But don't kid yourself. I happen to know you can't cook for shit."

"Memorial Day is only a month away," Charlie said gloomily. "We were already shorthanded, and now we're losing two of our best."

"So we'll hire some more help," Traci said unconvincingly.

"From where? The spring hiring fair was a bust. High school kids don't want to spend a summer sweating their balls off as lifeguards or caddies or housekeepers."

"Like you and I did," Traci put in.

"The locals are all going to tennis camp in Florida, or doing TikTok videos for an energy drink that costs eleven bucks a bottle. Have you seen all the businesses in the village with HELP WANTED signs in their windows? Everybody's hiring but nobody wants to work."

"Maybe we need to try something different," Traci said. "Can we recruit from farther away? We're a beach resort, Charlie. Who doesn't want to spend the summer at the beach?"

"We could, but where are these kids from Sumpter or Jacksonville going to live? It ain't like it was when you were growing up here. Do you have any idea what the rents around here are now? Folks who used to rent to our summer help have turned their cottages or garage apartments into short-term vacation rentals."

She swiveled her chair around and stared out the office window at the postcard-pretty view of the Saint Cecelia, the venerable beach resort and country club that had been founded by her late husband's grandfather in the Roaring Twenties.

Nestled on a tiny private island off the Georgia coast, the Saint, as it was known locally and formally, had been a mainstay destination for generations of upper-crust families who'd flocked there for over a hundred years. If Traci squinted, she could see the pink-and-white candy-striped cabanas that lined the beach. And if she leaned out her office window, she might spot white-garbed players whacking croquet balls on the "village green" that had been added to the resort in the postwar years. One thing that had changed little over the decades was the presence of designer-clad moms watching as their little darlings splashed in the pool, while dads sipped martinis and plotted business deals après-golf at the Watering Hole lounge.

The golf course was lush and green, and just beyond the beach club and pool was a wide, sandy strip of shore and the shimmering green Atlantic.

If she closed her eyes she could almost picture walking along the beach, hand in hand with Hoke, after their first real date. Even at twenty-nine, he'd been so awkward, so tentative, bumbling even, in an adorable way, as he pulled her behind a palm tree for a kiss. Reliving the moment, she felt the inevitable lump in her throat and was glad her back was to Charlie.

"Traci?" Charlie's voice brought her back to her present-day problems.

"I'm thinking."

"About?"

"Housing. What if we turned the old golf cart barn into a sort of dorm? Like the one everybody stayed in back in the day."

"The one from back in the day that was a firetrap? That the county would have condemned if your father-in-law hadn't paid off the inspectors?"

"Not like that," she said firmly. "There are bathrooms in the cart barn, right? One for caddies and one for guests?"

"There *were*. The roof on that barn is falling in, Traci. The electrical wasn't up to code when it was built, so it sure as hell ain't gonna meet code now. It wasn't fit to house golf carts, which is why we built a new one, and it sure as hell ain't fit to house our summer help."

"We'll put a new roof on it, bring the electrical up to code, get some of those splitter heat and air units, like the ones we put up in the cottages by the lagoon."

Charlie shook his head. "You want all that done in less than a month? You know what that'll cost? In materials and labor?"

"You know what it'll cost if we have to delay—or even cancel opening up by Memorial Day? How much money we'll lose? You remember the pandemic? We're still bleeding red ink. Now, we've got an almost fully booked summer season ahead of us, Charlie. We can't afford to take that kind of a financial hit."

His mouth opened to protest, but then he thought better of it.

"What's the absolute minimum number we need to be staffed up?" Traci pressed. "How many more bodies do we need?"

"Nine would be ideal. But I guess, if we offer overtime, and maybe come up with some decent signing incentives, we could do with seven. But no less than that."

"Some of the hotels out by the interstate are offering signing bonuses to new employees, or current employees who recruit someone new," Traci said. "Maybe we could try something like that."

"I can make some calls," Charlie said. "Chefs come and go all the time. We can find somebody in the kitchen, but as for the front desk . . ."

She swiveled back around. "I'll talk to Parrish."

"I don't know if that's a great idea," Charlie said slowly. "How will it look to the rest of the staff if you install your niece in a high-visibility job like that?"

"It'll look like this is a family-owned company and she's family," Traci said.

Charlie clearly wasn't in favor of the idea. "Didn't I hear something about her spending the summer in Europe?"

"I'll talk to her," Traci said firmly. "But if you see Ric? Don't mention it, understand?"

"Got it." Charlie didn't need to ask any more questions. He'd worked for the Eddings family all this time; he knew where all the bodies were buried. Literally. Like her, he'd grown up in the business. Traci knew he'd do whatever it took to keep the Saint afloat. Just as she would.

CHAPTER 2

* * *

PARRISH

Parrish Eddings watched from her bedroom window as her father's car sped backward down the sloping driveway. She heard the gears of the Porsche grind as Ric slammed it into first gear and raced away. Toward where?

"Anywhere but here," she whispered aloud. Downstairs, she heard her stepmother slamming things. Pots and pans in the kitchen. She heard the sound of a glass shattering. The front door closed heavily with a thud, then reopened and slammed again. And again.

Just another typical Monday. No telling what the fight was about. Madelyn's new kitten, a Himalayan, refused to use the litter box, preferring the clothes Ric inevitably left on their bedroom floor. Or maybe it was about Ric's late hours. She'd heard him creeping up the stairs at 3:15 A.M. on Sunday night.

More likely it was about money. Madelyn no longer cared about her husband's comings and goings. She'd known exactly what she was getting when she married Ric. Or so she thought.

Parrish went back to her packing. Her clothes were folded and arranged in tidy little piles atop her neatly made bed in her very adorable bedroom, which Madelyn had decorated without Parrish's consent or input, after marrying Ric.

She could never pin down why she hated this room so much. She loved soft teal, aquas, and pale pinks, which was the current color palette. The bed was big and soft, and the first time she'd brought a boy home to it, she'd delighted in imagining what Madelyn would say if she'd known all the things they'd done atop that fluffy down duvet.

It didn't matter. None of it mattered. Back to packing. She'd given herself a strict mandate: the medium-sized rolling suitcase, and her backpack. Anything more she needed in Europe, she could buy. With her own damn money. She couldn't wait to wave goodbye to the drama and the trauma of the Ric and Maddy show. Whee!

When her phone rang she almost didn't pick up, but when she saw the caller ID, her resolve softened.

"Heyyyy," Traci said.

Parrish's body relaxed at the sound of her favorite aunt's voice. Traci was on her side, always and forever. They were a team.

"Got plans for lunch?" Traci asked.

"I'm packing, but I guess I could take a break. What did you have in mind?"

"I'll pick you up in ten," Traci said. "And hey, this is just us. Right? Your dad and stepmom don't need to know our plans."

"As if," Parrish said. "I'll meet you down by the mailbox. You know what a sneaky little spy Madelyn can be."

Traci took the coast road and they ended up at BluePointe, a new planned development fifteen miles north of the Saint.

"Checking out the competition?" Parrish asked as they walked toward the restaurant, which was located in the middle of the resort's faux village of expensive shops and food trucks.

"Something like that. I'll tell you after we've ordered."

Parrish's spidy-sense antennae were activated. Her aunt was being deliberately evasive.

They waited at the hostess stand for five minutes before a harried server rushed up and showed them to a table, handing them vinyl-covered menus that were sticky with what smelled like maple syrup.

"Ick." Parrish pushed her menu away, squirting her hands from the tiny bottle of hand sanitizer she kept in her purse. "Since when does a fine dining restaurant hand customers a plastic menu? These aren't exactly Waffle House prices, right?"

Traci was watching the server, who looked to be around Parrish's age: petite, with white-blond hair chopped chin-length, and a tattoo of some sort peeking out from the short sleeve of her uniform blouse. "Looks like they're shorthanded too. No valet parking. No hostess." She nodded toward the steam table prominently displayed in the middle of the room. "And a lunch buffet. Not a healthy sign."

"Mmm-hmm," Parrish said. "Thanks but no thanks to the wilted iceberg lettuce and freeze-dried bacon bits and your gross gravy-covered chicken. I'll just have a nineteen-dollar club sandwich. They can't screw that up. Right?"

Traci laughed. "Nobody would ever know you were raised in the business."

The server reappeared. "You ladies want the buffet? We have baked cod today. And fried shrimp!"

Parrish shuddered. "Just a club sandwich. And iced tea."

"I'll have the same," Traci added. "No mayo on my bread."

"Fries or coleslaw?"

"Fries," the women said in unison.

They watched the girl hurry away. "How long has this place been open?" Parrish asked.

"Not even a year. You wouldn't believe all the free publicity they got when they opened. The Atlanta paper sent reporters down. *Southern Living* did a piece because they hired some fancy chef away from a restaurant in Buckhead." She looked around the dining room.

"See that wallpaper, and those window treatments? That's Scalamandré, the paper and the fabric, done in a custom colorway too, which makes it even more ungodly expensive. I priced that same fabric out when we redid the garden room at the hotel years ago, and when I gave Hoke the quote he almost had a myocardial infarction."

Parrish laughed. "Yeah, Uncle Hoke was not one to throw money around, that's for sure."

"All the same, that year, for my birthday, he had a pillow made out of that same fabric, sort of as a joke, but I loved it. Loved that he remembered, loved that he made the gesture," Traci said.

Parrish needed to change the subject before her aunt got all misty-eyed the way she still did, even though Hoke had been gone for four years now.

"That poor girl," Parrish murmured, nodding in the direction of their server as she hustled back toward the kitchen. "I think she's the only one working this dining room today. I hope they at least let her keep all her tips."

Their server brought their orders a few minutes later. Traci lifted the top slice of bread on her sandwich and sighed. "I knew it. Absolutely plastered with mayonnaise." She set the bread aside and attacked the sandwich with knife and fork.

Parrish held up a pale, limp French fry. "Straight out of the freezer bag. I guess they must have waved it in the direction of the deep fryer before they plated up this mess."

"Never mind," Traci said, sipping her tea. "I've got something important I need to discuss with you." She took a deep breath.

Parrish felt her stomach do a flip-flop. She grabbed for her aunt's hand. "Traci? What's wrong? Are you sick?"

"No, no, oh honey, no. I'm fine."

Parrish was still skeptical. "You sure? You know you can tell me. I mean, you've been looking kind of pale lately, and distracted. Dark circles under your eyes . . ."

"I swear it. I'm healthy as a horse. Could use a little more sleep, a little more sunshine, and a lot less worry, but that's not it at all."

"Wow. You had me scared for a minute there. So then, what's this super-secret emergency lunch about?"

"Mehdi's quit. And Sam's going with her."

"Oh no." Mehdi was the head chef at the Verandah, the Saint's signature restaurant, and her impeccable cooking had earned the restaurant its first Mobil five-star rating, making it one of only two such restaurants in the state. And Sam, Mehdi's husband, was the hotel's guest relations manager. He was smart and warm, and like his wife, seemed to have made himself indispensable in the half dozen years since he'd come to work at the Saint.

"The timing couldn't be worse," Traci said. "We were already seriously shorthanded going into spring, but now, unless I can find some more staff, specifically a chef and someone to run the guest relations desk, I honestly don't know if we can open."

"Where's Mehdi going?"

"Some resort in Hilton Head hired them both away. Charlie said they offered stupid money. Look, I hate to ask, but I'm out of options. I really, really need you back at the Saint this summer."

Parrish was already shaking her head. "No way. You know I'm doing this program in Europe this summer. I'm already registered for my classes. I'm leaving Thursday. You're always shorthanded at the Saint. Every year, and somehow you manage. Sorry, but you're just gonna have to find someone else."

"There *is* no one else," Traci told her, desperation creeping into her voice. "I can't just hire someone off the street to run guest relations. We've got to have someone who knows the property, knows the guests, knows how we do things at the Saint. The person running that desk is the image of our family business."

Parrish found herself shredding the paper napkin in her lap, her face arranging itself into what everyone in the family called her "cement face." Her eyes were dead, staring straight ahead, jaw stubbornly set, arms folded across her chest.

"You think I'm exaggerating?" Traci asked. "We're in the same boat as every other business on the coast. So I'm going to have to offer something those other businesses can't. On-site housing. More money. Recruiting bonuses. Hopefully, that'll bring in some bodies, but the one body I absolutely have to have this summer is Parrish Eddings."

Parrish was unmoved. She leaned into the table, her resolve steely. "I have worked at the Saint every year since you started me scooping ice cream in the Parlour at fourteen. You promised that after I graduated, I'd be liberated. I did everything y'all asked. Majored in hospitality management, got good grades, didn't get arrested. And now it's *my* time."

She slapped her hands together as though wiping them clean of an invisible noxious substance. "I am done with working in the family business." She *would not* cry. "And I can't believe you, of all people, would try to guilt-trip me into coming back. Do you know what it's like? Living in my house? Dad's sneaking around seeing someone again. Madelyn knows, I know, and he knows we know. It's gross. And the idea of working at the hotel with her? Bad enough I have to live under the same roof. I just want to start living my own life."

"Oh, Parrish," Traci said, her voice low and soft. She really knew how to work the sympathy angle. "I hate dumping this on you. But I'm out of options. I can't open the Saint without enough staff. But I can't *not* open, because, just between the two of us, we've been bleeding red ink. Hoke committed us to spending millions on the renovations, borrowing heavily. And you know what the past few summers were like, coming out of the pandemic. It's been brutal. We've got to start recouping some of our losses—or there won't be a Saint."

Parrish didn't allow the cement face to crack. Not even a little. "Not my problem." She picked the bacon from her sandwich and nibbled on a corner of it.

"Except it is your problem. Like it or not, Parrish, you're an Eddings. The Saint is your legacy. Those are *your* little-bitty handprints on the patio outside the dining room. Your grandmother pressed them into the concrete the day you started walking. Do you want to see this place, that's been around for over a hundred years, taken over and run by bankers and venture capitalist vultures from New York?"

"You're exaggerating," Parrish said, but dammit, she could already feel the tiniest fissure working away at her façade.

"Am I? Come into the office. You're a smart girl. Take a look at the books. Talk to Charlie. You know he won't sugarcoat it. Look, what about this? We postpone your summer program. I'll pay the cancellation fees or whatever. You come to work at the Saint. Did I tell you we're turning the old cart barn into a dorm for summer staff? You wouldn't have to live at home, and I'll make sure Madelyn keeps her distance. She's never around that much, anyway. Who knows what she's actually up to? You'll get your own room at the dorm. You'll be well paid. And you'll have fun. And after this summer, I swear, Parrish, you can go do your Europe program. I'll pay for it. All of it."

"A dorm?" Parrish's upper lip curled delicately. "I haven't lived in a dorm since I was a college freshman."

"Or you could stay with me," Traci said. "And Lola," she added.

Lola was her aunt's gassy, wire-haired dachshund. "Oh God, no," Parrish said quickly. "I'd rather live in a dorm."

She could already feel her summer in Europe slipping away. Coming out of the pandemic, the past few summers, even she could tell that business was way off. If she didn't do what her aunt wanted, maybe the Saint actually *would* close. And then what?

Time to cut a deal. She couldn't let Traci totally off the hook. Especially if it meant living in a freakin' dorm for the summer.

"I want to be paid what you paid Sam," Parrish said firmly. "And you're gonna have to explain this whole deal to Dad."

She grinned, just thinking about *that* awkward conversation. Her father was civil to Traci, but just barely. He'd be absolutely livid about the nonrefundable fees he'd already paid for her trip. But mostly he'd be majorly pissed that Traci had outmaneuvered him.

"Then you'll do it?" Traci let out a long sigh of relief. "Okay. I'll talk to your dad. He won't like it, but at least I'll be able to breathe again." She looked around the dining room, catching the server's attention, motioning for her to bring the check.

"All set?" the girl asked, handing her a leather folder with the bill inside. She looked down at the mostly uneaten food on the table and lowered her voice. "I'm so sorry about your sandwich. I did put the no-mayo on your order, but we've got a new guy on the grill, and I think he gets off on screwing over the servers."

Parrish rolled her eyes in sympathy. "Ugh. The worst."

Traci reached for her billfold. "Parrish, why don't you go ahead out to the car. I'll just be another minute here."

"Uh, okay."

CHAPTER 3

* * *

OLIVIA

Olivia noticed the woman at table six looking at her oddly. Early forties, probably. On the skinny side, kinda pale, with dark blond shoulder-length hair with those cool balayage streaks Livvy couldn't afford. She was definitely rich, judging from the size of the big honking diamond on her left hand, and also that Fendi purse.

The woman kept glancing at her. But there was no time to obsess over it, because the two other girls who were supposed to work lunch had both called in sick, and her manager was being a total dick about it. So she basically ran her legs off, and somehow got food to her tables and managed not to spill anything or get the orders wrong.

It wasn't until she dropped the check at the woman's table that she realized the problem. The younger woman had only eaten the bacon off her club sandwich, but the other woman had lifted the top slice of bread off her sandwich and set it aside, which is when Livvy saw that it was slathered with mayonnaise.

Eddie. He was screwing with her again, just because she'd threatened to rat on him for texting her dick pics. She was pretty sure it wasn't even *his* dick, not that she ever intended to find out.

"I'm so sorry about the sandwich," Livvy told the woman, after her daughter had left. "I can take it off your bill if you want."

"It's fine," the woman said, tilting her head and giving her a full-on stare. Livvy was getting more than a little freaked out now.

"Uh, is there anything else? Maybe you want an iced tea to go?"

"No thanks. It's just that you look like someone I used to know. Are you from here?"

"No, ma'am. I'm from Bonaventure. It's a little town just south of here," Livvy said. Obviously this woman was a tourist. BluePointe had only been developed like a year or two ago. Five years ago, this had all been pine trees and palmettos.

"That's funny. I'm originally from Bonaventure too.

"Livvy, right?" the woman said, pointing to the name badge Mr. Godby made all the servers wear.

"It's Olivia, but nobody ever calls me that."

"Nice to meet you, Livvy. I'm Traci. I couldn't help but notice you're the only server working today. Is that unusual?"

"No, I mean, yes, ma'am. There are usually at least two other girls working the weekday lunch shift, but they both called in sick, so today it's just me."

"You did a good job, though," the woman said thoughtfully. "Can I ask you a personal question?"

Livvy shrugged.

"Do you enjoy working here?"

She had to think about that. She didn't mind waiting tables. The money was decent, and she knew it would get way better when the season started and all the tourists came back. But she was tired of trying to dodge handsy grill cooks, and they totally did not have enough servers to get them through the season, plus her boss was a major jerk.

"It's okay," Livvy said.

The woman hesitated. "Normally I wouldn't go into another restaurant to poach their help, but these aren't normal times. The reason I ask is, I'm looking to hire staff for a resort near here. And I was wondering . . ."

"Which resort?"

"The Saint," the woman said, smiling. "We're the oldest resort on the coast. The business has been in my late husband's family since the nineteen twenties."

Livvy sucked in her breath. How dumb could she be? This woman was Traci Eddings. *The* Traci Eddings. Before she could say anything else, she could see Mr. Godby gesturing for her to get back to the hostess stand, where a party of six was waiting impatiently.

"Nice to meet you, Mrs. Eddings, but I gotta go."

The woman nodded, then pressed something into her hand. "Call me," she said, in a low, urgent voice. "We're hiring. Whatever you're making here, I'll pay two dollars an hour more, plus a hundred-dollar bonus, plus free, on-site housing."

"Liv!" Mr. Godby's voice was sharp.

The rest of her shift was a blur. She waited on a bridesmaids' luncheon with twenty women. Half the girls were her age or younger, all of them wearing clothes she could never afford, sloppy little drunks who brought their own cheap-ass grocery store sheet cake, which they then demanded that she cut up and serve to them. Then the bride's bitchy mother had the nerve to take her aside and complain that the restaurant shouldn't have tacked on the 15 percent gratuity for a party over ten, even though the menu clearly stated that was the restaurant's policy.

Livvy just stared at the woman.

In the end, Mr. Godby had intervened in the dispute, and even though none of it was Livvy's fault, she could tell he was pissed at her. So unfair.

She had a pounding headache and blisters on both feet from her new work shoes by the time she limped back home at four.

Her mother was still at work at the hospital, thank God. Even though she was almost twenty-one, Livvy still felt guilty about pouring herself a glass of wine to sip while she soaked in a bubble bath.

Shannon had found religion and had let it be known that she didn't approve of alcohol. Well, good for her. It wasn't like Livvy was running wild in the streets. She liked an occasional glass of wine to relax, that's all.

It wasn't until she'd toweled off and was emptying her uniform pockets before putting them in the laundry that she found Traci Eddings's business card.

The paper was heavy and embossed, the type elegant and in gold. TRACI EDDINGS, CEO, THE SAINT CECELIA. There was a phone number, and an email address.

Livvy pulled on a pair of gym shorts and a T-shirt and stretched out on her bed, phone in hand. She glanced around her bedroom. It was small, like the rest of the house, which was a cinder-block box painted pale yellow, on a street full of houses all just alike. This had been her grandmother's house, and Shannon had lived here all her life. Bright pink potted hibiscus trees flanked the front door, which was painted the same shade of pink.

Her mother was a clean freak, liked everything new and shiny and pristine. Shannon never left the house with so much as a dirty coffee mug in the sink, or a damp towel on the floor. Her mother had rules. Shoes were to be removed as soon as you came inside. Kitchen counters were to be sprayed and wiped down with Lysol every morning and every evening before bed. Shannon wouldn't even allow trash to sit in her house for twenty-four hours.

She ran a fingertip over the business card, getting a subversive electric thrill as she considered the offer Traci Eddings had made. Two dollars an hour more than what she was making at BluePointe? Plus a hundred-dollar signing bonus? That was nothing to sniff at.

With that kind of money, Livvy could save up enough to transfer to a college out of state. She could even maybe buy a new-to-her secondhand car. But most important was that last bit Mrs. Eddings had mentioned at the end of her pitch.

Free, on-site housing. It wasn't that Livvy didn't love her mom. Shannon had been a single mom, and she'd never let Livvy forget that she had sacrificed everything to raise her. But she was twenty now, for Pete's sake, still living with her mom and her mom's strict rules. She longed to live on her own, paint her walls whatever color she pleased, maybe even leave a sweater on the back of a chair.

Was that so wrong?

Twice she started to call the number on the card, and twice she chickened out. She took a long swallow of wine, then, finally, made herself take the leap. She sat up, cross-legged on her bed, called the number on the card, and when instructed, left a rapid-fire voice message.

"Um, hi, Mrs. Eddings? This is Olivia Grayson. I waited on you today, at BluePointe? Anyway, I wanted to talk to you about the job you offered me. You can call me back at this number. Thanks."

Just as she was about to disconnect, the front door opened. Her mother was home. Livvy felt her face burn with shame mixed with relief. She'd done it! And it felt fine.

"Liv?" Shannon opened her bedroom door without knocking. Why should she knock? This was Shannon's house, Shannon's rules. For now.

They were at the kitchen table eating dinner—Stouffer's mac and cheese and bagged salad—when Livvy's phone rang. She glanced at the caller ID screen and grabbed for it before the call could go to voice mail.

"Who's that?" Shannon asked, her eyebrow quirked.

"Just somebody returning my call about a job," Livvy said, pushing away from the table and heading for her room.

Shannon frowned. "Tell them to call back. You know how I feel about using your phone at mealtime."

"Can't," Livvy said.

"Just a moment, please," she said into the phone, before closing and locking her bedroom door.

"Hi, Livvy. This is Traci Eddings. I hope I'm not catching you at a bad time, but I was so happy to get your call earlier. Do you have a moment to talk?"

"Yes," Livvy said, sinking down onto her bed. "Now is good."

"Okay," Traci said. "As I told you earlier, we're starting to staff up for summer, and I have several positions open at the Verandah."

"The Verandah?"

"Yes. That's the main restaurant on the property. There's also a men's grill, and an ice-cream shop too. Have you ever visited us here?"

"Don't think so."

"Well, we'll have to fix that. When could you come in for an interview?"

"I could come in tomorrow. Any time before four," Livvy said.

"Perfect," Mrs. Eddings said. "You won't have a problem with drug testing, right?"

"No, ma'am. Can I ask you a question?"

"Of course."

"You mentioned something about on-site housing for employees?"

"We're renovating an existing building on the property," Mrs. Eddings said crisply. "We'll provide a dorm-type experience. Furnished, private rooms but with two shared communal baths."

"Sounds good," Livvy said, trying to sound casual.

"The dorm won't be ready for at least another two weeks, but if your interview goes well, and I have no reason to believe it won't, we'd want you to start training immediately. Will that work for you?"

Livvy took a deep breath and chewed at her cuticle, a bad childhood habit she'd never outgrown. Things were moving so fast. But maybe that was good. Change was good, right?

"Livvy?"

"Yes, ma'am. That will work."

"Wonderful. Tell me your full name again? I'll let Charlie Burroughs—he's our GM—know to expect you tomorrow, and I'll leave you a parking pass at the security gate."

"It's Olivia Grayson."

"Did you say Grayson?"

"Yes, ma'am. G-R-A-"

"Never mind," Mrs. Eddings said hastily. "I know how it's spelled. Looking forward to seeing you tomorrow, then."

After she disconnected, Livvy sat very still on her bed, wondering what the hell she'd just gotten herself into. She'd worked at

BluePointe since they'd opened. Mr. Godby had hinted about the possibility of a raise, after a year. She liked the other girls she worked with well enough . . .

Her phone dinged, notifying her of an incoming text.

She looked down. The photo was blurry, but the subject was unmistakable. A man's unzipped fly with an erect penis, followed by a series of hot dog emojis interspersed with tongue emojis.

It was just the sign from the universe that she needed, gross but convincing. Livvy tapped the photo to download, then forwarded it to management@bluepointe.com. With a brief message. *Hi. Olivia Grayson here. The attached photo was sent to me tonight by your grill cook, Eddie Argentau, who sexually harasses all the waitresses at your restaurant. I quit. I'll turn in my uniform when I pick up my last paycheck.*

Livvy smiled as she pressed Send. No turning back now.

CHAPTER 4

* * *

SHANNON

Shannon tried Livvy's bedroom door and was annoyed to find it locked. She rapped on the door, twice. Livvy had been acting strangely during dinner. In fact, for the past few weeks her daughter had been quieter than usual. Shannon's mama-mind went to a dark place, imagining all the possibilities.

Livvy opened the door and Shannon stepped inside.

"Liv? Honey? Who was on the phone? And what's this about a new job? I thought you were making good money at BluePointe. Why would you want to leave?"

Livvy flopped backward onto the bed. "Let's just say there are issues. Like today, two girls called in sick, and Mr. Godby didn't cut me any slack, even though I was working my ass off. Anyway, one of my customers today was super impressed by how hard I was working. She's shorthanded at her business, and she's made me an amazing offer. Which I just accepted. I'm going over there tomorrow for an interview, but she's already told me it's just a formality."

Shannon sat down on the bed beside her daughter and tucked a lock of Livvy's still-damp hair behind her ear. Livvy's natural color was a gorgeous shade of chestnut. She hated this new hair color; the obvious bleachy blond was just plain trashy in Shannon's opinion, but she didn't dare share that assessment.

"You're quitting? Just like that? Without even a week's notice?"

"I emailed Mr. Godby. Told him I'd pick up my last check when I turn in my uniform. It's a done deal, Mom, so don't even try to talk me out of it."

"That's a terrible thing to do to an employer, Olivia. Word gets around, you know. What if your new boss calls over to BluePointe to ask for a referral?"

"They won't," Olivia said, with a snotty attitude that Shannon didn't at all care for.

Livvy had never given Shannon a moment of heartache, not even when all her high school friends were out getting tattooed and noses pierced and running wild in the streets—much the way Shannon had at Livvy's age. She was a good, sensible girl.

"You're so lucky to have a daughter like Livvy," her nurse friends from the hospital would say. "My daughter never has a civil word to say to me," her friend Angela said. (Which was true. Angie's daughter Bree was a total brat.)

Maybe it was Livvy's time of the month, Shannon rationalized.

Livvy read her mind. "And before you ask, no, I am not on my period. God! Can't I just stand up for myself without you handing me a box of tampons?"

"I don't understand," Shannon said. "It's irresponsible to quit a job this way, without even giving notice. And don't forget, Angie was the one who put in a good word for you at that restaurant. If you up and quit, it's gonna make her look bad."

"I don't care," Livvy said, stony-faced. "My mind is made up. I've had a really sucky day, and now I'd really appreciate it if you'd butt out of my business. Just leave me alone, okay?"

"Young lady!" Shannon said sternly. "You're living under my roof. As far as I'm concerned, your business is my business. Now please explain to me why you're being so irrational about all this."

"Irrational?" Livvy jumped up and began pacing around the room. She stopped in front of her mother.

"Okay, Mom. Here's the deal. If my new boss asks, I'll tell her my old boss gives me the worst shifts because he's sleeping with one of the other waitresses on the side. And also, the grill guy keeps sending me dick pics. I think she'll understand."

"Whaaat?" Shannon shrieked, clutching her chest. "What did you just say?"

"Eddie, the grill cook, has been sexting me. He just texted me a picture of his dick. Or somebody's dick. He's a shrimpy little guy, probably doesn't weigh a hundred pounds, so I doubt that's actually his real package. Anyway, he grabs my ass every time we're alone in the kitchen, or tries to shove his tongue down my throat. So no, I'm not going to keep working there, no matter what you say."

"Livvy!" Shannon exclaimed. "Why didn't you say something? Have you told Mr. Godby? That's . . . criminal. We'll report him to the police."

"Mommm," Livvy said. "Drop it. No way Godby is going to fire Eddie. Experienced cooks are too hard to find. Tomorrow, I've got an interview for this new gig, and I'm super excited. Can't you be excited for me?"

"Where is this new gig?" Shannon asked. "What's the job? And how do you know they're actually going to hire you? Have you considered what happens if this supposed sure thing falls through? How will you pay your tuition? And your car payment?"

"I'm going to work at the Saint," Livvy said. "It's a done deal. I waited on Traci Eddings today, and she was super impressed . . . offered me a job on the spot."

"The Saint?" Tiny black spots floated in front of Shannon's eyes and her pulse was racing. She would put a stop to this here and now.

She grasped her daughter by the shoulders. "No. Absolutely not. You're not going anywhere near that place, and you're not going to work for that family. Ever. Do you hear me?"

Livvy shook her off. "What is wrong with you? Why is this such a big deal?"

"Never mind. I won't let you do this, Livvy. There are plenty of other places you can work around here. Like the hospital. They're always looking for aides, and the pay's decent. If not there, you could work for your uncle. Decent hours, and . . ."

"You're not listening!" Livvy shouted. "I don't want to work at your shitty hospital, or any other place, and I'm definitely not working at Uncle Joe's boring insurance office. You can't stop me. I'm almost twenty-one. I can make my own decisions."

"No," Shannon insisted. "You don't know those people. They're rich and charming on the surface, but the reality is that they're rotten. All of them. I absolutely forbid this."

"Forbid?" Livvy laughed. "This isn't the eighteenth century, Mom. You don't get to forbid me to do stuff. What are you going to do? Put me in time-out?"

"Is this funny to you? Because it's not funny to me. I'm dead serious, Liv. Do not do this. These people—"

"These people what?" Livvy challenged her. "I'll tell you what. These people are going to pay me a lot more than I'm making now. And they're giving me a free place to live, on site. As far as I'm concerned, it's a done deal."

Shannon's breathing went shallow; her mouth was dry. "So you're moving out too, just like that?"

"As soon as the new dorm is ready, I'm out of here," Livvy told her.

CHAPTER 5

* * *

FELICE

Deion was gone. The pickup was gone, and more importantly, Caribbean Soul had gone with him.

Stunned, Felice slumped down to the pavement in the motel parking lot, clutching her face in her hands, softly moaning and cursing, first in English, then French, then Creole.

Thirty minutes she'd been gone. That's all. Just thirty minutes. She'd walked to the Shop and Go to buy coffee and sweet rolls, and by the time she returned, De had vanished.

At first, she'd had a fleeting thought. Maybe some redneck cop had run him off. No telling what her hotheaded fool of a boyfriend would say or do if challenged by a cop. He had a gun. A little pistol he hid rolled up in a pair of socks that he didn't think she knew about. She tried calling De's phone, but he wasn't picking up.

But she knew; yeah, she knew. His stuff was gone from their room. All his clothes, his stash, and yeah, his kicks, ten fucking pairs of designer sneakers. Thousands of dollars' worth of shoes. He wore them in rotation, and after every wearing, would sit down and lovingly clean them off with baby wipes.

Felice sleep-walked into the motel office, where a chubby white girl with stringy black hair, bad skin, and a worse attitude sat behind the desk.

Felice's voice shook with a combination of anger and fear. "Our food truck? Have you seen it?"

The girl was watching something on her laptop computer. She didn't even look up.

"You mean that fugly trailer with the pineapples and palm trees and shit painted all over it? I seen that dude light outta here earlier. Good thing, too. My daddy was gonna tell y'all to get that thing outta our parking lot. Y'all can't be running some shady shit outta here."

"Shady shit? Caribbean Soul is a food truck. Perfectly legal. We have a permit from the Health Department . . ."

The girl shrugged. "Well, looks like your man has moved on. Maybe you oughta think about doing the same thing. You're only paid up through today."

Felice reached for her pocketbook. Thank God she'd taken it with her to the store. She pulled out her billfold and thumbed through the thinning stack of currency. Her Visa card? She scrabbled around in her purse, sifting through the contents: lip gloss, pens, her notebook—the red spiral-bound one with all her recipes.

Then it struck her. Two days ago, she'd handed the Visa to Deion so he could gas up the truck. And now De was gone. With her Visa card, and her future.

"I, uh, I think my card has been stolen. I'll call Visa and get a new one issued. In the meantime . . ." Felice took four twenty-dollar bills from her billfold and pushed them across the counter to the girl.

The girl smirked, enjoying her misery, and shoved the bills back, watching as they fluttered to the filthy carpet. "Sorry. No vacancy. Checkout time is ten, by the way."

Felice traveled light. Out of necessity. Out of habit. She reached into the bottom of the duffel and for reassurance, touched her one treasure. Her knives. Deion had his shoes. Well, Felice had her knives. They were snug in their felt-lined pockets inside the leather roll that was tied up with grosgrain ribbon.

The knives had been a graduation present from the kitchen crew at Shanahan's, the steakhouse she'd worked at in Hialeah. All six of them had gone in on the gift; no telling how much they'd saved out of their own shares of the crappy tips that came their way.

She slid her fingertips over the smooth steel of the knife handles as she called Visa to report that her card had been stolen. Already, the fraud squad told her, someone had used the card at a Walmart, spending just over three hundred dollars. There was a charge at a Starbucks, twelve dollars, and thirty-two at a McDonald's.

Who spends thirty-two bucks at McDonald's? Solo? De must have ordered one of everything on the menu. It would have been funny if it hadn't been so freaking infuriating.

Thank God, Felice told herself, she'd never shared her PIN with him. She didn't have much in her checking account, less than three hundred dollars, but that was two hundred more than she'd had when she left home eight years ago at seventeen.

Stranded again, she thought, rolling up her panties, some shorts, three T-shirts, and her spare pair of jeans, stuffing them into the bag. She went into the bathroom—puke-green tile, one of those plastic shower stalls that never looked clean—and swept the thimble-sized containers of shampoo, conditioner, soap, and hand lotion into her toiletry bag.

She zipped the duffel, slid the strap over her shoulder, and headed for the door, tossing the plastic key card onto the dresser. Catching a glimpse of herself in the mirror, she stopped, then dug in her wallet and placed two one-dollar bills beside the key. One thing she'd learned early on, working in the business jokingly called hospitality. Never stiff the help.

CHAPTER 6

* * *

KJ

One minute he was minding his own business, sprawled facedown across his bed, and the next minute his old man was in his face, yelling like the house was on fire.

"Get up, goddammit," Spencer Parkhurst said, yanking the sheets back. KJ looked up, bleary-eyed, and tried to cover his naked form.

"Huh? Whuut's wrong?"

His father wasn't a large man, but when he was mad, like he was now, his rage made him seem ten feet tall.

"Wrong? You tell me, son. Tell me why your mother has to find out from Christine Foyle that you've flunked out of school? Tell me why you've been lying through your teeth since the day you got home a week ago?"

"Shit." KJ pulled the sheet over his face, and his father quickly snatched it back.

"Get up," he repeated. "I'll see you in my office in ten minutes. In the meantime, take a shower and get yourself sobered up. Your mother doesn't need to see you like this."

Kevin John Parkhurst was always the man with the plan. Take every Advanced Placement test available at Westminster Academy, the elite Atlanta prep school he'd been enrolled in since the age of six. Go out for the tennis and lacrosse teams, win a place on the most competitive travel team in the southeast. Date the hottest girl at Westminster. Get accepted for early admission at Duke, Vanderbilt, Wake Forest, and his old man's alma mater, Penn, even though he had no intention of going to school there. Earn a lacrosse scholarship. Rush the best fraternities, get bids from all the top houses, and eventually, inevitably pledge the hardest-partying house on the Wake Forest campus.

And it had worked. Mostly. Until it hadn't.

KJ couldn't figure out when it had all gone to hell. His first-semester grades had been crappy, averaging barely C−, which came as a shock, because he'd always aced his high school classes. But college was different. The lacrosse practices came at a brutal pace, and the frat's social schedule was killer.

He'd gone home over Christmas break and lied to his parents about his grades. They'd happily accepted his story because why not? Hadn't KJ Parkhurst always been awesome at everything?

His coach had warned him—pick up the grades, or leave the team—and he'd been newly motivated. Until he wasn't. Until organic chemistry kicked his ass and he hadn't been able to get his term paper on beat poets written because he didn't get beat poetry and anyway, the library was closed by the time he got done with practice . . . and it was just as easy to borrow an old term paper from one of his fraternity brothers, except his prof recognized it and reported him to the university honor court for plagiarism, and he'd been put on academic probation.

Then, as if his life hadn't already gone completely to shit, in February, he'd blown out his left knee, and had to come limping home at the end of the semester, a total washout. In more ways than one.

When he was out of the shower, he scraped a razor across his chin and combed his wet hair. Better. He picked up the pill bottle, shook two tablets into the palm of his hand, and paused. He had six left, and NO FURTHER REFILLS was stamped in bold letters across the bottom of the label.

"Fuck it," he mumbled, and swallowed both. He could easily get more, and anyway, he'd need something to take the edge off the coming shitstorm brewing right down the hall in the old man's office.

KJ's mother turned sorrowful eyes on him from the armchair opposite the desk. It was a textbook Betsy Parkhurst move. The passive-aggressive "we're not mad, just disappointed" expression she'd used to great effect his whole life.

It was Tuesday, so she was still dressed for tennis, in her cute little pleated skirt and Piedmont Driving Club logo top. Her Tretorns were spotless, her peppy silvery hair and understated makeup unmussed. KJ had never seen his mother looking less than perfect.

Spencer was seated behind the desk, the sleeves of his starched blue dress shirt rolled up, waiting to pounce, so KJ sized up the situation and made a pre-emptive strike.

"Look," he said, with a long exhalation of penitence. "Mom, Dad. I'm sorry. I should have come clean with you guys right away. I know I screwed up. Big time. I just . . . didn't know how to tell you what was going on with me this past year."

The old man rolled his eyes and snorted.

"KJ, what happened?" his mother asked softly. "All of this? It's so unlike you. If you'd come to us, and told us you were struggling in school, we would have tried to help. I thought you understood that. Your dad and I are always one hundred percent behind you."

"I know," KJ said, pushing back a shock of blond hair that was brushing his eyebrow.

"This is all just bullshit," Spencer barked. "Enough. Bad enough you flunked out of school. But the rest is just as bad. Honor code probation for cheating?"

How the hell? KJ thought.

"I talked to your coach as soon as your mother came home to tell me what Christine Foyle told her this morning at their tennis match."

"The most humiliating moment of my life," Betsy put in. "I wanted to die. Christine sat down beside me between sets and patted my hand, like I'd just lost a kitten or something. 'Jenny told me about KJ's having to leave school, and that must be so upsetting for you.'"

"That bitch," KJ muttered.

"Never mind her," Spencer said. "You couldn't have told your parents you got kicked off the team?"

"What?" Betsy yelped. "When did this happen?"

"My knee," KJ said, clutching it for effect.

"Which it turns out you also lied about," Spencer said. "According to your coach, you didn't actually hurt it playing lacrosse. He tells me it was a car wreck? Off-campus? Jesus Christ, son! When did you turn into a pathological liar?"

KJ was waiting for the meds to kick in, but these days, it seemed the more he took, the less they worked. His bad knee was throbbing, his eyeballs itched, and he kept shifting from one foot to the other, unable to stand still.

"I'm sorry, I'm sorry, I'm sorry." He clasped and unclasped his hands behind his back.

"Do I want to know what actually happened?" Spencer asked.

"Definitely not," KJ mumbled as a wave of shame pinked his cheeks.

"What's the plan, then?" the old man demanded. But before KJ could get in a word edgewise, his father plowed ahead.

"I'll tell you *my* plan. You're not gonna lie around feeling sorry for yourself all summer. I put in a call a little while ago, to Ric Eddings. He says he can put you to work at the Saint."

"The Saint?" KJ leaned down and rubbed his knee, wishing again he'd listened to the surgeon who'd tried to set him up with a physical therapy regimen. "Like, down on the coast?"

His family had spent just about every summer of his life at the Saint. Every May, as soon as school let out, they'd pack up his mother's van and drive the five hours south, staying in Betsy's family's cottage—if you could call a five-bedroom house with its own pool a cottage—with his grandparents and a rotating cast of aunts and uncles and cousins. His dad would come down for long weekends, and in between, his mom played tennis and golf and bridge with her friends, who were mostly the same friends she palled around with back in Buckhead.

"Yes, that Saint," his father said. "Do you know any other place called that?"

"Ohhhh-kayyy," KJ said. "So, what? I'd work at the Saint, and stay at the cottage?"

"You'll stay with the other summer help in a dorm they're building."

"A dorm?" KJ blinked. "Like, sharing a room with strangers?"

"Exactly. You'll stay in a room with strangers, and you'll suck it up and work hard and let all your rich, entitled friends treat you like the minimum-wage jerk you're gonna be."

"Spencer!" Betsy piped up. "That hardly seems reasonable . . ."

"I don't give a damn about reasonable," the old man snapped. "Maybe if your son sees what life is like for the other half he'll make more of an effort to stay in school and use his brain so he doesn't have to spend the rest of his life waiting tables or caddying. At the very least, it'll make a man of him."

KJ raised his eyes to meet the old man's. "Say, Dad, did you ever do that kind of work? I mean, didn't you tell me you and Aunt Wendy spent every summer swimming and sailing all day every day up on the Cape?"

His father's face purpled. He came around the desk and smacked KJ's face with such force it sent him reeling backward. He stumbled, and nearly fell to the floor, then righted himself.

Something warm trickled down his chin. He touched his mouth and saw the blood.

"Spencer, for God's sake!" Betsy cried. She rushed to her son's side, but KJ shook her off.

"It's okay, Mom."

"Get out of my sight," the old man said through clenched teeth.

CHAPTER 7

* * *

The morning sun was already blisteringly hot. Traci wiped a bead of perspiration from her chin and pointed to a spot near the roofline of the old golf cart barn.

"What's that? Tell me it's not rot." She lifted damp hair from her neck and exhaled a quick "hfff" to dispel the cloud of gnats swarming her face.

The Saint's construction foreman gave a rueful laugh. "C'mon, Traci. You want me to lie? Yeah, we got some rotted boards up there, but I'll get the framing crew up there this afternoon and we can patch and paint it so it's good as new."

Javi Guerrero was three inches shorter than Traci Eddings, and built like a fire hydrant, with a full head of graying hair and massive forearms covered in tattoos. He'd worked at the Saint for as long as Traci had. There had been some rough patches after Hoke's death, when Javi clearly resented working for a woman, but they'd slowly developed an easy working relationship.

"What about inside?" she asked, walking toward the open barn doors. "How's that coming along?"

"See for yourself," he said. "We've got new doors on the way, and then we'll get started framing in the new entrance."

Even before they walked inside they could hear the whine of saws and the rapid fire of nail guns, and smell the pine scent of fresh-cut sawdust.

Already she could see the skeletal outline of the cart barn's transformation. A wide hall ran down the center of the barn, and the framing for the dorm rooms was almost completed.

"The electrician ran into town for some more cable, but he swears he'll have everything roughed in by end of day. If he gets that done, my guys can start hanging drywall tomorrow," Javi said, walking beside her.

She threaded her way through the corridor and poked her head inside one of the framed-in bedrooms. It didn't look like much at this stage. Concrete block walls, concrete floors, a dimly lit nine-by-twelve cell. Still, it was an improvement on the dumpy dorm room she'd lived in at the Saint at the age of nineteen.

Back then, the "staff quarters" consisted of a long, narrow wood-frame building in a swampy corner of the property. The rooms were tiny and stifling, barely big enough to hold the army surplus single bed and three-drawer dresser that were the only furnishings. No closet, just hooks on the wall, and no air-conditioning, just a box fan she'd bought for herself to stick in the window.

Traci sighed at the memories of that time, her last summer of innocence, and the foreman gave her a questioning look.

"Just thinking about the old days," she confessed. "Did you ever live in the dorm back then?"

"No," he said, his usually amiable expression hardening. "Old man Eddings didn't want the white kids mixing with the Blacks and the wetbacks."

"Oh God, that's right. It never occurred to me at the time to wonder why everyone in the dorm was white. We were so clueless."

"And the old man was such a racist. Hard to believe Hoke was his son. He was a good man, Traci."

"Thanks, Javi," she said lightly. "He wanted to do the right thing. He didn't always succeed, you know, what with his dad and Ric siding against him, but at least he tried."

"I paid ninety bucks a month to live in a garage apartment in town," Javi reminisced. "Shared it with two other Guatemalans. I was the oldest, so I got the only bed and the other two shared the pullout sofa." He laughed. "That said, it was a hell of a lot better than that crappy dorm of yours. We had a little kitchen with a fridge and a two-burner stove. Even had a window AC unit. Man, come Friday, we'd pool our money, get some beer, order pizza, crank up our boombox, and party down! We thought we were living high on the hog."

"And I was just excited to have a real job and be able to live on my own. I guess we were all young and dumb and ready to be grown up."

"Speaking of young and dumb, whatever happened to that friend of yours, you know, the cute little lifeguard, the one the old man fired after that poor little kid drowned?"

CHAPTER 8

* * *

2002

It had been a long, hot, boring afternoon at the Saint's swim club. Traci's head pounded and her stomach growled. She and Shannon had spent the previous evening at Pour Willy's, the local hangout in the village, and both the girls were feeling the unhappy effects of Wednesday-night happy hour. She had been watching a group of teenaged girls who'd struck up an improvised game in the shallow end of the pool, batting an inflatable plastic basketball around, shrieking and carrying on and generally annoying the moms with their little kids who'd established their base camp down there.

Traci was about to blow the whistle and order the girls to stop when Hudson, a skinny, little eight-year-old pain-in-the-ass began shouting and waving his arms from where he'd been clinging to the side of the pool in the deep end, not far from the diving board.

Normally, Shannon would have been on the lifeguard stand down there, but she'd just sprinted toward the bathroom with her hand clamped over her mouth, gesturing for Traci to keep watch over her station.

"Gahhh!" Hudson gagged and pointed at the surface of the water near two boys his age who'd been competing in a cannonball contest. One of the kids, a boy named Mike, was usually Hudson's pool buddy, but it appeared that today he and Hudson were on the outs.

"Gross!" Hudson hollered. "One of these guys pooped in the pool!"

Traci climbed down from the lifeguard stand, shaking her head. "Goddammit," she muttered. "Not again." She blew her whistle and picked up a megaphone. "Code brown! Everybody out of the pool. Right now! Code brown!"

The pool emptied in record time, with moms snatching their babies out of the water, and kids running and screaming like they'd just seen a twelve-foot hammerhead shark instead of a two-inch turd.

Just then, Shannon emerged from the bathroom, green around the gills and puzzled by all the commotion.

"Code brown," Traci yelled, pointing at the surface of the water near the ladder.

Shannon picked up her own megaphone to yell at a couple of girls who acted like they hadn't heard the code brown alert. "C'mon y'all, out of the pool. Right now!"

She grabbed the long-handled skimmer and headed for the deep end, handing it off to Traci before returning to her own post.

Traci swept the skimmer over the surface of the pool. She was getting ready to toss the offending item into the trash when she got a closer look. A friggin' Tootsie Roll.

"Hudson!" she yelled, looking around for the little troublemaker. But he seemed to have vanished into the crowd of people ringing the perimeter of the pool.

She reached for her megaphone. "Okay, y'all. Sorry about that. False alarm." She blew her whistle and started to climb back onto the lifeguard stand. "Open swim."

"Traci!" one of the moms screamed, and pointed. A small figure was thrashing around in the water beneath the diving board. She recognized the close-shorn strawberry-blond hair. A moment later, she saw his body go still.

"Hudson!" she hollered, stomping around toward him. "You're not funny. Cut it out. I mean it." But the child didn't turn his head and laugh. Now he was floating, face up in the water. Panicked, she dove into the pool, reaching him in seconds. His eyes were rolled back in his head, his body limp. She looped an arm under his narrow shoulders and swam for the side, keeping his head above the surface. Treading water, she lifted the boy out of the water and onto the side of the pool.

Shannon was sprinting toward them, and as soon as Traci clambered breathlessly out of the pool, she saw that Shannon was already crouched alongside the boy, attempting mouth-to-mouth.

"Somebody call nine-one-one," Traci yelled. She knelt beside the child, placed her hand on his bony, sunburnt chest, touched her fingertips to the base of his neck. Nothing.

"Get a doctor over here," she heard a woman shout. "Where's his mom? Someone needs to find his mom."

"Chest compressions," Traci whispered, wild-eyed. For the next five minutes they frantically worked on the child, pumping his chest, turning him on his side, trying everything they remembered from their lifesaving class, all while surrounded by a crowd of onlookers who'd gone deathly silent.

Finally, after what seemed like hours and hours, they heard the shrill *waaaah* of an approaching siren, and over that, the high-pitched keening of a woman. "Hudson? Where's my baby? Where is he?"

Traci's eyes met Shannon's. It was too late. They both knew it was too late.

CHAPTER 9

* * *

"Traci?" A man's voice echoed in the high-ceilinged barn. Ric Eddings stood in the cart barn doorway, his arms crossed over his chest. "Can I speak to you for a minute? Outside?"

"Uh-oh," Javi said in a low voice. "This can't be good, chica."

Ric's face was rigid with barely suppressed anger. As always, seeing him gave Traci a momentary startle. In passing he looked so like his younger brother: brown-blond hair, deep-set hazel eyes set beneath a high, wide forehead.

The brothers were only sixteen months apart, and Helen, their late mother, had told Traci that until the boys were eight or nine years old, people often mistook them for twins.

As they grew older, the similarities lessened. Ric, short for Frederic, named for his father, was taller and heavier, and his hair was much blonder—helped along, Traci had always suspected, by peroxide. Ric was an extrovert, the life of every party and the star quarterback at the private prep school he had attended, while Hoke was quieter and preferred hiking and fishing to organized sports. Hoke, Traci thought, was Eddings Classic, while Ric was Eddings XX.

And right now, Ric was seething. "Goddammit, Traci," he said, once they were outside. "What do you think you're doing?"

"Me? I'm building a dorm so the summer staff will have a place to live."

"You know what I'm talking about. Going behind my back and pressuring Parrish to cancel her summer abroad and work here instead. How dare you?"

"I didn't pressure her. I explained the bind we're in, with Mehdi and Sammy leaving so close to our opening weekend, and I pointed out the problem we're having finding help. I offered her a free place to live, a hundred-dollar signing bonus, and the best pay on the coast."

"You know just the right buttons to push with that kid," Ric said. "She wants to please her aunt Traci. Always has. She told me you also offered to pay for her program in the fall.

"You bribed her to do what you wanted, without even having the courtesy to discuss it with me."

Traci had to bite back the retort she wanted to give. "Your daughter is twenty-one. She's an adult, Ric. Anyway, Parrish doesn't have to be bribed to do the right thing. She's keenly aware that this business is her heritage, and she wants to make sure the Saint survives so that her generation of the family can continue to run it."

"With you leading the charge. Right, Traci? No kids of your own, so you have to lean on mine."

He'd struck a nerve and he knew it. She and Hoke had tried almost everything, including four rounds of IVF, but nothing had worked. They'd begun discussing adoption when the twin-engine jet he'd been a passenger on went down following a fishing trip to the Bahamas. There were no survivors.

Traci wouldn't let herself react to her brother-in-law's ugly taunts.

"Help me out here, Ric. Seriously. Why are you so pissed about Parrish working for the family business? Isn't this why you paid for her to go to business school at Georgetown?"

He shook his head, as though that might physically shake her away.

"Parrish has a perfectly good home, right here on the island," he said, abruptly changing the subject. "I don't want her living in some dorm with whatever random strangers you've hired for the summer. I know the kind of crazy, dangerous stunts kids get up to in the summer, when they're away from home."

"Is that a shot at me? Because your brother and I started dating the summer I lived in the dorm here? Are you afraid Parrish might mix with townies like you and Hoke did back then?"

"This is different," Ric insisted. "Parrish has gone to private schools her whole life, she's been sheltered. She's never been around . . ." He faltered, realizing how he sounded.

If only he knew the truth about his daughter, Traci thought. About the pregnancy scare Parrish had her senior year of high school, about the boyfriend who'd turned abusive, and the minor brush with the law during Parrish's freshman year at college, all of which she'd confided to Traci. Ric had no idea just how un-sheltered his daughter really was.

"What? Poor white trash? Just another Ain't, like you considered me to be?"

He rolled his eyes. "Talking to you is a waste of time. Obviously, I can't stop Parrish from working or living here. But I'm putting you on notice, Traci. If something happens to her . . ."

"It won't." Traci stopped him. She looked over her shoulder to see that Javi was waiting to finish their punch list. "Are we done here? I've got stuff to do."

"Yeah, we're done," Ric said. "Oh. One more thing. I got a call from Spencer Parkhurst yesterday. He mentioned his son KJ is taking some time off from Wake Forest, so I told him to send him down here and we'll put him to work."

"Who gave you the right to make my hires?" Traci demanded.

"It's a family business, remember?" Ric taunted. "Spencer Parkhurst is a longtime friend and business associate of our family. If his son needs a summer job, you'd do well to give him one. He's a good kid. Plays lacrosse. Polite, respectful."

"Great. Let him work for you at Saint Holdings."

"His dad doesn't want him at some cushy desk job. He wants to give him a taste of real life. You keep talking about being shorthanded, here's your solution. Make KJ a lifeguard, or put him on a grounds crew, or make him a caddy. I don't give a shit. Just put him to work."

Traci sighed. She knew this was Ric's way of paying her back for hiring Parrish.

"Fine. I assume he'll live at their family cottage on Sand Dollar Lane?"

"Nope. His dad thinks it'll be good for him to live in this new dorm of yours. I think he'll be down here in the next couple days."

"Swell," she said. "If it's not too much trouble, tell him to report to me by Friday."

CHAPTER 10

* * *

The problem wasn't a lack of jobs. Nearly every business in this dinky town of Bonaventure had a NOW HIRING sign in the window— from the Walmart out by the interstate to this very coffee shop Felice had been camped out in for two days, surfing their Wi-Fi and slowly nursing the one mug of fancy coffee she allowed herself per visit—just for the sake of using said Wi-Fi. Everybody needed summer help.

No, the problem was a simple matter of economics. All those employers were offering minimum wage, or barely above. Which meant that after paying for food, her phone, and gas for her fifteen-year-old Nissan, not to mention her student loans, there would be nothing left to live on. Or in. The cheapest studio apartment she'd seen advertised online wanted an eye-popping $1,100 a month, plus security deposits. Even a rickety double-wide in the laughably named Oasis Mobile Home Manor, way out in the country, twenty miles from civilization, cost $800 a month—plus utilities.

And then there was the matter of the note she'd cosigned when she and Deion bought the food truck. Thinking about that bastard made her head throb and her stomach burn.

Felice idly turned the page of the free local advertising shopper she'd plucked from a rack near the coffee shop's cash register. Squeezed in between the pancake house, tanning salon, and putt-putt advertisements, a small display ad caught her eye.

EXECUTIVE CHEF—Immediate position open for creative and experienced chef for exclusive local resort. Pay commensurate with experience. Position includes free on-site housing and meals. Uniforms provided. References required. $100 signing bonus.

"On-site housing" was the magic phrase. She'd slept in the Nissan for the past two nights. Her back might never recover. Felice wasn't what you'd call petite. Nearly six feet tall, and her braids added another two inches to her height.

She didn't need much. Growing up in her auntie's two-bedroom apartment in Liberty City along with her two little brothers and a herd of cousins, Felice had never had the luxury of needing much. Maybe that explained why she'd so easily fallen for Deion's line of bullshit. He'd offered her an escape, a glittering glimpse of what life could be.

Now she picked up her phone and called the number in the ad.

Traci had read the applicant's résumé with mounting excitement, tempered with more than a little trepidation.

The young woman, who'd called earlier, then followed up with her résumé, had impeccable credentials. Formal training at a respected culinary institute, stints at two high-end Miami hotel restaurants. But her last job, at a chain steakhouse in Hialeah, gave Traci pause. What was a woman like her doing at a place like that?

Traci had hired and fired enough staff over the years to be wary of those kinds of gaps. They could mean nothing, or they could mean a stint in rehab, jail, or worse.

Charlie poked his head inside the doorway. "You need me?"

"Just a heads-up. Ric informed me yesterday that he has effectively hired Spencer Parkhurst's son, for a yet-to-be-determined position."

"Oh. Well, it's not like we can't use an extra set of hands around here," Charlie said.

She sat back in her desk chair. "Wait. Did you know about this?"

"Saw Ric at the tennis courts yesterday. He mentioned it in passing."

"And you didn't think to mention it to *me*?"

"You beat me to the punch. It's no big deal, Traci. One less hire for you to worry about."

"But I *do* worry about it. That's the point. We don't know a damn thing about this kid, except that his father's rich and Ric apparently owes him a favor."

"So start him as a parking valet, or in the pro shop. If he flames out after a week or two you can fire him and send him on his way."

"And then I'll be right back where I started," Traci said, fuming.

Charlie raised an eyebrow. "Maybe you shouldn't have hired his daughter without discussing it with Ric. You know how he is about her."

"He's a giant pain in my ass. And you, Charlie? I can't believe you're siding with Ric."

"I don't side," Charlie said. "I merely opine."

"Go opine someplace else then," Traci said, making a shooing motion. "I've got a hot chef prospect coming in for an interview."

"Anyone local?"

"Nope. She's young, but she sounds pretty good on paper."

"Don't they all," he said as his parting shot.

Felice followed the signs pointing to the executive offices, housed in a low, vaguely Spanish-looking stucco wing of the hotel, painted shrimp pink with a red tile roof. Felice wiped her sweaty palms on the seat of her pants, took a deep breath, and stepped into the air-conditioned building, where she was directed to Traci's office off the hotel lobby.

"Mrs. Eddings? I'm Felice Bonpierre."

"Hello, Felice," Traci said. "I'm so grateful you could come in today for a chat."

The applicant was not what Traci had expected. She was very tall, for one thing, with long braids that spilled down the back of her jacket, and curious eyes that peered out from behind oversized tortoiseshell-framed glasses. Despite the glasses, she looked very young.

"I'm glad too," Felice said. "I was admiring your grounds as I drove in. Such a beautiful place. It would be a pleasure to work here."

Traci smiled and pointed to the chair across from her desk. "Please. Tell me, Felice, what do you like to cook?" she asked, as soon as the girl was seated.

"Excuse me?"

"I'm wondering what kind of dishes you enjoy preparing," Traci said, enunciating each word as though she thought Felice was deaf or stupid or both.

"I . . . I . . . cook whatever kind of cuisine your guests like," Felice said, stammering because she'd been caught off guard. "French, of course. Asian fusion? New American? Also, high-concept Southern. I went online and saw a couple menus from the Verandah, your fine dining restaurant. That's in the hotel?"

"Correct," Traci said, waiting.

"I can, of course, fry chicken . . ."

"No, no," Traci interrupted, deliberately putting Felice off balance. "I mean, what do you like to cook, for yourself? Your favorite dishes?"

Felice clasped and unclasped her hands, which were folded on her lap. "Me? I cook simple at home. Fresh fish or crab when I'm in Florida, of course. I do a very nice roast chicken, and I love whatever fresh vegetables are in season. Fruit too. I do have a sweet tooth . . ."

"What would you cook for me? For lunch, today?"

"Maybe something light. Fresh local greens with a simple herbed vinaigrette. Some poached shrimp, slice of avocado. Some nice sliced tomatoes if they are ripe."

"And if I don't care for shrimp? Or seafood?"

Felice wrinkled her brow. They were at the coast. Who didn't like seafood at the beach?

"Well . . . I do a nice peach and watermelon salad with burrata, dressed with reduced balsamic vinegar, that could be topped with some poached or grilled chicken, maybe sprinkled with some toasted, chopped pecans. Benne seed crackers too," she added.

"What else would you add to our menu?"

"Hmm. What about a soft-shell crab BLT, on small brioche buns, with microgreens and an herb mayonnaise? If you have a reliable source, what about frog legs instead of wings, in a nice butter-lemon sauce? If your guests simply must have a burger, I'd offer Wagyu beef sliders with quick-pickled red onion slaw, or a deconstructed salmon burger served atop sourdough bread."

Traci's stomach rumbled. The protein shake she'd whipped up at home this morning seemed light-years away. And if this woman's cooking was as good as she sounded, she felt heartened that she'd found her new chef.

"That all sounds very interesting. And inventive. Now, tell me a little about you. Your credentials look good. I called the GM at the Flamingo Club in South Beach, and he had lovely things to say about you."

"Jerry. Nice man," Felice said. "Best boss I ever had."

"If he was so nice, why'd you leave a hit restaurant like the Flamingo to take a job at a less prestigious chain steakhouse?"

Felice flinched. "I had . . . family demands."

"I see. Are you married? Do you have children?"

"No." Felice felt her palms starting to perspire, but she'd be damned if she'd be pressured into explaining about her aunt's illness and the shattering effect it'd had on her large, extended family. It was nobody else's business.

Traci noted the applicant's reluctance. She fiddled with the cap of her gold Montblanc pen. It had been a wedding gift. "I realize these are fairly personal questions, but this is an incredibly high-pressure, time-consuming position. So, if you're a single parent . . ."

"I'm not," Felice said, feeling her cheeks burn. Why did every white woman assume every Black woman her age was a single mother? She decided to plunge ahead with questions of her own.

"Your ad mentioned a competitive salary. Could you be more specific?"

The salary Traci Eddings mentioned made Felice's eyes widen. "That's . . . not bad," she said. It was almost on par with what she'd been making when she left the Flamingo Club, back before Sherise's cancer diagnosis. Before Felice moved home to take care of the aunt who'd been like a mother to her.

"Your ad also mentioned on-site housing," Felice continued. "Could you tell me about that?"

"We're just completing a staff dormitory down near the golf course," Traci said. "We're only set up for singles right now. You'd have a private room, of course, and there's a communal lounge with seating and television, dining area, kitchenette, and laundry. Separate men's and women's bathrooms."

"Oh." Felice longed for a place of her own again.

"Mind if I ask what happened to your most recent chef?" Felice asked.

Traci shrugged. "She and her husband, who worked in the hotel in guest relations, both took jobs with a brand-new resort just up the coast. We hated to see Mehdi go, but the salaries she and Sammy were offered were ridiculous. Not something we could match."

"Okay," Felice said. "So, now what?"

"Now, we send you over to my HR person. He'll get your paperwork completed, see about uniforms, and then you can go tour your kitchen."

"Really?" Felice beamed. "I'm hired?"

"Pending a drug test," Traci said.

"That won't be a problem. And what about housing? When can I move in?"

"The furniture is supposed to be delivered later today, and I'll have a final walk-through this evening. If everything shows up on time, I'd say you could probably move in Friday," Traci said.

She stood up, held out a hand to her new executive chef. "Welcome to the Saint."

CHAPTER 11

* * *

GARRETT

A cool breeze wafted off the ocean as Traci Eddings sat at her usual table on the patio at the Verandah.

Garrett, her favorite waiter, appeared moments later, carrying a glass of iced mineral water with a lime slice.

"Thanks, Garrett," she said, looking down at the notes she'd made back at the office.

"Can I bring you your usual, Mrs. E?"

Her usual was a lobster Cobb salad, but all that discussion of menu options from her newly hired chef had her thinking of trying something different.

"I'm feeling sort of adventurous today. What's your favorite thing these days?"

"I love the crab cakes with remoulade, and we've also got a nice little fillet if you're looking for something heartier."

"How long have those crab cakes been on our menu?" she asked.

Garrett would know. He'd started working at the Saint while he was still in high school.

"We were serving them when I started working here before my senior year."

"So, at least ten years. Can I ask you another question?"

"You're the boss, Mrs. E."

"How's the morale among the restaurant staff? Are folks happy? Content? Anybody thinking of following Mehdi to her new job?"

He looked away. "Uh, well . . ."

"So, people are restless," she said, reading his expression. "Go ahead and bring me the crab cakes." He started to walk away, but she put out a hand and touched his shirt sleeve.

"Wait. Garrett, you're not thinking of leaving us, are you?" She tried to tamp down the desperation in her voice.

Garrett was everyone's favorite, both with the barnacle-encrusted regulars who'd been staying at the hotel for what seemed like centuries, and who appreciated that he always remembered their cocktail orders and their grandchildren's names, but also the younger set, especially the women, because, with his mop of dark ringlets, twin dimples, deep brown eyes, and slender build, he was undeniably easy on the eyes.

His cheeks colored. "It's a really good offer, Mrs. E. Mehdi says the customers there are younger, and bigger tippers. I mean, I don't wanna leave. Y'all have been great to me . . ."

Traci unfolded her napkin and smoothed it across her lap. "I get it. Loyalty doesn't pay the bills, does it? But you live right around the corner here, don't you?"

"Yeah. I rent a room at my sister's. But it's so close, I can ride my bike to work most days, unless there's a hurricane blowing."

"So, how would you get to Surfside? It's at least a thirty-minute drive from here."

"That's a problem, for sure," he admitted, shoving both hands into the pockets of his waiter's apron. "My car needs new tires, brakes, the works."

"What if . . ." Traci started. "What if I raise your pay to what Surfside is offering?"

He grinned.

"You're kinda the senior guy around here, right?"

"I guess."

"Okay. How's this? We make you headwaiter, starting now. We'll also give you a hundred-dollar signing bonus."

"I like the sound of that," Garrett said, the grin widening.

"Just out of curiosity. Are you happy with your living situation?" she asked.

"Not so much, but Thea only charges me like a hundred bucks a week. I mean, I'd love to get an apartment, but no way I can afford to live around here. Not on my own."

"Have you heard about the new staff dorm?"

"Yeah. I checked it out the other day. Looks like a pretty sweet setup. How much are you charging people?"

"Nothing. It's all free. Including the Wi-Fi."

He looked dubious. "Why? I mean, what's the catch?"

"No catch. I don't have to tell you, housing in the village is outrageously expensive. So this is an incentive, and a way for us to compete with the Surfsides of the world."

He looked around, then pulled out the chair across from hers and sat down. "Are you saying—are you telling me I could live there? For free?"

"Absolutely," Traci said.

"Okay, lemme get this order in for you. And about that dorm. If you're serious, how soon could I move in?"

"The furniture is being delivered this afternoon. How does tomorrow sound?"

"Fucking awesome!" He pumped his fist in the air, then shrugged as he realized who he was talking to. "Sorry. My sister stays on my ass about my potty mouth."

She laughed. "I tend not to trust anyone who doesn't occasionally let an F-bomb fly. I'll let HR know about your raise. Hopefully move-in is this weekend."

CHAPTER 12

* * *

"Traci Waci!" Madelyn Eddings bore down on Traci with a force that belied her diminutive size.

Traci reflexively ground her back molars. "Hi, Madelyn. What's up?"

As usual, her sister-in-law was dressed to impress: dark hair coiffed high and gleaming, the jacket of her suit cut close and worn without a blouse to expose an inch of cleavage, the skirt tight and short, wicked-expensive Jimmy Choo spike heels, and as always, fluttery lash extensions and acrylic nails.

Madelyn's voice belied her business barracuda appearance. It was breathy, babyish even. "What's this I hear about you taking that nasty old golf cart barn and turning it into a staff dorm?"

"Ric told you, huh?"

"It would have been nice if *you'd* told me," Madelyn said, pouting. "Really, Traci, I can't believe you didn't even consult me before you began this project. And now, Ric says it's almost done. As director of design I should have had some input into this project." She shook her head, conveying her deep disappointment.

"There were no design decisions to be made. A lounge, a kitchen, two bathrooms, and some bedrooms. Once I realized we needed to do something to attract summer staff, there was no time to waste."

"Still, I should have been consulted. Window placement, flooring, bathroom fixtures, all those kinds of aesthetic decisions come under my purview," Madelyn protested.

"Anyway, I need to talk to you about the Pederson wedding. Nathalie, our bride, hates the ballroom wallpaper. And I agree. It's so . . . formal." She tapped her pen on the notebook, cocked her head, and flashed Traci a winning smile. "And dated. It just screams nineteen fifties. I was thinking instead we install a nice grass cloth maybe, or a more contemporary paper."

Traci cut her off. "We are *not* changing out the ballroom wallpaper for one spoiled-brat bride. That is a custom de Gournay mural, with all the flora and fauna native to this part of the coast. God only knows how much it cost when Helen had it installed."

Madelyn fluttered her lashes. "You know, Traci, time does march on." She gazed around the lobby. "We don't want to give our guests the impression that we're stuck in a time warp, do we? It seems to me that our post-Covid event bookings are a little . . . tepid. Ric thinks—"

Traci didn't care what her brother-in-law thought about the hotel's décor, or the health of the Saint's event bookings. "Let me remind you that before you joined the company, we'd just finished a massive property-wide renovation project, and our designer specified that the de Gournay should stay. We spent several thousand dollars having it restored and repaired."

Madelyn wrinkled her cute little nose.

"You don't have to get so defensive, Traci. I realize that the restoration project was Hoke's little baby, but really, you need to be more objective about matters like this. Ric and I are only trying to help keep our family's legacy alive."

Traci felt the heat rise in her cheeks at the mention of Hoke's name. Ric and Madelyn had been attempting to meddle in the way the hotel was run ever since the plane crash.

Before her father-in-law, Fred, became totally incapacitated with Parkinson's, he had finally caved to Ric's demands that his wife should be given a role in the company's management. The old man installed Madelyn as the family holding company's "design director," a nebulous title that seemed to allow her free rein to pass judgment on everything from the look of the Verandah's printed menus to signage for her husband's exclusive new townhouse development to, apparently, the appearance of the hotel ballroom. This despite the fact that the woman's only recent job experience was as assistant manager of a high-end menswear shop.

Which was where Ric and Madelyn had met. Her brother-in-law liked to order custom tailored shirts and bespoke suits from H. Capaldi's in Atlanta. Madelyn had apparently suited Ric just fine. They'd dated in secret until her divorce was finalized, then married quietly in Atlanta and honeymooned in Provence.

Parrish, not surprisingly, had taken an instant dislike to her new stepmother.

"Thanks for your concern, Madelyn, but you can assure Ric that the hotel is in good shape. I've hired a new chef for the Verandah, and earlier this week, Parrish agreed to step in as guest relations manager for the summer."

Something flickered in the other woman's eyes. "Parrish? That can't be right. She's headed for Europe. She's already packed."

Traci wasn't surprised Ric hadn't told his wife this bit of news.

"I persuaded her to put off Europe—just 'til the season's over. Great news, right?"

Madelyn pursed her lips.

"As for the event bookings," Traci continued, "we've got two new conferences coming in July, and they've already reserved half our rooms. And I know we have every weekend in June and July, as well as some weekdays, solidly booked with weddings. So it's all good, right?"

"We'll see," Madelyn said, her tone pessimistic.

"Okay," Traci said briskly. "Glad we had this little chat, now I need to get back to my office. But feel free to keep me updated on the new signage for the beach club."

CHAPTER 13

* * *

Traci closed her laptop, glanced at her phone, and stood. It was after eight. If she didn't hustle, she'd miss sunset, which was an unforgiveable sin at the Saint.

Hoke's mother had started the tradition shortly after she'd married into the family. Helen Parrish Eddings was from landlocked Iowa, and she never stopped marveling at the technicolor displays of sunsets over the river that divided the resort from the mainland.

Leo, the senior bellman, held the door as Traci entered the hotel lobby, crossed the nearly empty space, and stepped out onto the cobblestone courtyard of the Riverside Patio.

The bartender saw her approaching and handed her a glass of prosecco. "Thanks, Kendra," Traci said.

She joined a knot of folks standing at the edge of the patio, facing the river. Some of them, the old guard who didn't live at the Saint but maintained their family club memberships, greeted her with hugs and waves. A sunburnt family of six—grandparents, she assumed, with their grown children and two young grandchildren—stood slightly apart, not quite sure of the protocol. Hotel guests, Traci surmised, or maybe they were renting one of the bungalows for the week. She greeted them, directed them to the bar for their complimentary glasses of prosecco, then joined the regulars just as the sun hovered at the water's edge.

Suddenly, a trumpeter stepped forward, and just as the sun slipped from view, he played the first bars of "Retreat." Glancing around, Traci raised her glass and the other spectators followed suit. "Here's to another beautiful summer at the Saint," she called.

"Here, here!" The others joined the toast and drained their glasses.

She slipped quietly from the patio, walked back to her car, and as dusk settled over the island, she drove the winding roads, yet another ritual Hoke had insisted upon at the close of a business day.

"Why?" she'd asked, dumb as a rock at the age of nineteen, the first time she'd joined him on the golf cart ride around the property. "You have about a hundred employees working here. Why not let them do the tour? Why can't we just go to the movies like normal people?"

"Granddad always did the rounds, and then Dad, and now it's my turn," he'd said, patting her knee. "Besides, this is something I enjoy. It's the time of the day when I can really get a good look at the property. If a tree branch has fallen, or the trim on one of the bungalows needs paint, I can see it, make a note, and then address it first thing in the morning."

It wasn't until they'd been married nearly a year that Traci began to comprehend everything that went into running a historic family-owned resort like the Saint.

Nothing, it seemed, was too small a detail for Hoke to notice, and address. The soap in the men's grill restroom (hand-milled in England), the thickness of the beach towels at the beach club (sourced in Italy, monogrammed locally), the slightly faded armchair fabric in the lobby of the hotel, all of it was important to him. And gradually, over the years, it became important to her too.

She drove slowly, with the Mercedes' windows rolled down, inhaling the intoxicating scent of night-blooming jasmine. A possum skittered across the road in front of her, its eyes glowing red. She reached for her phone and dictated a note to ask the landscapers to make sure the creature hadn't dug up any flowerbeds in the area.

As she rounded a bend in the road she noticed some roof tiles missing from Plumbago Cottage, and added that to the note. A few cottages away, lights burned at the largest of the two dozen bungalows scattered around the property. She pulled into the short driveway of the Gardenia. A Kia with faded blue paint was parked under the carport.

Traci knocked lightly on the door and a petite older woman answered.

"Hi, Alberta. I was just passing by and thought I'd drop in. Is he awake?"

"Hi, Traci. Come on in. This is good timing. He's just had his bath and his meds."

She opened the door wider and Traci stepped inside. The television was on, and there was a tray with a sandwich and a glass of iced tea on the coffee table.

"I'm sorry to interrupt dinner," Traci apologized. "I won't stay long. How's he doing?"

The caretaker shrugged. "About the same. Honestly, I don't think the new meds are making a difference. In fact, I think maybe they make him feel more drowsy."

"Okay. I'll speak to the doc. If they're not helping, what's the point?" She touched Alberta's shoulder. "Go back to what you were doing. I'll say hi, then I'll get out of your hair."

Traci glanced around the living/dining area. All the original furnishings had been moved out once her father-in-law finally accepted the fact that he could no longer live independently in the grand Spanish Colonial revival mansion his own father had designed and built on the ocean side of the resort. The winding stairway that led to the villa's massive carved wooden front doors was one of the many features that made the house inaccessible, once the diagnosis of Parkinson's disease was pronounced, and confirmed by two more doctors.

Fred fought the move for months, but after he'd fallen and spent a brutal night alone, sprawled out on the floor of his bathroom, only to be found naked in a pool of his own urine the next day by his housekeeper, he'd had no choice.

Within two weeks, the Gardenia had been retrofitted with wider doorways, a wheelchair-accessible bathroom complete with shower lift, and private living quarters for the old man's favorite house-keeper, Alberta, who'd tended to him with quiet devotion since his wife's death eight years earlier. Madelyn had planned and engineered the lightning-fast remodel, and Traci had grudgingly admired her ruthless efficiency.

Traci stepped into the bedroom, which was illuminated by the soft light of a bedside lamp. The head of the hospital bed was raised.

Parkinson's had diminished Fred in so many cruel ways. Though he was once a vigorous athlete who'd played A-level team tennis and scratch golf well into his eighties, the man she saw before her now was nearly unrecognizable.

His skin, pale and liver-spotted, was stretched tautly over his skull, where only thinning tufts of white hair remained of his once glossy mane. Bony collarbones were visible beneath his cotton pajama top, and his skeletal arms were arranged stiffly on top of the sheet.

Hooded eyes flickered when he saw her. Colorless lips moved, but no words emerged.

She sat in the chair beside his bed. "Alberta tells me the new meds aren't helping much. Maybe I'll ask the doctor to take you off them?"

He blinked once, which she took to mean yes.

"Sorry I haven't been by this week. I've been super busy because we're ramping up for opening weekend. Trying to hire enough staff. Mehdi, do you remember her? Our head chef? She and her husband, Sam, who was head of guest relations in the hotel, left to take jobs up the coast at that new resort."

His expression was unchanging.

"I sweet-talked Parrish into postponing her Europe semester. She's agreed to take over Sammy's job. Ric is furious with me, but wouldn't you think he'd be pleased to have the next generation of the family in such a front-facing position at the Saint? I think it's a control issue."

The old man's lips turned up slightly. Was it a smile, or merely a cruel symptom of the Parkinson's?

Fred was intimately familiar with control issues. For sixty years he'd ruled the family business and his sons with an iron hand.

Somehow, Hoke had avoided turning into a carbon copy of his father. He was decent, caring, and warm, like his mother.

Fred snorted.

"Has Ric been by to see you lately?" she asked, her tone innocent.

She doubted he had. Ever since the Parkinson's diagnosis, her brother-in-law avoided seeing his father, claiming it was too depressing. Ric had begun researching nursing homes after Fred's fall, but Traci and Parrish had put a stop to that plan, instead insisting on moving Fred into Gardenia, where he had round-the-clock care.

Two years ago the doctors said Fred probably had less than six months to live. Yet here he was.

The old man's head slowly swiveled back in her direction, his eyes blazing.

"I'm sorry," she murmured. "I know he's been . . . busy."

Traci looked around the room. The wall-mounted flat-screen television was on, tuned to Fred's favorite financial news network, with the volume muted. It was an endless scroll of numbers—the highs and lows of the stock market, banking news. This, she supposed, was the only thing that regularly gave him joy—watching his net worth grow.

Such a depressing thought.

"Okay, I'm gonna go now," Traci said, standing. "Sleep well."

As soon as she walked in the door of her own bungalow, she collapsed into the nearest chair, overcome with guilt—for not doing more for Fred, even though she knew he silently detested her, and grief—oh God, the grief, the endless, relentless waves that rolled over her at the most unexpected times, and every day threatened to submerge her back into the darkness of that first, unbearable year after the plane crash.

And now, once again, she was wrestling with those two demon emotions. Hoke had been painfully aware of his father's many failings, as a father, a husband, an employer, but to Hoke, family loyalty was everything. So she tried to treat her father-in-law with compassion.

But every encounter with the old bastard left her with this . . . rage. Why should this dreadful man still be alive, at his age, while Hoke, her first and only love, a truly decent man who had so much to give to the world . . . why should *he* be the one moldering in a grave? Where was the fairness in that?

Traci went into the kitchen, opened the door of the under-counter wine fridge, and reached for the nearest bottle, a nicely chilled bottle of sauvignon blanc. She was about to pour herself a glass, but paused.

Rebecca, her therapist, had warned against using alcohol as a crutch at times like these. Mindfulness, Rebecca counseled. Practice mindfulness.

She heard her cell phone ringing.

UNKNOWN CALLER. She clicked Connect anyway.

"Hello? This is Traci Eddings."

A woman's voice, husky, vibrating with fury. "What the hell do you think you're doing?"

They hadn't talked in decades, but she recognized that voice in an instant.

"Hi, Shannon," she said. "How lovely to hear from you after all these years."

CHAPTER 14

* * *

The sound of Traci's voice—the recently acquired creamy, nuanced accent of a card-carrying country club Junior Leaguer—triggered something in Shannon.

"We need to talk," she said abruptly.

"So talk. I'm listening."

"I meant in person. Livvy's in the next room. She's already pissed at me for interfering."

"Shannon, I've had a long, brutal day. I just want to take off my bra, run a bath, and get in bed with a book. I frankly don't see what difference—"

"You *owe* me this much," Shannon said, cutting her off. "Meet me at Pour Willy's. I can be there in fifteen minutes."

Traci let out a long, aggrieved sigh. "I need twenty minutes."

"Twenty minutes. Back booth," Shannon said, and she disconnected.

Shannon hadn't been back to their old hangout in years. Not much had changed. Loud tunes blared from the jukebox. The same old neon Pabst Blue Ribbon signs blinked in the windows. It was a weeknight, so no bouncer met her at the door. Or maybe they didn't have bouncers now? The floor was still sticky; probably hadn't been mopped since the last time she was here. She hadn't been to *any* bars since she quit drinking, but as soon as she pushed open the heavy wooden door at Pour Willy's, Shannon found herself craving a beer.

"You don't really want a drink," she scolded herself as she shouldered through the throngs of young people standing three deep at the bar, waving away the haze of cigarette smoke. The county had adopted a ban on indoor smoking years earlier, but the news had apparently escaped the crowd here.

The back booth, their booth—the one just past the jukebox, closest to the bathroom—was occupied by a gaggle of college girls with a table full of sickly-sweet-looking parasol drinks. Back in her day, you'd have been bounced out of the place if you'd asked for anything other than a shot or a beer. These chicks were all sloppy drunk and definitely underaged.

Shannon fixed the kid seated at the near edge of the booth with an icy stare. The girl's makeup was smeared and her eyes were glassy. She looked up at the stranger with a goofy grin.

"Heyyyy. What's up?"

"I need to see some ID," Shannon said, holding out her hand.

"You're not a cop," one of the girls piped up. "If you're a cop, show us your badge."

This one had dyed red hair cut short to the scalp with half a dozen visible piercings—nose, upper lip, ears, and God knows where else. Shannon reached over and grabbed the girl's arm, deliberately spilling her drink.

"Heyyyy!" the girl protested, yanking her arm away.

"Damn straight I'm not a cop. I'm from the county beverage control board. I need to see a valid ID from every one of you little juvenile delinquents. Then I'm going to call the cops, who'll arrest all of y'all for being minors in possession," Shannon announced.

"You can't do that," the mouthy redhead shot back. She pointed her cell phone at Shannon, but Shannon was quicker and plucked it out of her hand.

"Oh, look," Shannon said. "I just did it." She tossed the phone into the pool of booze.

"Shut up, Marlee," a blond girl at the other side of the booth said. "Come on, y'all. Let's go. If I get caught drinking again my dad will never let me off restriction."

One by one, the girls scooted out of the booth. Marlee took her own sweet time. When she stood, she deliberately bumped against Shannon. "See you next Tuesday," she said loudly.

A woman's voice whispered in her ear. "Nicely done, Shan."

She whirled around. Traci was standing beside the bathroom door, laughing as the teenagers filed past.

She was dressed in a pale pink tank top that displayed tanned, trim arms; white leggings; and those pricey Jack Rogers sandals that showed off a French pedicure. Her streaky blond hair was pulled back in a high ponytail and her makeup was flawless.

Shannon, on the other hand, was squeezed into a pair of shredded jeans, a Mumford & Sons concert tee, and flip-flops. Her right-outta-the-box auburn hair color needed touching up, and the only makeup she wore was some Carmex lip balm.

Traci set two beers on the table the girls had just vacated and sat down at the booth.

Shannon sat on the opposite side, but pushed one of the beers away. "I don't drink."

"Since when?" Traci took a sip of her beer.

"None of your business. Just so you know, this isn't a reunion, and it's not a social call. I just need you to un-hire my kid."

"Un-hire. That's a novel concept. Just out of curiosity, why would I do that?"

"Why would you hire her to work at the Saint? Did you wake up this week and just decide to push my buttons, after all these years?"

Traci laughed. "I know you might find this hard to believe, Shan, but not everything is about you. I happened to take my niece Parrish to lunch at BluePointe earlier this week. They're obviously understaffed, like everybody I know in the hospitality business, and frankly, not very well managed. But our server was excellent. When she figured out the kitchen had screwed up our order, she apologized and tried to make things right. I offered her a job on the spot and didn't figure out until she told me her name that she was your daughter."

Shannon leaned against the back of the booth. "Livvy doesn't want to work at the Saint. And she definitely doesn't want to work for any member of the Eddings family."

"She's a grown-up. I think she can tell me that herself, if it's true, which I doubt. She recognized my name as soon as I handed her my business card, so she knew who I was. She called me back that same night to accept the job, which was a huge relief."

"Why are you doing this? There are hundreds of kids looking for jobs in this town. Hire one of them. Hire one of those little idiots I just chased outta here."

Traci cocked one eyebrow. "Did Olivia tell you I'm paying her two dollars an hour more than her previous employer? Giving her a signing bonus? And providing her with free on-site housing? I'd think you'd be glad for her to have an opportunity like this."

"An opportunity to be exploited? To be preyed on by assholes and jerks like your other employees, or even worse, your 'member-guests'? And oh yeah, tell me about this posh 'dorm situation' you expect my kid to live in. I heard it's actually the old golf cart barn."

Shannon gripped the edge of the tabletop with both hands. She really, really wanted a beer, or any kind of a buzz that would help her calm down and resist the urge to lean across the table and pluck out Traci's luxuriously long eyelashes one by one.

"So that's what this is really about," Traci said finally. "It's not about Olivia at all. It's about you, and your grievance with Hoke's family. And me. Twenty-one years later, and you're still pissed that you got fired instead of me after that little boy drowned, even though I tried to tell everyone who'd listen that it wasn't your fault. I even went to Hoke's dad and begged him to listen to me, but he'd already made up his mind."

She leaned across the table. "Shan, we were best friends. Or, I thought we were. I told you *everything* that was going on in my life. About my dad losing his job and my mom's breast cancer. I even told you about my dad's affair—which I never told anybody about. My own husband never knew about it until years later! I told you the first time Hoke kissed me, and the first time we did it. But you? I didn't even know you were dating anybody, let alone sneaking around and sleeping with some guy. You didn't even tell me you were pregnant. You completely cut me out of your life."

Traci's blue eyes bored into hers.

"You wouldn't have understood," Shannon said. "I know you, Traci. You would have judged me. Or tried to talk me into getting rid of the baby. My life was complicated enough."

"See!" Traci threw her hands into the air. "I would never have judged you. Never! I mean, neither of us were virgins. So what? Maybe if you'd trusted me, just a little . . ."

Shannon released her grip on the table and took a deep breath. "You're wrong about this being about me. I want Liv to have better choices and make better decisions than me. Her going to work— and live—at the Saint, working for the Eddingses? No. Livvy doesn't need that."

"What is your deal with my in-laws?" Traci demanded.

"You crossed over to the dark side when you married into that family," Shannon insisted. "What they did to me was totally unfair. That kid, Hudson? He was at the pool nearly every day that summer. He swam like a fish. So how did he suddenly drown? And why did I get the blame? I was doing my goddamn *job*, getting everyone out of that pool."

"I don't disagree," Traci said quietly. "You got screwed over."

"The old man paid off people to keep their mouths shut and look the other way after Hudson. There was no police investigation. It didn't even make the news," Shannon said.

Traci drained the last of her beer. "You're still blaming me for something I had no control over. I'm not them, Shannon. Yes, I agree, the old man was and is a horrible person. And if it makes you feel any better, he's dying and has nothing to do with the day-to-day at the Saint. Ric is also a piece of shit, but he's on the real estate side of the business. He didn't hire Olivia. I did. I'm the one running the

Saint, and I'm the one that will see to it that Olivia and our other new hires, including Ric's daughter Parrish, are treated fairly."

"Riiiight," Shannon drawled.

"Okay, I'm done here," Traci said, standing up. She threw a ten-dollar bill onto the table. "By the way, if you want to check out the new dorm, be my guest. Gimme a heads-up and I'll leave you a pass at the security gate."

Shannon watched as Traci wove her way through the crowd of twenty- and thirtysomethings, still turning heads as she went. "See you next Tuesday," she muttered.

CHAPTER 15

* * *

Thirty minutes later, Traci stood in the shower, trying to rinse the stink of cigarette smoke and beer out of her hair, and still fuming about the encounter with Shannon.

It was all so unfair. They'd grown up together, graduated from high school, gotten in and out of trouble together. They were both Ain'ts, from working-class families, living in the shadow of a five-star resort their families never could have afforded.

Traci stepped out of the shower, toweled off, and pulled on her nightgown. When she opened the bathroom door, Lola was crouched in front of it, waiting for her to emerge. She gave a short, happy bark, wagging her whole body in ecstasy. Traci scooped her up and deposited her onto the bed. Lola was a rescue, an anxious senior dog nobody wanted, part dachshund, part Velcro, sticking to her side for every waking hour she was at home.

She glanced at the clock on her nightstand. It would have been laughable, if it hadn't been so pathetic—she and Shannon, meeting tonight at their old hangout, then home and in bed, alone, before ten o'clock.

Two decades later—oh, how the times had changed.

She and Shannon had planned that summer of '02 in minute detail. Job one was to move away from home. They were both nineteen, with a year of community college under their belts. Job two was to land one of the prized lifeguard positions at the Saint and start saving money for their own apartments. Job three was to meet a cute, rich guy. There was never a shortage of those sons of families who "summered" at the resort.

Things went according to the plan. At first. Traci and Shannon hadn't just shared a room at the staff dorm, they'd shared everything, from clothes to confidences. Saint employees were specifically forbidden to consort with guests, but both of them had managed short-lived, furtive flings early in the summer.

But then everything changed, almost overnight on a Friday night. Armed with newly minted fake IDs, they'd gone to Pour Willy's together, but Shannon had hooked up with a guy almost as soon as they'd entered the bar, leaving Traci to fend for herself.

She'd just come out of the bathroom and wasn't looking where she was going; in fact, she was trying to zip up her Daisy Dukes—technically, they were Shannon's shorts, which was why the zipper seemed to be stuck.

The next thing Traci knew, she'd run straight into a guy who was, unfortunately, holding two flimsy plastic cups of beer, which collapsed and splashed all over her. And him.

"Oh, geez, my bad," he'd said, taking a step backward. He was four inches taller than her. He was wearing geeky Clark Kent–style horn-rimmed glasses, and dressed all wrong for a dive bar: khakis, navy blazer, an unknotted striped repp tie, and a button-down dress shirt that was now soaked in beer.

He'd stammered out an apology as he was gingerly mopping the beer off her boobs with an honest-to-Gawd handkerchief, and she'd started giggling, uncontrollably. "Oh man. I'm sorry. I, uh . . ."

Traci felt bad for the guy. Had he wandered in here from an undertakers' convention?

"It's okay. I think it was my fault 'cuz I wasn't looking where I was going because I was trying to zip up my shorts." She couldn't help herself, she looked up at him and brazenly batted her eyelashes. "Maybe you could help me out?"

He blushed violently. "Uh, well, I'm not sure. I mean, now my hands are all sticky with beer, and I wouldn't want . . ."

"Never mind," she'd said sharply, abruptly turning her back on him and returning to the barstool she'd abandoned earlier. She'd made an outrageous play for the guy and he'd fumbled badly, and she felt totally humiliated.

Ten minutes later, she felt a light tap on her shoulder. It was Clark Kent again. He'd ditched the blazer, and the necktie.

"Hey. I think I kinda blew my shot back there."

She raised an eyebrow. "Ya think?"

"I'm terrible at this kind of stuff," he confessed. "I don't have a single good pickup line, and zero smooth moves."

"Sad but true," Traci agreed.

"Give me a do-over? Let me buy you a drink, or a burger or something?"

"They don't have burgers here," Traci informed him. "Just greasy nachos, which I don't recommend." She tilted her head and appraised him. He had too-short dark hair with a silver streak, and a strong jawline. There was something about him—he was appealingly vulnerable. Not her usual type at all, and definitely not a regular at Pour Willy's.

"Maybe we could go somewhere else to get a drink, and maybe some food too?"

"Like where? They roll up the sidewalks in this dumpy town right about now."

He nodded thoughtfully. "Right. Of course. What about the Saint? The Verandah doesn't close for another hour yet, from what I hear."

Her spirits perked up. "So . . . you're a member there?"

"Yeah. I am. What do you think?"

"I'd love to, but they've got really strict rules out there—about the staff consorting with guests. And it'd be just my luck to get caught."

"Oh. You work at the Saint? What do you do there?"

"Lifeguard," Traci said.

"That's cool," he said. "Well, I wouldn't want to get you fired, but I think there's a way around the rules. What about . . . if we go to my bungalow? I can call ahead and order dinner to go. You can stay in the car, and nobody has to be any the wiser."

"Your bungalow? You *own* a house out there?"

"It's been in the family for a while," he said, sounding apologetic.

He blushed again. Traci'd never been with a guy who blushed before, and she had to admit it was kind of a turn-on. That, combined with the fact that he owned a house? At the Saint? Wait until she told Shannon.

"Let's go."

"Just like that? What about your friend? Won't she be worried about you?"

She narrowed her eyes. "How'd you know about my friend? Have you been stalking me all night?"

"What? No! I mean, I saw you with that other girl, earlier, is all. I'm really not a pervert."

"Which explains why you were lurking outside the bathroom at a bar. Textbook perv move. Next thing I know, you'll offer me some candy if I'll get in your car, and next month, my picture will be on milk cartons and billboards. HAVE YOU SEEN THIS GIRL?"

His face turned an even brighter shade of crimson. "Oh my God! I keep making things worse. Never mind. I'm leaving now, before you report me to the police."

He turned to go, but Traci reached out and caught his hand. "Hey, wait up."

"You still want to leave with me? After all that?"

Traci laughed and linked her arm through his. "You're not smooth enough to be a pervert. My name's Traci, by the way. What's yours?"

"Hoke."

She willingly climbed into his Jeep, which was parked outside, and it wasn't until they pulled up to the gate at the resort, and the security guard stepped outside and snapped to attention with a respectful "Evening, Mr. Eddings," that Traci realized she'd accidentally managed to get herself picked up by Hoke Eddings, whose family owned the whole damn place.

Wait 'til she told Shannon.

CHAPTER 16

* * *

Olivia placed her suitcase into the trunk of her car and slammed the lid, guiltily enjoying the stricken look on her mother's face.

Shannon had watched, silently, as Livvy packed up her stuff. She stood, stone-faced, as her daughter made trip after trip out to the car.

"Okay, that's it," Livvy said, returning to the living room. "Gotta get going. After move-in I've got orientation and training, and I'm working the dinner shift tonight."

"Good for you." Shannon gave Livvy a peck on the cheek, but drew back when her daughter tried to hug her.

"Mom, don't be like this," Livvy wailed. "I'm not joining a cult or going to prison. I'll be six miles away. Why can't you be happy for me?"

"Because I can't. I can't pretend when it comes to those people. That place. Liv, please. I'm asking you . . ." Shannon's voice broke.

Olivia stuck her fingers in her ears. "Can't hear you. Lalalalala." She shook her head as she walked away. "I'll call you next week to let you know I'm still alive."

Her back was to Shannon, so she didn't see the haunted expression on her mother's face.

Traci Eddings stood in the lounge area of the new staff dorm on move-in day. As she sipped a mug of coffee from the kitchen's Keurig machine, she looked around and liked what she saw. Everything was just right, because she'd taken charge of the project herself, much to Charlie and Madelyn's annoyance.

"We have people for this kind of thing, Traci," Charlie had said when he encountered her instructing the maintenance crew on how she wanted the bamboo blinds installed.

"I know. But I want to do this. It's a creative outlet for me—much more rewarding than staring at spreadsheets and rack-card rates."

He'd muttered something unintelligible and wandered away.

She wondered if her employees were experiencing the same mixture of excitement and apprehension that had flooded her all morning.

The first to arrive was Felice, her new chef. She carried a single duffel bag and a pillowcase bulging with what Traci suspected was her laundry.

"Where do you want me?" Felice asked.

"Everyone's room has their name on a little brass plate on the door. Your room is at the back, on the right-hand side. I hope you like it."

Before Felice could reply, the front door opened and the others entered: Olivia Grayson, Garrett, and a well-muscled twentysomething hunk who was dressed for a fraternity party in salmon-colored Vineyard Vines shorts, a loose-fitting, untucked white dress shirt, and Topsiders. He had to be KJ Parkhurst.

No sign of Parrish, which was a bad look for a family member.

Garrett, who was the senior-most in terms of employment at the hotel, and obviously regarded himself as the unofficial leader of the dorm residents, gave her a wide, assured smile as he strolled down the hallway, pausing in the kitchen to look around. "Hey, Mrs. E. This place turned out sweet."

"Glad you approve," Traci said. "All right, everyone. Please take a seat in the lounge. I know you all have shifts coming up, so I won't take up too much of your time."

The front door opened and Parrish walked in, looking as though she'd just pulled an all-night rager, clutching a can of Red Bull in one hand and tugging an enormous hard-sided aluminum rolling suitcase with the other. Three pairs of eyes stared at her.

Sorry, Parrish mouthed, sensing her aunt's annoyance. She scurried to join the others.

"First off," Traci said, "everyone has been assigned a room, and your name is on a small brass plaque on your door. You're all adults here, so I'll expect you to behave accordingly. You'll be responsible for keeping your own bedrooms clean and orderly. Upkeep of the communal areas, like this lounge, the bathrooms, kitchen, and laundry area, will be your responsibility as a group, although housekeeping will stop in once a week to do heavy cleaning. I'd suggest you work out a schedule to share cleaning responsibilities."

She pointed a finger at the men: Garrett and KJ. "It might surprise you to learn that the summer I was nineteen, I lived in a staff dorm here on the Saint property. What I remember vividly from that experience is how little the guys did of their share of the grunt work. Maybe times have changed. I hope they have. But just in case, I want to repeat that you all share equal responsibilities for upkeep of this facility."

The women in the group exchanged knowing nods.

"Similarly, this communal living arrangement is an experiment. An expensive experiment. It only works if all of you respect one another and yourselves. Illegal drug use will not be tolerated and will be cause for dismissal. Sexual harassment of any kind—also cause for dismissal. Again, respect—for one another's privacy, for boundaries, for the greater good of this little community here—is absolutely essential."

She felt her phone buzzing from the pocket of her jeans, a reminder that she had an important meeting back in her office in five minutes. "That's it," Traci said. "Have a good summer, and please don't make me regret this arrangement."

As soon as the boss was gone, KJ picked up the remote control from the coffee table and flicked the television on. "Cool. Premium cable package."

An awkward silence fell over the room as the others glanced at each other.

"Okay," Garrett said finally. "Hey, y'all. I'm Garrett. I've worked here for the past ten years. Mrs. E just promoted me to headwaiter at the Verandah." He pointed at the latecomer. "Don't I know you?"

Her smile was tight. "I'm Parrish. I've worked at the Saint in different capacities since I was a kid. I'll be working guest relations at the hotel, but only for this summer."

"Parrish? Aren't you Ric Eddings's daughter? Mind if I ask why you're living here with us commonfolk?" Garrett asked. "Especially since you have that sweet house up on the bluff?"

She pushed a strand of hair behind her ear and sighed dramatically. "Yes, I'm Ric's daughter, and Traci's niece, and yes, I mind if you ask questions that are none of your business," Parrish said. She got up and walked down the corridor, suitcase in hand. She stepped into the room and closed the door without further comment.

"Oh . . . kay," KJ Parkhurst said. "That was awkward. I'm KJ. I'll be working in the pro shop, but I might fill in as a valet attendant, or anyplace else I'm needed, according to my supervisor."

Garrett fetched a can of Coke from the fridge. "Parkhurst? Are you related to Mr. Kevin? He's like an OG golf member, right?"

"That's my granddad," KJ said, leaving it at that.

"So what . . . your family has a mansion that looks out on the golf course but you're slumming it with us this summer for shits and grins?"

KJ grimaced. "I *was* a sophomore at Wake. Fucked up my knee playing lacrosse, got kicked off the team, flunked out, pissed off my old man. This," he said, waving his hand expansively around the room, "is his idea of making me man up."

He slumped backward and nodded at Livvy. "Your turn."

"Olivia Grayson. Everybody calls me Livvy. I'll be a server at the Verandah, so I guess Garrett maybe will be my supervisor?" She shot him a tremulous smile. "I was working at BluePointe, and I waited on Mrs. E one day at lunch, so she recruited me to work here. I'm a local, grew up in town here. I've been going to the local community college, but I've got plans . . ."

"Plans," Felice muttered. "Ain't we all got some goddamn plans."

"You're the new chef, right?" Livvy asked. "I think I saw you in the kitchen when Mr. Burroughs was giving me a tour of the place."

"Felice." She obviously wasn't the smiley kind. "I'm from Miami, well, Hialeah, I work hard, I mind my own business." She glared at the men. "And I don't want my kitchen messed up. Like Mrs. E said, if you cook something, clean up after yourself. And don't nobody touch my stuff, especially my kombucha that's in the fridge, and we'll get along just fine." She sat back, her arms crossed over her chest.

CHAPTER 17

* * *

WHELAN

Whelan got to town on Tuesday morning, and by that afternoon he'd rented a grubby, overpriced, furnished efficiency above a surf shop in the village. It wasn't much—a pullout sleeper sofa, kitchenette, and tiny bathroom—but he didn't need much.

On Wednesday, he activated his Uber app and started accepting fares. It was a good way to figure out the lay of the land, the money was semi-decent, and it allowed him the flexibility to do what he needed to do.

First stop was the Bonaventure sheriff's office, located half a mile from the causeway that led to the resort. It was a picturesque pink stucco building designed to look like an annex of the Saint, complete with fake minaret and a wrought-iron balcony to nowhere. The place could have been mistaken for one of those cutesy cupcake bakeries.

Inside, the lobby looked more like a dentist's office than a cop shop. A young, uniformed female deputy sat at a desk in the center of the room.

"Hi. How can I help?" Whelan found her unnervingly cheerful. For a cop.

He told her what he was looking for and she handed him a form to fill out. He scribbled in as much as he knew: the date of the incident, the victim's name, and the location.

"Driver's license?"

"Huh? He didn't have a license. He was only eight."

She laughed and held out her hand. "I meant your driver's license."

He handed it over, and she scanned it on some kind of box on top of her desk and began typing on her computer, her long nails clicking as her fingertips flew over the keyboard.

"Found it," she said. A minute later she pulled a document from the printer and showed it to him. "That'll be twenty dollars. And we don't take credit cards."

The 2002 incident report told him little he didn't already know. The name of the responding officer, estimated time of death, the name of the witness who'd called in the report.

"Where's the rest of it?"

"Excuse me?"

"I'd like to see the officer's supplemental report, witness statements, coroner's report. The whole file."

Her smile evaporated. "I'm sorry, this is all the information I'm authorized to share with a civilian. Department policy."

Whelan felt himself losing his cool. "It happened more than twenty years ago. What possible reason could your department have for keeping this file under wraps?"

"Sir?" Her tone had gained an edge. "If there's nothing else, I'd like you to leave now."

"Screw it," he mumbled. "I'll file a Freedom of Information Act request."

"Help yourself." She pretended to busy herself with the papers on her desk, but he could see her watching him as he left the building and got into his Tahoe. Probably running his license plate, he thought, as he pulled away.

The Bonaventure County Public Library building was not nearly as scenic as the sheriff's office. A bland, beige brick box wedged in between a nail salon and a Piggly Wiggly supermarket in a strip shopping center. It was quiet inside, with only a couple of senior citizens sitting at tables reading newspapers.

He told the librarian, a middle-aged Black man in a bow tie, what he was looking for and explained that he'd already done a database search on his own, which yielded nothing.

"We can access digital copies of the Atlanta, Jacksonville, and New York newspapers here," the librarian said. "I can show you how to do that, if you like."

Whelan gave it some thought. "What about the local paper? Do you have those here?"

"The *Island Express*? Afraid not. They went out of business a few years back. Unfortunately, their files were never digitized. All their bound copies are kept at the historical society. I can give you directions if you like. It's just over in the village. Five minutes from here."

"Thanks, I can find it," Whelan told him. "Maybe I'll just search the bigger papers first."

As he'd suspected, the big-city papers contained nothing helpful. Why would they care? Shootings, stabbings, political unrest made the headlines of the day. The drowning of an eight-year-old boy at a posh resort on the Georgia coast was definitely not newsworthy. To them.

Whelan decided to grab lunch before hitting the historical society. Pour Willy's was located two doors down from his apartment, and it wasn't busy. Perfect.

He sat at the bar, looked at the menu written on the blackboard, and ordered nachos and a Heineken. The bartender wore a T-shirt that read I WILL PUT YOU IN A TRUNK AND HELP PEOPLE LOOK FOR YOU. STOP PLAYING WITH ME.

"Cute," he said, pointing to her chest when she brought his beer.

"I absolutely mean it," she said, looking him over. "No offense or anything, but aren't you kind of old to be hanging out in a place like this?"

He looked in the mirror in the bar back. He'd let his hair grow out and it was streaked with silver and almost touched his shoulders. He wore a St. Louis Cardinals baseball cap, and one of the many

Hawaiian shirts in his collection. His mustache needed a trim, his skin was weather-beaten, and his sunglasses dangled from a string, resting on his chest.

"I could say the same of you," he pointed out. She had long, frizzy gray hair and tinted granny glasses perched on the end of her nose.

"True that," she said. "But I've got family to support. I work here a couple days a week as a side hustle. And I fill in sometimes at the Saint."

He raised an eyebrow in question.

"You know. The Saint Cecelia. The big pink hotel?"

"Ohh. Right." He pretended to be surprised. "I keep hearing about that place. Maybe I'll take a ride over there to check it out."

"You can't."

"How's that?"

"Unless you're a member or a hotel guest or a guest of a member, you can't get in. There's security. And they're real particular about who they admit as members."

He chuckled. "So, that's a nice way of saying they'd never admit a lowlife like me?"

"Around here, if you belong, you're a Saint, and if you look like you and me . . ." She pointed at her faded T-shirt and worn jeans. "You're an Ain't."

"Guilty," he said. "Guessing you're a local?"

"Grew up here, never got around to leaving."

She went to the kitchen and brought back a plastic basket with his nachos nestled in a wax paper liner.

The place was empty, except for a couple of blue-collar types who were sitting at the end of the bar, watching a rerun of *Cheers*. The bartender busied herself near him, unloading glasses from a dishwasher rack.

After a few bites, he blotted his lips with a paper napkin. "Hey, uh, since you're local, you ever hear of a little kid drowning out there in the pool at that pink hotel? Would have been back in the summer of '02."

She screwed up her face as she considered his question. "Let's see. Two thousand and two? That's the summer I split with my husband. The first time, anyway."

"Were you working at the Saint back then?"

"Nah. I was working day shift at the paper plant."

"So. The drowning?"

"Well, now that you mention it, I do remember that. I was kinda seeing a guy on the side who worked as an EMT back then. He was working that day. By the time they got down to the pool, the kid was dead."

"Huh." Whelan set his beer down on the bar top and twirled it between his hands.

"Where did you say you're from?" she asked, not bothering to hide her curiosity.

"Me? I've lived all over the place. Most recently, Orlando."

"Since I'm being nosy, what brings you to a backwater like Bonaventure? And why're you interested in something that happened so long ago?"

"I just took early retirement. My mother passed away recently, and while I was cleaning out her condo, I found some old letters and stuff. Things that made me think maybe it's time I figured out the answers to questions that I've been wondering about for a long time."

"And you think the answers might be here?"

"Could be. I got nothing better to do. And this seems like an okay place to do nothing." He stuck out his hand. "By the way, I'm Whelan."

She shook, briefly. "Cool. Like Waylon Jennings?"

"Different spelling, but close."

"And I'm Marie."

"Like Marie Osmond?"

That gave her a laugh. Not even.

"Hey," she said, after a moment. "You looking for work?"

"Might be. What do you have in mind?"

"You could try out at the Saint. They always need help."

"Maybe I'll check it out."

"You, uh, might want to think about spiffing yourself up a little first. They're real persnickety about how the help looks."

"Oh." He swept his hair back under his cap. "I got ya."

She pointed at the tattoo on his right forearm. Semper Fi with the Marine Corps screaming eagle.

"You served?"

"Yup."

"Good for you, but you're gonna want to cover that up. The GM has a bug up his butt about that kinda stuff. No tats, piercings, long hair. You apply for a job, you need to look like one of them clean-cut Mormons that go around door-knocking and handing out Bible tracts."

By the following Monday Whelan was wearing a set of coveralls in what he'd come to find out was the ever-present Saint signature pink. His hair was shorn, mustache gone, and the tattoo was hidden beneath long sleeves—at least until he started work and ditched it.

They'd made him an assistant supervisor on a landscape crew, which he found surprising, but not challenging.

This week they were weeding the miles of colorful flower beds that lined the roadway leading to the resort. It was hot, backbreaking work, but he found the mindlessness suited him. Weeding, planting, mowing, blowing; there was a rhythm that appealed to him. He clocked in at seven and out at four. Then he went back to the apartment over the surf shop, showered, and cooled down. Some nights he fixed himself a sandwich for dinner and watched a Braves game, other nights he grabbed something at one of the bars or restaurants in the village before turning on his app and driving.

He usually stopped accepting fares at eleven, because he'd quickly learned that anyone he picked up later than that was more than likely an obnoxious drunk.

Other nights, he sat at the tiny table in his crummy apartment and went through the papers he'd found in his mother's condo.

There hadn't been a lot. She wasn't the sentimental kind. Or maybe she was, but just not about him.

He'd been going through Kasey's clothes, tossing things into a box to donate to charity, when he came across an old Christmas card box. Now that was a surprise. She wasn't a Christmas card kind of person. Never once had she sent one to him. In fact, he couldn't ever remember her sending him a birthday card. He'd been about to throw the box in the trash, but something made him stop. He could feel things inside, sliding around.

What he found inside the box—those little scraps of paper, a few baby pictures, and a notebook written in girlish handwriting, a kind of journal, he supposed you'd call it—that was the real reason he'd come to Saint Cecelia. It was time he found some answers.

CHAPTER 18

* * *

Parrish was still getting set up at the guest relations desk in the lobby on Wednesday when the mom arrived—with three tow-headed children surrounding her. Technically one child, who looked like a four-year-old boy, was attached to the hip of her lime-green-and-pink Lilly Pulitzer shift, and sucking on the edge of a disgusting-looking gray blanket. The other two, twin girls, maybe six years old, were circling the woman's legs, slapping at each other and whining. They were dressed in miniature versions of their mother's dress.

"Hi!" Parrish chirped, trying to sound cheerier than she felt. "How can I help you?"

"Day camp," the woman said. She had an enviable super-toned body, with shiny dark hair falling below her shoulders. "I called the desk last night to sign them up, but the guy who answered the phone, who, by the way, was very rude, said there weren't any more openings. We chose this resort because my friends all said the kids' day camp was excellent."

"Hmmm," Parrish said, trying to sound concerned. "Let me just check." She tapped some keys, found the page for the Saint's Little Minnows Day Camp, and looked up. "I'm so sorry, but that's correct. The day camps fill up super early in the summertime, which is why when you booked your stay, you should have been sent a link to preregister online."

The woman shifted the blanket-sucking kid to her other hip, and let out a long, beleaguered sigh. "Well, my idiot husband booked our cottage, so that explains a lot. The only thing he's interested in signing up for are blowjobs and tee times." She waved her hand at the computer. "Can't you, like, squeeze them in anyway?"

"I wish I could," Parrish said. "But there's already a waiting list for this session."

"What am I supposed to do with these three now?" The mom gestured at the girls, who had somehow managed to steal the blanket from their brother and were using it for a game of tug-of-war, while the little boy was sobbing, "Banky. I need my banky." The woman reached down and swatted both girls' butts. "Sidney! Sloaney! Stop it!" she hissed. "Give Sutton his blanket back. Right now, or you're not getting any ice cream."

Parrish craned her neck to look out the French doors that led to the veranda. "Looks like a beautiful day for the beach. And of course, the pool is open, and the playground. Also, if I hurry, I can sign you all up for the nine-o'clock nature walk with Miss Anne, our in-house naturalist. You'll see the roseate spoonbill rookery . . ."

"Birds?" The woman's shrill voice echoed in the high-ceilinged lobby. She leaned into the desk until her face was only inches from Parrish's. "It's already eighty-five degrees outside. Do I look like someone who wants to drag these three on a walk to see some fucking birds?"

"To be honest, you don't."

"Babysitters? Surely you people have a babysitting service."

Maybe just drop them off at the nearest fire station, Parrish thought. *Wonder if there's, like, a Tinder, but for childcare?*

"I'm afraid not," Parrish said finally, trying to sound sympathetic. "But I can add your name to the Little Minnows waiting list, and if something comes up . . ."

"Hrrumppph." A man with graying hair stood a few feet behind the mom and her kids.

"I'll be with you in a moment," Parrish said, hoping this would signal the woman that her time was up.

"Mommmmmmy," the little boy wailed. "I tee-teed!" Sure enough, there was a suspicious, spreading wet spot on the front of the mom's dress.

"Perfect!" the woman said. "Just perfect." She grabbed both her daughters' hands. "Come on. We're gonna go find Daddy on the golf course."

Felice picked up the sea bass fillet and sniffed. It wasn't off—yet—but it definitely wasn't fresh, and had, in fact, probably been sitting on ice for at least a couple of days.

"Eighty-six the sea bass," she called to Rocky, her sous-chef.

"What? Why? It's the lunch special." He pointed to the wall-mounted computer screen. "Look. We've got six orders already."

"It's gone bad," Felice said. "When was this mess delivered?"

"This morning. First thing. From our regular fishmonger."

"What's his name?"

"Tommy Betz. We buy all our fish from him. He's been around forever."

Felice picked up the tray of sea bass and tipped the whole thing into the trash. "This *fish* has been around forever. We're not sending this out of *my* kitchen. No, sir."

"What do we tell the servers?" Rocky asked, desperation in his voice and on his face.

She turned to the walk-in cooler and pulled out another tray of prepped fish fillets, lifted the plastic, and sniffed.

"Grouper, right?"

"Yeah."

"This is okay," she said, placing the tray on the stainless steel table. "Did it come from that same guy?"

"Tommy? I guess."

"Okay, well, tell the servers that we had a problem and we're going with the grouper for the special instead. Same preparation, herb-and-citrus gastrique, and what else on the side?"

"Grilled asparagus and cheese grits," Rocky said. "These fancy people love their grits."

Felice could remember a time when the only thing her aunt Sherise could afford to buy and cook was grits. Three times a day, sometimes supplemented with some greens cooked with a little bit of fatback. Grits were definitely not what she'd consider a delicacy.

"All right. They can have their grits." She wiped her hands on a kitchen towel. "Later on, me and Mr. Tommy Betz, we're gonna have a little talk."

"KJ? KJ Parkhurst? My man! Is that you?"

He had been dreading this moment. It was inevitable that one of his friends, either from prep school in Atlanta, from college, or a neighbor, or anybody, really, from his past, would find him here, in the pro shop, dressed in his Saint-branded shirt and shorts, folding and refolding shirts, shorts, and socks.

He spun around and found himself facing a guy about his age, shorter and chunkier, with Oakleys pushed back into his shaggy hair. He was with an older man, his father, probably, and KJ knew he knew him, sort of. Maybe this guy had played lacrosse for a rival Atlanta school—Lovett, or maybe Marist?

"Oh, hey . . ." KJ's voice trailed off. He was hoping the guy's name would come to him. "How's it hanging?"

"Goin' good. I mean, I stunk up the front nine, but it's all gravy, right?"

"Absolutely. It's just a game, that's what my granddad says."

The other guy. Maybe his name was Nash? Yeah. Nash something. He'd coached the kid in a summer junior league camp put on at Westminster.

The older man moved to the other side of the shop to examine the selection of putters and wedges.

"So, uh, are you, like, working here now?" Nash asked.

KJ straightened up. "Hell yeah. The money's good and the hours don't suck. Gives me time to work on my game, ya know?" He lowered his voice and nodded at Olivia, who'd been drafted to fill in when someone called in sick. "And the ladies are fine, ya know what I'm sayin'?"

"I hear that," Nash said, giving him a fist bump. "Say, KJ, I heard from my buddy Miles that you'd quit Wake. I told him that can't be right."

"Taking a little sabbatical is all," KJ said. He gestured at his leg. "Messed up my knee this year, so I thought, what the hell, might as well head down to the Saint, catch some rays. But I got bored just sitting around my granddad's house, playing video games all day. The boss here is an old family friend, and he'd been bugging me to come work for him, so I finally said okay."

"Cool," Nash said. He reached down, unfolded one of the polo shirts KJ had just folded, studied it, then tossed it aside before rejoining his father at the cash register.

"Good seeing you, man."

KJ picked up the shirt and refolded it. "You too, asshole," he muttered.

Livvy was brazenly eavesdropping on KJ's conversation with the customer.

What a load of bullshit, she thought.

The night before, while KJ and Garrett were hanging out in the lounge area, sucking down beer, KJ had tipsily admitted that he'd been kicked off the lacrosse team and flunked out of school. He'd also confessed that his presence in staff housing was a direct result of his father's "sentencing" him to spend the summer working and getting his shit together.

Livvy didn't actually dislike KJ. Yes, some of the time he acted like the rest of the entitled assholes who made up a certain percentage of the Saint's guests, but unlike them, he could, on occasion, be generous, even thoughtful, offering her the last slice of pizza, or, as last night, stopping to give her a ride home when he encountered her walking back from the restaurant.

He'd even offered her a ride this morning, after she got the call directing her to report to the pro shop instead of the Verandah.

Livvy rang up the customer's purchases: two golf shirts, a golf club, and a leather belt with a design of embroidered whales. The total came to a whopping $1,422. The old man gave her a noncommittal nod and left the shop while Livvy fumed.

Traci Eddings hadn't hired her to work as a sales clerk. She'd been hired as a server in the restaurant, where, if her customers had spent that kind of money on a purchase, she would have easily made a 20 percent tip. Instead, she got a lukewarm smile, which wouldn't help pay her bills.

She moved over to where KJ was rearranging the shirts. "Do you know those people?"

"I know the son. His name's Nash. I coached him in a summer league lacrosse camp."

"His father just spent almost fifteen hundred dollars here. How rich are they?"

"I wouldn't say they're mega rich. Maybe ordinary rich. Why?"

"I can't get over how much money you people spend on stupid shit," Livvy told him. "Why does a golf club cost, like, a thousand bucks in here? I see golf clubs at the Goodwill for ten bucks. And why does a Saint logo on something make a twenty-dollar shirt worth a hundred and fifty?"

KJ gave her his best, most dazzling smile. "I'll have you know that shirt is made of one hundred percent organic yarn-dyed Sea Island cotton. Hand-sewn right here in the US by artisans using patterns custom-designed for this resort."

"You're full of shit," Livvy told him.

"Guilty."

"What about you? Are you regular or mega rich? And what's your real story?"

"Me? I'm not any kind of rich. I mean, my parents and my grandparents have money, but I'm working here, aren't I?"

She didn't want to admit that she'd been eavesdropping—last night or just now. And she wouldn't point out that he'd neatly evaded her question.

"Working in here is boring as hell," she complained.

"But it beats waiting tables, doesn't it?"

"Not really. At least I'm not standing twiddling my thumbs between customers. When I'm working at the Verandah, I'm moving. The shift goes fast, I'm making decent tips, and I'm not bored out of my gourd. I mean, what do you even do in here all day long?"

KJ whipped out his phone and showed her his gaming apps, two screen-loads of them.

Livvy rolled her eyes. "Dude. Get a life."

CHAPTER 19

* * *

Traci worked through the morning, eating lunch at her desk. Shortly after one, she got a call on her desk phone from an old high school classmate whom she occasionally ran into around town. They were friendly, but hardly best friends.

"Traci? It's Hannah Styles. Is this a good time?"

"Um, sure. What's up?"

Hannah lowered her voice to a whisper. "I could get fired for this, but I thought you should know that I'm pretty sure your brother-in-law is up to something sneaky."

Traci pushed her salad aside and felt a cold chill move down her spine. "Like what?"

"I'm not sure. All I know is, Ric called my boss late yesterday and asked him to go out to the Saint to meet with your father-in-law."

Traci knew Hannah worked as a legal secretary for a local lawyer. "Are you still working for Reeves Corbett? But he's not the family's lawyer. Andy Plankenhorn's firm handles our legal work. He has for years."

"That's what I remembered," Hannah said. "I worked for Andy when I first got out of college, until I went on maternity leave."

Traci tapped the pen against her chin. "And you have no idea what this is about?"

"Reeves asked me to find him a videographer to go out there with him. So I gave him the name of the woman who shot my little sister's wedding last summer."

"Who's the videographer? Do you think she'd talk to me?"

There was a long pause at the other end of the call. "Uh, you know what a small town this is. I wouldn't want it to get back to my boss that I talked to you. It's kind of a breach of confidentiality. I could get fired, you know?"

"Okay, no, you're absolutely right. I'll keep this to myself," Traci said, her mind racing at all the possible skulduggery Ric Eddings might be up to. "Thanks, Hannah. I owe you one."

"The reason I called you was because I can't stand that bastard Ric, excuse my French."

Traci laughed. "Sounds personal."

"Oh, it is. Back when I was a penniless college student, Ric sideswiped my poor little Chevy in the parking lot at the mall. He was driving the Saint's black SUV with the logo on the door. Ripped the right rearview mirror clean off my car, and he didn't even slow down. When my daddy called Mr. Eddings to complain about it, Ric straight up called me a liar."

"That sounds exactly like him," Traci said. "I'm gonna quietly ask some questions, and I'll definitely keep your name out of it, but if you hear any more details, will you let me know?"

"You got it, girlfriend."

She left a message on Andy Plankenhorn's voice mail, telling him she had an urgent matter to discuss.

He called back fifteen minutes later. "Traci? What's so urgent?"

"I can't tell you how I found out about this, but I understand my brother-in-law may have retained Reeves Corbett to do some legal work that involves Fred."

Plankenhorn let out a long, low whistle. "If he has, this is the first I've heard of it. Ric certainly hasn't notified me that your family is changing law firms."

"He hasn't notified me, either," Traci said. She told him about Reeves Corbett and the videographer. "That's pretty concerning to me, given Fred's current medical status."

"It's damn concerning," Andy agreed.

"You and I both know that if Ric has hired an outside law firm, it means he's up to something nefarious," Traci said.

"I can't say I blame you for having this reaction. Let me make some discreet inquiries and see what I can find out. In the meantime, when was the last time you saw Fred?"

"I check in on him at least once a week. The last time was two days ago. He's no longer ambulatory, and he's nonverbal these days, you know."

"Does he seem mentally alert?"

"I suppose so. He watches the financial news all day, every day. One thing that makes me suspicious about Ric is that he rarely bothers to visit his dad. Says it's too depressing. So why, all of a sudden, is he inviting Reeves Corbett—along with a videographer—for a drop-in?"

"I'm wondering the same thing," Plankenhorn said. "Stay tuned."

CHAPTER 20

* * *

"Miss Eddings?" Parrish recognized the voice—and the scent of its owner—before looking up. It belonged to Colonel McBee, the military retiree who, in only a week, had quickly become Parrish's least favorite guest.

The Colonel smelled like a combination of cheap aftershave and mothballs, and his pronounced Southern drawl reminded her of Foghorn Leghorn.

He slapped a folded newspaper onto her desk with such force that it sent a stack of real estate brochures flying. His yellowing mustache quivered with outrage.

"Thee-us," he snapped, "is a day-old *Wall Street Journal*. I need you to find me today's paper."

Parrish sighed. She'd suffered a variation on this same theme for three straight days.

"I'm sorry, Colonel, but as I explained yesterday, print versions of the big national newspapers are flown in here every evening from Atlanta. They're not available same-day here on the coast. However, all of them are available online."

"Online?" His upper lip curled, as though the word was as distasteful as something from a porn novel. "I can't read that small print. I must have a real newspaper."

"There's a computer monitor in our library," Parrish said, in the kind of soothing voice she'd heard mothers use on the screaming toddlers having meltdowns out by the pool. "I can show you how to enlarge the print with the click of a mouse."

"Never mind," he said. "All those advertisements swimmin' around and poppin' up give me a migraine."

She gave a weak smile. "Sorry. Is there anything else I can assist with?"

"The maid. My wife is certain the girl was rummaging through her jewelry. When we came back from dinner last night, the things she'd left on the bathroom counter had been moved."

Parrish bit her lip. "Was anything missing?"

"Well, no. Also, I don't understand why these people don't speak English . . ."

"Sir?" She let her voice take on a hint of frost. "I feel very, very sure that our housekeepers haven't been 'rummaging' through your wife's jewelry. Each evening, during turndown service, they tidy up bathroom vanities so that they can clean every surface, and generally freshen your suite. If you don't require turndown, you can simply hang the 'Do Not Disturb' sign on your door. Or place your valuables in the safe in your closet."

"Hmmmph. We'll see about that. And another thing. The television in our suite doesn't get the right channels."

"Are you sure?" Guests who couldn't understand how to use the smart televisions in their rooms, especially elderly ones, were the bane of her existence. The Colonel was the third guest this week who'd complained about not being able to access the premium cable channels.

"Of course I'm sure. All I can find are your dreadful local channels. What kind of five-star resort doesn't get the BBC? My wife is missing her baking programs."

She scribbled something in her blue notebook. "I'll send up someone from engineering to take a look. All right?"

Before the Colonel could answer, Charlie Burroughs walked up. "Colonel McBee," he said. "Good to see you again, sir. I trust our Parrish here is treating you right?"

"You trust wrong," the Colonel snapped. He grabbed his newspaper and left. Again.

"Hey, Mr. Burroughs," Parrish said wearily.

"What's got the Colonel all worked up today?" Charlie asked.

"Let's see. Day-old newspapers, housekeepers who don't speak English and move his wife's stuff during turndown service, and, oh yes, his television doesn't get premiere cable channels, which is ridiculous, because I know for a fact that we just bought all-new, top-of-the-line smart TVs, right?"

"Right," Charlie said.

"The old fart probably just can't figure out how to work the remote," Parrish said. "But he's the third person to complain about a television this week. I told him I'd send engineering up to take a look, but in the meantime, I think I'll ask Traci to check on where those televisions came from. Maybe the vendor sent the wrong ones?"

"Your aunt's got enough on her plate this week, with the Beach Bash coming up. I'll look into it myself, okay?"

"Sounds good," Parrish told him.

"Miss?"

Parrish rolled her eyes and went back to work.

Livvy took an extra shift after lunch was over, finally dragging herself back to the dorm at six. She took a long, hot shower, pulled on shorts and a T-shirt, decided against a bra, and ambled into the kitchen to look for a beer.

It was quiet. Mostly because KJ and Garrett weren't around. Parrish was sitting in the lounge, nursing a chilled glass of wine and staring down at her phone. Livvy flopped down onto the sofa next to her. She'd fixed a bag of microwave popcorn and held out the bag, offering some to Parrish, who looked startled.

"Thanks," the girl said, taking a handful of the hot, buttery popcorn and stuffing it into her mouth. "I didn't have time to eat today."

"Yeah, we were slammed in the restaurant too. I guess the season is officially in full swing," Livvy said. She took a long pull from the beer bottle.

Parrish put her phone facedown on the coffee table and propped her bare feet on the table's edge. "The season is definitely here. And all the whiny Karens and bossy Bitsys have checked in with the express purpose of making my life a living hell."

"I've been meaning to ask, what exactly do you do in that lobby all day? I mean, explain guest relations to me."

"To quote my aunt, my job is to make sure our guests have a perfect experience. Like, today? Colonel McBee was standing at my desk, waiting, when I got there."

Livvy groaned. "Ugh! McBee. Everyone at the restaurant calls him Captain Crunch."

"It's like he sits around and dreams up things to bitch about. Yesterday he complained that the landscape crew was making too much noise. Does he think we mow the grass with nail clippers? The day before that, the ice-cream shop didn't have soft serve. Ruined his whole day!"

"I can top that," Livvy said. "Earlier in the week, he asked to speak to the restaurant manager because he said we shorted him a shrimp in his shrimp cocktail. Who counts shrimp?"

Parrish sipped her wine and munched on her popcorn.

"Hey," Livvy said softly, "is it okay if I ask you something?"

"Depends on what it is."

"Soooo, I think my mom and your aunt used to be besties back in the day. They even worked here, together, as lifeguards, the summer after they graduated from high school."

"Oh yeah?" Parrish was intrigued. "What's your mom's name? I'll ask Traci."

"Shannon Grayson," Livvy said.

"Never heard her mention a Shannon. What was her maiden name?"

"Grayson. She's never been married," Livvy said, as bright pink bloomed on her cheeks. "All I know is, my mom and your aunt Traci went all through school together. They were really tight. But not anymore. My mom blew a valve when I told her I was coming to work here."

"That's so weird," Parrish said. "Do you have any idea why they broke up?"

"I have a sneaking suspicion it has something to do with that last summer they worked here. Which was when my mom got knocked up. And had me nine months later."

"Oh my God," Parrish said. "So . . . can I ask? Who's your dad?"

"You can ask. I've been asking my whole life, but my mom refuses to tell me."

"Seriously? And you have no idea who it might be? How can she keep a secret like that from you? Doesn't she think you have a right to know who your father is?"

Livvy let out a long sigh. "You'd have to know my mom to understand. As far as she's concerned, it's her secret and it's none of my business."

"Just . . . wow," Parrish said, flopping back against the sofa cushions. "Now you've got me intrigued. I'm gonna ask Traci about this when I meet her for lunch tomorrow."

"No! Don't. I don't wanna stir up anything. Not when I just started working here."

"Do you think Traci knew who you were? That day you waited on us at BluePointe?"

"Not sure. When she called to offer me the job, and I told her my last name, she sounded kinda weird. Like, maybe she did?"

Parrish took another handful of popcorn and chewed slowly. "Okay. I'll play it cool, but I'm definitely gonna see if I can find out what happened back then."

"Let me know what you hear."

CHAPTER 21

* * *

Traci sensed something warm beside her in the bed, a head on the pillow next to hers. She smiled, sleepily turning toward him, forgetting, again, for only a moment, that he was gone.

In the weeks and months following the plane crash, Hoke's absence, the crushing loss, the overwhelming grief, was something that she carried everywhere, like a lead-weighted collar. Almost every morning, in those weeks, she would awaken to that moment of remembering, after she'd finally managed to fall asleep and forget that he was gone, that he wasn't right beside her in this very bed, hogging the covers, spooning against her back, his warm breath tickling her neck.

Eventually, she remembered to stop forgetting. According to her therapist, that was progress, wasn't it?

A wet nose burrowed into her neck, and then the licking started.

"Lola, no," she mumbled, still half-asleep. But resistance was useless. She turned her head and stared into the dachshund's dark, unblinking eyes. "Whyyyy?"

In answer, Lola licked her nose.

"Okay," she said, yawning. "I get the message. Breakfast it is."

She padded into the kitchen, started the coffee, and filled Lola's water and food bowls.

While the coffee brewed and Lola ate, Traci checked the weather forecast for the upcoming weekend. The Beach Bash was only two days away, and she was praying for sunny, dry weather.

The weather odds for Saturday looked iffy: sunny in the morning, highs in the mid-eighties, with 30 percent chance of afternoon scattered showers.

"No lightning," Traci prayed.

After she'd showered and dressed, she steered her golf cart in the direction of Gardenia Cottage. She needed to get a handle on what Ric was plotting.

Alberta seemed surprised to see her so soon after her last visit. "Something wrong?"

"I'm not sure," Traci admitted. "I heard Ric was here earlier in the week, and that he brought a new lawyer."

"He did," Alberta said. "I never seen that man before. And he got Mr. Fred all riled up. His blood pressure spiked something scary. Brought a movie camera lady with him."

"Did Ric tell you who the lawyer was, or what he was doing?"

Alberta pressed her lips together. "You know Mr. Ric don't tell me nothing. I'm just the help to him. Somebody to wipe his daddy's butt and dose his medicine."

Traci nodded. "I'm not asking you to tattle, exactly, Alberta, but did you happen to hear anything that Ric and the lawyer were discussing with my father-in-law?"

"Oh, no. Mr. Ric told me to go ahead and take my lunch break. It was only eleven o'clock—and he knows I don't go nowhere when I have lunch. I sit in the living room and watch my stories. But that day, he hands me a twenty-dollar bill and tells me lunch is on him."

"He definitely didn't want you to know what he was up to," Traci said.

"When I got back from lunch, they were still in there, talking to Mr. Fred. Then, Mr. Ric said they need me to witness something. So I went on in there, and the lawyer handed me some papers to sign, and the video lady asked me to say my name. Made me repeat it twice."

"What kind of paper? A will?"

"Maybe? Bunch of legal words."

"Did you see Fred sign anything?"

"You've seen how bad he shakes, but they put a pen in his hand, and he managed to make some kind of a chicken scratch with Mr. Ric holding on to that paper they had."

Traci drummed her fingers on the kitchen countertop. What was Ric up to?

"Won't be long now," Alberta muttered.

"What makes you say that?"

"I can just tell. He's sleeping more, don't hardly drink that liquid supplement. He's skin and bones. New doctor told me he thinks maybe his organs are starting to shut down."

"New doctor?" Traci said sharply. "What happened to Dr. Forney?"

"I guess maybe she retired or something. This new man is way younger, I'll say that."

"A new doctor and a new lawyer. He's definitely scheming something," Traci said.

Alberta walked her to the door, pausing to put her hand on Traci's shoulder. "Been meaning to ask. How about you? Are you taking care of yourself? You know, I was about your age when my man Bennie passed. I was blessed, 'cause I had my two kids, but those were some lonely times. Especially early in the mornings. For the longest time, I'd wake up and expect him to be right there beside me."

"You too?" Traci asked.

"Yes, ma'am," Alberta said softly. "When you got good husbands, like we had, I think the body remembers. And that's not a bad thing, is it?"

Traci called Andy Plankenhorn as soon as she got back to her office. "I just came from Fred's house. Alberta confirmed what I'd heard about Reeves Corbett, and the videographer."

"Tell me exactly what she told you," the older lawyer said.

"Ric didn't want Alberta overhearing what they were saying to Fred, so he sent her out to get lunch. When she got back, they brought her in and filmed her witnessing him sign a document of some sort, while Ric held the paper. She said it was chicken scratch."

"Interesting."

"Have you heard anything new?" she asked.

"I checked into Reeves Corbett. I understand he's Ric's fraternity brother."

"That can't be good," Traci said.

"Corbett went to a decent law school, but most of his experience is in real estate, which explains a lot. He knows about as much about trusts and estates as I know about criminal law."

"Do you think Ric is rewriting Fred's will? How will that affect me? Honestly, Andy, with the way things are going at the Saint, I just don't think I can take one more worry."

"I'm sorry this is causing you such anxiety, Traci dear," Andy said, his deep, courtly Southern voice already soothing her jangled nerves. "We can't know what might or might not be in Fred's new will, but I can tell you that as I understand Hoke's will, and his intentions, it would be impossible for Ric to outright strip you of your ownership rights in the Saint."

"Thank God," she said fervently.

"However . . ."

"Ughhhhh. I don't want to hear 'however.'"

"Nobody ever does. I can't ethically discuss the terms of the will our firm drew up for Fred, but there are other tangible assets, the disposition of which could be affected by any new will. And that's all I can say about that."

"I don't understand a word of what you just said. But it doesn't sound good."

Plankenhorn cleared his throat. "The good news here is that your brother-in-law and this Reeves Corbett appear to have bungled whatever it is they are attempting to do. Having a videographer there to film with Ric—who would most certainly be a beneficiary of any new will—present, and assisting his father in signing a new document, would probably be proof of undue influence. And, of course, if Fred is not fully mentally cognizant, well, that would raise further questions at probate."

"Is this your way of telling me it's not all bad news?" she asked.

"Well, er . . ."

"Never mind. Thank you, Andy. I think."

CHAPTER 22

* * *

KJ and Garrett strolled into the staff dorm together shortly after nine o'clock on Thursday night. "Hey, y'all," Garrett called loudly. "Who's ready to party down?"

They found their dormmates, Parrish, Olivia, and Felice, sitting in the lounge area, watching their favorite true-crime show and sharing a plate of messy nachos.

"Shhh!" Livvy said. She was dressed in gym shorts and a ratty tee, with her wet hair wrapped in a towel. "*Dateline* is on. 'Mystery of the Missing Mom.'"

"I've seen this one," Garrett said. "The husband did it. It's always the husband."

Felice glared at him. "I'm fixin' to bitch slap you if you don't hush up your mouth." She pointed the remote control at the television and turned up the volume.

"Come on, y'all," Garrett pleaded. "You don't really wanna sit around here all night, do you? The night is young, and so are we. Let's get wrecked and go have some fun."

Livvy fluffed her damp hair. "The only party I'm having is in my pj's." She gave Garrett the side-eye. "You worked the same hours as me. How do you have the energy to go out?"

He patted the pocket of his shorts. "I got a little friend here that helps me out when I need a little sumthin' sumthin'."

Felice set her mug of herbal tea down on the coffee table. "Boy, you keep up that shit and you're gonna wind up dead. Or fired, or in jail, or all of the above."

Garrett took a swallow of beer with whatever was in his hand. He belched forcefully. "Come on, Felice. You telling me you never need a little pick-me-up? I been working in restaurants since I was fifteen. I never met a chef anywhere who didn't do coke. Or something."

She smiled her Cheshire cat smile. "Didn't say I *never* did coke. These days I don't mess with stuff I can't afford. That includes men, drugs, booze, and any combination of the above."

"Well, hell, dude. If you're handing out the good stuff . . ." KJ winked and extended his palm. "Count me in."

Garrett placed a pill in his hand and KJ dry-swallowed.

"Say, Kaje," Garrett said. "Let's ride into town and see what's shakin' at Pour Willy's. I waited on a table of fine young ladies today, and they were talking about checking out the local scene. I told 'em me and my buddy would meet them there."

"Better not. My supervisor at the pro shop stays on my ass. I can't be rolling in there with a hangover tomorrow."

"Well, damn," Garrett said, his shoulders sagging. "Talk about a bunch of wet blankets."

Parrish waved her hand back and forth. "Helloooo? I'm sitting right here. I'll go."

Garrett looked dubious. "Really? The boss's daughter is gonna party with the help?"

Parrish stood slowly and stretched. "First. She's my aunt, not my mom. Second, fuck off, loser. I work as hard as anyone in this dorm, and I don't need your attitude."

She was halfway to her bedroom when Garrett called out, "Hey, can't you take a joke? C'mon, don't be mad. I was just kidding. Let's be friends, okay?"

Parrish didn't answer for a moment. She turned. "Okay, but I drive."

"Cool with me," he said.

When she emerged from her room she was wearing a short, pale blue sundress that showed off her tan, and her hair fell softly to her shoulders.

"Day-yummm," Garrett said. "You look fine."

Pour Willy's was slammed. People were standing in clusters on the sidewalk outside, drinks in hand, and the night air throbbed with loud music. Parrish circled the block twice before finally finding a place to park her Audi convertible. "Nice wheels," Garrett said, sliding an admiring hand over the bumper after he clambered out of the car.

"It was either a graduation gift or a bribe. From my darling daddy," Parrish said, wrinkling her nose. "Depending on your point of view."

"And what's your point of view?" he asked.

"Bribe. Definitely."

There was a bouncer at the door, a burly woman with a backward ball cap topping an impressive mane of bright red hair.

"Sarebear!" Garrett called, drawing out the name.

"Garrett, baby! Get your sweet ass in here." She hugged him, then looked Parrish up and down. "This your new lady?"

"He wishes," Parrish said.

The bouncer's braying laugh nearly drowned out the music. She held the door open. "Have fun, then."

The bar was shoulder-to-shoulder jammed. Garrett placed his hand on the small of Parrish's back, then jerked it away when she shot him a withering look.

"Just trying to help steer you through this traffic," he said, shouting to make himself heard. "Hang on to my shirt, then."

She grabbed a handful of his shirttail and they waded into the fray, elbowing their way to the bar, where people stood three deep. Three different times, people called his name, paused to slap him on the back, or wave hello.

Somehow, he managed to shoehorn himself at the edge of the bar, and seconds later, the bartender was standing in front of them.

"Hey, man," he said, nodding at Garrett. "What can I get you two?"

"The usual for me," Garrett said, turning to Parrish. "What about you?"

"Tanqueray and tonic."

The bartender fixed her drink, then slid it across the bar to her. He poured a shot of tequila, and drew a beer from the tap. Garrett tossed the shot back with one gulp.

She squeezed the lime into her drink and took a sip before looking around. "See your friends anywhere?"

Garrett leaned against the bar and surveyed the room. "Lots of ladies here tonight, but I don't see them."

"Is it always this mobbed?" she asked, leaning close to his ear in order to be heard.

"What? You've never hung out at Pour Willy's?"

"Not really. I mean, I was away at college, and then when I came home, I mostly just got drinks at the club with my friends."

"Ohhh. Riiiiiight," he drawled. "I guess Pour Willy's would be slumming for an Eddings."

"Are you gonna keep up with that snobby rich girl stuff?" Parrish asked. "'Cuz if you are, you can just catch a ride home with Sarebear or one of your other homeboys who work here."

Garrett held up both hands in a sign of surrender. "Damn. Sorry if I offended."

He took a long slug of beer, and she stirred her drink with the straw.

"Garrett!" a sunburnt blonde called from a few barstools away. "Where you been all week? We missed you Tuesday night."

"Sorry, had to work," he yelled back.

"Call me, m'kay?"

"I will. Totally," he said, turning back to Parrish.

She raised an eyebrow. "Who's that girl, and what happens Tuesday nights?"

"That's just Courtney. Tuesday night is darts league. But I don't play every week. Now, what were you about to say?"

Parrish pulled her long hair behind one ear. "It's really tiresome, having people make assumptions about me all the time. I raised my share of hell, but I didn't try to sneak in here underage because I was afraid of what would happen if I got caught."

"What? You'd get shunned?"

"More like screamed at for embarrassing the family." She looked around the room. "How do you know all these people?"

"Lived here all my life, went to school with some of 'em, worked with a couple of the guys and drank with most of 'em . . ."

"And slept with half the ladies?"

He grinned sheepishly. "Not quite half."

The bartender held up a bottle of Gran Patrón Platinum. "You ready?"

"Hit me," Garrett said, holding out the shot glass. He knocked it back and blinked. "Burns so good."

"How about the lady?" the bartender asked, holding up the bottle of Tanqueray.

Parrish covered her glass with her hand. "No thanks. Still working on this one."

Garrett had been scanning the room, but now he tapped her forearm. "Hey, there's an open high-top over there. I'll settle up here and you can go claim it." He pushed a ten-dollar bill across the bar. "Jamie, my man, that's for you. Now, why don't you go ahead and fix a freshie for the lady, and then gimme a double, rocks this time."

"Drink up," Garrett urged, pushing the new drink across the high-top to Parrish.

"Don't rush me," she said. "Still don't see your friends from the Verandah?"

"Screw 'em. I'm having fun with you."

She raised an eyebrow. "Seriously?"

"Yeah, why not? Tell me something about the mysterious Parrish Eddings."

She thought about it. "Well . . . I'm tone-deaf. Totally. Which is why I don't do karaoke."

"No karaoke," he said solemnly. "I'll make a note. What else?"

"I don't like seafood. I can't stand guys who smoke. I speak fluent Spanish, I like to drive fast, and I have every episode of *Friends* downloaded onto my iPad. I watch them late at night, when I need cheering up."

"Who's your favorite guy on *Friends?*"

"Joey," she said quickly. "Who's your favorite girl?"

"Phoebe."

"Really?"

"No. C'mon. I'm Team Rachel. All the way."

"That makes me sad. I would have respected you more if you really did like Phoebe."

"But she's so dumb," Garrett protested. "And Rachel was way hotter."

"Men. You're all pigs," she said.

"Do you think you'll keep working at the Saint? After this summer?"

She pulled on a strand of hair, twisting and twirling it. "Everybody kind of expects me to. I only agreed to work there this summer because Traci convinced me things were pretty dire."

"How so?"

She shook her head. "I shouldn't be talking about this stuff. It's family business."

"Hey. We're roommates, right? Don't you think I deserve to know what's what?"

She stirred her untouched drink. "Okay, but you can't tell anyone. Promise?"

"Of course."

"There are money issues. Big ones. The year before he died, my uncle started this huge renovation and expansion project at the resort."

"That's old news. They totally remodeled, added that new wing, and rebuilt the pool house. I almost went broke because the place was closed for, like, fifteen months. I had to get a second job driving for DoorDash."

"According to my dad, Uncle Hoke got way over his skis, financially. He took out a lot of loans . . . and then he was killed in that plane crash."

Parrish's eyes welled up. "Losing him nearly killed Traci. She and Hoke, they were so in love. A real team."

Garrett nodded, then emptied his drink. "But there was, like, insurance, right?"

"My dad, Mister Know-it-All, says Hoke should have had key man insurance."

"What's that?"

"It's insurance for the company, that says if, like, the president of the company dies—something that would really hurt, maybe even bankrupt the company—the insurance will pay off the company's debt. Hoke didn't have it. And now there's still *so* much debt."

"That shouldn't hurt your aunt, though, right? I mean, business is good. Like, at the restaurant we're booked solid all day every day. The pool is packed . . ."

"It's not that good. She tries not to show it, but I know Traci's worried sick."

"Come on," Garrett said. "I've seen that car she drives. I've seen the house she lives in."

"Appearances can be deceiving," Parrish insisted. "Her car? Yeah, it's a Mercedes, but it's six years old. And Traci's house is not that big inside. It was my grandparents' house when they first got married. My grandmother gave it to Hoke. They were finally going to build a bigger house, on one of the ocean lots, but then Hoke died, and Traci told my dad to sell it."

Garrett jiggled the ice cubes in the glass he'd just drained, and a server magically appeared at their table with another pair of drinks.

"Thanks, Bunny," he told the girl. "Keep 'em coming."

Parrish pushed her drink away, untouched. "Jesus, Garrett, you must have a hollow leg."

He poured the half-melted ice from his empty drink into the full one and gulped half of it. "Practice makes perfect."

Then he returned his attention to Parrish, eying her with undisguised envy. "Why wouldn't you want to work at the family business? Sounds like the sweet life to me."

"Let's talk about something else. Like, how do you get what I count as at least six shots of very expensive top-shelf tequila—and my two drinks—for free?"

He gave her a broad wink. "Trade secret, baby! Hey, you wanna dance?"

The jukebox was playing the kind of '60s rock you always heard at beach bars, and the tiny dance floor was crowded, but before Parrish could refuse, he'd downed the rest of his drink, then slid off the stool, nearly tripping in the process before quickly regaining his footing.

Garrett tugged at her hand, dragging her in the direction of the music. Parrish smiled despite herself. It was the song "Be Young, Be Foolish, Be Happy." She'd heard it played her whole life, at Saturday night dances at the Saint.

Garrett grasped her hand and they wedged themselves into the crowd. For a minute or two they did a respectable version of the Carolina shag. He was a good dancer, smooth and loose-limbed. But when he tried to execute a tricky turn, everything went to shit. He stumbled, collapsed onto the floor, and pulled her down on top of him.

Parrish jumped up, red-faced and furious, but the other dancers seemed oblivious to the debacle. She looked down at Garrett, who was still on the floor, glassy-eyed, grinning, and flailing around like a beached flounder.

"Get up, dammit," she said, extending her hand. He took it, and pulled her down again.

This time the crowd parted, and when she looked up, all she saw were a couple dozen faces, pointing at them and laughing hysterically.

"I'm gonna fucking kill you," she said through gritted teeth. She stood and stalked away.

"Parrish! Hey, Parrish!"

She grabbed her purse from the back of her barstool. After that, she didn't stop, didn't slow down, until she was on the sidewalk outside the bar, fumbling for her car keys.

Garrett burst through the bar's door. "Hey, wait up!"

CHAPTER 23

* * *

Parrish took a few wobbly steps, then looked down to see that the heel of her left sandal was broken. "Dammit." She stooped, dropped it in a trash bin, and began limping toward her car, with Garrett following behind, weaving from side to side on the sidewalk.

"Wait up," he called. "C'mon. Slow down. Why you gotta be so mad?"

She stopped and waited for him to catch up. "Look what you did!" She gestured at her dress, stained from the filthy barroom floor. "My favorite dress is ruined, thanks to you. My shoe is broken, and I just flashed my panties to about fifty strangers at that bar back there."

Garrett awkwardly reached out his hand to brush away some of the dirt on the back of her dress, but she slapped his hand away.

"Leave me alone." She stopped, removed the other shoe, and pitched it into a patch of nearby shrubbery before resuming her trek.

"Where you going?"

"Back to the Saint. It's late and I have to work in the morning." She turned and glared at him. "I should leave you right here. It would serve you right."

He threw his arm around her shoulder. "Aww, Parrish, you wouldn't do me that way, would you?"

She shrugged out from his embrace, and kept walking.

"Hang on," he called. "Gotta water some flowers."

He walked over to the side of a building and, with his back to her, unzipped his fly.

"Gross!" she yelled.

"All done," he reported, still fumbling with his zipper.

"Are you crazy?" Parrish asked, grabbing him by the elbow. "You're so completely wasted you're gonna get yourself locked up for public drunkenness, and indecent exposure."

"Nah. I know all the cops in town. We play darts together."

On the way back to the Saint, the silence in the car was deafening.

Garrett yawned and tried to look penitent. "Aww, Parrish, don't be mad at me. I didn't mean to get drunk. And I'm sorry I messed up your pretty dress. You want me to wash it?"

"No," she snapped.

"Listen, there's something I feel really bad about."

"You should."

"No, it's not the dress. Earlier, you asked me how come I got all those drinks for free. If I tell you something, do you swear it'll be just between us?"

"I won't swear to anything until I know what it is."

"Fuuuuck," he sighed. "Look. Your aunt has been good to me, the whole time I've worked for her. So I feel kinda shitty about it, you know?"

"About what?"

"The thing is, some of us at the Verandah, we got an arrangement with some places around town. Which is why I get to drink for free."

"What kind of a deal?"

"They, uh, buy liquor from somebody at the Saint. Kinda out the back door."

Parrish pulled the Audi to the side of the road. "You're saying someone at the Saint is selling our liquor—liquor we pay for? Jesus, Garrett. That's stealing. Outright theft. You've got to tell me who it is."

He ran his fingers through his hair. "I shouldn't have said anything."

"Yes, you should have. How many people are involved?"

He shifted uncomfortably in his seat. "I don't know."

"How long has it been going on?"

"Look, it's not that big a deal. Everybody in the restaurant business does this kind of stuff. The guy who told me about it said if I kept my mouth shut, I'd be taken care of."

"Taken care of, how? Kickbacks?"

"Not, like, in cash. Like, the bars I hang out at, I drink and eat for free. That's all."

Parrish pulled at a strand of her hair, twisting it until it was almost knotted. "That is a kickback, Garrett. You know it and I know it. You just told me how good Traci has been to you, and that's how you repay her? Looking the other way while somebody rips her off?"

He grabbed her hands. "You can't tell anyone I told you about this stuff. Promise me, Parrish. I could get in big trouble."

"You're *in* big trouble, asshole."

"I'm not the one dealing the booze," he protested.

"No. You're protecting whoever is stealing from us. That's called, what? Accessory?"

"Please, Parrish? If you rat me out, I'll lose my job. At the very least. And I need this job. Big time. Please? Promise me."

"I don't know," she said reluctantly. "I'll have to think about it." She started the car again and pulled onto the roadway.

"Fuuuck." Garrett pounded the dashboard with both fists. "You're gonna get me killed."

When they got to the dorm, Garrett slumped against the doorframe while Parrish keyed in the code on the front door. He lurched inside, mumbling something unintelligible as he stumbled to his room.

Parrish watched him go. "What an asshole," she whispered.

Back in her own room she got undressed, tossing the blue dress into the trash can, and changed into an oversized Georgetown

T-shirt. She tiptoed to the bathroom, washed her face, and brushed her teeth.

She climbed into bed, but she was too wired to sleep. Something was going on at the Saint. Garrett's drunken confidence about stealing liquor was just the tip of the iceberg.

Parrish pulled out her blue notebook and scrawled some hasty notes. She had no idea what any of this meant, but she did know it wasn't good. She yawned, then dug a sleep gummy out of the bottle on her nightstand and chewed it. Next she texted her aunt.

*Hey, Traci. Can we meet up
ASAP? Got something serious
we need to discuss. About the
Saint.*

She was drifting off to sleep when she heard her phone ding with a response. So Traci was up too. Was she worrying about the fate of the hotel?

*Gah! Now I'm worried. How
about Sunday breakfast, my
house, 10 am?*

Parrish texted a thumbs-up emoji, yawned, and fell asleep.

CHAPTER 24

* * *

On Friday morning, KJ was in the stockroom, opening boxes of new merchandise. He'd been working for two weeks and was astonished by how much there was of it, and how fast it sold in the Saint's pro shop.

He scored the flaps of a cardboard carton with a box cutter and lifted out the packing slip, indicating the shipment contained sweaters from a company called Suki Smith. Inside were layers and layers of cellophane bags. He opened the first bag and out slid six women's cashmere sweaters. They were impossibly soft to the touch and in a rainbow of vibrant and pastel hues. He set them on the table and opened the next bag, and then the next.

When he'd emptied all the boxes, he went back over the packing slip with a yellow highlighter, marking off each of the items in the shipment. When he got to the description of the sweaters, he had to force himself to slow down and concentrate. Each color had a different name and style number and price. There were V-neck sweaters and button-down cardigans and half-zips and mock turtlenecks. Who knew that many kinds of sweaters existed?

And the colors. Jadeite. Hibiscus. Orchid. Azure. Cerise. Pearl. What the hell?

Also, the numbers seemed to be off. According to the packing list, he should have unpacked two bags of each color and style of sweater, which would have made for 144 sweaters. But he only counted 120. He recounted and the number came out the same.

Marcie, the shop manager, had given him a sheet of the shop's computer-generated price tags and the pricing gun. He stuck the gun in the back pocket of his carefully pressed logo shorts. The clothes were definitely a perk of the job. Marcie had stressed that he wear the shop's clothes every day when he reported to work. And he had to be carefully groomed, she'd warned, looking him up and down that first day.

"Trim up those sideburns, get rid of the five-o'clock shadow, and don't let me see you in here looking wrinkled or messy. As far as I'm concerned, you're a walking mannequin. We want our customers to want to look like you. Understand?"

He found her behind the cash register, chatting with a woman who was asking questions about golf shorts for her son. He waited until the customer had wandered away. "Hey, uh, Marcie. You know those Suki Smith cashmere sweaters?"

She was sorting through a stack of the previous day's receipts. "What about them?"

He showed her the packing list. "I don't understand these color names. Like, what's 'cerise' and also, 'azure' and 'pearl'?"

She glanced at the list. "Don't they teach vocabulary at that high-priced college of yours? Cerise is like a pinky-purple. Azure is blue. Pearl is off-white. Orchid is light purple."

He laughed. "Why can't they just call it those colors? Why have tricky names?"

"Because those sweaters retail for just over a grand apiece," she said. "People don't want to pay that kind of money for a plain green sweater. So it's called jadeite. Got it?"

"Yes, ma'am," he said.

She looked annoyed when he didn't leave. "Anything else?"

"Well, yeah. The packing list says we should have received one hundred forty-four sweaters, but I counted. Twice. And it looks to me like we only got one hundred and twenty. You want me to call the company?"

Marcie plucked the packing list from his hand and lowered her voice. "You just leave that to me. Get the sweaters priced and put them out here on that front table. And be quick about it, because I need to run an errand and I can't leave the shop while you stand around in the stockroom with your thumb up your ass."

"Bitch," he said, under his breath, when she hurried from the pro shop. Marcie was sweet as pie with the customers, to whom she brazenly sucked up at every opportunity. But when they were alone in the boutique, she was a pint-sized Mussolini.

Barely five feet tall in her stylish wedge-heeled sandals, Marcie had a set of boobs that, even to KJ, did not look like original factory equipment. He marveled that she was able to stand upright. But right from the start, he could tell his boss had it in for him.

Take today. He spent the rest of the shift hustling, keeping all the displays neat and restocked, writing up reorders and ringing up customers. It had been a productive day. He'd sold a hella lot of logo shirts, windbreakers, and even an entire set of golf clubs—to the tune of $3,200. But every time he looked up, he caught his manager giving him the stink-eye.

He wondered what he'd done to earn her wrath today. Finally, ten minutes before closing time, she approached a father-son duo who'd been perusing a rack of last season's marked-down winter jackets.

"Sorry, folks," she said. "But we're closing a little early tonight to do inventory."

As soon as they were gone, Marcie locked the plate-glass door. She turned to KJ.

"I need to speak to you in the stockroom."

He followed her into the stockroom with dread in his heart. What now?

She leaned against the pricing table in the center of the crowded room and pointed a finger at him, her voice shaking with barely suppressed rage. "First off, don't you ever dare question me about inventory issues while we have guests in the shop."

"Oh. Okay," KJ said eagerly. "Sorry. I just—"

She raised her hand, palm out, like a traffic cop, to stop him.

"Second. You should know that from the beginning, I was against having you work here. I thought it was a bad look, hiring a member's son, but I got overruled. And I'll admit, until today, I had started to come around. You're attractive, our guests seem to like you, and you seem to have a knack for the upsell."

"Oh, uh, thanks. I think?"

Marcie had explained the art of upselling on his first day of work.

"Say you sell a pair of golf cleats. That's a nice sale, right? Couple hundred bucks. But it's not enough. Here's what you do. You show the customer one of our custom-designed imported leather belts with the Saint logo. That's a hundred twenty-five. You ask how he's fixed for socks. No man has ever had enough socks. He'll need one of our shoe totes too, to keep the cleats from getting dinged up. Then you show him the shirt selection. Tell him they just came in today and they're flying out the door. Create a sense of urgency. And mention that if he buys two, he's going to get one of our awesome stainless steel insulated travel coffee mugs. Thirty-dollar value."

KJ had nodded enthusiastically, taking it all in, the way he'd never absorbed anything taught in his boring college classes.

"It's like a game, see," Marcie explained. "And now, you've taken a simple hundred-and-seventy-five-dollar purchase and upsold it to an easy six hundred dollars' worth of add-ons. If you've done it correctly, your customer is going to actually be grateful for the chance to spend more money. And that, my friend, is called the upsell."

Now KJ was watching Marcie's face, waiting for the ax to fall.

He didn't have to wait long. She raised a finger. "You need to understand, what goes on in this shop stays in this shop. Right?"

He was still puzzled. "I'm sorry. I don't get it. If you're mad about the sweaters, I counted them twice. I just thought you'd want to know we were missing a couple dozen. Because of how expensive they are and all. I wanted you to know . . ."

Her eyes narrowed. "So now I know, and that's the end of this discussion."

KJ nodded that he understood. He looked around for his messenger bag, getting ready to leave, but Marcie wasn't finished.

"And KJ?"

"Yes, ma'am?"

"Since we're letting each other know about stuff, I should let you know that I saw you, Tuesday night, leaving the Back Porch."

He could feel the ice in his veins and the heat rising in his face. He forced himself to give her the patented dumb jock face he'd perfected over the years.

"Back Porch? Must have been somebody else. I've never heard of it. Never been there."

She chuckled. "Oh, sweetie. It was you, all right. You had a ball cap pulled down over your face, but I recognized your walk. The slight limp when you favor your bad knee. And your shoes."

Marcie pointed at the shoes he was wearing today. His favorites. The neon-gold-and-black Nikes with the Demon Deacon logo. "Pro tip, KJ. If you're trolling a gay bar and you want to be incognito, go for something a little more understated."

He was staring down at the damned shoes. Frozen in his tracks. When he looked up at her, he felt like he might puke.

"Don't worry, hon," she purred. "Your little secret is safe with me. I don't judge. But your folks might. And your granddaddy? I know the man. He'd definitely judge, and I'm thinking he wouldn't like knowing his grandson and namesake was a sneaky little queer."

CHAPTER 25

* * *

Shannon's supervisor, a sour-faced older woman named Ruth, stopped her as she was leaving her patient's room. "You have a visitor downstairs."

"Me? What kind of visitor? It's not about Olivia, right?" She grabbed her phone from the pocket of her scrubs, but there were no recent texts or calls from her daughter.

"I'm not your receptionist, Shannon," Ruth snapped. "All I know is there's someone here to see you. I suggest you take your break and deal with it."

"Understood," Shannon said.

Scott Whelan recognized Shannon Grayson from the old photos he'd seen online, as soon as she stepped off the elevator. She wore pale green scrubs with black Crocs, and her reddish hair was in a tightly pulled-back ponytail. She was pretty in a fresh-faced way, with freckles and high cheekbones.

"Miss Grayson," he said, approaching her with a smile and an outstretched Starbucks venti.

"Do I know you?" She didn't take the coffee, just crossed her arms over her chest in a defensive posture that told Whelan she wasn't going to make his life easy. Not today.

"You don't. Yet. My name is Whelan, and I was hoping you could maybe give me ten minutes of your time?"

"Why would I do that? I don't need life insurance or an extended warranty on my car. So, who are you and what do you want from me?"

He gestured toward a seating area near the lobby window that looked out onto the hospital's meditation garden. "Could we sit over there so I could explain?"

Shannon took a seat and Whelan sat beside her. He set the coffee on the table between them, along with some sugar packets, creamers, and wooden stir sticks. "That's for you, by the way."

She removed the lid of the cup, dumped in a creamer and a sugar, and took a sip. "Ten minutes."

"I'd like to talk to you about something that happened in 2002, the summer you were working as a lifeguard at the Saint Cecelia."

Her expression darkened, so he rushed ahead, wanting to get it out before she changed her mind and went scurrying back upstairs to her patients.

"I'm interested in what happened to a little boy named Hudson back then. He drowned. At the pool where you were a lifeguard."

Shannon gasped. Her hands were shaking so badly she had to clasp them in her lap to keep them still. "It was an accident. A horrible, horrible accident."

Whelan's pale blue eyes were unblinking. "I want to understand what happened that day. I've looked at the police reports—as far as I can tell there was a strictly perfunctory investigation. The local newspapers had only the briefest mention of it. I think the story was hushed up by the owners of the resort. And I want to know why."

"Did you know they fired me? I was just nineteen. I gave him mouth-to-mouth, did chest compressions. Everything I'd been trained to do. And I didn't stop, even after it was clear he was gone."

"According to the police reports, there were two lifeguards on duty that day."

"Yeah. But only one of us got blamed."

"Why was that?"

"That part's not a mystery. The other girl happened to be engaged to the boss's son."

"Can you tell me what happened that day?" he asked.

"It was a long time ago. And you still haven't explained why you're interested in digging up this ancient history," she said.

"Hudson was my little brother. Well, half brother. And I know he knew how to swim, because I'm the one who taught him."

He pulled out a folded sheet of paper. A photocopy of an old, faded color snapshot he'd found in his mother's papers. It showed a younger version of Whelan, standing in chest-high water with a skinny, sunburnt Hudson perched on his shoulders, grinning into the camera.

"This was taken at his father's house, in their pool in Atlanta. Hudson had been around pools all his life. There's no reason he should have drowned."

"And yet he did," Shannon said. "I was there."

"Did you ever meet Hudson's mom? My mom?"

"Sometimes she'd come down to the pool with him that summer, but mostly not. When she was there—wow! She was an eyeful. She could really rock a string bikini. The dads couldn't take their eyes off her, and let me tell you, the other moms didn't like that. At all."

Whelan smiled at the memory of his mother, who, even in her forties, loved nothing better than shocking the prim and proper mothers in her Buckhead neighborhood. He pulled another sheet of paper from his pocket, this one a photocopy of the last picture he had of his mother.

"This was my mom. Her name was Kasey, by the way. I think it was taken a few months before she died."

The photo was blurry but showed an emaciated woman with thinning white hair worn in a badly executed bowl cut. Her eyebrows were drawn on crookedly, her cheeks sunken, lips barely parted over toothless gums. It was a shocking photo. And that was the point.

"Oh my God," Shannon exclaimed. "That doesn't look anything like the same woman. How old was she when this was taken?"

"Just barely sixty-six," Whelan said.

"Wow. She looks like about a hundred years old. What happened to her?"

"Her little boy died. Her husband blamed her and she blamed herself and this is how she ended up. Alone, haunted by that loss," Whelan said. "So. Anything you can remember about that day would really be a help to me."

She looked out at the garden, where butterflies fluttered above bright pink blooms.

"I hate to tell you, but that kid was a big pest that summer. Always getting into trouble. And it didn't seem like he had a whole lot of adult supervision."

Whelan nodded. "Hudson's father, Brad—my mother's second husband—wasn't around much back then. I think my mom was basically a single mom that summer."

"Yeah. I don't know if I ever even saw the dad," Shannon agreed. "And when I did see your mom, she usually had a cocktail in her hand."

"Sounds right," Whelan agreed.

Shannon closed her eyes as she thought back to that day. "Seemed like he was in some kind of feud with his little buddy who he usually hung around with. Mike something."

"Michael Sullivan?" Whelan had found the name, scrawled in childish handwriting, on a sympathy card among his mother's belongings.

She nodded. "That sounds right. Mike and another boy were down at the deep end, having a cannonball contest to see who could make the biggest splash. You could tell Hudson was mad about not being included. At some point, he was sitting on the side of the pool. And all of a sudden, he starts screaming and making these gagging noises, yelling that one of the kids had pooped in the pool."

Shannon rolled her eyes. "It was textbook Hudson. Of course, then Traci—that was the other lifeguard—and I had to get everybody out of the pool. Code brown, we called it. I went and got the skimmer, to scoop up the poop, only it wasn't really poop. It was a Tootsie Roll."

"Hudson's idea of a practical joke," Whelan said. "He was always a little trickster."

"It wasn't funny to us," Shannon retorted. "Traci started yelling at him to get out of the pool, but then he was flailing around, splashing and pretending that he was drowning, which really pissed us off. And then, he kinda stopped moving. And his head rolled back . . ."

She wasn't looking at the butterflies anymore, Whelan noticed. She was looking up at the ceiling, dredging up that very bad day, and her eyes were damp.

"I was down at the shallow end, yelling at kids to get out. Traci jumped in, still thinking maybe he was faking us out again. But his lips were already turning blue . . .

"Traci and I, we took turns working on him. All these people were gathered around us, yelling for someone to call nine-one-one. And then, I heard this woman, screaming. Just, the most piercing, awful howl I ever heard. And she was screaming . . . 'My baby. Save my baby.'"

Shannon looked over at Whelan. She was still clenching and unclenching the hands that had been resting on the knees of her scrub pants. "But it was too late."

When he'd set out on this mission, Whelan had convinced himself that he could approach it, all of it—including hearing a firsthand account of his little brother's death—with the kind of clinical objectivity he'd possessed during his previous career in the military.

But he hadn't reckoned for this—his instant recall of his mother's high-pitched wail, the utter despair in her voice when she'd called to tell him about what had happened.

That summer, he was sharing an apartment in Charlotte with two other guys, sweating his balls off working on a construction site, bored and considering joining the military.

Kasey had been hysterical, crying so hard he could barely make out what she was saying. Just . . . "Hudson" and "my baby" and . . . "drowned."

It hadn't made sense then and it still didn't make sense all these years later.

That July day had been the beginning of the end for Kasey. For years, he'd been too selfish, too wrapped up in his own drama to recognize the fact of her rapid demise. Now, though, he owed it to her, and to himself, to find out the truth.

He reached across the end table and lightly touched Shannon's hand. She flinched.

"I'm sorry to bring this back up again. It's painful for me, and I wasn't even there. I just have a couple more questions."

"Okay, but make it quick. I'm on the clock and my supervisor hates me."

"You said you ran and got the pool skimmer, after Hudson hollered about the fake poop. Was there anyone else in the pool?"

"Not in the deep end. Traci and I blew our whistles and yelled at everybody to get out of the pool."

"What about the kids who'd been on the diving board? Where did they go? Could one of them have pushed Hudson underwater when you weren't looking?"

"No. Traci was watching. She would have yelled at them."

"You're sure? I mean, you said you went to get the skimmer. Maybe, while your back was turned, and while Traci was clearing the pool, one of those boys, just horsing around, pushed Hudson in and held him underwater?"

"I'm telling you, my back wasn't turned but a few seconds. And when I got back to the deep end, Hudson was the only kid in the pool."

She stood abruptly. "I gotta get back. Ruth is probably writing me up right this minute."

Whelan couldn't let her leave. "Did you and the other lifeguard, that girl Traci, did the two of you talk about it, afterward? I mean, maybe she saw something you missed?"

She headed for the elevator bank and stabbed the Up button. He'd lost her. She was stony-faced, shut down. "Me and Traci didn't talk at all after that day. About anything."

Whelan followed her to the bank of elevators. "Really? You'd just witnessed what had to be the most traumatic event in your lives, and you never talked about it? At all?"

"At all," she said, pressing her lips together. The doors opened, she stepped inside, and a moment later the doors closed and she was gone.

CHAPTER 26

* * *

By late Saturday afternoon on the day of the Beach Bash, Traci was on the phone in her office, frantically trying to stave off a chain of minor disasters that threatened to ruin the event.

"Traci?"

Charlie Burroughs's expression was glum. He sat down in the chair opposite her desk and gestured to his cell phone. "We've got a shituation down at the beach club."

She sighed and disconnected. "What is it now?"

"Just got off the phone with Gary in maintenance. Someone flushed an entire roll of toilet paper in each of the commodes down at the beach club."

"Oh God. What do the plumbers say?"

"Plumber. Singular. It's just Marvin, and he says it's not good. Six plugged-up commodes. We gotta shut the bathrooms 'til it's fixed. And he doesn't know how long that will take."

"Okay," Traci said. "Plan B. Call Cindy over at Royal Flush. Ask her if they can get us some portalettes delivered to the beach club ASAP."

"That ain't gonna be cheap," Charlie said gloomily.

"We've gotta have bathrooms down there. Other than toilets, how's everything else looking?"

"Okay. They're setting up the tables down there now."

"Mrs. E?"

Felice, the new chef, stood in the doorway of her office, holding a small bowl covered with plastic wrap.

Charlie bristled. "Felice? Now is not a good time."

Traci waved away his objections. "Hi, Felice. Come on in, but please tell me you don't have more bad news."

Felice stepped into the office and held out the bowl, removing the plastic wrap. Inside were a handful of grayish, foul-smelling shrimp.

"Gah!" Traci pushed the bowl away.

"The whole order is like this," Felice said angrily. "I called that Tommy Betz and told him we're not paying for this mess. He hung up on me. I went down to the docks in town myself and bought some fresh stuff right off the boat."

"Good thinking," Traci said.

"We need a new fishmonger," Felice said.

"Felice?" Charlie said. "Let's just get through tonight. Okay? Monday, you and I will have a talk with Tommy. I'm sure he wouldn't intentionally send us bad shrimp."

"That's what you think," Felice said. She turned and left.

"I know you hired her, Traci," Charlie started, "but I don't think that girl grasps how important our business relationships are. The Betzes have been supplying our fish since—"

"Happy Beach Bash Day!" Madelyn Eddings swept into the room, clutching her ever-present planner. "Wanted to let you know the flowers for the centerpieces were just delivered and they are stunning, if I do say so myself."

"Centerpieces?" Traci eyed her sister-in-law warily. "What happened to just using pineapples and palm fronds on the tables, like we always used to do?"

"Traci, must you cling so tenaciously to the clichés of the past? Wait until you see what I've done. Three different kinds of orchids, bromeliads, tuberoses. It's absolutely heavenly."

"And I bet the florist bill will be hellish," Traci snapped, out of patience.

"The Saint is a five-star hotel, and we must give our guests a five-star experience," Madelyn said, waving away her sister-in-law's objections. "And now, I'll just scoot along down there to supervise, and then I'll see you out front at five."

Traci and Parrish stood in the entryway to the hotel lobby, dressed in coordinating Hawaiian-print dresses, their arms full of leis. The plan was that promptly at five, the doors would be opened and they would begin greeting their guests and offering the leis.

"About your text," Traci told her niece. "How worried should I be?"

"Not here," Parrish whispered, as one of the valet parking guys jogged past. "Have you seen my dad? Or Madelyn? Shouldn't they have been here by now?"

"Madelyn came by the office earlier . . ." Traci said.

"And here she is now," Parrish said, nodding as her stepmother approached. "Jesus! Will you look at what she's wearing? I swear, I can see the tops of her nipples."

"Oh my," Traci whispered back.

Madelyn Eddings's dress was made of the same eye-popping floral fabric as the other two women's dresses, but that's where the resemblance ended. Her own dress was a short, shirred, skin-tight tube of fabric, and her breasts spilled aggressively over the top. She wore beaded orange sandals with five-inch heels.

"Traci-Wacy! Parry-Warry. Look at you two," Madelyn exclaimed, clapping her hands in glee. "Totes adorbs."

"Yes," Parrish deadpanned. "Just look at us. Can I ask you a question, Mads?"

"Of course."

"What happened to the rest of your dress? And also, how do you plan to walk on the beach in those fuck-me pumps?"

Madelyn's smile vanished.

"Parrish! Such a potty mouth. For your information, I won't be here that long. I just dropped by to be part of the family welcoming committee."

"Where's Dad?" Parrish asked. "I thought this was supposed to be an all-hands-on-deck family-fun day."

Madelyn shrugged. "Ric has a scheduling conflict. He sends his regrets."

"How's it looking down on the beach?" Traci asked, as Charlie walked up wearing his own Hawaiian shirt.

"It's all good," Charlie assured her. He looked over at Madelyn and blushed violently. "Hi, Madelyn. Is Ric coming?"

"Big meeting with investors," Madelyn said, shaking her head.

Charlie motioned for Traci to give him her armful of leis. "I swear, everything is under control. Why don't you get a glass of prosecco and try to relax?"

"Relax? What's that?" Traci's stomach was in knots. Coming out of the pandemic, they'd canceled the annual Beach Bash for the past three years. This was her first time running it without Hoke by her side, and she was quietly terrified. The back of her dress was already clinging from perspiration, despite the fact that they were standing inside in the air-conditioning.

She stepped forward as Charlie unlocked the heavy carved wooden doors. A swirl of tropical-garbed guests quickly flooded into the lobby, and Traci, Parrish, and Madelyn began greeting them and placing leis around their necks.

A couple in their early fifties approached Traci and her niece. The husband wore a violently patterned Hawaiian shirt, baggy Bermuda shorts, and a wide-brimmed straw hat. His wife was reed-thin, with a deep, leathery tan. She was wearing skin-tight white jeans, kitten-heeled sandals, and a low-cut embroidered Mexican cotton shirt.

"That's the Logans," Traci whispered. "He's vice president of our bank . . ."

"I know," Parrish replied. "The lifeguards all call her Mahogany. I got it." She turned to the guests. "Palmer! Sherry! So good to see you again." She draped leis over their necks. "Sherry, have you signed up for next week's tennis clinic? We've got a new coach, and just between us, he is smoking hot!"

Traci turned to her niece after the guests had moved on. "You were born for this, you know."

By seven, the party was in full swing. Four hundred and fifty guests in varying versions of beach attire dotted the beach and pool area. The servers, dressed in their coordinating tropical-print dresses and shirts, busily circulated, offering appetizers and drinks. People wandered around, seated at cloth-draped tables, or standing, sampling the Low Country boil and barbecue, drinking and catching up. Traci mingled among the guests, gritting her teeth every time someone patted her shoulder and asked, in a concerned voice, "How are you doing?" It had been four years, and although she appreciated the thought, she was really tired of the pitying expressions.

By eight, the steel drum band had swung into faster-tempo music. Guests had discarded their shoes, and couples and singles were dancing, barefoot, in the sand and on the tiled pool deck. Children splashed in the water and raced around, faces sticky from the ice-cream sundae dessert bar.

Traci stood in front of the pool house, glancing anxiously at the darkening sky. Sunset was an hour away, but purplish-black clouds loomed on the horizon. "It's gonna rain. I just know it. Things were going too good."

"Maybe not." Charlie handed her a plate of food. "C'mon. Eat. You need to taste the barbacoa pork. That spicy pineapple salsa is great."

Parrish joined them. "I can't tell you how many members have come up to tell me how much they like Felice's food."

"Good to hear," Traci said. She popped a bit of pork in her mouth and chewed. "You're right. Really good. So different from Mehdi's food." She turned to Charlie. "I think we need to do whatever it takes to keep Felice happy, which means finding some new vendors."

"We can talk about that later," Charlie said.

Just then Garrett and KJ passed close by with trays of the signature Saint cocktail that Felice had concocted for the event. Parrish snagged two cups and handed one to her aunt.

Traci took a sip and gasped. "Wow! What the hell is in this? I don't want anyone getting pie-eyed here and then getting in a collision on the way home." She looked around, then discreetly dumped the remainder of the drink in a potted palm.

Parrish took a gulp from her own drink. "Oh, don't be such an old lady, Traci. I think it's awesome. Fruity but not too sweet. Anyway, they're offering a nonalcoholic version too. Most people are being responsible. They're behaving themselves."

"Oh yeah?" Traci pointed to the beach, where Sherry Palmer, aka Mahogany, had ditched her shoes and was now twerking with a wide-eyed Garrett, whom she'd yanked onto the dance floor as he passed by with an empty drinks tray. Her husband watched, stormy-faced, as his wife grinded against the waiter's crotch.

"Oh my God," Parrish yelped. "I just snorted curaçao and passion fruit all over myself."

"Maybe you better go rescue poor Garrett," Traci said.

Parrish's merry expression darkened. "He's a big boy. He can handle himself."

Traci studied her niece and was about to say something when she heard the low rumble of thunder, followed by a jagged bolt of lightning.

"Crap! I knew it," Traci said.

A lifeguard's shrill whistle sounded, the music stopped abruptly, and an announcement came over the club's public address system: "Everyone off the beach and out of the pool, please."

Guests began to move toward shelter as fat, warm raindrops began to fall.

"Rain plan is a go," Traci said as she turned to her niece.

But Parrish was already sprinting toward the beach, helping the lifeguards and servers herd guests toward cover.

By nine, the beach and pool had been cleared out. A few die-hard guests huddled together under the shelter of the pool house, but the majority had left, leaving around sixty people crowded around the hotel lobby, grumbling about the long wait for their parked cars to be returned.

Colonel McBee approached Parrish, who was standing behind the guest relations desk, working the phone, frantically trying to summon the island's few cabs for guests who hadn't been able to call a rideshare.

"Miss Eddings," he boomed, holding up a waterlogged garment. "My wife's dress is soaked. She's upstairs in tears. Absolutely inconsolable."

Parrish counted to three before replying. "Colonel, I'm sorry, but here at the Saint, we don't actually have any control over the weather. Now, how can I assist you?"

He shook the dress at her, spraying rain droplets onto the desk and her computer monitor. "You people can reimburse me for the cost of this dress, of course. It's my wife's favorite designer, and she paid good money for it in New York."

Back in the Reagan administration, Parrish thought, eying the limp cotton dress.

"And also, the rain forced us to leave the party before we were served our desserts, so I believe we are owed at least a partial refund of the fifty-dollar ticket price, which, of course, was an outrageous amount to spend on such a paltry dinner offering."

"A refund?" Parrish took a deep breath. This old man was going to break her, she knew it for sure. "I'm sorry, Colonel, but I'm not authorized to offer that. What I can do is send your wife's dress out to the cleaners, and I'll see if the kitchen can't send something sweet up to your room as soon as things settle down here."

"Absolutely not acceptable," he snapped. "Where is your aunt? I need to speak to her immediately."

"Mrs. Eddings isn't available right now," Parrish told him. "But I'll let her know about your concerns."

By ten, the lobby had cleared and the rain had stopped as abruptly as it had begun.

"Afterparty," one of the valet guys, named Juan, whispered to KJ. "Tell the others. At the Shack."

"Where's the Shack?" KJ asked.

"Ask Garrett, and tell him to grab a golf cart to help carry the booze."

"Afterparty," Angela, one of the room service servers, whispered as she passed Olivia, who was walking up the beach with an arm-load of foil-wrapped trays of leftovers. "And bring that food, okay?"

"Where?" Livvy asked.

"The Shack," Angela said, hurrying away before Livvy could ask for more details.

She found Parrish as she was heading for the lobby door. "Hey, where are you going?"

"Home," Parrish said wearily. "But all the golf carts are out, so I guess I'll have to walk back to the dorm."

"That's because everybody's taking them to the afterparty. KJ just passed me on the way there with a cooler full of punch, but he promised to come back for us."

"Not me," Parrish said. "I'm toast."

"Oh, come on," Livvy urged. "Loosen up and live, right?"

KJ pulled the cart alongside them. The back was loaded with coolers and stacks of foil-wrapped food trays. "Get in, losers," he called cheerily. "Partayyyyyy!"

Parrish laughed despite herself and hopped onto the back seat. Livvy pulled out her phone, leaned in, extended her arm, and shot a selfie of the two of them, grinning in their matching flowered dresses and leis.

The golf cart bumped and rocked as it left the paved road and swerved onto a mud-soaked path through a dense thicket of palmet-tos and kudzu-draped pines.

"Do you know about this place, Parrish?" Livvy asked.

"It used to be the landscaping shed. When I was a little girl, my friends and I used it as a clubhouse, until Granddaddy found out we'd made a bonfire to cook hot dogs, and in the process, nearly burned the place down. He padlocked it, but a few years later, when I was in high school, we used a hacksaw to open it back up. We used to hang out here and drink and smoke weed and . . . you know."

"Ohhh," Livvy said.

"The good old days," KJ put in. He slowed the cart and pointed to a clearing ahead, where a motley crew of the Saint's staffers stood around a small fire, clutching beers and Solo cups. People were swaying to loud rap music and a pungent haze of smoke drifted their way. "Smells like teen spirit!"

CHAPTER 27

★ ★ ★

Parrish stood at the edge of the crowd, already feeling like an outsider. She recognized most of the partygoers as her coworkers, and the members of the steel drum band. KJ took her by the hand, dragged her closer to the fire, and handed her a Solo cup of the punch. She downed it quickly, hoping it would numb her sense of awkwardness, and it went down so smoothly, she drank a second cup, finally feeling a comforting buzz.

She spotted Garrett on the other side of the crowd. He was smoking a joint, and had his arm around the waist of the petite singer from the band. Their eyes met, and he whispered something in the girl's ear. She pouted for a moment, then kissed him passionately on the lips.

He moved lazily toward her, and Parrish thought briefly of commandeering a golf cart to make an escape. Even though they lived under the same roof, they hadn't exchanged a single word since that night at Pour Willy's. He'd been so very drunk—did he even remember what he'd told her about the liquor thefts?

"Hey," he said casually when he reached her side. He looked her up and down approvingly. "Nice dress."

"Thanks."

"All you girls and your aunt in matching dresses? How cute."

Such an asshole. "What do you want, Garrett?"

He took a drag on the joint and handed it to her. Was this a dare? She took a hit and let the smoke slowly swirl through her nostrils before handing it back.

"Okay, sorry. That was mean. Let's start over. You really do look pretty tonight."

"Uh-huh." She gulped down some punch, and then some more, waiting.

"Did you, uh, say anything, to anyone, after, uh, the other night?"

"What? You think I ran right back to my aunt to tattle about your little side hustle?"

His face flushed. "It's not *my* side hustle. I told you that. And you still haven't answered my question. I need to know if I'm in some kind of trouble."

Parrish took the joint back, finished it, and coolly flicked ash down the front of his half-unbuttoned shirt, giggling at the spectacle of Garrett trying to brush away the burning ash.

"Do you think you're the only one running an operation at my family's hotel? I've got news for you, you're not. I've been watching, and taking notes. And it's all up here." She tapped her forehead and gave him a loopy grin. "And in my little blue book."

"Geezus, what an amateur. You are stoned out of your mind after two hits."

"Drunk too," she agreed, draining her drink and handing him the Solo cup. "Get me another, m'kay?"

"Get it yourself, bitch," he said. "I'm officially off duty."

Okay, so maybe she was stoned. And drunk. It had been a minute since she'd smoked any weed. And that punch? Lethal. She joined the rest of the crowd standing around the fire, swaying to the music. Someone handed her a lit joint. She didn't really want it, but she smoked half, then dropped it to the ground and carefully stubbed it out with the heel of her sandal.

Bored, she made her way over to one of the golf carts, which had been set up as a makeshift buffet cart, with the foil trays of leftover shrimp and barbecue laid out on the seats.

Parrish peeled a shrimp and popped it in her mouth, surprised by how peppery it was. She grabbed a can of beer from an open cooler and sipped, mostly to wash away the spice.

She hadn't realized how hungry she was. There'd been no time to eat earlier. She ate some chips and guacamole, and was munching on a brownie when one of the band members sidled up to her.

"Hi, pretty," he said. "You having a good time?" He had a slight, lilting accent. Jamaican, maybe?

He plucked a joint from the pocket of his shirt, lit it, and handed it to her.

She took a hit, and then another and another, hoping to mask her shyness around him.

"Having a great time. I like your music."

"And I like your dress. Do you work at the hotel?"

"Yeahhhh," she said, realizing she was slurring the word. "What's your name again?"

"Cedric. Don't you remember me? Let me get you another drink. Be right back."

Five minutes later he returned with another cup of punch. She'd finished the joint, and drank the punch, this time sipping more slowly. People were milling around, laughing and talking. Cedric was saying something she couldn't quite understand.

The inside of her mouth felt funny, like wet wool, and she was suddenly unbearably hot. And dizzy. And she needed to pee. "Could you excuse me for a moment, please?"

She walked unsteadily away, toward the Shack. "Need to pee," she muttered. Was there still a commode in the shed? She couldn't remember. When she got to the door, she heard voices from inside.

Ohmygod, I will wet my pants, she thought. She leaned against the doorjamb for a second, then staggered to the rear of the Shack. There was a thick clump of palmettos a few yards away. She could roll down her panties, tinkle, and nobody would be the wiser.

Just a few more steps, Parrish told herself. But the landscape tilted and spun crazily, then began to slide and fuzz, like a carnival funhouse. She tried to hurry, but now everything was in slow motion. Were there footsteps behind her? Thrashing through the underbrush? She sank down to her knees, aware of the thick, cool mud. Then she lay down and closed her eyes, willing the spinning to stop.

"Parrish?" A soft hand stroked her forehead, brushing back her bangs. She was eight, and had taken a bad fall on her Rollerblades. Her granny smiled down at her. "Come on, now, honey. We've got to take you to the doctor to see about that arm of yours."

"Granny?" Parrish reached out a hand, then felt it drop woodenly to her side, as her grandmother's face melted into nothingness.

CHAPTER 28

* * *

Traci bustled around the kitchen of her cottage, setting out coffee mugs and bowls. She had homemade granola from her favorite bakery in the village, fresh blueberries and peaches, and Greek yogurt. Lola dozed in her favorite sunny spot near the back door.

Her laptop was set up on the pine kitchen table, and she started reviewing the notes she'd made after returning home from the previous night's event so she could go over the hits and misses with Charlie on Monday, but her mind kept returning to Parrish's text message. *Something serious*. What the hell did that even mean?

When Lola started scratching at the back door to go out, she was surprised to see it was ten thirty.

She frowned and checked her phone to make sure she hadn't missed a text from Parrish, who, unlike most of her generation, was habitually prompt. Nothing. She picked up her phone to call, but was sent directly to voice mail.

"Parrish? Coffee's ready. Where are you? Call me, please."

As the minutes ticked by, she felt a prickle of unease. She drank half a pot of coffee, and tried to concentrate on work, to no avail. After an hour, she called and left another message.

Should she call Ric, to ask if he knew anything about his daughter's whereabouts? But the thought of hearing his voice conjured up unpleasant thoughts about the nefarious scheme her brother-in-law was cooking up in what she was sure amounted to some kind of power grab.

At noon, she got in her golf cart and rode over to the staff dorm. Parrish was probably in her room, having overslept after the party. When she arrived, she saw her niece's Audi was parked in the gravel lot. So she was there. Wasn't she?

Traci was about to punch the door code into the keypad when Felice pulled up and stepped out of her car, dressed in a pastel flowered dress, with a wide-brimmed straw hat.

"Mrs. E?" Felice looked flustered at seeing her employer here, on a Sunday, so out of context. "Something wrong?"

"Hello, Felice. You look very pretty. I'm just a little concerned. Parrish and I had a breakfast date this morning, and she never showed, which is very unlike her. She hasn't returned my calls or texts. Have you seen her this morning?"

"Me? No, I left for church at nine and nobody else was up. I think everyone had a late night at the afterparty last night."

"Afterparty?"

She followed Felice inside. The dorm was quiet. A heap of muddy sneakers and flip-flops sat beside the door. The television in the lounge was turned on, but muted, and she could see that the dining table and kitchen counter were littered with dishes and discarded takeout containers. A bag of trash sat in the middle of the kitchen floor, and a half-eaten pizza had been left on the coffee table in the lounge, and she could definitely detect the smell of weed.

For a moment, she was transported back to that hot, creaky staff dorm that she and Shannon had lived in all those years ago. Same pizza boxes and dirty dishes. But this time with air-conditioning. And premium cable.

"It's kind of a mess," Felice apologized. "I fuss at those guys, but you know . . ."

"Don't worry," Traci said. "I'm not here to inspect. I just need to check on Parrish."

She knocked lightly on her niece's door. "Hey, kiddo. You awake in there?" After a minute, she opened the door and stuck her head inside.

Parrish's bed was unmade. A laundry basket was overflowing with rumpled clothes and her nightstand held a phone charger and a can of Red Bull. No sign of the room's occupant.

Felice was still waiting in the hallway. "Not here," she told the chef.

"Maybe she's in the shower," Felice said. "I'll just check." But she was back, a moment later, shaking her head. "Nobody there."

Traci fiddled with her engagement ring, twisting it around and around.

"You want me to wake up the others and ask?" Felice asked.

She did and she didn't. "Maybe so," she said finally.

Felice stood in the center of the hallway and bawled loudly in her distinctive accent. "All y'all, wake up now! Come on. Mrs. E is here and she's looking for Parrish."

A door popped open and Olivia poked her head out. "Parrish? Isn't she here?"

"Nope," Felice said.

A moment later, KJ emerged from his room, yanking a T-shirt over his head. Garrett stepped out of his room, bare-chested and bleary-eyed.

"I'm sorry to bother you," Traci said, trying to mask her mounting anxiety. "But Parrish missed a breakfast date with me this morning and I'm a little worried. I'm wondering when was the last time any of you saw her."

She noticed a wary glance passing between the two men.

"I saw her last night, at the Beach Bash," Garrett offered. "We, uh, had a little get-together after the Beach Bash. A few beers, a few laughs."

"An afterparty," Traci said. "Where was this? And was Parrish there?"

"She was there," Olivia said. "We rode over together, with KJ. There were a lot of people there, and I'm not sure the last time I saw her."

"Again. Where was the party? Come on, you're not in trouble. I just need to know where Parrish could be."

"The Shack," Garrett began. "It's this old—"

"I know where it is," Traci cut in. "When did you see her last?"

Garrett ran his hands through his hair. "I don't know. Maybe around one?"

"She was talking to one of the guys from the band," KJ volunteered.

"And then what?" She turned to the chef. "Felice, did you see her last night?"

"I came back here and soaked my feet and went to bed. Last time I seen Parrish was down at the beach, right when the storm came up, telling everyone to move inside."

Traci turned to the others. "And she didn't come back here with any of you?" She recognized that her tone was sharper, because she was growing desperate.

"Not with me," Livvy said. "Tommy, one of the other servers, gave me a ride back."

"Me and KJ rode a golf cart back here together," Garrett said.

"So. What was the last time anyone saw Parrish last night?"

"Maybe one thirty?" Livvy was apologetic. "Just a guess. My phone was dead by the time I got off work."

"Hey. Maybe try calling her phone here. Maybe she forgot it or something," KJ said.

Traci made a show of tapping her niece's number. "It's still going directly to voice mail. Which means she either turned it off, or it's dead."

KJ shifted uncomfortably from one foot to the other. "Do you want me to go out to the Shack to look for her?"

"That's a great idea," Garrett said quickly. "Me and KJ will go scout around."

"I'll go with you," Traci said.

"Well, it's super muddy out there after all that rain last night," he said. "If you'll just let us borrow your golf cart, we can run out there, check, and come right back."

"I don't know." She was raising a welt on her ring finger from all the twisting and turning. "I don't have a good feeling about this. Maybe I should call the police."

"You don't wanna do that," Garrett said. "I mean, how embarrassed would she be if she was, like, with a guy? Also, have you checked at the hotel? Maybe she decided to go in early to work and just forgot."

"Not likely," Traci said. "But I'll walk over there and check. You two go out to the Shack. Call me right away if you find her."

The area around the Shack looked like a dump truck had overturned, spilling out beer cans and bottles, cigarette butts, lighters, and discarded Solo cups. The ground was muddy and matted down around the fire pit. Flies buzzed around half-empty foil pans of food, and the sickly sweet smell of rot lingered in the swampy summer air.

"Man, what a mess," KJ said, surveying the site.

"Come on," Garrett urged, handing him one of the plastic garbage bags they'd brought from the dorm. "We gotta get the place cleaned up. If Mrs. E sees this, we'll all be in deep shit."

The two men began loading trash into the bags. It was hot, miserable work.

KJ tossed a full bag of trash onto the back of the golf cart. "I'm just gonna take a look inside the Shack, make sure she's not in there."

They removed the broken padlock from the door. Rusted hinges squeaked as he pulled on the door handle. He stepped inside. "Jesus!"

CHAPTER 29

* * *

KJ slammed the door hard and jumped backward, the color drained from his usually ruddy face.

Garrett, motionless, stared at KJ. "Is it . . . her?"

"Christ, no! It was a rat! The biggest freakin' rat I've ever seen. Like, the size of a cat. And it ran right across my foot." He shuddered and moved away from the Shack. "Let's go. We need to call Mrs. E and get the fuck outta here."

Garrett glanced around the area, picking up a beer bottle and a discarded vape pen, which he dumped into a trash bag and slung into the back of the golf cart. "Okay, I guess. You go grab the rest of the bags and look around the back and make sure we didn't miss anything."

"Oh hell no. There's probably a whole nest of rats back in there." KJ tossed the remaining bags onto the back of the cart and Garrett got behind the wheel and they drove off.

Traci paced back and forth outside the hotel lobby, getting increasingly frantic.

She picked up on the first ring when Garrett called.

"No sign of her here, Mrs. E. Was she at the hotel?"

"No." Traci's voice cracked. "Nobody's seen her here since last night." She twisted her engagement ring around and around, the phone cradled in the crook of her neck. "I guess I'd better call her dad."

"Sorry, ma'am," Garrett said. "You want us to bring the cart back to you there?"

"Yes, please," she said. "I really appreciate the two of you looking. And if you could just spread the word around, if anyone has seen Parrish, or heard from her today, have them call me, please."

"Will do."

After he disconnected, Garrett steered the cart past the hotel entrance and onto a service road that looped around the rear of the hotel, toward the restaurant's service entrance. Garrett pulled alongside the dumpster and turned to his friend. "Chuck those bags in there, okay?"

"Better not be no rats," KJ muttered as he clambered out.

Traci's heart was racing as she tapped Ric's name on the contact list in her phone.

Her brother-in-law finally picked up on the fourth ring.

"Hey," he said. "I'm about to tee off on the fourth hole. Can this wait?"

"No. It can't. Ric, have you seen Parrish today?"

"No. Why?"

"She was supposed to meet me for breakfast this morning and she didn't show. I'm really worried."

"So? She probably overslept. Or maybe she's blowing you off like she does me all the time."

Traci bit her lip. "She wouldn't blow me off without calling. She didn't oversleep. I've called, and her phone goes right to voice mail. I've been over to the staff dorm. Her car's there, but she's not, and none of the others have seen her since last night."

"Get a grip, Traci. She's a grown-up. Parrish doesn't have to report in to you every day."

"I never said she did. I'm telling you, Ric, something is wrong. She texted me yesterday and said she had something she wanted to talk to me about. In private."

"Probably just a boyfriend problem, but then, you'd know more about that than me, since you've managed to completely alienate my daughter from me."

Traci wanted to scream, but somehow managed to tamp down her rage.

"She's not dating anyone, Ric. And unlike you, Parrish's not a hookup kind of girl."

"What the hell is that supposed to mean?"

"You know exactly what it means. But this isn't about you. It's about your kid, and I am worried sick about her. Can you just tear yourself away from your precious golf game for a few minutes to help me figure out what's going on? Can you call Madelyn and ask her if she's seen Parrish?"

"Call her yourself," Ric snapped.

"I did. Several times. She didn't pick up."

"Okay," he said finally. "I'll call Madelyn, and then I'll head over to the house to see if she's there."

"I did that already," Traci said, fighting back tears. "Nobody answered the doorbell."

"Maybe she's out back by the pool, listening to music on her earbuds. I'm sure you're getting worked up over nothing."

"This one time, I pray you're right," Traci said.

Her next call was to Ray Bierbower, the Saint's head of security. She filled him in on Parrish's disappearance.

"I'm on it," Ray assured her. "I'll go out there to the Shack myself and take a look around, and I'll send a couple of my guys to do a thorough search of the grounds. Don't you worry, Mrs. E. If that girl is here, we'll find her."

Traci paced around the hotel lobby, absent-mindedly greeting guests until she retreated to her office for more pacing. Finally, she called Charlie Burroughs at home. He answered on the fourth ring.

"Hey, Traci. Congratulations. Despite the rain, it was—"

She cut him off quickly. "Charlie? Parrish is missing."

"You're sure?"

"Absolutely. Nobody has seen her. Not Ric, not the kids in the dorm. I've got Ray Bierbower and his men combing the property. I know it's your day off, but—"

"I'm on my way," he said.

She'd just disconnected the call when Ric burst through her office door. "Nobody's seen her," he said breathlessly. "I've talked to Madelyn, her friends, everyone I can think of."

Her phone rang again.

She grabbed it up and glanced at the caller ID. Ray Bierbower.

"Ray?"

"Mrs. E?" His voice was low and mournful. She sensed what was coming.

"I'm afraid I've got some bad news."

CHAPTER 30

* * *

Wordlessly, Traci handed her phone to her brother-in-law.

Ric's face was impassive as he listened and nodded, his Adam's apple working as he swallowed the emotions he seemed unable to speak. Finally: "Yeah. I understand. You're sure it's her? Yeah. I'll tell her."

Ric disconnected the phone, threw it onto the desktop, and doubled over, burying his face in his hands, his shoulders heaving with each muffled sob.

Traci waited, her heart pounding in her chest, for the news she'd been dreading all day. Parrish was gone. She hadn't known how or why, but the same black cloud that had descended after Hoke's plane went down was back.

After his sobs seemed to have subsided, she spoke. "Ric?"

He raised his tearstained face and took a deep breath. "Ray says . . . he found her. My beautiful, my baby girl, is gone. Oh my God. Parrish is dead."

"Where?" Traci whispered.

"She was behind the Shack all this time. Ray says . . ." He gulped and started over. "He said he spotted a woman's shoe in the overgrown bushes behind the Shack, so he kept searching and it looks like she must have fallen down into a kind of ravine."

He stood abruptly. "I've gotta go. I've gotta get to my little girl."

"Ric, wait," she called, but he was already out the door.

———

By the time Traci reached the Shack, the woods were alive with lights: blue lights from the Bonaventure sheriff's department, the red lights of an ambulance, and the swirling white lights from the Saint's security patrol cars. Her heart pounded and she felt the blood rushing to her head. This was real.

Yellow crime scene tape had been stretched in a wide perimeter around the Shack. Inside the tape, Ric stood stiffly at the edge of a knot of law enforcement types.

A uniformed sheriff's deputy stepped forward as soon as Traci alighted from her golf cart, and motioned for her to stop.

Traci tried to brush past the woman. "I'm Traci Eddings, the president of the resort, and that's my niece, Parrish, the girl who—"

"Sorry for your loss, ma'am, but this is an active crime scene investigation. You need to stay right here."

"Can you . . . tell me anything? Like, what happened?"

Just then, Ray Bierbower walked up and ducked under the tape. "I'm so sorry, Mrs. E."

He removed his aviator sunglasses and pinched the bridge of his nose. "This was the last thing I wanted to find."

"Who called the sheriff?" she asked.

"I called it in, as soon as I found her, but I don't think your brother-in-law is too happy with me for doing that."

"Don't worry about it. You did the right thing. Do they know what happened?"

"They're not telling me nothing official. But I can tell you, when I found her, she wasn't shot or stabbed or anything like that, at least as far as I could tell. She just kinda looked like she'd fallen asleep."

Traci felt bile rising in her throat. She ran to a thicket of palmetto and vomited; dry heaves that brought her to her knees as she retched and sobbed. When she tried to stand, she felt faint. Somehow, she managed to stagger to her feet. She was leaning against a slash pine tree when Bierbower found her, her eyes closed, a cold sweat forming on her flushed face.

He handed her a neatly folded handkerchief and looked tactfully away as she dabbed at the snot and sweat dripping down her face.

"Your niece seemed like a real nice girl, every time I had dealings with her," he said.

"She was . . . amazing. I don't know what I'm going to do without her. Parrish was like a daughter to me."

"Traci? This is Sheriff Coyle. He needs to talk to you." Ric turned and walked away without another word.

The sheriff could not have missed the hostility in her brother-in-law's attitude.

"Very sorry for your family's loss," Coyle said. "As I understand it from Mr. Eddings, there was some kind of party here last night? What can you tell me about that?"

"Not very much. I only found out about it this morning, from some of my staff who share a dorm with Parrish."

She dabbed at her face and neck with the handkerchief and fanned at the halo of swarming gnats.

Coyle whipped a notebook from his pocket. "I'm gonna need to talk to all those folks."

"Our general manager, Charlie Burroughs, can provide you with everyone's . . ."

Traci was aware that her voice was trailing off, and she was beginning to do a kind of slow-motion sway. Coyle touched her arm. "Are you okay?"

"No," she whispered. It sounded like her voice was coming from far, far away.

"Lean on me," Coyle said. The next thing she knew, she was stretched across the bench seat of her golf cart with a cool towel pressed to her neck and a cold bottle of water being rubbed across her forehead.

She opened her eyes to see Ray Bierbower, Charlie Burroughs, and the sheriff staring down at her.

"You passed out," Bierbower said.

"Dehydrated, probably," Coyle said, handing her the water bottle. "Drink."

"Have you eaten anything today?" Charlie asked.

She shook her head.

"Let's get you out of this heat," Coyle said. "Is there someplace we can go to talk?"

"My office. It's at the hotel," Traci said.

"I'll join you," Charlie offered. "In case the sheriff here needs any questions answered about staff."

"That's okay," Coyle said pleasantly. "For now, I'll just need Mrs. Eddings."

Traci sipped a glass of iced tea that someone had sent in from the restaurant, and nibbled at a saltine cracker while Coyle questioned her.

"I just can't wrap my mind around this," she said, crumbling the cracker between her fingertips. "You're seriously thinking it was foul play?"

"We can't really know until the medical examiner weighs in, but your niece was a healthy young woman. Only twenty-one, right? So it seems like a stretch that her death could be from natural causes."

"But who? Who would want to hurt her?"

"That's what we need to find out. Was there a boyfriend, or an ex, someone like that she might have gotten crossways with?"

"Not really. She dated a boy at the beginning of her senior year of college, but by Christmas they were broken up. She hadn't seen him in months."

Coyle jotted something on a pad of paper. "What kind of work did she do here?"

"Guest relations, which covers a lot of ground. In a nutshell, Parrish was responsible for seeing that our members and guests have nothing less than a stellar experience here."

"What's the difference between a member and a guest?"

Traci blinked. "Sheriff, how long have you been in office here in Bonaventure?"

"This is my first term," he said. "I guess you can tell I've never spent any time on your property. Not much call for us, what with you people having your own security."

"A guest is someone who's paying to stay at the resort, which means they have access to most of our on-site amenities, like the pools, golf course, and tennis courts. For members, we offer two kinds of memberships; residential and nonresidential."

"Would she have had any problems with your guests?"

"I mean, some guests can be difficult and demanding. A lot of them have been coddled and catered to their entire lives."

"Entitled assholes," Coyle said.

"You said it, not me."

"Tell me about her coworkers. You said she was living in a sort of dorm, here on the grounds of the resort? Did she get along with those folks?"

"Yes, as far as I knew. They'd only been living there a couple weeks."

Coyle shifted gears without warning. "What's Parrish's dad's role here?"

"Ric is CEO of Saint Holdings. It's the real estate arm of the family company. My late husband, Hoke, was CEO of the Saint Cecilia resort, and I assumed that role after his death."

"Why was Ric Eddings's daughter living here, in a dorm? I saw his house earlier. It's a mansion."

"I think that's something you should address with Ric, not me. I had the old cart barn remodeled into staff housing earlier this spring so that we could offer free housing to some employees. With rents in this area as high as they are, it was a way we could recruit summer help."

"Including your niece Parrish? Her father seems to think you bullied her into coming to work for you."

Traci turned her eyes on the detective. "Ric told you that?"

"He seems pretty angry at you."

"He's been angry with me for a while. I'm sure he already blames me for her death." She took a deep breath. "Maybe Ric's right. Maybe it is all my fault."

Coyle leaned forward in his chair, his voice calm. "Mrs. Eddings, take my advice. It's early days yet. Don't go there with the guilt. It'll eat you alive, if you let it."

She managed a wan smile.

"Tell me about that Shack," he said.

"It used to house the landscape maintenance equipment. My father-in-law built a modern barn a few years ago, and the Shack was left to deteriorate. At some point, we realized people were using it as a sort of illicit party destination, so we had it boarded and padlocked."

"When was the last time you were out there?"

"Years, probably. You saw how overgrown the woods around it were."

"Would a lot of your staff have known about the place?"

"I suppose so."

Coyle doodled something on his notepad. "Tell me about this Beach Bash that was held Saturday night. Who all was there?"

"It's an annual celebration to kick off the summer season. I think we had over four hundred paid reservations. Guests of the hotel, of course. And members."

"All those people would have had to pass through the security gates, right?"

"Yes. Although members have QR code decals on their vehicles, so they don't even have to slow down at the gates. Resort guests are given parking passes that allow them to come and go at will."

"You said people had to make reservations for this party? Who would have that list?"

Traci's eyes began to well up again. "Parrish would have had the list. On her work computer, I suppose." She pulled a tissue from a nearby box and dabbed at her eyes.

Charlie Burroughs knocked lightly on the office door and stepped inside. "Traci, how are you feeling? You still look kinda peaked."

"I'm . . . overwhelmed," she admitted. "Sheriff Coyle was asking about a list of folks who were at the Beach Bash last night."

"I can help with that," Charlie said.

Traci turned back to the sheriff. "I'm sorry, but do you think we could continue this later?" She handed him one of her business cards. "I just need some time to process this. Charlie here can help you with whatever else you need."

"Fine," Coyle said. "I'll be in touch."

CHAPTER 31

* * *

The lounge of the staff dorm was uncharacteristically quiet as Sheriff Coyle looked around at the four gathered employees. The only sound was the soft dinging of incoming texts to Garrett's phone. Felice flashed him a death stare and he reached into his pocket and silenced it.

Coyle stood in front of the flat-screen television, expressionless.

"I know y'all have heard the unfortunate news about your friend Parrish. And I'm sorry for your loss, but we need to get to the bottom of what happened last night, especially since her body was found at the location of that afterparty everyone here attended."

"Except me," Felice said loudly. "I wasn't there. I came back here right after the Beach Bash was over."

"Understood," the sheriff said. "But you were at the Beach Bash, correct?"

"I was working, yeah."

"When was the last time you saw Parrish?"

"I guess it was maybe a little before ten, the last time I saw her. She was helping a mom who had two crying kids on her hands."

"All right. Noted," Coyle said. "I'm gonna want to talk to all of y'all individually, but first things first. I couldn't help but notice how tidy that crime scene was today. I mean, you'd never know a party, with what, maybe forty, fifty people went on in those woods last night."

Garrett and KJ averted their eyes, staring intently at the floor, apparently fascinated by their own choices in footwear.

"Obviously, somebody went out there at some point today and cleaned up. And in the process, they managed to ruin and contaminate a crime scene. Anybody here got any information on how that happened?"

KJ spoke up first. "Okay, so we did pick up all the beer bottles and cans and trash. Not because we were trying to hide anything. We just didn't want to get in trouble, because, you know, of the mess from the party."

"We really did look all over out there for Parrish," Garrett added. "Like, all around the Shack. But we didn't see any sign of her."

Coyle pinched the bridge of his nose and tried not to show his mounting frustration.

"Y'all couldn't have looked too hard, or you would have seen that shoe that the hotel's security chief found, less than a hundred yards from the back of that shed building."

"There was a rat!" KJ protested. "A huge rat. No way I was going digging around in the weeds after we saw that thing."

"Okay," Coyle said wearily. "What did you do with all the evidence you two geniuses picked up?"

"We didn't find anything that was, like . . . suspicious. It was just a lot of beer bottles and paper plates and leftover food from the Beach Bash. We loaded it all into garbage bags, then we tossed the bags in the dumpster behind the restaurant," Garrett said.

Coyle swore softly to himself as he pulled out his phone and walked out of the dorm.

Five minutes later, the sheriff was back. "I had one of my deputies check that dumpster. Apparently, the trash was picked up about an hour ago. On a Sunday, no less."

"We have a contract with a private sanitation company. Because of the smell from all the seafood and stuff in hot weather, the trash gets picked up every couple days," Felice volunteered.

"Great," Coyle said, slapping the palm of his hand on his leg. "That's just great. Any evidence we might have collected at the scene is now headed for a landfill."

"Sorry," KJ said, looking sheepish. "We were just trying to stay out of trouble, you know?"

"Never mind that," the sheriff said. He pointed to KJ. "You. I want to talk to you in private. Everyone else can scatter to your rooms, until I call for you."

An hour later, Coyle left the dorm and the members of the group drifted back into the lounge area.

Olivia went to the fridge and came back with a bottle of flavored seltzer. She popped the top and sipped while the others flopped down onto the sofas. Her eyes were noticeably red from crying.

"What did the sheriff ask you?" she said, pointing at KJ.

"He had some crazy idea that just because my old man is friends with Parrish's dad, and because he kinda got me this job, that maybe Parrish and me were like, a thing. I told him, 'Dude, the first time I met that chick was when I walked into this dorm three weeks ago.' Why would I want to hurt her?"

"Parrish's dad got you your job?" Garrett asked. "Figures."

KJ shot him a look. "Who cares? I work hard, and up until now, I've managed to stay out of trouble. Jesus. I wonder if we'll all get fired when Parrish's dad hears what we did."

"Me and Olivia had nothin' to do with that stupid stunt you two pulled today," Felice said. "Anyway, Ric Eddings didn't hire me. Mrs. E hired me, and as far as I'm concerned, she's the only one who can fire me."

"Me too," Garrett said.

"And me," Olivia agreed.

"So, Liv, what did the sheriff ask you?" Garrett asked.

She sniffled a little. "He asked if Parrish and I talked about guy stuff. Like, who we were dating and whatever. But we didn't. She was kinda private about that stuff, and since I haven't dated anyone lately, I didn't have anything to discuss. And then he asked if you guys were into Parrish, and I told him not that I know. I mean, we were all just friends, right? Like the TV show, but without the great apartment in New York or a cool coffee shop."

Olivia considered Garrett for a minute. "Wait. The two of you didn't hook up, right?"

"Hell, no," Garrett said.

"But not because you didn't try," Felice interjected.

"Yeah, I made a play. But she wasn't into me, so I dropped it. Plenty of pretty ladies around who would be interested, so that wasn't a problem."

"Gag me," Olivia said, rolling her eyes.

"So into yourself," Felice agreed.

"Hey," Garrett said, his tone sharpening as he pointed at Felice. "You keep saying you weren't at the afterparty, and that you were here. But how do we know that's true? For all we know, you could have been creeping around out in those woods, while the three of us were back here, sleeping it off."

"Come on, Garrett," Livvy said.

"Actually, someone did see me here last night. The DoorDash driver who delivered my order of potstickers and pad Thai at about ten thirty." Felice held up her phone to show the open DoorDash app.

"But you could have gone out after," Garrett insisted.

Olivia punched his shoulder. "What is *wrong* with you? Felice didn't kill Parrish. None of us did."

"Then who did? And why?" KJ asked.

"Obviously, it had to be someone who was at the party last night. I saw her talking to that guy with the crazy dreads from the steel drum band, and she took a hit off his joint, but then later, I saw him leaving with some girl I didn't recognize," Olivia said.

Felice bristled. "Oh. Now you gonna say the Black dude must've been the one who murdered Parrish? You know, because he's Black and probably a stone-cold killer?"

"No! I'm not saying that at all. I just said I saw them together. That's all," Livvy protested. "I swear, I'm not a racist."

"Okay, calm down, Felice," KJ said. "I saw Parrish with that dude too. Doesn't make us racists. They didn't really talk that long, but then it looked like she got mad at something, and she went stomping away."

"Okay," Felice grumbled. "Maybe I was jumping to conclusions."

"Maybe?" Garrett rolled his eyes. "Look. Maybe it wasn't anybody who was at the afterparty who did it. Last night, this place was crawling with people."

"We had reservations for four hundred and fifty people," Felice said.

"And the hotel was packed to the gills with overnight folks. Parrish told me we were sold out weeks ago and a lot of members were bitching that they couldn't get a room because of all the 'tourists,'" Livvy added.

"Maybe one of those pissed-off guests took out their frustrations on her," Garrett said.

"More likely, it would have been Parrish taking out one of them," Felice said. "Like that old cracker McBee."

Livvy shook her head vigorously. "You're thinking about this all wrong."

"And you know a lot about investigating murder?" Garrett asked.

"I kinda do. I've probably listened to more true-crime podcasts and read more true-crime books than anyone else in this whole state."

"So that makes you a detective?" he asked.

Livvy started to say something, but Garrett cut her off. "Stay out of it," he advised. "Keep your head down, do your job, and let the cops do theirs."

CHAPTER 32

* * *

Traci sat alone at her desk. Her office door was closed, but she could hear guests talking outside in the lobby, discussing the day's shocking events in hushed tones.

Mostly the noise was a gray buzz as she scrolled through the pictures of her niece on her phone's camera roll.

The most recent photo had been taken just the day before—Traci and Parrish posing, dressed in their matching floral Hawaiian sarongs. Parrish looked so fresh-faced, happy, even glamorous, with a hibiscus tucked behind one ear as she laughingly vogued for one of the reception desk clerks who obligingly snapped photos for them. There were other photos too, of the Saint staffers, standing in the lobby, all dressed in their Beach Bash outfits. Parrish and Livvy and Felice, Garrett and KJ stood arm in arm, smiling widely.

These photos, Traci realized with a jolt, were the last she would have of her niece.

Before that, there was a picture of Parrish on her first day of work, standing behind the guest relations desk dressed in her pink Saint polo shirt, with her name badge pinned on her chest. She looked so grown-up and efficient, with her hair pulled back in a severe bun.

Farther back than that on Traci's phone, there were photos of Parrish at birthday parties, Christmases, on the beach, at the pool, gathered arm in arm with her college friends. The photo that took Traci's breath away was the one taken during Parrish's senior year of high school. That year, she and Hoke had treated their niece to a last-minute ski trip to Aspen.

A lifelong Southerner, Parrish adored the novelty of all the snow and was, like Hoke, a natural athlete who took easily to ski-ing, spending long days racing her uncle down the slopes. In the evenings, they'd hit the hot tub on the deck of their chalet, enjoy-ing hot cocoa, and treat themselves to lavish dinners at the resort's lodge.

"Best vacay evah!" Traci could still hear Parrish's raucous laugh-ter as she and Hoke set off on another trip up the ski lift.

"Hey, maybe you could help me get a job here next winter," Par-rish had suggested at dinner their last night at the resort, after the general manager, an old friend of Hoke's, stopped by their table to say hello.

"What?" Hoke had raised an eyebrow. "Skip college?"

"Not skip. Maybe work here for a semester. Think what great experience it would give me when I come back to work for you guys at the Saint."

"I'm thinking about the grief your old man would give me if I sanctioned something like that. He's already pissed that you came on this trip with Traci and me," Hoke said.

"Instead of going to Palm Beach with him and Madelyn? Gross. I would rather have stayed home with Grandpa than go anywhere with those two," Parrish had said. "Please, Uncle Hoke? Pleeeaassse? Just talk to him about it. Please?"

Ric had, unsurprisingly, vetoed the idea of Parrish postponing college for even a semester, and it had only caused yet another crack in Hoke's already eroding relationship with his younger brother.

With her fingertips, Traci enlarged the photo of the three of them with the snowy Aspen mountains in the background. And she realized, with another fresh wave of grief, that it was the last photo that she had of the three of them together. Six months later, Hoke's plane had gone down.

She put her head down on the desktop. Unable to maintain her composure, she began to sob, her tears wetting the papers on her desk.

All day, she'd been unable to stop thinking about what Parrish's last moments must have been like. The cops hadn't said what killed Parrish, but Traci was sure this was not a death from natural causes. Was Parrish terrified? Had the killer watched and stalked her? Had he stood by in the dark while she drew her last breath? She rubbed her waterlogged eyes, wishing she could scrub away the tortuous thoughts that had haunted her all day.

And then she cried some more. She cried for Parrish, for the bright promise of her future, for her open and loving heart, for her love of Taylor Swift and cute, wildly inappropriate shoes, and iced coffee, and scary slasher movies.

Selfishly, she cried for herself, for the overwhelming sense of loss. First Hoke and now Parrish. For the past four years she'd felt as though she were walking through life dutifully, but in an emotional fog, which had only in the past few months started to lift. Now she felt achingly alone and empty. Again.

Traci tensed when someone knocked at her closed door. She fumbled in her desk drawer, found a tissue, and blew her nose.

Oh God. She was a blubbering mess. She should have gone home to have her breakdown in private.

"Mrs. Eddings?" A man's voice.

"Just a minute." Traci blew her nose again, dabbed the tears from her cheeks.

"Come in."

It was Sheriff Coyle. "Just wanted to let you know we've done a pretty thorough search of that dorm, including your niece's room."

Her eyes widened. "Did you find anything?"

"Nothing that gives us any clue about what happened to your niece," he said. "I've spoken with her dormmates, and I'd say they were as helpful as they could be, under the circumstances."

"That's good to hear. I'm sure they're all upset about what happened."

"Your general manager gave us the guest list from your event last night." He held up a stapled-together sheaf of printer paper.

"I'd like you to take a look at this and see if any names stand out. Maybe someone who had a beef with your niece?"

"Now?"

"The sooner the better. Understand, we don't want to be in your hair any longer than is necessary, but we do have a death investigation to conduct."

She took the list and gazed down at it, but none of the names caught her eye. "Nobody on this list would have a reason to hurt Parrish. Sheriff, should I be concerned? For our guests' safety, or for my staff?"

His expression remained neutral. "At this point, we still don't know what killed your niece."

"When will we know what happened? I mean, to Parrish. It's so painful, not knowing."

That muscle in his jaw twitched again. "Your brother-in-law has political pull in this county. I've already gotten a call from the county commission chair, wanting to know when we'll have this investigation wrapped up. From what I understand, phone calls were made and favors were called in. The medical examiner is scheduled to do the autopsy first thing in the morning."

"Ray Bierbower, our head of security, told me there was no sign of violence that he could see," she said.

"No *visible* signs," he corrected. "Look, I can't talk to you about an ongoing investigation."

"But I'm family," she protested.

"Speak to Ric Eddings," the sheriff said. "I'm going out to the dining room now, to talk to some of your staff. Is there a room where I can talk to people, in private?"

"The Azalea conference room, closest to the restaurant, is available," Traci said, picking up her phone. "I'll have it unlocked for you."

"What the fuck do you want?" Ric Eddings stood in the half-open doorway of his home, glaring at her. His usually precision-styled hair was matted to his head; his eyes were bloodshot. He was dressed in baggy gym shorts and a faded white undershirt and he held a half-empty tumbler of what she assumed was scotch in his right hand. From the smell of him, it wasn't his first drink of the day. Not even close.

Traci had prepared herself for this kind of greeting.

"Ric, I know you and I have been at cross-purposes lately, but I was hoping we could forget our differences, considering what's happened. Parrish wouldn't have wanted—"

"You don't know shit about what Parrish wanted," Ric said, his voice hoarse. "How dare you show up at my home like this?" He pointed a trembling finger at her and his speech was slurred. "My daughter is dead because of you. If you hadn't guilt-tripped her into working for you this summer, hadn't bribed her to move into that goddamn dorm with those low-lifes and pervs . . ."

"Hey!" she interrupted. "You want to know why your daughter was so eager to move out? I'll tell you what she told me. She was tired of your lying and cheating and fighting with your wife and running around on her. I didn't have to bribe her."

Ric swayed a little, sloshing the scotch over the side of the tumbler he was clutching.

"I'm sorry," Traci said, contrite. "I really don't want to bicker with you. I'm sorry I talked Parrish into working for me this summer. Maybe if I hadn't . . . And I know you're in pain, but you have to know what Parrish meant to me, and to your brother. We loved her too, you know." She tried to blink away a fresh wave of tears.

"Just one more thing. If you and Madelyn need help, you know, making funeral arrangements . . ."

Ric downed the rest of the scotch in a single gulp.

"I think I've had about enough of your help to last me a lifetime, Traci. Now get the hell off my porch. And don't come back."

He slammed the door in her face.

CHAPTER 33

* * *

Whelan was only partly surprised to learn that there were seventeen Michael Sullivans living in his targeted geographical area, which consisted of Georgia, Florida, and South Carolina. Of those seventeen, just six had been born between the years of 1991 and 1993, the years bracketing Hudson's birth.

One of the Mikes (that's how he thought of them: Mikes) was deceased, killed, as Whelan had read in the online obituary, by a rare childhood blood cancer. The other five Mikes didn't fit the profile for the Mike he was seeking—a kid whose parents had been Saints; that is, a family wealthy enough to be a member-guest at the Saint back in July of 2002.

These Sullivans all seemed to be working-class families—or in the case of one, the product of an unmarried mother who'd gotten pregnant at the age of sixteen.

Which left him with just one Mike: Michael Thomas Sullivan, age thirty-two, who was, as luck would have it, living in a suburb of Jacksonville, Florida, which was less than a two-hour drive away from Bonaventure, Georgia.

Whelan was skittish when it came to social media. He'd occasionally check in with the guys who'd been in his unit in Afghanistan. They had a Facebook group where they'd post updates on their families, jobs, and social life, something Whelan rarely did.

But he'd learned early that social media was an invaluable research tool. To that end, he'd been cyber-stalking Michael T. Sullivan of Avondale Park for the past week. He'd learned Michael loved paddle-boarding with his golden retriever Gladys, grilling out, and posing for selfies with a group of handsome, tanned men who always seemed to gather in a bar or at a beach. Michael's BFF or "work wife" was a young brunette named Jill who worked at the same bank in down-town Jacksonville. He knew Michael lived in a fixer-upper ranch, and that he'd been slowly doing a DIY renovation of his kitchen.

On Sunday afternoon, Whelan hit the road around four, reason-ing that if Michael had been out paddleboarding or beaching it with his friends, he'd probably be back home by six that evening, getting ready for a Monday workday.

The day was scorching hot, ninety-eight according to the readout on the dash of his Tahoe. But he was listening to '80s rock on his radio and the trip was so uneventful, the traffic on I-95 so light, he managed to pull up to the curb in Avondale Park shortly before six.

Sullivan's house was clearly the nicest on his block, with extrava-gant beds of pink, blue, and white New Guinea impatiens nestled in swaths of bright green asparagus fern. A porch had obviously been added on to the front of the house, supported by modernist-looking columns.

Whelan rang the doorbell and heard a deep-throated series of barks. A voice emerged from the Ring doorbell.

"Yes?"

The barks continued. "Hush, Gladys," the voice said. "How can I help you?"

Whelan flashed what he hoped was a warm, sincere smile. Sometimes, warmth was a stretch for him. "I'm looking for Michael Thomas Sullivan?"

"That's me," the disembodied voice said. "Who are you?"

"Hi. Sorry to bother you. My name is Whelan, and I'm looking for the Michael Sullivan who spent time at the Saint resort in the summer of 2002."

The door opened and a man peered out at him. He was very tanned, and bare-chested, with a mane of swept-back dark brown hair, wearing loose-fitting white linen pants. A fine gold chain hung around his neck.

"I was there that summer, but I was, like, nine. What's this about?"

"It's kind of a long story, and it's hot as shit out here," Whelan said, feeling the perspiration dripping down his back. "Would it be possible for me to come inside and talk?"

"Are you some kind of cop or something?"

"Not anymore. I can assure you, I'm legit."

Sullivan held out his hand. "Okay. Give me your driver's license."

Whelan handed it over. Sullivan closed the door. A moment later, he opened the door again, snapped a photo of the visitor with his phone, and then handed Whelan's license back. Again he closed the front door. A minute passed. Whelan heard a door opening on the side of the house. He watched while Michael Sullivan sprinted, barefoot, across his sculpted green lawn, paused in back of Whelan's Tahoe, and snapped a photo of his license tag.

A moment later, Sullivan opened the door again. "Okay, cool. Come on in."

"Smart," Whelan commented, as he returned the license to his billfold. "Good for you, being so security conscious when a stranger shows up at your door."

The interior of Michael Sullivan's house seemed to consist of one large, airy room. The ceilings were vaulted, the back of the house consisted of a series of French doors, and everywhere there was a living jungle of vivid green plants. "Nice house, by the way."

"You can sit there," Sullivan said, pointing toward a low-slung kidney-shaped loveseat. "When you've been on as many gruesome Grindr dates as I have, you start to be careful. I mean, you could, theoretically, still kill me and eat my kidneys with some fava beans and a nice chianti, but if you do, my best friend Jill has those photos of your driver's license and your car tag, so at least there's that."

The dog sat on the terrazzo floor directly in front of Whelan, who wondered if he'd encountered the only mean golden retriever in existence.

Sullivan sat down on a sofa that matched the loveseat, and tucked his legs beneath himself. He was wearing a shirt now. The dog jumped up beside him and put her head in his lap. "So. Spill the beans. Why do you want to know about my traumatic summer at the Saint, way back then?"

"What was traumatic about it?"

Sullivan waggled a finger at him. "Nuh-uh. I asked first."

"Fair enough. That summer, my half brother and my mom and her husband rented a cottage at the Saint. And . . . that was the last summer of his life. I want to know why."

"Oh. My. God!" Sullivan clutched his chest with both hands. "Are you telling me your brother was Hudson? Oh my God!"

"Half brother," Whelan said.

"But you're so much older. I mean, you're, what? In your fifties?"

"Almost. My mother had me in her mid-twenties. Her first marriage."

"You don't look anything like Hudson. He was blond and spindly and you're not that."

"I'm told I look like my father's side of the family."

"Mmm-hmm." Michael stared intently at his visitor. "So. Your mom. Wasn't her name Kasey? And, Lord, what was Hudson's dad's name? Even at nine, I knew he was a real tight-ass."

"Brad. His name was Brad Moorehead."

Sullivan snapped his fingers. "Right. I remember now."

"What else do you remember about that time? Especially the week Hudson drowned."

The younger man squeezed his eyes shut as he tried to summon the past. "Well . . . I hate to speak ill of the dead, but Hudson was such an annoying little shit." He opened his eyes and gave Whelan a rueful shrug. "Sorry, but that's the truth. There were only a few kids around our age that summer, so we basically hung out together because there wasn't anyone else."

"No kids whose names you remember?" Whelan asked.

Sullivan's face stretched into a wide grin. "Ah. Yes. There was this group of fabulous older girls—and by older, I mean they were maybe fifteen or sixteen. And when Hudson wasn't around, these girls would let me sit with them at the pool. I was like their mascot. They let me pretend I was one of the cool kids instead of the pathetic little sissy boy I was in real life."

"But you and Hudson were buddies, right?"

"Some of the time."

"Tell me about that day. All of it, please," Whelan said.

"Let me think," Sullivan said. "Do you want something cold to drink?"

"No thanks. I'm good."

"Just as well. I promised myself I was going on the wagon today. Okay . . . I think I met up with Hudson that morning at the game room. They had a jukebox in there, and a Pac-Man and a Ping-Pong table. We played Ping-Pong, but Hudson got pissed when I beat him. I remember, after I won, Hudson deliberately stomped on the Ping-Pong ball, and the game room attendant kicked us out."

"What happened then?"

"I guess we left?" Sullivan absent-mindedly stroked the dog's ears. "No. Wait. We were both on our bikes. We spent that whole week on our bikes, and I thought I was hot shit, because I could pop a wheelie on mine. We got on our bikes, and I think Hudson called me something, maybe a shithead? I popped a wheelie, and started to ride away."

"What did Hudson do then?"

"You know? I was gonna say he rode away too, but now that I think about it, I remember I circled back, because I'd thought of some other incredibly rude name to call him. But just then, this flashy red car pulled up alongside Hudson's bike, and the window came down and the driver was talking to him."

"What kind of car?"

"I was nine. I didn't know a Ford from a French fry. I remember I thought it was a cool car. And I was kinda jealous, because your brother knew someone with a cool car. Then, the driver handed Hudson a paper bag and he drove off, and I pedaled away too, to go to the pool because I was all hot and sweaty."

Whelan leaned forward, his elbows planted on his knees. "You said the driver was a guy?"

"Did I? Hmm. I guess, now that you mention it, we saw that car around the Saint a lot that week."

Sullivan snapped his fingers again. "Yeah. In fact, those cool girls I told you about? Lisa and Jessie, and oh, what was the name of the redhead with the big boobs? I don't know. But they were always watching for that red car."

"Whose car was it?"

Michael wrinkled his nose. "Maybe, like, a lifeguard? But maybe not. Maybe it was just one of those rich guys who were always around at the Saint."

Whelan tried to hide his frustration. "Okay. Maybe that's not important. Let's talk about what happened later, at the pool."

"Ugh. Let's not," Michael said promptly. "You asked me what was so traumatic about that summer? That. What happened at the pool. I still have nightmares about it."

"I'm sorry to bring it up, but this is really important to me," Whelan said.

Sullivan looked at him with something like pity. "Why? Why is it so important, all these years later? It's been, like, twenty years. Why go dredging up all that mess?"

"The day Hudson died, that's the day my mom's life started to unravel. She blamed herself, because she told her son to get out of her hair and go play. And her asshole husband, who, by the way, was on a golf course at the time, blamed her too. They split up a few months later, and even though Brad had tons of family money, he made sure Kasey got almost none of it. I'll spare you the details, but she was never the same after that."

"Is she still . . . with us?"

"No. She died last year. We hadn't really been very close in a long time, but after her death, I went to Spartanburg, that's where she'd been living, to sell her condo. While I was cleaning it out, I found some papers, in a box in her dresser, that made me think there was more to Hudson's death than any of us knew about. I decided I owed it to Kasey to find out the truth."

"Okay, I get it. So, that day, a new kid showed up at the pool. And don't ask me his name because I have no idea. We were jumping off the diving board. Having a cannonball contest. We'd been there around half an hour, and then Hudson shows up."

"He didn't go off the board with y'all?"

"No. He sat on the side of the pool at the deep end, yelling stuff, splashing water at us. Heckling us, I guess you'd say. We just ignored him. Which I think pissed him off even more. At some point, Hudson stood up and he started yelling and waving his arms and screaming that we'd pooped in the pool."

"Right," Whelan said. "And the lifeguards. Do you remember what they did then?"

"Shannon and Traci," Michael said promptly. "Such cute girls. Traci was on the lifeguard stand at the deep end where we were, and Shannon was down at the shallow end. Traci yelled something like, 'Code brown, everyone out of the pool,' and then she and Shannon were blowing their whistles to make everyone get out of the pool."

"And did you and the other kid get out?"

"Shit, yeah. They were the law. Plus, poop in the pool? Gross!"

"What did you do after you got out?"

"I don't know. I guess we were standing there, trying to explain that we *didn't* drop a deuce in the pool. I mean, it was bedlam."

"And where was Hudson? At what point did he get in the pool?"

Michael ran his hands through his hair. "Honest to God, I never did know. The cops kept asking me, but I never saw him get in the water. I think Traci, or maybe it was Shannon, saw him there, and screamed at him to get out of the water. He was, like, flailing his arms and he kept going underwater—you know, like he was pretending to drown."

The younger man shook his head. "I just thought it was typical Hudson, trying to prank everyone. I mean, it turns out he'd deliberately put that Tootsie Roll in the water to get us in trouble. And I know those two lifeguards thought the same thing, that he was faking it, because they were yelling at him to cut it out."

Michael stood abruptly. "Fuck it. I really, really need a drink now. You?"

"Just water," Whelan said.

Gladys the golden followed her master toward what Whelan assumed was the kitchen. A moment later, Sullivan returned, with a highball glass filled with what Whelan assumed was gin or vodka, with a twist of lime, and a can of carbonated water for Whelan.

He sat back down and sipped his drink, and Gladys joined him on the sofa.

Sullivan placed his hand over his heart. "I swear to God. Nobody else was in that pool when Hudson drowned. For a long time, people thought I shoved him in, or pushed him under or something. Hell, I think my own mother thought that, may she rest in eternal torment, the bitch. But I swear, on Bette Midler's life, I never touched your brother. I don't know how or why he drowned. I just know it wasn't anything I did."

"Okay," Whelan said. He popped the top of the can and took a long drink of the cold, bubbly water. "Okay. I believe you. And if it's any comfort, that's the same thing Shannon told me, earlier this week."

"Shannon? The lifeguard? You talked to her? You mean she's still around?"

"She is. In fact, she's a nurse. She still lives in Bonaventure."

"Wow. Just . . . wow. I can't believe you managed to track her down after all these years. Come to think of it, how did you track me down? How did you even know about me?"

"I'm pretty good at what I do," Whelan said. "I found a sympathy card from you in my mom's things. More importantly, I had to threaten to sue the Bonaventure sheriff's office, but they finally gave me access to the old incident reports from that day. And you were listed as a witness. Michael Sullivan, age ten."

Sullivan gulped down more of his drink, then jiggled the ice cubes at the bottom of the highball glass. "Sometimes, I wonder what my life would have been like, if I hadn't been there that day. If I'd let Hudson win at Ping-Pong, or if I'd told him, sure, come on, you can be in the cannonball contest. Maybe he wouldn't have pulled that stunt. And maybe . . ." His voice trailed off, and he finished off the last of his drink. "Maybe I wouldn't have spent thousands of dollars in therapy. Maybe I would have come out sooner . . ."

"And maybe, things would have been the same," Whelan said. "I think something else happened that day. Something that could explain why Hudson died. What you just told me? About that red car? And the guy that handed him a bag? This is the first time I've heard anything like this. Did the cops ask you the same questions I just did?"

"No. They just asked about what happened in the pool. That's all."

"Figures." Whelan stood up slowly. His knees, he'd begun to notice, had started to get creaky. He set the drink can down on the table.

"Better shove off," he said. "And I guess you better let your friend Jill know the stranger didn't kill you, or cannibalize you."

Sullivan stood too. "Yeah. Guess I will. Hey, since you know where to find me, can you let me know? If you find out what happened to Hudson? I'd really appreciate it."

"Sure thing," Whelan said.

CHAPTER 34

* * *

Olivia was running late for work on Monday, so when she stepped outside the dorm and spotted the golf cart, which KJ or Garrett had used over the weekend, with the keys still in it, she hopped on.

On a normal day it was only a ten-minute walk to the Verandah, but it was already hot and sticky, with temps in the high eighties. So she turned the key in the ignition and took off, fretting about being late for her lunch shift.

Her cell phone was in the cup holder, and when it rang, with the distinctive ringtone she'd assigned to her mother, her heart sank.

"Mom, before you start . . ."

"Jesus, Mary, and Fred," Shannon cried. "Why didn't you tell me Parrish Eddings was murdered? Why did I have to hear about it on the news this morning instead of from you? Killed right there at the Saint! What did I tell you, Livvy? Didn't I tell you those people were evil and that place is cursed?"

"Mom! Stop!" Livvy begged.

"No. You stop. I want you out of that damned place. Right now, and I don't care how much they're paying you, it's not worth it."

"Please, calm down."

"I can't. I can't calm down knowing my only child is in danger there."

"I am not in danger," Livvy insisted. "If you'd just listen, for once. The police are all over the place. Like, everywhere. And Parrish wasn't killed at the dorm. They found her behind the Shack, a place way off in the woods . . ."

"I know all about the Shack. It's where we all went to party, back in the day. But what was she doing clear out there? The news didn't give any details. Just that she was dead, under suspicious circumstances. Wait. If Parrish was at a party, were you there too?"

"Yeah. But it was no big deal. Just a bunch of us getting together after the Beach Bash."

"Who do you think you're talking to, Olivia? You forget I lived that life. I was right there when I was your age. I know y'all were drinking, probably smoking dope too, right?"

Livvy said nothing.

"That's what I thought. Don't even bother to deny it. I swear to God in heaven, Livvy, if you don't quit that job right today and come home, I'll—"

"You'll what? Take away my car, like you did in high school? Mom, we've been over this. I'm legally an adult. You're totally overreacting. We still don't know what happened to Parrish. It could have been anything. I'm safe. Nobody is coming after me. There are two big strong guys living in the dorm, and I'm pretty sure Garrett has a gun. We lock the doors every night. Besides, nobody gets onto the property past the security guards at the gate."

"Somebody *did* get past those guards, though. And they killed that poor girl. I'm never gonna sleep again until you return to your senses and come home."

Livvy was approaching the turn-off for the service entrance to the restaurant. "I *am* home, Mom. I'm sorry you're so worried, but I am not going to let you guilt me into quitting my job. Look, I'm already late for work, so I gotta go now."

She disconnected and dropped the phone back in the cup holder.

Garrett met her at the back door to the kitchen. "Hey. I just tried to call you."

"Sorry. I was on the phone with my mom, who is wigging out because she's convinced there's a maniacal killer on the loose over here." Livvy laughed nervously.

"I was calling to tell you that Mrs. E wants to see you in her office."

"Me? Am I in trouble?"

"Don't think so. She came into the restaurant a few minutes ago to get a salad and asked me to tell you she'd like to see you."

"Olivia, hi," Traci Eddings said, pushing away what looked like an untouched plate of salad and covering it with a linen napkin. "Thanks for coming in so quickly."

The boss did not look like herself today, Livvy thought. Her hair was lank, there were huge dark circles under her eyes, and her face was unnaturally pale. She wore no makeup, not even lipstick, and the dress she was wearing, although obviously expensive, looked rumpled, as though she'd picked it up off the floor.

"Sit down, please," she told Olivia.

"Did any of you get any sleep last night? I understand the police searched the dorm? I hope it wasn't too upsetting for you all."

"I don't think anyone got a lot of sleep," Livvy admitted. "We're all so sad about Parrish, and it seems so surreal. We didn't mind about the search. We want the cops to figure out what happened to Parrish."

"So do I," Traci said. "I want you to know, I've asked Ray Bierbower to have extra security details patrol regularly past the staff dorm. At least until we catch this person."

"Oh good. That'll make my mom feel a little better," Livvy blurted without thinking.

"Shannon," Traci said. "Lord. She's even more upset with you now, right?"

"Yeah. I told her she's overreacting, but I guess you know how she gets."

Traci sighed. "Your mom wasn't always like that, Olivia. She used to be so much fun. She was wild and always up for anything."

"And then along came me," Olivia said. "And she turned into my grandma."

"Don't be too hard on her," Traci said. "Being a single mom, raising a daughter alone can't be easy, but from what I know about you, she did a superlative job. That's not what I called you in to talk about, though."

She bit her lower lip. "I've got to have someone working the guest relations desk. As you might imagine, our guests are rattled. They're nervous, and having a police presence here, asking questions, has them worried and on edge. And as soon as the news broke about Parrish, we started getting cancellations."

"Oh man. That's awful," Livvy said. "Like you don't have enough on your plate."

"Honestly, if I could, I'd close the Saint, today. Losing Parrish is like losing a part of myself. Again."

Livvy felt herself tearing up, seeing the pain in her boss's eyes.

"But I can't afford to close down the Saint. We have bookings and commitments, a wedding coming up next weekend . . . and then there's our staff. We're the biggest employer in this county. My staff is like family to me, and I believe they need us, as much as we need them."

Traci looked over at the framed wedding photograph on her desk. "Besides. This place is my husband's legacy. It's all I have left of him, so I guess I'm just gonna suck it up and keep going. Because I don't have any other choice."

"Good for you, Mrs. E," Livvy said. "How can I help?"

"You can take over for Parrish on the guest relations desk," Traci said. "I've already talked to the dining room manager, and Garrett. He's called in someone who can take over your shifts for now. That is, if you agree."

"But . . . I've never done that kind of work before," Livvy said. "Are you sure there isn't someone more qualified?"

"Positive," Traci said firmly. "You're the right girl for the job. You're hardworking and loyal and you're a fast learner. So, will you do it?"

"Yes, ma'am," Livvy said. "When do I start?"

"Now's as good a time as any," Traci said, rising from her desk. "I'll train you myself."

CHAPTER 35

* * *

By the end of the day, Livvy felt she'd had a crash course in customer care from a woman who had refined it to an art form.

Even as heartbroken and grief-stricken as Traci Eddings was, she somehow managed to present a sunny and serene face to the hotel's guests.

"Oh hell," Traci whispered, when she spied Colonel McBee tap-tapping his way across the lobby in their direction. "That's Colonel McBee. He was the biggest pain in Parrish's butt."

"I know him," Livvy said. "He was unanimously voted most likely to send back his meal. Every. Single. Day."

"Right," Traci said, pasting on a smile. "Here's what you do. Smile and be accommodating, but if he demands to have his room moved, yet again, politely explain that it's impossible."

The Colonel stopped in his tracks when he saw not one, but two new faces standing behind the guest relations desk.

"Good afternoon, Colonel," Livvy chirped.

The old man frowned. "What are you doing here? Why aren't you in the dining room? And where's the other girl?"

Livvy and Traci exchanged a look. Livvy cleared her throat, but it was Traci who spoke first.

"I'm afraid my niece Parrish met with a tragic accident over the weekend, Colonel, which is why you might notice a police presence on our property. But I want to assure you and Mrs. McBee that you're perfectly safe."

McBee's mustache twitched. "Accident? What kind of accident?"

"I'm not at liberty to say," Traci said. "Olivia here will be happy to help you with whatever you need."

"But she's just a waitress," he griped. "What does she know about taking care of my wife and me?"

"What exactly can I help you with?" Livvy asked, taking a cue from Traci.

"The mattress in our room. It's terrible. The other girl promised to see about replacing it, but nothing has been done, and my poor wife's sciatica has her in excruciating pain."

"Mattress?" Livvy gave her boss a sidelong glance.

"Yes. *Mattress.* Are you deaf?" he shouted, pounding his cane on the floor. "The other girl wrote it down in her book. She wrote everything down in her book. Just check it and you'll see."

"I don't know anything about a book," Traci said. She glanced down at the shelves below the desktop and saw brochures for local attractions, a stack of coupons for area restaurants, even bound menus for the resort's own restaurants, but nothing resembling a book.

"It was blue. Find the book and you'll see every single thing she was supposed to take care of. Like the mattress, which I want replaced immediately."

"I know we bought all new mattresses within the last six months," Traci said. "Maybe, somehow, the one in your room didn't get replaced. I'll look into it myself. You'll hear something from Livvy by the end of the day, I promise. Now, is there anything else?"

There was, of course, much, much more. Livvy found a pad of paper and a pen and dutifully wrote it all down: room too cold—she promised to send someone from engineering to check the thermostat. Not enough towels—she would have housekeeping send up additional towels. Not enough envelopes and stationery. Livvy wondered just how many of the hotel's guests actually wrote letters on stationery these days, but she promised to send up more.

"One more thing," the Colonel said. "The most important thing, actually."

Great, Livvy thought. *Finally, we get to the bee in Colonel McBee's bonnet.*

"It's these damn kids. They're everywhere. Causing a fuss in the dining room, tracking in sand from the beach. Just this morning, when I was trying to swim my laps in the pool, one of these little urchins actually jumped on top of me! Where are the rules? Why are these little menaces allowed to roam the property at will?"

"What time was this, Colonel?" Traci asked.

"Approximately eleven hundred hours."

"Oh dear. That's the problem. You see, we have dedicated lap lane swimming every day from seven to ten A.M. After that, the pool is open to everyone, including families with children," Traci explained.

"That's ridiculous. Mrs. McBee and I have been coming here for decades and I never heard of such a rule." He pointed a gnarled finger directly at Traci. "This place has gone all to hell. Nothing has been the same since Hoke Eddings died."

Livvy gasped. She watched as the smile faded from her employer's face as she absorbed the blow of the old man's spiteful remark.

"Colonel?" Traci's tone was even but her expression was steely. "You should know that my staff and I strive every day to meet my late husband's exacting standards for the Saint. But if you're truly unhappy with your accommodations, you're welcome to check out early. We will refund you the cost for the remainder of your stay."

"What? Leave early? Not at all. Mrs. McBee and I always stay 'til mid-June. I have no intention of changing our plans this year."

"As you wish," Traci said. "Livvy here will do her best to address the issues you've raised. But I must insist, sir, that you treat her—and all my staff—with the same courtesy and respect which you expect to be shown by them."

He raised one bristling white eyebrow, started to say something, then changed his mind. "Respect," he huffed, and turned and walked away.

———

"Hateful old dinosaur," Traci muttered, watching his departure. "I'd almost pay him to leave now, but that could set a dangerous precedent."

She turned to Livvy. "Did you ever see Parrish with a notebook like the one he described?"

"Come to think of it, I did. It was like one of those old school composition books we used to have in high school. Parrish called it the 'bitch book.' I'll look around and see if I can find it. But maybe the police won't want us going through her stuff in her room, or at the dorm?"

"I'll ask the sheriff if it's okay for us to go into Parrish's room now," Traci said. "And I'll also ask if they found the notebook. I'd be interested to see what's in it."

"Colonel McBee's gripes probably take a whole chapter," Livvy quipped.

She opened the lid of the laptop computer on the desktop and began clicking through the tabs. "Okay. Here's the McBees' room number. I'll put in a work order, like you showed me, for engineering and housekeeping. What should I do about the mattress?"

"Check in our warehouse and see if we actually have any new ones in our inventory, and if we do, ask engineering to deliver it. They'll need to remove the old one, and then housekeeping will need to go make up the bed with fresh linens, ASAP," Traci said.

"I'd go up there and supervise the switchover myself, but I've been out of my office too long, and I dread seeing the mountain of phone calls and emails that have piled up in my inbox. As soon as you hear from engineering that they have the mattress, I'd like you to go up there and personally supervise the replacement. But have you even had a lunch break yet?"

"Actually, I haven't."

"Go ahead and take your break, and then you can check on the great mattress switcheroo. I want to know exactly what's wrong with that thing."

"Yes, ma'am," Livvy said. "But how do I tell if a mattress is good or bad? I've spent my whole life sleeping on a mattress that was my mom's when she was a kid. In fact, it was probably even older than that. Could have been my grandma's, even."

"You should be able to tell whether or not it's new. But take a photo of the old one before engineering takes it away. And in the meantime, when I get back to my office I'm going to ask Charlie to look at the purchasing orders to see if we can get to the bottom of this."

Shortly before Livvy's shift ended, Reginald, the hotel's engineering chief, called to say that the new mattress was on its way to the Mc-Bees' suite.

"Okay, I'll let housekeeping know, and then I'll meet you up there," Livvy said. But out of the corner of her eye she saw a regal-looking older woman in a wheelchair being pushed across the lobby by a much younger man, and from the look of it, they were heading straight for the guest relations desk. Mrs. Dahlberg had become one of her favorite guests as soon as Livvy started working at the Verandah.

"Ohhhh," she said. "Cancel that. I've got an incoming guest."

"What do I do with the old mattress?" Reginald asked. "I'm fixing to clock out."

"Don't throw it away, please. Mrs. E wants to see what was so awful about it."

"Okay. I'll stack it against the wall in the warehouse, but you better get down here fast to take a look, 'cause I don't like a cluttered workspace."

"Thanks, Reggie. I'll get over there as soon as I can," Livvy said.

When she looked up, Mrs. Dahlberg was parked in front of her desk, with a large square box placed in her lap, and Livvy saw that her grandson Walker was at the wheelchair's controls.

"Mrs. Dahlberg, so nice to see you," Livvy said.

"Why, Olivia, what on earth are you doing here?" the older woman asked. "I was just telling Walker we missed you at lunch today."

"I've been promoted. Sort of. Now, how can I help you?"

"I'm in a terrible pickle." Mrs. Dahlberg pointed to her head, which was wrapped in a colorful silk scarf. "It's my hair," she confided. "Or, rather, my wig. My real hair is mostly gone now. Chemo, you know."

"I'm sorry to hear that," Livvy said.

"Oh, well, it wasn't very pretty hair to start with, so no great loss." She tapped the box on her lap. "My daughter bought me this marvelous wig, which is what you're used to seeing me wearing, but I'm hopeless at styling it, and my girl in the village who usually does it is out on vacation. I've called all over the island, and I can't find anyone who'll give me a last-minute hair appointment. I have to be at an important function tonight, and I simply can't go with this dreadful scarf on my head."

Livvy glanced at the clock on her desk. It was 5:05, and she knew that Beauté, the hotel's hair salon and spa, closed at five.

"Oh no," Livvy said. "Our in-house salon is closed."

"It's my sister's engagement party tonight," Walker confided. "Isn't there someone you could call?"

"Anyone at all?" Mrs. Dahlberg pleaded.

"Let me see what I can do," Livvy said, dialing the hair salon just in case. "Pick up, pick up," she whispered.

"Beauté. This is Gigi," a woman's voice said.

"Hi, Gigi. This is Olivia from the guest relations desk."

"Ohhhh. I heard about Parrish. So sad. And scary! What's up?"

"I know you're supposed to close at five, but I'm wondering if there's anyone there who could do a quick restyling of a wig? Our guest has an important event tonight at six thirty."

"I wish I could, hon, but all our stylists have gone home."

"Hey. Would it be okay if I ran over there with her? I'm no stylist, but I used to do hot rollers and hairspray on my grandma's wig all the time."

"There's no written policy against it, but our salon manager might not like the idea."

"But Mrs. E would like it. You know how she feels about keeping our guests happy, and this particular guest is a longtime Saint member."

"Okay. I can give you thirty minutes, and then I really gotta get home to my kids."

Livvy looked over at Mrs. Dahlberg, who was waiting expectantly. "Okay. I think I have a solution. I used to set and comb out my grandma's wig all the time when I played beauty shop. What do you think? Are you game?"

The older woman giggled. "If you're game, I'm game. So let's get going."

When they got to the salon, Gigi waved them inside. "I've got your hot rollers plugged in over there. Remember. Thirty minutes, then I have to throw you out."

"Thank you, sweetheart," Mrs. Dahlberg said.

Gigi smiled at the guest. "Can I pour you a little prosecco while you wait?"

"Oh, I shouldn't. But then again, it's not as though I'm driving, so I believe I will."

Twenty minutes later, Livvy removed the hot rollers from the wig, which she'd placed on a wig form on the counter of the station, and began attacking it with a brush and hairspray, styling the short silver curls into a loose, feathery coiffure.

"What do you think?"

"It's wonderful," Mrs. Dahlberg said. She began to unfasten the scarf, but then stopped.

"Now, close your eyes, please, Olivia. I hate for anyone to see this ugly old bald head of mine."

"I will," Livvy said, obeying the guest's request. "But I don't believe you could ever be anything other than beautiful, Mrs. Dahlberg."

"All right, you can look now," Mrs. Dahlberg said a moment later.

Livvy opened her eyes. "You look amazing," she said. "Gorgeous, even!"

The old woman batted her pale eyelashes. "I do, don't I? And it's all thanks to you." She reached for her pocketbook, opened it, and brought out her billfold.

"Oh no," Livvy protested. "I'm not allowed to accept gratuities."

"It's not a gratuity," Mrs. Dahlberg said. "It's payment. I'm sure you should have gone home by now, but you stayed to do me a huge favor, and it's only right that you are paid."

"Seeing you happy is enough payment for me," Livvy said. "And I can't wait to hear all about the party tomorrow."

It was nearly six by the time Livvy returned to the guest relations desk.

"Shit," she murmured. "I still gotta go look at the Colonel's damn mattress."

She commandeered one of the golf carts parked near the service entrance, and motored over to the engineering and maintenance warehouse. Only one car was in the gravel parking lot. Livvy tried the door, but it was locked.

She pounded on the heavy metal door. "Hey! Anybody in there? Let me in, okay?" She pounded again, sweat dripping down her back in the hot, humid air.

Finally the door opened and a skinny teenager in a dirty uniform shirt peered out at her. "Hey," he said warily. "What's up?"

"I'm Olivia, from guest relations, and Reggie was supposed to leave a mattress here for me to look at, so if you'll just let me in, I'll take a look, snap a picture, and get gone."

He blinked and pushed a strand of sweat-soaked hair from his forehead. "Mattress?"

"Yeah. You know, the flat thing you sleep on? Reggie brought it back from the hotel."

"I ain't seen no mattress," the kid said. "But you can look around for yourself."

Livvy stepped inside the cavernous metal building. She toured a machine shop, passed pallets of shrink-wrapped goods and towering rows holding rolls of carpet and cartons of coffee makers, micro-waves, and televisions, but there was no sign of a used mattress.

"I don't understand," she told the kid. "Reggie promised he'd keep it here for me."

"Reggie's gone home," the kid said. "I gotta go too. You know?"

Her shoulders slumped as she left the warehouse and stepped onto the golf cart. Ugh. Only her first day in guest relations, and she'd somehow managed to screw up the one thing she'd promised Mrs. E she'd attend to.

CHAPTER 36

* * *

Livvy was waiting, and when Felice finally returned to the dorm just after ten that night, she pounced.

"Hey," she greeted her colleague. "How was work?"

"It was work," Felice said, dropping down onto the sofa and kicking off her Crocs.

Livvy patted her own lap. "Here. Put your feet up and I'll rub them like my mom used to do for me before I moved in here and she disowned me."

"And why would you do that?" Felice asked, her suspicious nature taking over.

"Because I have something I need to talk to you about. And also, I'm a nice person."

"I'm not that nice a person," Felice said, but she swung her legs up onto the sofa.

"Be right back." Livvy went to her room, and when she returned she carried a bottle of scented lotion and a towel. She went into the kitchen and ran hot tap water over the towel.

Back on the sofa, she wrapped the towel around Felice's feet. "Close your eyes."

Her coworker did as she was directed. Livvy removed the towel, squeezed a dollop of lotion into her hands, and went to work, rubbing and kneading Felice's feet, cracking her toe joints one by one, and massaging the lotion into the skin.

"Oh God, that's nice," Felice croaked, keeping her eyes shut.

She opened one eye and fixed it on Livvy. "Now. What's so important you think you have to bribe me with a foot massage?"

"Can you keep a secret?"

"Yeah. Sure. Spill it, girl, 'cause I gotta get to bed pretty soon."

Livvy took a deep breath. "I want you to help me figure out who killed Parrish."

"You don't know she *was* killed. Maybe she had a heart attack or something."

"Come on. The cops obviously think there was foul play. We wouldn't do anything illegal. Just, you know, look around, ask some questions. Observe."

"No way," Felice said, swinging her legs back down onto the floor. "You do you, Livvy, but I am out. Ask one of the guys if you wanna go playing detective. Where are those two clowns, anyway?"

"It's hospitality night tonight at Pour Willy's. Two-buck beers," Livvy said. "And just between the two of us, I think KJ and Garrett are okay, and I don't really think they would have done anything to purposely hurt Parrish. But I also don't totally trust them."

"The answer is still no," Felice said.

Livvy wasn't so easily deterred. Her mother used to compare her to a rat terrier when she was after something she wanted. "Hey. Remember that blue composition book Parrish used to carry around with her?"

"I guess."

"She called it her little blue bitch book. She kept notes in it about all the guest complaints and requests she dealt with. Mrs. E wants to find it. And so do I."

Felice's expression remained stony. "I got no idea where something like that would be."

"But you could help me look for it," Livvy suggested. She turned and pointed toward the door to Parrish's room, where the yellow crime scene tape had finally been removed.

"The cops must have finished looking in there while we were out today. So, what would it hurt if we went in there—just to look for the bitch book, which Mrs. E wants."

"You already said the part about Mrs. E, and I keep telling you, there's no 'we,'" Felice repeated. "I am not fixing to become your sidekick, accomplice, or coconspirator."

"But you could be my lookout, right?"

Felice gave a martyred sigh. "All right. But you're gonna owe me another foot rub when I get off work tomorrow."

"You got it."

Livvy winced when she saw the room's state of disrepair. Parrish had furnished the room with gorgeous designer linens, monogrammed bedding, even a slipcovered chair that matched the bed's dust ruffle. The inexpensive dresser held a silver-framed photograph of Parrish, in pigtails, her arms around a brown-and-white dog.

The police search had been thorough; all the drawers in the dresser had been pulled out, their contents tossed onto the thick rug. The tiny closet had been emptied and the mattress pulled off the box spring. Suitcases had been pulled out and sat on top of the bed frame, exposing dozens of pairs of expensive designer shoes.

"Oh man," Felice said, pointing at one of the suitcases. "Look at all those killer shoes. I bet those Jimmy Choos cost more than my car."

"Mine too," Livvy said, as she knelt beside the bed and poked her head beneath it.

"Nothing under here," she reported, sitting back on her heels. "If you were Parrish, where would you keep something like a notebook?"

"My purse, or my desk at work, or my nightstand," Felice said.

"I think the cops took her purse, and it's not in her desk at work, and I checked the nightstand first thing."

"My car," Felice added.

Livvy stood up and snapped her fingers. "The Audi. I should have thought of that."

"Which the cops towed away this morning," Felice said.

Livvy moved to the dresser and began picking up clothing, carefully folding each item and placing it in one of the suitcases: Parrish's silk thong panties, the matching bras, shirts, shorts, bathing suits.

"What are you doing, and why?" Felice asked.

"I don't know," Livvy admitted. "Someone from Parrish's family—maybe her dad, or that stepmother of hers or even Mrs. E, is going to want to come in here and pack her stuff up." She began folding dresses. "And they're gonna feel so awful, and so sad, when they see this mess." She gestured at the floor, still littered with the dead girl's clothes and other belongings.

Felice nodded and silently began picking up clothing, following Livvy's example.

Within ten minutes, they'd packed everything into the suitcases.

"Give me a hand with this," Felice said, grabbing one side of the mattress.

Together, they replaced the mattress and by unspoken, mutual agreement, began stripping the bed, folding the high-thread-count sheets, then the quilted coverlet, even folding the down comforter and placing it at the foot of the bed.

Felice pointed to the mound of decorative throw pillows stacked beside one of the nightstands. "That girl sure loved her pillows. Must be at least a dozen."

"And they're all so pretty," Livvy said, picking one up and placing it against the headboard.

"Not like that." Felice grabbed the smaller pillow and replaced it with a large, square Euro sham. "Parrish always had these big square pink-and-white-striped ones against the wall."

"Yeah, you're right," Livvy said, placing the matching Euro on the other side of the bed. "But how do you happen to know how she made up her bed?"

"Some days, after she'd left for work, I'd sneak in here, just to look," Felice admitted. "She had it fixed up like something from a magazine. Not like our rooms with those crummy Walmart bedspreads."

"I used to do the same thing. Parrish had such great style. Without even trying."

"Rich-girl style," Felice said. "You think she was born with it?"

"Maybe." Livvy picked up a pair of matching slightly smaller pillows, patterned with green vines and pink flowers, holding one in each hand.

"Hey," she said, dropping the pillow in her left hand and holding up the one in her right hand. "This one's heavier."

She searched the pillow's flanged seam and found the invisible zipper, sliding it open. As she did so, a slender blue-and-white composition book slid onto the floor.

Both women stood staring down at it, before Felice picked up the book and handed it to her coconspirator. "Looks like the bitch book to me."

CHAPTER 37

* * *

On Wednesday morning, the Chapel by the Sea was full to overflowing. Traci made a conscious decision to arrive late, slipping into the last available seat in the last row of pews in the tiny nondenominational church.

The woman seated on the aisle looked up and glared at Traci, resolutely refusing to slide over, so Traci stepped over her and her husband and son and managed to squeeze into the middle seat.

She knew the family, of course. Jolene and Pete Woods were Ric Eddings's neighbors. Their son Pace had been in Parrish's class in elementary school, until Ric sent his daughter to boarding school in Virginia.

Traci sat erect in her seat, eyes straight ahead, clenching and unclenching the wad of tissues in her hand.

She wasn't surprised that the Woods family had literally given her the cold shoulder, and hadn't been surprised when she'd learned that morning, strictly by accident, that Parrish's funeral was being held later that day.

Charlie had arrived in her office that morning, holding the thick, buff-colored invitation in his hand. "Did you get one of these?"

Traci took the card in her own hand and read: *Celebration of Life: Parrish Helen Eddings, beloved daughter of Frederic Eddings and Heather Eddings Goldstein. Wed., June 14, 5 p.m., Chapel by the Sea.*

She ran a thumbnail over the engraved words. "This is the first I'm hearing about it. As you know, Ric isn't speaking to me."

"Oh. Sorry. I just assumed . . ."

"What? That Ric would do the decent thing? I'm afraid you over-estimate him." She patted the older man's arm. "It's all right. But thanks for letting me know in time. I'll clear my afternoon calendar."

He looked startled. "You're going anyway?"

"Yes," Traci said firmly. "Don't worry. I won't make a fuss or a scene. Today isn't about Ric or me. It's about honoring Parrish. I won't let her father's petty grievances keep me from that."

She held up the invitation. "May I keep this, please? I think Par-rish's dormmates would want to honor her memory too."

Charlie raised an eyebrow. "Is that really wise? I mean, I've talked to Ric, and he seems to think . . . well, with Parrish and that party . . ."

"None of them would have harmed her," Traci said flatly. "They're kids. Good kids. And they cared about her. I'll ask them to be discreet, and I know they will be."

Soft organ music was playing something vaguely ecclesiastical. A white-robed pastor appeared on the altar and led the congregation in prayers and scripture readings. Traci zoned it all out. The tears had started with the first chord of organ music, and she'd had to choke back her sobs, ignoring the pointed side-eye given her by Jolene Woods.

Charlie was right, she thought. This was a mistake. She felt pan-icky and would have fled the church, but one look at the stubborn set of Jolene's jaw let her know she was trapped.

She closed her eyes and tried to meditate, tried to slow her breaths and focus on better, happier times. But the church was packed, and the warmth from all those bodies and the scent of Jolene's overpow-ering perfume felt suffocating.

The pastor began his eulogy, and it was all Traci could do to stay seated and not run screaming out of the chapel. Working from notes, he mentioned Parrish's family, talked about her beloved dog Patches, her love of the water and the beach, et cetera. She deliber-ately zoned out, catching only random phrases, but it was clear that this man, although well-meaning, had never met her niece.

This chapel had been Helen Eddings's idea. She'd commissioned the architect who'd drawn up the design, and Fred had paid for the construction. He'd dutifully attended services there, but after his wife's death had abandoned any pretense at being a man of faith.

Traci was fairly sure that this was Ric's first time back in this church since his first wedding two decades earlier.

She gazed around the church and easily spotted the uncomfortable-looking dormmates, Olivia, Felice, and KJ. Garrett, she assumed, must be working in the restaurant.

As she looked around the sanctuary, she saw dozens of familiar faces—old Eddings family friends, some of Parrish's classmates, longtime hotel staffers, and club members. Some gave her sad smiles. A few turned away quickly, refusing to allow their eyes to meet hers.

It was a small town, she told herself, and Ric had been vocal about blaming her for his child's death. Still, the snubs stung.

There was another reading. More organ music. Traci relaxed, sensing the service was over. But then, the pastor stepped aside and a lone woman, clutching a guitar, took a seat on a high stool in front of a mike stand and started strumming and singing in a pure, clear voice.

She recognized the song at once, Eric Clapton's poignant "Tears in Heaven," but it was the singer/guitarist who was the surprise. It was Heather, Parrish's long-absent mother.

Traci heard a soft, barely suppressed gasp from the congregation as they recognized her too, when Heather started to sing. She glanced to her right and found grim satisfaction in noting Jolene's shocked expression.

She almost didn't recognize her former sister-in-law. Heather's once long, lustrous dark hair had been chopped short, and was now entirely silver. And she was at least thirty pounds heavier than the former rock goddess Ric Eddings had been transfixed by all those years ago.

When Heather played the last plaintive guitar chord and sang the last verse, the church fell silent, and then, the artist was met with scattered, restrained applause.

Jolene grabbed her husband's arm. "Come on," she said in a stage whisper. "We've got to get over to Ric's so I can start putting out the food for the reception."

It was a relief, watching everyone else leave the chapel. Traci lingered, not wanting to get caught up in the logjam of mourners who she knew, from painful personal experience, would be filing past Ric and Madelyn, expressing their condolences.

Finally, she slipped out a side door and was headed for her car when she heard a woman calling her name.

"Traci?" She turned and saw Heather hurrying toward her, the leather guitar case slung over her shoulder.

When Heather reached her, the two women stood inches apart, awkwardly sizing each other up. They hadn't been close, not really. They'd see each other at family events; birthdays, holidays. Traci was busy with her job at the hotel, and Heather, at first, had a career of her own, as the lead singer in a band.

That's how she'd met Ric Eddings, playing at a wedding reception at the Saint. He'd been instantly smitten by the exotic Heather and had pursued and won her in a matter of months. They'd married and Heather got pregnant not long after. She'd miscarried that first child, and then, within a year, had Parrish.

Three years later, when her daughter was in preschool, Heather left, telling Ric that life as a wife and mother was "stifling and soul-deadening."

"Hi," Heather said now, holding out a hand.

Traci took her hand, squeezed, and released. "Hey."

Her former sister-in-law sighed. "Hey. I, uh, heard about Hoke, and I was so, so sorry. I wanted to call, but you know how it is. But lucky you, marrying the good brother."

Traci bit her lower lip. "Heather, I don't know what to say. Except that Parrish was amazing. In every way. She was smart and kind and fabulous. Maybe she got that from you."

"Maybe. Guess we'll never know, huh?"

With the back of her hand, Heather brushed her bangs from her eyes. She looked around. Mourners entering the parking lot were openly staring, then giving them a wide berth.

"Wow. It's like we're a couple of Typhoid Marys from the collective stink-eye people are giving us, huh? You wanna get out of here? Maybe go get a drink. Not at the hotel, though, okay?"

"There's a dive bar a couple blocks from here. Pour Willy's."

"I remember the place," Heather said. "Meet you there."

Traci found a two-top booth near the back of the bar, and five minutes later, Heather slid into the seat on the opposite side of the table.

"Place looks about the same," she commented, and nodded at Traci. "And so do you. But don't bother trying to tell me I haven't changed. We both know I'm older and fatter, and only maybe a little bit wiser."

Their server, a girl barely out of her teens, in cut-offs and a tank top, arrived and took their orders.

"She reminds me a little of Parrish," Heather said wistfully.

Traci looked up, surprised. "When was the last time you saw her?"

"Graduation. I saw you there, from across the room, but Parrish didn't want me anywhere near the rest of the family. She knew her dad would be pissed that I was there."

"I had no idea you'd been in touch with her."

"That was the general idea," Heather said.

Their drinks arrived, club soda for Heather, wine for Traci, along with a basket of French fries.

"She found me on Facebook," Heather confided. "The year Ric and Madelyn got married. I hadn't posted anything on that page in ages, but for some reason, I looked at my page the week after the wedding, and saw that she'd private-messaged me. My heart about stopped."

"I'll bet," Traci said, sipping her wine. "Can I ask? Where've you been all this time?"

"All over. I sang with different touring bands. After a couple years, I got tired of the road life and got a job as a booker. Married the boss and moved to Vermont."

"Vermont," Traci said wonderingly.

"I like it there. We have a big vegetable garden and I have chickens and a donkey. It's quiet, but it's good."

"Still married?"

"Yeah. I finally figured out I should stay clear of bad boys."

"Did you ever have any more children?"

Heather sipped her drink. "Nope. I didn't think I had the right to bring any more kids into the world after I walked away from my own daughter."

"Can I ask? Why did you walk away?"

"It's complicated. I was so damn unhappy. With Ric. With myself. I was self-medicating for depression. My own mom was a shit show; a bad drunk, emotionally and physically abusive, and I could see myself following that path. I was messed up, and I was terrified I'd mess Parrish up too."

"Well, I can't pretend to understand that, but I can tell you this—Parrish turned out great." Traci found herself tearing up again.

Heather plucked a napkin from the tabletop dispenser and handed it to her. "She was crazy about you too, you know. You were way more of a mom to her than Madelyn ever was."

"She saved my life, after Hoke was killed. None of this seems real—her being gone like this. I really don't know how I'm gonna make it without her now."

"You will," Heather said calmly. "You're strong, Traci. I always admired that about you. When the old man and Ric treated you like shit, you'd just shrug it off and keep going."

Traci laughed. "I always thought you thought I was stuck-up, although God knows I didn't have anything to be stuck-up about."

"The truth is, you intimidated me. You seemed to have your shit together. And Hoke so obviously adored you. Unlike my own husband, whose fascination with me faded fast."

Heather made a face. "I almost didn't come back for the funeral, excuse me, celebration of life. But I made myself do it."

Heather propped her elbows on the table and leaned forward. "It's no accident, us running into each other like this. I've kind of been stalking you."

"Me? Why?"

The other woman's gray eyes were unblinkingly focused on Traci's. "I want answers. About Parrish. And I have a feeling you're the only one who can give them to me."

"I want answers too," Traci said. "Has Ric told you anything at all?"

"He thinks I forfeited the right to mourn my child the day I walked away," Heather said.

"Well, excuse me, but fuck him," Traci said passionately.

"I do love a nice Southern gal who can drop an occasional F-bomb," Heather said, chuckling. "Ric mentioned a party, way out in the woods?"

"Something like that," Traci said, quickly filling her sister-in-law in on the missing elements of the rudimentary story she'd been told.

"Ric would like to blame it on her dormmates, but I just can't see any of them wanting to harm Parrish. Most of them were there today, in the chapel. They're a decent bunch of hardworking kids. They remind me a lot of my friends and me at that age, just really hustling, trying to make a living and have fun."

"Could it have been drugs? Was she mixed up in anything like that?"

"I doubt it," Traci said. "Parrish was sort of an old soul. Pretty conservative in her attitudes, for her age. Maybe she did a little recreational weed now and again, like we all did when we were that age, but I one hundred percent don't think she was a heavy drug user."

Heather shook her head violently, her eyes brimming over with tears, and she pounded the tabletop. "Then, why? Why her? Just when her life was starting. So full of possibilities . . ."

Traci placed both her hands over her former sister-in-law's hands. "I feel the same way. And I promise you, I'm gonna do my best to get some answers. For both of us."

"I better go," Heather said abruptly. "My flight leaves in three hours, and I still have to turn in my rental car in Jacksonville."

She held out her hand. "Here. Give me your phone. I'll put my number in. Promise me you'll call, or text, with any news. Anything at all."

Traci handed over her phone and watched while Heather typed in her contact info.

"Hey, Heather? How'd you get Ric to agree to let you sing today? It was beautiful, by the way, so touching and appropriate."

"Thanks. I didn't really give him a choice. When he called to tell me about Parrish, I just flat told him, I'm coming, and I'm singing. Not for you. For her. To her. I used to sing to her all the time when she was a baby. Totally inappropriate songs, and no matter how bad a tantrum she was having, the sound of my voice always seemed to calm her down."

"I'm glad," Traci told her. "I'll never hear that song again without thinking of you, singing one last time to our girl."

CHAPTER 38

* * *

When Livvy, Felice, and KJ got to the back of the chapel, Felice deftly guided them out the door and away from the family receiving line, where Ric and Madelyn were shaking hands and being patted on the back.

"Man," KJ said, glancing over at the long line of mourners. "This is the first funeral I ever went to. Pretty intense, huh?"

"You've never been to a funeral?" Felice asked with disbelief. "All y'all's folks just stay alive? I've been to a bunch of funerals. My mama's, aunt's, granddaddy's, my uncles', my big brother . . . but in my church, we call 'em homegoings."

"I still remember my grandmother's funeral," Livvy said. "I was about eight, I think, and it didn't strike me until a couple days later that she was really gone and that she was never coming back."

"Kinda depressing, right?" KJ loosened his tie and removed the sport coat he'd worn.

"I need a drink. And some food," Livvy said.

"Okay by me," Felice agreed. "It was cool of Mrs. E to give us time off for the service. I say, let's make the most of it while we can."

"You ladies go ahead," KJ said. "I'm gonna have to take a raincheck."

"But you're our ride home," Livvy pointed out.

"Can't you just Uber back?"

"An Uber back to the island costs, like, sixteen bucks," Felice said. "That's not in my budget."

"Mine either," Livvy chimed in.

"Fine." KJ sighed dramatically and whipped a twenty-dollar bill out of his money clip. "The ride's on me."

"You mean it's on your daddy," Felice said, plucking the money from his fingers and tucking it in her purse.

The two women watched the Jeep pull out of the parking lot. "Where do you think he's headed tonight?" Livvy asked.

"I think he's got a boo thang he's sneaking around with," Felice said.

"Who do you think he's hooking up with? Maybe a married woman?"

"Could be," Felice said guardedly. "But you notice, he never talks about his love life."

"Unlike Garrett, the total man ho who loves to talk about his hook-ups," Livvy agreed.

They ended up at Pour Willy's by unspoken agreement. They found a table near the front of the bar and ordered: rum and Coke with lime for Felice, a margarita for Livvy, and hamburgers for both of them.

Livvy looked around the long narrow room, which was starting to fill up, and leaned across the table to whisper. "Just think of it. Parrish's killer could be right here in this bar."

Felice shuddered. "I don't wanna think like that. I wanna think about sinking my teeth into a big, juicy burger." She turned and pointed at the server, headed in their direction with two plastic baskets containing their burgers and fries.

Livvy dumped ketchup onto her pile of French fries, then attacked her food. The two women ate in silence broken only by the sound of Livvy slurping her margarita.

When her burger was half-eaten, she took the blue notebook from her purse and opened it.

"Well?" Felice asked.

"I can only read like every other sentence, her handwriting was so bad, but I can't believe the petty crap people complained to Parrish about." She flipped a few pages in the notebook and paused. "Here's a woman bitching that the counselor at Little Minnows didn't put enough sunblock on her kid. Isn't that the mom's job? The woman wanted the counselor fired!"

Livvy turned another couple of pages. "Here's another. A guy complaining the air-conditioning vent was too close to his bed. Parrish actually had to send engineering up to their room to show him how to adjust the thermostat. And use the down comforter in the closet."

"That's the kind of crap *you'll* be dealing with now," Felice said. "But did you find anything like a clue in that bitch book?"

Livvy flipped more pages. "Maybe? The mattress thing is kind of a puzzle. Colonel McBee wasn't the only one complaining about that. Parrish logged two more complaints."

"What else?"

"Some of the rooms on the new wing got a lot of complaints about the air-conditioning."

"Those rooms get direct sun in the afternoon. It makes sense that they'd be hotter, and harder to cool down," Felice pointed out.

"Parrish must have thought there was more to it than that. She's got a lot of detailed notes about BTUs and stuff I don't understand, plus her handwriting is really hard to read."

Felice finished her burger and wiped her hands on a paper napkin. "Let me see it."

Livvy handed over the notebook and Felice paged through it, shaking her head.

"You're right. Parrish had serial-killer handwriting. I don't see how you could read anything in there, but from what you say, there's nothing in there that would give anyone a motive to kill her."

Livvy took the notebook back and patted the cardboard cover. "I feel like there are all these little puzzle pieces in here, but I'm missing some big ones. So far, none of it makes sense."

"You're not a real detective, Livvy," Felice said. "Just a girl with this creepy true-crime obsession. Watching every episode ever of *Dateline* and listening to all those murdery podcasts don't make you an expert."

"I still think we could figure this out," Livvy insisted. "Didn't I find the bitch book? You saw how those cops turned Parrish's room upside down, and they missed it."

"Weirdo," Felice said. "Finish your burger, then let's head back to the dorm."

CHAPTER 39

* * *

Traci gazed at her half-full glass of wine with regret. She'd ordered and drank a second glass after Heather's departure. She wasn't sloppy drunk, but she wasn't cold sober either.

What she was was melancholy, morose even, looking around the now-crowded bar full of lively, much younger customers, talking, laughing, dancing, flirting. How long had it been since she'd had a night like that?

Stop with the pity party, she told herself. She pushed the wine-glass across the table and flagged down her server to ask for her check.

She was reminded of those summer nights she and Shannon had spent right here at Pour Willy's, shamelessly trolling for rich, cute guys who might offer to buy them drinks; guys they'd flirt with, dance with, and yes, occasionally leave with, although Shannon had been much more successful at that than Traci.

Her car was still parked at the chapel, but she knew it would be unwise to drive, buzzed as she was. Instead, she pulled her phone from her purse, tapped the app, and summoned an Uber.

Whelan hadn't intended to drive that night, but the Braves game was on a rain delay and he'd read the last of the paperback mysteries he'd bought by the bagful at a local thrift store.

He tapped the Uber app on his phone, and by the time he got downstairs to his Tahoe, he had a ride waiting. Fortunately, the pickup spot was two blocks away. Unfortunately, it was Pour Willy's. Another night he might have declined the fare, but tonight his passenger, someone named Traci, was headed out to the Saint, easily a twenty-dollar ride, and hopefully a decent tip. He accepted the trip.

Whelan pulled up to the curb outside the bar and groaned when he saw two guys, dead drunk and sprawled on the sidewalk with their phones in their hands.

But his mood brightened when an attractive woman, wearing a black dress and heels, nimbly sidestepped the drunks and approached his car. He lowered his window. "Traci?"

She nodded and got into the back seat.

Before pulling away from the curb, he turned to get a look at his passenger. Early forties, nicely put together. "You want a bottle of water or something? It's awful hot tonight. There's some in the cooler on the floor there."

"No thanks," she murmured, leaning back in the seat. "Thanks for coming so quickly."

"I just live around the corner," he said. "You having a good night?"

"Hmm?"

He raised his voice. "I said, hope you're having a good night."

She didn't reply. He was watching her in his rearview mirror. Her eyes were closed, and at first he thought she was dozing, but then he noticed her wiping at the tears flooding down her face. She was weeping.

"Hey, are you okay?"

She nodded. "I'm fine."

A moment later: "That's a lie. I'm not fine. I've had a really sucky day, and suddenly, it's just all . . . too much." Her eyes met his in the mirror. "Sorry." She gave a rueful smile. "I'll try to pull myself together. You can just pretend I'm not here."

"You wanna talk about it?" Whelan asked. This was unusual for him; he didn't really engage with passengers. He liked a nice, clean transaction, but there was something different about this fare. She looked like she could use a friend.

"Something bad happen back at that bar?" he asked.

"No, it wasn't the bar. It was what happened earlier." She sniffled. "I was at a funeral. For my niece."

"Oh. Damn. Sorry for your loss. How old was she?"

"She would have been twenty-two in September."

"So young." Whelan shook his head in sympathy. "What a shame."

She was quiet for a while, and again, Whelan thought, even hoped, she was asleep. He didn't know what to do with a crying woman. It was a complication he didn't need.

"Her name was Parrish."

"Pardon?"

"My niece. Her name was Parrish."

Whelan was afraid to ask for details. Because details would invariably bring more tears.

"Nice name" was all he could come up with. Stupid thing to say.

"She was named after her paternal grandmother, Helen, but Parrish was her mother's maiden name."

"That's a real Southern thing, huh?"

"I suppose so." The passenger, whose name was Traci, he recalled, blew her nose on a tissue and stared out the window. They were on the causeway that crossed from the mainland to St. Cecelia Island. There was a full moon and it was mirrored perfectly in the river's smooth black surface.

"Nice night." Weather, he thought, was always a safe topic.

"At least it didn't rain. On the funeral, I mean."

"It was raining hard in Atlanta. Delayed the Braves game."

"Oh. You're a Braves fan?"

"Yeah. Grew up listening to the games on the radio with my granddad."

"That's funny. So did I. Where are you from?"

"All over," Whelan said. "My folks split up when I was a kid, so I went to live with family in Greenville, South Carolina, then went in the military, started and sold a business. Retired a few months ago, and decided to try out island life for a while."

He waited for a minute or two. "How about you? You staying out at the Saint?"

"Yes. You could say that." She didn't elaborate.

The ball was in her court. "Do you drive full-time? Or is this a sort of side hustle for you?"

"I've got a full-time job, so yeah, driving is just to make walking-around money. And, to tell you the truth, I'm new in town. I don't know a lot of people, so this gets me out and learning the community." This was partially true, so he didn't feel guilty about the part that wasn't strictly true.

"Walking-around money," she mused. "I like that."

"With my job, I mean, the money is okay, but living in a resort town ain't cheap."

"Tell me about it. What exactly do you do in your job?"

"I'm a supervisor for a landscaping crew. Out at the Saint, actually."

"Interesting," she said. "Do you like your job?"

"Yeah. I kinda do. It's hot, sweaty, physical work, but I don't mind that. The main problem is, we don't have enough reliable help. You get someone good on the crew, and damn if, a few days later, they've gone to work someplace else, for more money."

"How well I know," she murmured.

Whelan liked this woman. She was easy to talk to.

"And what do you do, that you can afford to stay someplace as fancy as the Saint?"

"I'm in the hospitality business," she said.

They'd reached the security gates at the Saint. Whelan pulled forward and lowered his window to address the security guard, a redheaded woman he'd seen around the property, although he still didn't know her name.

"Got a hotel guest," he started to say, but in the meantime, his passenger had rolled down her window and leaned out.

"Oh, hi, Micki," she said.

The guard snapped to attention. "Mrs. Eddings! Sorry, I didn't recognize your car."

Whelan turned his head to stare. "So . . . you're Traci *Eddings?* My boss?"

She gave him an apologetic shrug. "Yeah, I guess I am."

"Glad I didn't say anything bad about my job here," he muttered.

"I'm glad too. People think I'm exaggerating, but our staff is our greatest asset here. I want all our employees to be treated fairly and paid a living wage. But, as you say, it's hard in a place like this with the cost of housing as high as it is."

Whelan let his GPS guide him to her cottage. He'd seen the place, named Wisteria, while working around the Saint's grounds, had even pruned some dead palm fronds at the front of her property, but he wouldn't have guessed it belonged to the resort's CEO.

Compared to some of the lavish multi-story, multi-million-dollar homes on the property, it was a fairly modest house: pale-pink-colored stucco in a Spanish mission style, low-slung with a terra-cotta tile roof, surrounded by a waist-high hedge of pittosporum.

"You can pull in here." She pointed to a break in the hedge. The driveway bisected a smallish lawn of thick St. Augustine grass, with beds of palm trees and oleanders outlined with flowing borders of green and white caladiums and pale pink and white impatiens. There was an arched porte cochere to the left of the front door, and beyond that he could see double garage doors.

He stopped the car in front of the front door and waited.

"Thank you, uh, Whelan."

"Ma'am?"

"Yes?"

"Did you have a car downtown?"

"Well, yeah, but I didn't want to drive after having a couple glasses of wine, which is why I called for an Uber."

"How are you going to get the car back tomorrow?"

"I guess I'll ask someone on staff to go get it and drive it back here."

He hesitated a moment, wondering why he should go out of the way to help her, and then pushed that thought aside.

"I was going to say, if you wanted, you could give me your keys tonight, and in the morning, when I come to work, I'll drive your car here, and leave it for you up at the hotel."

"Oh, I couldn't possibly impose on you like that," she said.

"No trouble. I'm coming back in the morning anyway."

She appeared to be considering his offer. "But . . . how would you get home tomorrow, after work?"

"Everybody on my crew lives on the mainland. One of them can give me a ride home."

"That would be a help," she admitted. "Of course, I'd pay you."

"Then, it's a done deal? I swear, I won't steal your car, or take it joyriding."

She laughed. "Well, if you were to take off with it, I'm pretty sure we have your personal information in our employee database, so we'd know where to find you. And also, Ray Bierbower, our head of security, is pretty darn good at what he does."

"Duly noted," Whelan said.

She reached into her pocketbook and retrieved a set of keys. After a moment, she removed a black plastic fob from the keychain. "It's a silver Mercedes, parked on the street near the Chapel by the Sea."

"Tag number?" he asked, and jotted down the number she gave him on the pad of paper he kept on the Tahoe's front seat.

"Good night, then," he said. "I'll drop the car off by seven tomorrow."

CHAPTER 40

* * *

On Thursday morning, Ray Bierbower poked his head inside Traci's office door.

He placed a key fob on her desktop. "One of your landscapers dropped this off at the front desk earlier, and I told the new girl I'd get it to you."

"Thanks." She looked up from her computer, where she'd been staring at the latest depressing booking figures. Cancellations had been dribbling in since the news of Parrish's death had broken.

"Anything else?"

"Yeah, actually there is something else." He sat in the chair opposite her desk, and for the first time she noted his grim expression. Her stomach clenched.

"What is it?"

"I just got off the phone with the sheriff's office. They're about to release Parrish's cause of death and he called to tip me off, as a favor."

"Go on," Traci said, steeling herself.

"They found traces of alcohol, which is no surprise. Plus, marijuana and fentanyl. The official cause of death will be drug overdose."

"Fentanyl?" She'd read all the headlines over the past few years about the growing number of deaths and accidental drug overdoses attributed to the synthetic opioid.

"How is that possible? Parrish wasn't some cokehead or pill pop-per. If there was fentanyl in her system, someone intentionally did that—to harm her."

"That's what the sheriff thinks too," Bierbower said. "So, now this is officially a homicide investigation."

She nodded, her mouth suddenly too dry to speak.

"Does Ric know?"

"Yeah. I just came from his place."

"And he still blames me," Traci said bluntly.

"We didn't get into that," he said. "The sheriff's investigators are headed back out here, now that it's officially a homicide investiga-tion. He wanted me to let you know. I'll have a couple of my guys 'assisting' them, just to make sure they don't, you know, alarm the guests and members."

"Okay," she said, waiting for the other shoe to drop.

"They want to talk to you again. I think it might be a good idea for you to have your lawyer sit in on any interview."

"Jesus, Ray. Am I a suspect?"

"He didn't say that, and I don't think he has any reason to suspect that you were involved in any way in your niece's death. I just think, out of an abundance of caution . . ."

She felt numb. "When are they coming?"

He glanced at his watch. "They're on their way here now."

Traci reached for the phone. "I'll call Andy Plankenhorn and ask him to meet me here."

"This could get really ugly, you know?"

"How is that possible?"

"Someone must have tipped off the news media. There's televi-sion vans from Savannah, Jacksonville, and Atlanta camped outside the main gate. My guys, of course, have been instructed not to allow them on the property, under any circumstances. But it looks like they're set up for the long haul."

She closed her eyes and envisioned the circus atmosphere that would greet guests arriving at the Saint's entry, and could already

anticipate the avalanche of alarmed phone calls, texts, and emails—
and more cancellations.

"And there's no way we can make them leave, right?"

"They're on public property, so no."

"All right," she said. "I'm gonna call the restaurant and have them
send up a cooler full of sandwiches and cold drinks for the reporters."

He stared at her in disbelief. "You're gonna feed those jackals?"

"I'm gonna kill 'em with kindness. Not treat them as adversaries.
In fact, as soon as Andy gets here, I'm gonna go up there and give
them a statement."

"That's a terrible idea, Traci. The press are like cockroaches. You
throw them some crumbs, they're never gonna leave."

"Maybe so, but I don't have anything to hide, and I don't want
anybody thinking we're covering up a crime here."

Bierbower rolled his eyes. "Okay, you're the boss."

"Yes. I am."

"That's a terrible idea, Traci," Andy Plankenhorn told her, when she
informed him of her intentions. "I think you should call the agency
that handles the Saint's PR and ask them to take care of this. Crisis
management, damage control, whatever you call it."

"There's no way to spin this or minimize it, Andy. Something
terrible happened here Saturday night. Hiding it or denying it only
makes it worse."

He was sitting in the same chair Ray Bierbower had vacated
only an hour earlier. His silvery-gray hair flopped over his eyes.
The lenses of his thick horn-rimmed glasses were smudged, and his
short-sleeved dress shirt had seen better days. Still, he was the best,
wisest lawyer she'd ever met.

"Traci, you need to understand how folks around here feel about
the Saint. Ever since Fred put up those gates out on the causeway,
people think you and everyone connected to the Eddings family are
just a bunch of uppity, rich, entitled billionaires. And some, not all

of 'em, get a morbid thrill, thinking about how some poor little rich girl got her comeuppance."

"That's . . . that's sick. Parrish never did anything to deserve what happened to her."

"You know it and I know it, but we also know why the locals talk about 'Saints' and 'Ain'ts.' It's the haves and have-nots," Plankenhorn said. "And it's only gotten worse over the past few years. Folks see all these big houses over here, lining the waterfront, they see the rich kids in town, raisin' hell and acting the fool, and it pisses 'em off."

"Andy, I used to be an Ain't," Traci protested. "But in the years since Hoke took over, and I took over from him, we've done *so* much good in this community. We're the biggest corporate contributor to United Way, we fund literacy programs, sponsor job training fairs, and donate excess banquet food to the food pantry . . ."

"All noble acts of charity. But some folks resent charity. They see the Eddings family as the Gotrocks, and your misery is their comfort," the lawyer said.

"Understood. But I still think the best way to handle this is to address it head on, now." Traci opened her laptop and turned to Plankenhorn. "Help me draft a statement, will you? And then let's call the sheriff and tell him we'd like to have an impromptu press conference when he gets here."

By the time she and Andy Plankenhorn made it to the Saint's entry gates, the number of reporters had swelled to roughly a dozen, with television news crews from three different network affiliates as well as CNN, plus print reporters from newspapers around the southeast. True to Ray Bierbower's description, they'd set up canopy tents to provide shade from the afternoon sun, and most sat around in folding soccer chairs, talking on their phones.

At roughly the same time the Saint's management arrived, two sheriff's cruisers arrived too, lights flashing, but sirens off.

Traci had sent Livvy as an advance team, to alert the media about the upcoming announcement, and to set up a wireless mike stand.

When Traci arrived, Livvy quickly showed her the makeshift staging area she'd arranged.

Flanked by the sheriff on one side and her lawyer on the other side, Traci stepped up to the mike and gave each man a nervous, sideways glance.

"Hello. I'm Traci Eddings, the CEO and president of the Saint Cecelia resort." She turned to the lawman on her right. "This, as you may know, is Bonaventure County sheriff Wynnton Coyle. He's agreed to give you an update on his ongoing investigation into the death last week of Parrish Eddings, which occurred here on the resort property."

Coyle, hands clasped at the waist, spine rigid, looking distinctly uncomfortable, gave a perfunctory nod, and then stepped up to the microphone.

"Today, we received the medical examiner's report regarding the cause of death of Parrish Helen Eddings, age twenty-one, recently of St. Cecelia Island, whose body was discovered in a wooded area on the Saint property, at approximately two P.M. last Sunday."

The sheriff stared straight ahead, seemingly oblivious to the clicking cameras and jostle of television camera operators aiming boom mikes in his direction.

"The autopsy revealed a large amount of alcohol in Miss Eddings's bloodstream, as well as marijuana and the synthetic opioid fentanyl. To that end, the medical examiner has declared the manner of death to be a drug overdose, believed to have been caused by an ingestion of fentanyl."

Traci forced herself to mimic the sheriff, eyes forward, face expressionless, although her gut was roiling.

"Our office is investigating this death as a homicide, and we'll have no further comments until our investigation has uncovered substantial new information." Coyle tugged at the collar of his shirt and stepped back from the microphone.

Reporters began calling out questions, but the sheriff, stony-faced, stood his ground. "I'm going to ask Mrs. Eddings to make a few comments," he said.

Traci stepped up to the mike to fill the void.

"Thank you, Sheriff. As you can imagine, the Eddings family and the staff and our longtime members and guests are deeply grieving the loss of my beloved niece Parrish, who started working here at the Saint as a young teenager, and who'd come back to work here this summer, after completing most of her college coursework with a major in hospitality."

Traci took a deep breath and continued. "We have given law enforcement our fullest cooperation in this investigation, and total access to any witnesses or evidence they might uncover as they work to solve this horrendous crime."

A reporter wearing a polo shirt with the logo of the Jacksonville FOX affiliate shouted a question. "Do your guests feel safe? Is this the start of a crime wave at your resort?"

Coyle grimaced. "I'll take that question. As far as we're concerned, this is a completely isolated incident. We've seen no evidence to suggest that any guests at this resort are in danger."

Traci gave him a wan smile. "Thank you, Sheriff. To add to your response, I'll say that the Saint's private security team has stepped up patrols on the property, because the safety of our staff, guests, and members is of paramount importance to me and this company, and of course, they will alert local law enforcement to any suspicious activities on our property."

She gave a meaningful nod to the sheriff, who picked up his cue. "The Saint management has generously authorized our office to offer a fifty-thousand-dollar reward for information leading to the apprehension and conviction of the party or parties responsible for the murder of Parrish Eddings. All information will be held in the strictest confidence. Anyone with information can call our hotline." He announced the number, repeated it, and then repeated it again.

A reporter from the Savannah NBC affiliate shoved his way to the area in front of the makeshift stage. "Mrs. Eddings? Is it true that illegal drug use is rampant among your employees?"

Traci bristled at the suggestion. "I have no reason to believe that's true. Our employees submit to drug testing as part of their job application process, and they understand that a condition of their continued employment is voluntarily submitting to random drug testing. That said, realistically, many of our younger, college-age staffers regard casual use of marijuana, which is legal in some states, although not Georgia, as a noncriminal offense. Still, we have made it clear to all our employees that drug use on company property is a firing offense."

Andy Plankenhorn gave her a subtle elbow nudge, and she noted his horrified expression.

Another reporter, a tall, intense white guy whose mike had the logo of the Atlanta CBS affiliate, stepped forward.

"Any truth to the rumor that Parrish Eddings had been sexually assaulted?"

Traci flinched as though she'd been slapped in the face.

Coyle leaned into the mike. "I can answer that. There was absolutely no sign of trauma, either sexual or physical, to the victim's body, which was fully clothed when it was discovered."

Traci found herself shaking uncontrollably when her lawyer whispered into her ear. She nodded and took another breath.

"That'll be all for today. Also, I would appreciate it if, in return for our willingness to communicate with the press, you would refrain from harassing or otherwise infringing on our members' and guests' privacy. Thank you."

CHAPTER 41

* * *

Whelan was on his hands and knees, ripping out a bed of faded annuals near the resort gatehouse, when he saw the news vans arriving.

Within an hour, they'd erected a small village, with pop-up tents, folding chairs, generators, and coolers.

Traci Eddings and an older man—her lawyer, he surmised—showed up at the scene within an hour, where they were met by two police cruisers from the sheriff's office.

His curiosity got the better of him, so he went to the landscaping truck, pulled on a clean T-shirt, and casually joined the knot of reporters gathering around for what looked like an impromptu press conference.

Whelan marveled at Traci's composure—even while she was discussing the loss of her niece, her voice stayed calm and steady. She was an impressive woman. He'd seen that already.

The night before, after he'd returned to his apartment, he'd gone online and done a deep dive on the background of the Saint's president—and his new boss.

It seemed she'd met her future husband, Hoke, at nineteen, working as a lifeguard at the resort, the same summer, ironically, Hudson had drowned in the Saint's pool.

He'd fetched the old police incident reports and been startled to realize that the teenaged Traci Davis who'd unsuccessfully attempted to save Hudson's life back then was now the CEO of the Saint.

Hoke Eddings was ten years older, the scion of one of the wealthiest families on the Georgia coast, and Traci was a townie, from a working-class family. Unlike her husband, who had an Ivy League education and a newly minted MBA, she'd graduated from the local community college and married Hoke Eddings before the ink was dry on her diploma.

The Savannah and Jacksonville papers he found online were full of breathless accounts of the whirl of parties and soirees hosted on behalf of the happy couple's nuptials, and a dozen years later, the headlines were about the multi-year, multi-million-dollar expansion of the Saint, rebuilding much of the hundred-year-old hotel complex originally built by Hoke's grandfather, and turning it into an up-to-date five-star luxury resort.

Then, just as the project was nearing completion, came the plane crash that had left Traci Eddings a widow and the CEO of the resort. Whelan could find no mention of children in Hoke's obituary. Maybe that explained why she was so close to her niece.

He watched now as she fielded questions, deferring to the sheriff, her expression neutral, until the shithead from Jacksonville asked if the dead girl had been raped.

Traci had recoiled as though she'd been slapped, leading the sheriff to step in and definitively quash the rumors.

When the press conference was over and the reporters had begun to pack up to leave, she'd spotted him at the back of the crowd and acknowledged him with a nod. Then, she said something to the older man and walked over to greet him, stopping to fetch a bottle of water from a tub near the makeshift stage.

She gave him the bottle and a weary smile. "I was hoping to catch you today, to thank you for bringing my car back this morning. It's been quite a day."

"I watched the press conference. You handled it like a pro."

"Really? I felt numb, like I was watching someone else speaking."

"It couldn't have been easy for you," Whelan said. "Especially after what that one jerk asked."

He uncapped the bottle and took a long drink. "Guess I better get back to work. We've got, like, a hundred flats of begonias to get in the ground today."

She looked over at the area where the rest of his crew had nearly finished.

"It's looking really nice."

"All the rain we've had helps," he said. He gave her a mock salute with the water bottle and started to walk away.

"Hey, Whelan? I don't know what time you get off, but I've got to run into town late this afternoon, and I could give you a ride, if you want."

She noticed the startled expression on his face, and felt the same surprise. What possessed her to make such an offer?

Maybe it was the memory of how kind he'd seemed last night? A stranger who'd shown genuine concern during her wine-soaked, regrettable near-breakdown.

Was she really that needy?

No matter. She'd made the offer on an impulse and it was too late to back out now.

"Really?" Whelan asked. He pointed to his clay-caked boots, mud-stained Carhartts, and only slightly damp T-shirt. "You don't want me riding in your nice car like this."

"It's fine," she assured him. "I might get you to put those boots in the trunk, though. Why don't you head up to the hotel around six."

By the time she returned to her office her inbox was flooded with emails, and her phone kept dinging to notify her of incoming text messages. All the news outlets had already broken the news of Parrish's cause of death online, and more reporters were calling with more questions. Maybe Andy Plankenhorn had been right. Maybe she really should have let the Saint's PR agency put a more subtle spin on the story.

She ignored most of the text messages and worked her way through the emails, replying "no comment" to all the queries from reporters, and answered at least a couple dozen emails from long-time members who wanted to be reassured that the Saint was no longer considered a crime scene.

It was past five when her phone rang and the disembodied voice identified the caller as Ric Eddings.

She was tempted to let the call go to voice mail, but knew it would only infuriate her always infuriated brother-in-law even further.

As soon as she tapped Connect, she regretted that decision.

Ric's voice was a low growl. "What the fuck do you think you're doing? I turn on the TV a little while ago and there you are, crying alligator tears and talking about my daughter—*my daughter,* and how she died because she was drinking and doing drugs and getting raped. I swear to God, Traci, if I could get my hands around your throat right now . . ."

His words were slurred, which meant he was probably deep into the scotch bottle.

"Stop right there," she said. "Someone leaked the coroner's report to the press, Ric. The news was already out and half a dozen TV vans were camped right outside our entrance before noon. They were gonna report it with or without a statement from me."

"So I'm supposed to thank you? For dragging my little girl's name through the mud?"

Traci felt her head beginning to throb. Maybe it was because she'd skipped lunch, or maybe this was the same fight-or-flight reaction she had every time she had an unpleasant encounter with her brother-in-law. And lately, they were all unpleasant.

"You're not supposed to threaten to do bodily harm to me," she shot back. "Especially when I'm doing my best to save this company. And to find out who killed Parrish."

"Shiiiit," he drawled. "All that reward money is gonna do is draw out every crackpot and nutjob who's looking for an easy payday."

"Or, just maybe, it'll motivate someone to tell us something that will help the cops solve this," she said.

"And maybe a frog will sprout wings and fly. Do me a favor, will you, Traci? Keep your mouth shut about my kid."

"I can't do that. I can't pretend her loss isn't devastating. And by the way, have you told your dad what's happened?"

"No. And I don't plan to. He's a sick old man. He's dying. I don't want him spending his last days on earth thinking about the horrible way his only grandchild died."

No, she thought. *You want him spending his last days rewriting his will to give yourself a jackpot after he's gone.*

"He's not senile," she pointed out. "He's gonna want to know why Parrish hasn't visited him. Unlike you, she went to see him every week."

"It's not your business to tell him. Stay out of it, Traci, or I swear to God, I'll get a restraining order to keep you away from him. Hell, I may do it anyway. Because I can."

Traci massaged her aching forehead with her fingertips. "You really are a miserable excuse for a human being, Ric. I still don't understand how Parrish turned out as decent and kind as she did—with you as her father."

"Maybe you should ask her so-called mother," he said. "Yeah, I saw you and Heather leaving the service together yesterday, which you were deliberately not invited to, by the way."

"I figured it was an oversight," she said. She glanced at the clock. It was past five and she decided she'd had enough torment for one day.

"Bye, Ric. Lovely speaking to you as always, but I've got a hotel to save now."

She allowed herself the distinct pleasure of disconnecting while he was still sputtering.

CHAPTER 42

* * *

Shannon was in the break room at the hospital, eating a dish of tapioca she'd rescued from a patient's untouched lunch tray, and half-heartedly watching *Days of Our Lives* on the wall-mounted television, along with assorted other nurses and aides who made *DOOL*, as they referred to it, their daily guilty pleasure.

Mostly, they watched it because they'd always watched it, or because their moms or grandmoms had always watched it, so the room was buzzing with the usual low-key gossip and whining and bitching.

But then there was a news break, and Shannon looked up to see what appeared to be a press conference, with Traci Eddings standing just outside the Saint Cecelia gatehouse, speaking earnestly into a microphone about the investigation into her niece's death.

She dropped a glob of tapioca down the front of her scrubs, and the dish went clattering onto the tabletop.

Shannon squinted up at the television, focusing on the figure of a young woman standing off to the side of the platform, gazing up at Traci and the local sheriff, who was saying something about a drug overdose, and she felt her pulse quicken.

"Shut up, y'all," she hollered, and the room quieted suddenly, as all eyes turned to the television. She grabbed the remote from a table near the television and turned up the volume.

Now the sheriff was saying something about no sign of sexual assault, and Shannon's heart rate flattened a little. But it was the sight of that girl, her daughter, Olivia, standing there that made the blood hum in her ears.

Then the sheriff was talking about a reward of $50,000 for tips leading to the apprehension of Parrish Eddings's killer. The news break ended and now there was a commercial for weatherproof siding.

Shannon flipped around to the other channels, but couldn't find any other news break mentioning what had happened at the Saint.

Briana, her best friend, who also happened to be her shift supervisor that day, was sitting at the table next to hers, working on a Sudoku puzzle.

"Bree, can you get someone to cover the rest of my shift?"

"But you get off in a couple hours," Bree said, not bothering to look up.

"It's about Livvy. And it's life or death."

"Go on." Bree waved her away. "I got you. But you're gonna owe me a batch of chocolate-chip cookies."

"Two batches," Shannon promised. Then she bolted for the parking lot with fire in her eyes and malice in her heart.

Traci had barely finished dealing with her brother-in-law when she got a call on her office phone.

"Mrs. E? This is Howie, up at the main gate. There's a lady up here says you know her."

Traci heard a familiar voice in the background.

"Tell that bitch she can't hide from me. Tell her if she doesn't let me in, I'm gonna set right here on the side of the road, and I'm not leaving 'til she comes out."

"It's okay, Howie," Traci said, massaging the back of her neck, where the headache had decided to commute. "Tell her to leave her car at the gate, and bring her up here on a golf cart."

"You sure you really want that?" The security guard lowered his voice. "She threatened to kick me in the balls if I didn't call you ASAP. She's kinda crazy-acting."

"That's not acting, that's Shannon," Traci said. "Bring her directly to my office, please. I don't want her causing a scene in the hotel lobby. And Howie?"

"Yes, ma'am?"

"Watch your crotch."

Ten minutes later, Shannon charged into Traci's office, with the wary-looking security guard trailing a few steps behind.

"Howie, I'll give you a call when our guest needs a ride back," she told him.

"So this is the seat of all the glory and the power," Shannon said, pacing around the office. She was still dressed in her hospital scrubs, with what looked like a lump of mashed potatoes directly over her heart, and her hair pulled back in a severe ponytail. The freckles sprinkled over her nose reminded Traci of their carefree teen years spent at the beach or the rec center pool.

Shannon stopped in front of a framed color portrait of Traci and Hoke on their wedding day. She started to say something, but stopped short.

Next she walked over to a vintage black-and-white photo of the Saint's façade, taken shortly after the hotel was completed.

"Y'all should have kept it like this," Shannon said, pointing to the photo. "Now this place looks like a cross between Cinderella's Castle at Disney World and Barbie's Dreamhouse."

Traci waited. She turned to the console behind her desk, opened the mini-fridge, and removed an eight-ounce glass bottle of Coke. She held out the bottle, and the bottle opener, to her old friend—an unspoken peace offering.

Shannon snatched the bottle from her hand, uncapped it, and drank.

"God, that's good," she said, when the bottle was half-empty. "I don't know when's the last time I had a cold Co-Cola right out of the bottle."

"What can I do for you, Shannon?" Traci asked, when the other woman finally stopped pacing and sat, abruptly, in the chair opposite the desk.

"You know what I want. I want you to either fire my daughter or encourage her to quit her job here."

"I'm not gonna do that, and you know it," Traci said. "Livvy is one of our most valued team members. She's been promoted to guest relations and given a raise."

"This place"—Shannon gestured toward the lobby—"is a snake pit. You can change the way it looks on the outside, but it's just like it was when we were kids. Rich assholes parading around their privilege like it's a badge. I don't want Livvy exposed to people . . . like all of y'all."

"Like me?" Traci gave a short, joyless laugh. "My husband's family has money, yeah, I won't deny that. I live a comfortable life. A bougie life, as the kids would say."

She leaned across the desk. "But I work my ass off here, Shan. Twelve-, fourteen-hour days are the norm, and if I'm lucky, maybe I get an afternoon to myself in the offseason. I haven't taken a vacation since Hoke died. I know you think I live in some mansion with hot and cold running servants, but I don't. I live in the same little bungalow his parents handed down to us when we got married. Three bedrooms, two baths. I bet your house is bigger than that. In fact, I know it was. Remember all the nights I spent there when we were kids?"

"So what? I don't want my daughter working here, especially since you've got a murderer running around loose. It's not safe. You've got my kid living in some dorm, partying with a bunch of drinkers and druggies. I don't want Livvy living like that."

Traci fixed her old friend with a level gaze. "You mean, like we lived when we worked here when we were exactly Livvy's age? I seem to remember you weren't opposed to getting drunk or high back in the day."

"It was different back then!" Shannon's face was pink with agitation. "Nobody back then was lacing weed with fentanyl."

"No, they were cutting it with other stuff, like rat poison, but luckily, neither of us ever ingested enough to get us anything worse than sick as a dog."

"Fentanyl can kill you," Shannon said. "You don't see all the people I see coming into our emergency room, either DOA or near death if they're lucky and somebody's around with a can of Narcan when they overdose."

Traci turned around and got herself a bottle of Coke, hoping that the caffeine would help her headache.

"I'm as terrified of fentanyl as you are. We've talked to all our employees about the dangers of buying or taking drugs from strangers, and we actually keep Narcan in the staff nurse's office, just in case."

Shannon's lips were pressed together in an uncompromising grimace.

"I know you don't believe me, but I am deeply, deeply concerned about the safety of Livvy and everyone else on this property. We've hired two additional security guards, stepped up patrols in every corner of the property, and tomorrow, we're installing Ring cameras outside the staff dorm."

"It's too little too late. How do we know the same maniac who killed Parrish won't come after my Olivia?"

Traci's forehead was pounding like a bass drum. She took an unopened Tylenol bottle from her top desk drawer, turned it this way, then that, trying unsuccessfully to align the tiny white childproof arrows on the cap.

"We don't," she said bluntly. "There are no guarantees. Anything can happen at any time to any one of us, despite all the precautions we take. Remember that little kid who drowned at the pool here? There were two of us, lifeguarding, and we were good at it. But that kid died anyway. It could happen to any of us. We could get struck by lightning while out on the golf course, or swerve to miss a slick spot in the road and end up wrapped around a telephone pole."

She got a letter opener and tried to wedge it under the cap of the pill bottle. "We could take a couple of Tylenol that some nutjob deliberately injected with cyanide. Or we could smoke a joint with fentanyl in it. Or go down in a plane crash on a perfectly cloudless day in June."

Shannon stared at her, slack-jawed.

"Your daughter is an adult, Shannon. I'm thinking you raised her to make responsible decisions. So maybe you should let her decide if she feels safe and wants to continue working here. Maybe don't poison her with whatever bizarre, personal feud you have with me and my husband's family. Or just ask yourself—it's been over twenty years—Isn't it time to let this shit go? Can we just call a truce?"

Traci rummaged around in her bottom desk drawer and finally found a tack hammer she'd used to hang the wedding portrait. She placed the Tylenol bottle on its side and gave it a vicious whack. The plastic collapsed and capsules went spurting out of the bottle. She picked up three and swallowed them down.

Shannon reached out for the ever-present box of tissues on the desktop. She blew her nose loudly.

"Let it go? You have no idea what you're asking me to do. None."

"Okay, then," Traci said. "I'll tell Livvy you came by. It's late. I guess she's already clocked out for the day."

"I'd rather you didn't tell her I was here," Shannon said stiffly. "She already thinks I'm a helicopter mom."

"Hmm. Wonder where she got that idea."

CHAPTER 43

* * *

Whelan did his best to make himself presentable in the locker room. He doused his head in cold water, scrubbed his hands and arms with soap, and donned his fourth clean shirt of the day. He found an old pair of sneakers in his locker and changed out of his boots.

He was combing his wet hair in the mirror when Shorty, one of his coworkers, walked by and gave him a teasing once-over.

"Got a hot date tonight?"

"Yeah. Britney and Beyoncé are dropping by after their big concerts tonight," Whelan said. "Hey, Shorty, can you give me a ride up to the hotel?"

"I guess."

Whelan shoved aside a pile of fast-food wrappers and energy drink cans and climbed into the passenger seat of Shorty's truck.

"What's up at the hotel?"

"Boss wants to see me," Whelan said.

Five minutes later, the truck stopped a few yards short of the hotel's porte cochere. "Management don't like us driving up here where the paying customers come in," Shorty explained.

Whelan hopped out. "Thanks, man."

Inside, the hotel lobby seemed quieter than usual. The desk clerk, a primly dressed middle-aged woman in her blue blazer and pink shirt, gave him a questioning stare as he walked past.

"Mrs. E asked to see me," he said.

———

At first, when he glanced inside Traci Eddings's office, he didn't see her. He knocked on the doorframe. "Hello?"

Nothing.

And then, a disembodied voice said, "Come on in."

He walked in and peered over her desk, which was when he spotted the Saint's CEO stretched out, flat on her back on the floor.

"Hey. Are you okay?" He stepped around the desk and gave her a hand as she scrambled to her feet.

"Just a killer headache," she said. "Compounded by a whole lot of concerned and pissed-off people."

"Listen, I can still hitch a ride home with one of the guys on the crew," he said, starting to back out of the room.

"I just had a little late-afternoon sinking spell. But I took three Tylenol and I'll be fine once I get up and start moving again."

He pointed at the smashed pill bottle and the capsules scattered around on her desktop and the carpet. "I see that."

"Yeah, I had a little trouble with the childproof cap," she said ruefully as she swept the capsules back into the bottle and stashed it in her purse. She brushed some carpet lint off her navy slacks. "Let me gather myself and we'll be off," she said.

"No offense, but you don't look so hot. Maybe you should go home and get some rest."

"I'm fine," she repeated. "Let's roll."

When they were buckled into the front seat of her Mercedes she handed him her cell phone. "Put your address in there, so I can get directions on Google Maps."

"It's not that complicated," Whelan said. "Follow the causeway off the island. When you get to the mainland, hang a left, and when you get to the traffic circle, take the second exit onto Beachview, then follow that into the village. I've got a studio apartment above the surf shop."

———

She didn't say much as she drove, but she kept yawning, and he noticed she kept pressing her fingertips to her temples.

"Would you mind if I drove?" he asked, when they were a mile down the causeway.

"I'm actually a very safe driver," she said, yawning again.

"But you're exhausted. And I do this for a living, you know, or at least as a paying side hustle."

"You're right," Traci said. "I feel like, excuse the expression, shit on a shingle." She pulled off the roadway and they switched places.

Once they were under way, she leaned back against the headrest and closed her eyes. A few minutes later, Whelan glanced over when he heard her breathing slow. She was asleep. A moment later, she was softly snoring.

Whelan turned the radio to an easy listening jazz station and followed his own directions into the village.

He pulled into the small parking lot in the lane behind the surf shop. It was posted NO PARKING, VIOLATORS WILL BE TOWED, but the shop was closed for the night and he knew for a fact that the shop's owners rarely summoned tow trucks. Anyway, he wasn't really parking. Just stopping and dropping off a passenger. Himself.

He cleared his throat. "Mrs. E?"

She didn't stir, but a thin ribbon of drool dribbled down her chin.

"Traci?" He waved a hand in front of her face. Nothing. He gently tapped her shoulder and in almost comical slow-motion style she slumped sideways until her nose was in his lap.

He shook her again. "Hey, Traci. Wake up. We're here. Can you wake up?"

In response she turned her head slightly, burying her nose in his crotch.

"Shit. Shit. Shit. What the hell kind of Tylenol did you take?"

He reached across his slumbering boss and picked her purse up from the Mercedes's floorboard.

Whelan hesitated. In his experience, no woman ever wanted a man digging through her pocketbook. Especially a man she'd just met. But he reasoned that this was an emergency.

He closed his eyes and felt around inside the purse until his fingers closed on a flattened plastic pill bottle.

"Ahh. Success." He squinted at the pill bottle and then glanced at Traci, who was still slumbering peacefully on his lap. "Tylenol PM. Case closed."

Somehow, half walking, half carrying, he managed to get her out of the car and up the metal staircase to his apartment. He leaned her up against the railing of the miniscule landing while he unlocked the door, and with an arm around her waist, guided her inside.

The apartment was hot and stuffy. He deposited her on the sofa, then switched on the window air-conditioning unit and the ceiling fan. When he turned to check on his guest, she'd slid sideways, so he lifted her feet off the floor until she was fully horizontal.

"Okay. Now what?"

Maybe, he thought, caffeine would help. He popped a pod of dark Italian roast in his coffeemaker, and filled up one of his two mugs. After it was brewed, he let it cool on the countertop.

He sat on the floor in front of the sofa. "Hey, Traci," he said loudly. "You need to wake up now. Wake up and have some nice coffee, okay?"

She smiled beatifically and rolled onto her side, facing the back of the sofa.

"This is not good," Whelan said aloud. He grabbed the remote for the television, which was already turned to the Braves game, turning the volume to high.

His guest did not stir.

He paced around the tiny studio apartment. He'd taken an early lunch break and now he was starved. There wasn't much in the fridge. A six-pack of beer, a nearly empty jar of pickles, some of the turkey lunch meat and cheddar cheese slices he used to make his bag lunches, half a jar of salsa, and some moldy grapes.

On the way into town, he'd decided to head over to the new Mexican place that had opened across the street. One of the guys on his crew claimed it was authentic Oaxacan cuisine. But did he dare leave Traci alone like this? What if she woke up in a strange apartment and thought she'd been abducted?

Instead, he dumped three bags of snack-sized Doritos onto a plate, tore up some of the cheese slices and scattered the pieces on top of the chips, and zapped it in the microwave, then dumped some salsa on top.

He sat at his table and scarfed down the nachos with a bottle of Modelo. Authentic desperation dinner, Whelan-style. At least he had a ball game to watch.

The Braves were playing at home, but losing 2–3 to the Mets, until the bottom of the eighth, when the rookie catcher slammed a three-run homer into the seats at Truist Park. "Dumbest bank name ever," Whelan grumped, not for the first time.

It was nine thirty. Traci Eddings had been passed out on his sofa for a solid two hours, and she showed no signs of waking up anytime soon. And now *he* was tired, bone weary after a full day of sweaty manual labor. Too tired to safely drive his boss back out to the island, and even if he tried, what would he tell the security guard on duty?

Oh, hi. I've got your drugged-up boss here. Where should I dump her? They'd probably have him arrested, especially given the circumstances of her niece's well-publicized overdose.

At ten, he took a hot shower and changed into a clean T-shirt and a pair of jogging shorts. He usually slept nude, but tonight that was not an option.

He'd half hoped she might be awake when he emerged from the bathroom, but instead she was snoring. And drooling on his sofa cushions.

It looked, he thought, like he was going to host a sleepover. And not the fun kind.

Whelan found a light blanket and draped it over her, and slipped her shoes off.

Since she was sleeping on the sofa that normally became his pull-out bed, he fashioned a pallet on the floor with a long-disused sleeping bag from his military days, with a throw cushion from the sofa as a pillow.

The floor was unforgivingly hard and the air conditioner wheezed in a way he'd never noticed before, and he was struck by how loudly Traci, a relatively petite woman, could snore. He lay awake for an hour, exhausted but too uncomfortable to fall asleep.

"Fuck it," he said finally, and helped himself to one of Traci Eddings's Tylenol PMs. He set the alarm on his phone for 6:00 A.M. and drifted off to sleep. In the morning, he told himself, everything would sort itself out.

CHAPTER 44

* * *

"Mom?" Livvy's voice was shaking with anger and embarrassment. "I can't believe you would come to my job today and create a huge scene."

"I did not make a scene," Shannon protested.

From the clanking of silver and china, Livvy could tell her mother was unloading the dishwasher. Which probably only contained one spoon, one bowl, and one glass, but in Shannon's world the dishwasher got run every day. No matter what.

"Oh really? You didn't threaten to kick a security guard in the balls if he didn't let you in to see Traci Eddings?"

Her mother didn't deny it. "Who told you?"

"Howie. The guard. He's a friend of mine. And one of the girls in the front office heard you shouting at Mrs. E. Mom, how could you? I'm so humiliated, I could die."

"I don't care. I'd rather you be embarrassed than murdered."

"Jesus, Mom! Why can't you get it into your head? I'm fine. I like my job, and the people I work with and live with, and I'm not quitting. And also, I'm perfectly safe."

"That's probably what Parrish Eddings told her mom too," Shannon said, unfazed.

"You're unbelievable, you know that? How would you like it if I showed up at the hospital and raised a ruckus the way you did?"

"If you went to my workplace, out of genuine love and concern for my well-being, as I did, then I would not have a problem with that."

"Well, I have a problem," Livvy said. "I do have a problem with you asking my boss to fire me, and with you coming into my place of business and insulting my boss. And, Mom—I'm warning you, if you keep this shit up, I'll . . ."

"You'll what?"

"I'll cut you off. I'll block your calls and texts, and I definitely won't see you. I'll totally ghost you."

"You wouldn't do that to me. I'm your mother, and everything I do for you—everything!—is out of love."

"Try me," Livvy said.

As soon as Felice walked into the dorm that night, Livvy pounced.

"Come see me," she whispered. "In my room."

KJ and Garrett had donned headsets and were playing *Grand Theft Auto* on their gaming console and slamming back beers in the lounge. They were barely aware of Livvy's existence, but she wanted privacy.

"Gimme ten," Felice said.

"Close the door, please," Livvy said when Felice walked into her room wearing loose-fitting cotton pajamas.

"The guys are gonna think we're in here having a lesbian hookup, but come to think of it, who cares what they think?" Felice did as she was asked.

"What's up?" She sat down at the foot of Livvy's unmade bed in her messy room. "And why all the secrecy?"

"Did you hear about the press conference today?"

"No. All I heard about today was 'My prime rib is too rare' and 'Is this fried chicken gluten-free?'"

"The medical examiner says Parrish died from a drug overdose. They found alcohol, marijuana, and fentanyl in her system."

"Fentanyl? That's some scary shit."

"Right? There was a lot of booze at that party. A lot of joints were being passed around. I took a few hits myself. So did KJ and Garrett. It could have been any of us."

"But Parrish is the only one who died," Felice pointed out. "So, what's your point?"

"My point is this wasn't an accident. Somebody wanted Parrish dead."

Felice fixed her with a stare. "Like who? And why?"

"That's what we're going to find out."

"Not me. Let the cops do their jobs. I'm out." Felice jumped off the bed.

Livvy grabbed her by the hand. "The local cops? They're a joke. You don't know 'em like I do. All they care about is busting speeders and jaywalkers. And giving out 'Just Say No' pamphlets at the high school. I bet they haven't ever investigated an honest-to-Gawd homicide."

"Neither have we," Felice countered, unclasping Livvy's fingers from her wrist.

"Mrs. E is offering a fifty-thousand-dollar reward for information leading to the arrest of whoever killed Parrish," Livvy added. "I mean, it wouldn't be about the money . . . but . . ."

"Dammmmmmn. Fifty K? Wow."

"Right?"

"All we gotta do is catch a killer. Like on *Dateline*, right? Easy peasy," Felice scoffed.

"We can do it. I know we can."

Livvy opened her closet door and pulled out a large cardboard tampon box, reached inside, and pulled out the notebook, which gave Felice a laugh.

"You really think somebody's gonna come in here looking for a notebook they don't even know exists? Like who? One of those two doofuses out there?" Felice nodded her head in the direction of the lounge. "Does this mean you don't trust KJ and Garrett?"

"It's not that I don't trust them. I just think we keep this on the down-low. For now."

Livvy leafed through some pages in Parrish's bitch book, stopped, and stabbed her forefinger on one particular page.

"I think I might have figured this one out. Like I said, her handwriting is barely readable, but this looks like it says something about liquor. A guest came to her and complained that they ordered premium Glenlivet at the Verandah bar and got something else, I can't read what it was. And her note says the customer said it happened a couple times. And then, this next bit, it says something like 'check liquor distributor.'"

Felice rocked backward on the bed. "Okay, I been around restaurants my whole life, and I know this scam. She thinks somebody's pouring well liquor and charging customers for the top-shelf brands."

"You know," Livvy said, "I think maybe the same thing is happening with our wine list. I've had a few customers send back their wine, complaining that it doesn't taste like it usually does. Like, a customer last week said his Beaujolais tasted . . . not right."

"What'd you do?"

"Brought him a different kind and took it off his check, like Garrett told me to do."

"Huh." Felice peered over Livvy's shoulder. "What else is in that bitch book?"

Livvy paged backward and pointed at a note, but Felice shook her head.

"I can't read that chicken scratch. But, are you hungry?"

"Have you met me? I'm always hungry."

"Skinny girls like you, eat like a horse and never gain an ounce, really piss me off," Felice said, getting up. "Be right back."

Ten minutes later, Felice entered the room with a tray holding two steaming bowls of noodles.

Livvy bent over the tray and inhaled. "Smells divine." She grabbed one of the bowls and a pair of chopsticks. "What all is in here?"

"A little of this, a little of that. Ramen noodles, some chopped tomatoes and basil from the restaurant's kitchen garden, some diced-up salmon left over from dinner service, some fish sauce, and a poached egg."

Livvy scooped up a pile of fragrant noodles and chewed. "Mmm. This beats the hell out of the popcorn I had when I got off work." She slurped up another bite and rolled her eyes in ecstasy.

"I ate a lot of ramen when I was in school and my mom was working the night shift, but I never knew ramen could taste like this."

"Oh yeah. Done right, ramen is like the little black dress of the cheap and fast dinner category," Felice said.

She looked over at her friend. "Hey, Livvy. Can I ask you something?"

"Go ahead."

"It's about your family," Felice started.

"I guess you heard about my mom showing up here today to make a complete ass of herself with Mrs. E," Livvy said, her face getting pink.

Felice shrugged. "I heard, but that's not what I'm wondering about. It's none of my business, but is there, like, a dad in the picture? My dad disappeared when I was a little kid, and he never married my mama anyway. And my aunt always says that was a blessing, 'cuz he was nothing but trash. Anyway, you don't have to talk about it if you don't want to."

"I've never known who my dad is," Livvy said matter-of-factly. "All I know is my mom got pregnant with me the summer she worked here. Parrish told me, right after we moved in here, that my mom and Mrs. E were best friends back then. They were both lifeguards, and a little boy drowned, but my mom was the only one that got fired. Anyway, whatever happened, I think it's part of why she hates the Saint, and especially hates the whole Eddings family."

"Really? You've got no clue who your father could be?"

"None. I used to get all sad that I didn't have a daddy, especially around Father's Day," Livvy said, her tone wistful. "But my mom would always say we were doing fine with just the two of us. When I got older, I quit asking questions about him."

"Seems like, now that you're an adult, you have a right to that information. It's half your DNA. Right?"

"At this point, I don't want to set her off," Livvy said. She scraped the last bit of ramen from her bowl and set it atop a stack of books on her nightstand.

Felice picked up a novel with an especially lurid-looking cover. "You really like to read all this scary serial murderer shit? Karin Slaughter? Is that the chick's real name?"

"She's my favorite. Her books creep me out, but once I start reading, I can't stop."

"You think there's something in those books that can help us figure out who killed our girl Parrish?"

"Parrish died because of something someone at that party gave her. I think we have to look at who was at that party, and figure out why they'd want to kill her."

"Well, I can't help much with that, since I wasn't there. Thank God."

"But I *was* there," Livvy said.

"Do you remember who she was hanging around with that night?"

"There were a whole bunch of people I didn't know, folks who work in housekeeping, landscape, reservations. The steel drum band guys were definitely there, and I saw Parrish talking to one of them, but then he walked away."

"When was the last time you saw her that night?"

"I'm not sure. We rode there together with KJ on the golf cart. But then we kind of got separated. I was talking to one of the other servers from the Verandah, and then some of us were standing around the bonfire, drinking, and I honestly lost track of time. When it got time to leave, she wasn't around. I just figured she hooked up with someone earlier."

"Okay," Felice said. "So the who is a big question mark. But what about the why?"

Livvy tapped the blue notebook. "My theory? Parrish figured out there was all kinds of shady stuff going on at the hotel. And whoever killed her was afraid she'd blow their cover. But who?"

"I guess that's what we gotta find out," Felice said.

"There's notes in here that say something about inventory at the pro shop, but it's literally just scribbles," Livvy said. "The lady who runs it is a real bitch, but maybe I can do a little snooping around. I've also gotta figure out this whole mattress thing."

"That's a start," Felice agreed. "I guess I can look into the liquor and wine situation. Maybe ask a couple of the servers if they've noticed anything. And then, I think I'm gonna try to figure out what's going on with our seafood and meat vendors. Something's definitely off there. They're selling us subpar product, at premium prices."

"Have you mentioned that to Mrs. E?"

"I tried, but it was the day of the Beach Bash and Charlie Burroughs cut me off. Said he'd discuss it with me later. Which he hasn't."

Livvy picked up a pen and jotted a note in the bitch book. "Let's make sure we look into that next."

"We?" Felice asked.

"Yeah. We're a team. Right?"

"I guess."

CHAPTER 45

* * *

Crunch. Crackle. Crunch.

Whelan lay very still. It was still dark outside. Where was that noise coming from? It might have been a mouse, but what self-respecting mouse would move into a hovel as small as this?

He rolled onto his side and looked up.

Traci Eddings was seated on his sofa, casually eating Tostitos out of the bag. Her hair was combed, her pale pink blouse looked crisp and neat. She looked remarkably fresh.

"Good morning," he said, struggling upright and stifling a groan from the pain in his lower back.

"Hi." She held out the bag of chips. "These are stale, by the way."

"Sorry. I didn't plan on having company last night. Or this morning. How do you feel?"

She ducked her head. "Embarrassed. I'm not used to waking up in a strange man's apartment."

"Don't be. Nothing happened. It was all completely innocent."

"Yesterday was a lot. First the press conference, and then my brother-in-law called and went off on me and basically threatened to strangle me, then my oldest friend, who now hates me, showed up in my office to remind me how much she hates me. I never got a chance to grab lunch, which is probably why I had such a fierce headache . . . which led me to overdose on this stuff."

She held out the smashed bottle of Tylenol PM and shook it.

"You figured that out, huh?"

"I've been awake for a while. You're out of coffee, by the way, because I drank the last pod."

"I tried to get you to drink some last night, but you were too far gone," Whelan said.

"Can't believe I slept for twelve hours straight," Traci said. "Sorry you had to sleep on the floor. You should have dumped me there."

Whelan stood up and headed for the bathroom. "I better get ready for work."

"What about breakfast? Honestly, if I don't get some real food . . ."

"Sorry, but as I mentioned, I wasn't expecting company."

"The least I can do to repay you for all the trouble I caused you is to buy your breakfast."

He started to protest.

"It'll be okay. I'll call your supervisor and explain I co-opted you this morning for an hour or so for some landscaping consulting work." She looked around the apartment. "I don't suppose you have a spare toothbrush I could use?"

He pointed to a stack of plastic bins near the door. "There should be one in there."

When Whelan emerged from the bathroom she was leaning over his tiny kitchen sink, brushing her teeth. "Much better," she pronounced, popping the collar on her shirt. "I have no business going out in public looking like this, but right now I'm so hungry I don't give a damn."

She grabbed her purse. "Have you been to Kory's Kitchen?"

Kory's was a greasy-spoon diner he'd seen in a nondescript strip shopping center about a mile from the downtown tourist district. "Uh, no."

"You'll love it. Best homemade biscuits in town, but don't tell our chef at the Verandah that I said so."

"We'll need to take your car," Whelan advised. "You're parked in a tow-away zone."

———

The interior of Kory's featured dark pine paneling, corny signs like BLESS THIS MESS and SLAP YO MAMA, numerous taxidermy fish, and an eclectic crowd that looked like a mix of casually dressed locals, suit-and-tie businessmen, and blue-collar laborers, many of whom seemed to know Traci Eddings on a first-name basis.

"Hey, Traci," a white-haired man in denim overalls said, stooping to bestow a kiss on her cheek. "Good to see you out. Real sorry about Parrish."

"Thanks, George. Give Bess my love."

Their server was in her twenties. "Mrs. E! Y'all want some coffee?"

"Hi, Chrissy. Yes, coffee for two, please."

She filled their mugs and left the thermos on the table after handing them menus.

"Chrissy worked as a counselor at Little Minnows, while she was in high school," Traci explained, sliding the menu to the side of the table. "You know what you want?"

"Whatever you're having," he said.

To his amazement, she ordered biscuits with sausage gravy, scrambled eggs, hash browns, and grits, and when the food arrived at their table shortly afterward, she tucked in like a . . . man. Which Whelan found refreshing.

She was slathering a packet of grape jelly on a biscuit but paused, the knife hovering above her plate.

"Whelan? What's your story?"

"Me? No story. Just a guy trying to make an honest living."

"C'mon. There's more to you than that. I just spent the night at your apartment. While you were asleep this morning, I looked around. Lots of books, some original artwork. No nudie magazines or neon beer signs . . ."

"Really, I'm not that interesting."

She took a bite of biscuit and chewed.

"I disagree. But also, what's with all the bins of random stuff? Like, there must have been thirty or forty toothbrushes and tubes of toothpaste and hotel-sized bottles of shampoo and hand cream in there."

Whelan debated trying to deflect her questions, but then decided to tell her the truth. What did he have to lose?

"I didn't just come here for a job," he admitted. "I came because I need some real answers."

"Existential questions?"

"You asked about the bins. They belonged to my mom. She died last year, and I found all that stuff when I went to clean out her condo. She'd turned into kind of a hoarder."

"I'm sorry," Traci said.

"Me too. We hadn't been close in a long time. My folks split up when I was a teenager, and I was sent to live with my dad's family. She remarried and then she and Brad, the new husband, had a baby together. Funny little kid. I wasn't around him that much, because by then I was an adult, and also because of Brad, but when we were together, he was like my shadow. And then, Hudson drowned, and my mom's life went to shit."

Traci's eyes widened. "Did you say your little brother's name was Hudson? And he drowned?"

Whelan nodded. "Summer of '02. At the Saint."

"Is this some kind of a stunt? I was one of the lifeguards on duty that day."

Whelan calmly poured more coffee in both their mugs. "I know."

"So what? You're here to try and pin the blame on someone?" Traci balled up her paper napkin and tossed it onto the table.

"I am sorry for your loss. I am. It was heartbreaking, for all of us. But we did everything we could that day to save Hudson. It was an accident. One minute he was goofing around, trying to prank us, the next minute he was drowning."

She pushed her chair away from the table, grabbing for her purse.

Whelan reached across the table and grabbed her wrist. "Don't go. Please. Hear me out."

She crossed her arms. "So talk."

"I'm not blaming you, or your friend, the other lifeguard. But I need answers."

"Why now? It was more than twenty years ago. Answers won't bring back that little boy and they won't bring back your mother."

"But maybe it'll give me some peace," Whelan said. "My mother's life went completely off the rails after Hudson. Brad blamed her. He left, and she basically came out of the marriage with nothing, because he made her look like a neglectful parent. She was never the same after that. She'd been this vibrant, outgoing woman . . ."

Traci's attitude visibly softened. "I remember her. Sort of. Her name was Kasey, right?"

He nodded.

"She was gorgeous. A knockout."

"She changed completely after Hudson. A shut-in. No friends. I'm ashamed to say I didn't bother to find out what had happened to her, until it was too late. And that's on me."

"You said you want answers. What are your questions?"

"First off, I want to know why did Hudson drown? He was a good swimmer. There was a pool at their house in Atlanta."

"I wondered about that too," Traci admitted. "He basically lived at the pool that summer. Like, all day, every day. He and this little buddy of his."

"Mike. Yeah, I talked to him last weekend."

Traci stared. "How did you find him?"

"It wasn't that hard. I had the original police report from that day, and his name was included on the list of witnesses. Luckily for me, he lives down near Jacksonville."

"Did he remember anything? He was like, what, eight or nine?"

"I was surprised by how much he remembered about that day. He and Hudson had a fight that morning, in the game room. Mike said he rode off on his bike, but then he circled back because he'd thought up another nasty name to call Hudson. Which is when he saw Hudson talking to a guy in a 'fancy' red car. He saw the guy hand Hudson something in a paper bag, and then he drove off."

Traci looked puzzled. "What's this got to do with what happened in the pool?"

"I don't know yet."

"Did Mike know what kind of a 'fancy' car this guy was driving?"

"No. But he said he remembered seeing it around the resort a lot. When Mike wasn't goofing off with Hudson, he said he hung out with this gaggle of teenaged girls who were intensely interested in that car and its owner. You don't happen to remember those girls, do you? Or a red car?"

"You're kidding, right? There was a constantly changing cast of bored rich girls hanging out at the pool or the beach that summer, but no way I could dredge up any of their names."

She toyed with a used packet of sugar, folding it in thirds.

"I'd tell you to ask Shannon, but that's a lost cause."

"She was one of the first ones I talked to when I came to town," Whelan said. "Not very friendly, and she definitely doesn't have anything nice to say about the Saint, but her account of what happened that day lines up exactly with the police report and what Mike told me."

"And I'm afraid I can't add much more to the story either."

Whelan again considered leaving it be. If he pressed Traci Eddings too hard, she might shut down totally. Might even have him fired. Which would be a shame, because he liked the work, and more important, he liked her.

But then again, he hadn't come to Saint Cecelia to make new friends.

"Maybe there is more you can tell me," he said finally.

"Oh?"

"Your in-laws managed to shut down the investigation into Hudson's death. And then they hushed it up. Fired the lifeguard who tried to save Hudson. You don't find that odd?"

Her face flushed. "They weren't my in-laws at the time. But of course they didn't want any publicity. It would have made the Saint look bad. Unsafe, even."

"Maybe. But last week when your niece was murdered on the property, that would have been even worse publicity. Yet you didn't try to hush it up. You called a press conference to announce what had happened, and you offered a reward. See the difference? It's like maybe they had something to hide back then."

Traci let out an exasperated sigh. "Hoke didn't agree with how his father handled the drowning. He wanted to let the cops do a real investigation, but Fred wanted it shut down. The sheriff and his family got a free, all-expenses-paid weeklong stay at one of the cottages every summer. He was beholden to Fred. And the Saint was the newspaper's biggest advertiser, back when we still had a news- paper here in town. My father-in-law probably didn't have to say a word to the sheriff or the newspaper publisher. They knew what was expected of them."

"But you're a different person," Whelan observed.

She lifted her chin. "I try to be."

"So? If I wanted to find answers to how Hudson drowned? You'd try to help?"

"I don't see how I can. It was so long ago. And don't forget, I've got a very real, very painful mystery of my own to get to right now. I won't rest until we find out who killed Parrish."

"That's fair," Whelan said. "Maybe we can help each other."

"You're going to play detective? In your spare time, between working full-time on a landscape crew, your side hustle driving for a rideshare, and trying to find out what happened to your little brother more than two decades ago?"

Whelan finished his coffee and reached for the check, which the server had tucked under the coffeepot.

"I'm actually pretty good at this stuff, you know. People open up to me. I guess they don't see me as threatening. Let me take a shot. Please?"

Traci snatched the check away from him. "I've got this. What else do you need from me?"

He took a five-dollar bill from his pocket and placed it under his coffee mug. "I'll get the tip. And what I could use from you are the names of those teenaged girls who saw that red car in the summer of '02."

"I told you, I don't remember."

"Tonight when I get off work, I'll look up my notes for the names of the girls Mike Sullivan mentioned. And then maybe you could check the hotel registry from that time."

She rolled her eyes. "That won't be any help now. Their parents would have been the ones the rooms were registered to."

"I'll call Mike Sullivan. Maybe he can come up with some last names for me. In the meantime, do you think Shannon might re-member the girls, or that red car?"

"I'm the last person she'd talk to about that summer," Traci re-minded him.

"I'll get back to her myself."

"Good luck with that."

Whelan checked his phone. "It's almost eight. I better get going. Can you drop me at my car?"

She turned onto Beachview and slowed when she came to the block where the surf shop was located.

Whelan pointed to the Tahoe. "That's me."

"I remember."

"See if you can get me copies of the sheriff's report on Parrish's death. That would be a huge help. I want to see what the witnesses who talked to him said."

"Doubtful he'd give that to me," Traci said.

"Try this. Pretend, just for a day, that you're Ric, or Fred Senior, when you ask him. Use your power for good, instead of evil."

CHAPTER 46

* * *

Lola was waiting at the door when Traci got back to her cottage, giving her the kind of reproachful, guilt-inducing glare Traci hadn't experienced since sneaking home after curfew as a sixteen-year-old.

The kitchen had a dog door that led into the backyard, but access wasn't the issue with Lola. Her absence was.

"I'm sorry," she told the dachshund, gathering her wriggling body into her arms and whispering into her floppy ears. "Very, very, very sorry. Did you think I'd abandoned you?"

She filled the bowl with dry dog food and then, as a peace offering, added a small scoop of canned wet food, the doggie equivalent of putting sprinkles on a cupcake. After Lola was done she leapt into her mistress's arms and covered her face in kisses.

In the bathroom, Traci stepped out of the clothes she'd been wearing for the past twenty-four hours straight and stepped into the shower.

While she lathered her hair she considered how quickly Lola, who depended on her for everything, had forgiven her for leaving her home alone for an entire day.

And then she thought of Fred, whom she hadn't visited in over a week.

Ric refused to tell her father-in-law that Parrish was dead, but as she'd pointed out, the old man was still mentally sharp. And he watched television most of his waking hours. Had he seen the news coverage of his granddaughter's murder?

Resolving to find out, she dressed quickly. Lola was waiting expectantly at the door, whipping her tail back and forth in anticipation of a walk.

"All right," she relented, grabbing her leash. "Just a quickie. Around the block and back."

While they walked she scanned her phone for missed calls or important emails. They were *all* important—and of varying degrees of urgency.

It could all wait, she decided. There was a soft breeze in the air and it ruffled the Spanish moss hanging from the branches of the nearest live oak as she turned the corner onto a street that faced the river.

Lola stopped short and sat on her haunches, quivering with excitement. She was staring at a huge blue heron casually pecking at something among the exposed oyster shells on the near side of the riverbank.

The dachshund gave a sharp yip and the heron responded with an unconcerned "whatever" expression before it rose, flapping its wings and flying off to the other side of the bank, where there were no annoying small dogs.

The breeze picked up suddenly and dark clouds scudded across the sky, blocking out the sun. Now fat raindrops dimpled the glasslike river surface.

"C'mon, Lo," she said, leaning down to scoop up the dog. "Let's make a run for home."

They made it back to the house just as the skies opened up. She toweled off the dog, refilled her water bowl, and tossed her a guilt cookie, then changed into what she thought of as her work uniform—slim-fitting pants, a silk tee, and a linen blazer. She fastened pearl studs in her ears, and at the last minute added a thin gold chain with a dangling gold heart charm. It had been a tenth-anniversary gift from Hoke.

———

She was sitting in the driveway of her father-in-law's cottage, wait-ing for the rain to subside, but suddenly, Alberta was standing in the doorway, waving to beckon her inside.

"He's real bad today," Alberta told her as soon as she was inside the house.

"How bad?" Traci gazed down the hallway toward Fred's room.

"Blood pressure's down. He won't eat. Just staring at the ceiling."

"What does the doctor say?"

"His *old* doctor told me to call his new doctor, and the new doc-tor's office says he's doing rounds at the hospital. The PA told me to up his anxiety meds. And the morphine drip."

"Did you do that?"

Alberta crossed her arms over her bony chest. "No, ma'am. He don't want nothin' else. He's made it clear. He's ready to go."

"Have you talked to Ric?"

Alberta's mouth tightened into a grim line. "Tried calling him, left a voice mail, but his assistant called back and said he's not avail-able. At a meeting up in Savannah."

"What about Madelyn?"

"That heifer ain't been here in months," Alberta said.

"Okay," Traci said. "Let me go see about him."

She tried not to look shocked at how dramatically the old man had diminished in just over a week. His eyes were sunken into his head and they followed Traci's movements when she entered the room.

"Hey there, Fred," she said, but there was no reaction from the old man.

Alberta stood watchfully in the doorway.

"Why is his television turned off?" Traci asked.

"Mr. Ric told me to leave it off because of you-know-who," the caregiver said.

Traci found the remote control on top of a dresser crowded with medical supplies and clicked it on.

"It's the only damn thing he can enjoy," she announced. "Let's leave it on, and you can tell Ric I overruled you, if he asks."

"All right then," Alberta agreed.

The old man's eyes flickered, his gaze resting briefly on her, but returning to the endless scroll of the stock market coverage. Traci chose to believe he was thanking her.

She pulled the only chair in the room alongside the hospital bed and leaned over, so that her father-in-law could see her. She took his hand. It was cool and paper dry to the touch.

"Fred? Would you like to listen to some music?"

His eyelids blinked rapidly.

"That means yes," Alberta translated. "He used to like to listen to that Seriously Sinatra channel on the satellite radio."

Traci found the app on her cell phone, downloaded it, then searched for the Sinatra channel. A moment later, the lush strains of the Nelson Riddle arrangement of "Strangers in the Night" filled the room.

"That's real nice," Alberta said approvingly. She nodded at the patient, whose rigid facial muscles seemed to have relaxed a fraction.

Traci glanced around the room, which was depressingly sterile and featureless. "Weren't there some family pictures in here before?"

"There were a bunch of 'em," Alberta said. "But Mr. Ric told me to put 'em away. He said they were germ catchers."

"Tell me where they are," Traci said, standing up. "I'll bring them in. I think it will give him comfort to see the faces he loved, don't you?"

"Sure do. But you stay here. I'll fetch 'em myself," Alberta said.

She returned with an armload of framed photographs, and Traci slid the hospital tray over the bed and the two of them arranged the family pictures so that the patient could see them from his prone position.

There was a color wedding photo of Fred and Helen Eddings, he with a thick head of dark hair, wearing a debonair white dinner jacket, gazing into the eyes of his bride, who wore a heavy satin ecru A-line gown and a fingertip lace veil. Helen's hair had been teased and contorted into the '60s bouffant style of that era. There were baby photos of Ric and Hoke, with Helen seated and the boys on her lap. Fred stood behind, his hands resting lightly on the shoulders of her dress.

There was a beautiful silver-framed photo of Helen that Traci had never seen before. Maybe it was her engagement portrait? There were candid photos of Fred and his teenaged sons, suntanned, shirtless, and relaxed, posing poolside at the Saint. There were high school graduation photos of both the boys, photos of Ric and Heather on their wedding day, and one of Fred and Hoke at the ribbon-cutting for the hotel renovation. But no photo of Hoke and Traci's wedding day, she noted.

Traci's throat caught when she spotted the last couple of photos. One of Helen, holding her infant granddaughter and namesake on her lap, and the most recent, a framed picture of Parrish, looking positively regal in a white formal gown and elbow-length gloves, posing on the arm of her grandfather, in black tie and tails, at Parrish's debutante ball.

"There now," Alberta said, when the last photo was tucked into place. "He's got all his people right here with him."

Traci looked down and saw a single tear glistening in the old man's eye. She reached over with a tissue and dabbed at it.

"I'm gonna step out and fix us some tea, Traci," Alberta said.

"That would be lovely. Thank you."

The stock market ticker continued its silent crawl across the bottom of the television. The Dow Jones was up slightly, the Nikkei was flat, and the NASDAQ had dropped, but Fred Eddings was no longer watching the fortunes of the financial world. His gaze was fixed on the family portrait gallery in front of him as Sinatra crooned about girls in summer dresses and broken hearts and flying to the moon.

Alberta returned with the tea and the two of them sat in companionable silence, while the storm continued to rage outside.

"The doctor's office finally called just now," Alberta said in a tone barely above a whisper. "He's got emergency surgery and won't be here for a while."

"Just as well," Traci said. "Anything from Ric?"

"He did call. On his way back here from Savannah, but there's a bad pileup near Darien. Traffic's moving slow."

Traci took the old man's hand again. His eyes flickered and his colorless lips moved slightly. He closed his eyes.

His breathing grew raspy.

"I think he's ready to pass on now," Alberta said gently.

Traci felt suddenly uneasy. Was there something more that should be done?

"Should we call someone? Like nine-one-one?"

"No, ma'am. This here is God's will. His will too. We don't need nobody rushing in here and ruining this old man's peace."

Traci sat back down, but the old man's hand had grown colder.

Alberta placed her fingertips on his wrist. "He's with Jesus now." Gently, she pulled the sheet up over her patient's face.

Traci had known that her father-in-law's death was imminent, and she hadn't been sure how she'd feel about it. He'd been civil to her while his son was alive, but had made no secret of his growing antipathy toward her in recent years.

In moments of weakness, she'd told herself she'd feel nothing at his passing. But that wasn't quite true. She didn't feel grief. More like pity. He'd been such a vigorous life force, but in the end, cruel Parkinson's had reduced him to nothing more than a bitter, scheming shadow.

She picked up her phone to switch off the music, but the next song had Sinatra in a distinctly blue mood that seemed appropriate for the moment, singing about the wee small hours of the morning. So she lingered at the old man's bedside until the song was almost over, until Alberta touched her arm.

"Mr. Ric just called. He's at the gatehouse."

"I'm gonna leave," Traci said, standing and hugging the older woman tightly.

"Thank you for being here with him," Alberta said. She began clearing away the photos.

CHAPTER 47

* * *

It was still drizzling, so there was no planting to get done that morning. Whelan was dumping bags of cedar mulch into the planting beds on the first traffic circle after the main gate when an ambulance sped past, lights flashing, no siren.

He turned and watched, and then, his curiosity piqued, he jumped in the cab of his work truck and followed, at a safe distance.

About a mile down the main road the ambulance turned onto a residential street bordering the golf course, and then it made another turn, at the end of which was a broad cul-de-sac.

Whelan paused at the stop sign and watched while the ambulance slowed and then backed down the driveway of Gardenia Cottage, a handsome single-story stucco bungalow.

There were three cars parked at the curb in front of the house, and a sleek black Porsche parked in front of a two-car garage. A man in a dress shirt and tie stood near the front door, shielded from the rain by a pink-and-white-striped Saint golf umbrella.

Two attendants hopped out of the ambulance and the man walked over to speak to them. After a minute or two, they went around to the rear of their unit, pulled out a gurney, and leisurely rolled it into the house in a way that suggested they weren't there on an emergency mission.

The man with the umbrella didn't follow the EMTs inside. Instead, he paced back and forth outside, talking animatedly on his cell phone.

Whelan pulled out his own phone, found the website for the county tax assessor's office, and tapped in the home's address, which was 267 Golfview Lane. According to county records, the home was owned by Fred Eddings.

Could umbrella guy be Ric Eddings, Traci's brother-in-law? It seemed likely. He'd seen photos of Ric, but the guy's face was obstructed by the angle at which he held the umbrella.

Whelan was a little worried that Eddings or whoever it was would wonder why one of the Saint's landscape trucks was parked a few hundred yards away, but he needn't have been concerned, because umbrella man was oblivious to everything except his phone.

After thirty minutes or so, the front door opened again and the EMTs slowly wheeled out a stretcher containing a zippered body bag.

An older woman with salt-and-pepper hair, wearing pink scrubs, followed the attendants out of the house. Just before they put the gurney on the lift, she stepped up and lightly patted the body bag. Then, she nodded at the attendants and stepped aside. The man with the umbrella walked over, and raised it over the older woman's head, not touching her, but standing silently. This time, when the ambulance pulled out of the driveway, there were no lights and no siren.

The weather report wasn't promising. Scattered thunderstorms for the rest of the day and into early evening. His supervisor had already sent the rest of the crew home with instructions to report back in the morning, but Whelan lingered, puttering around the landscape barn, cleaning, inspecting, and putting away equipment until noon, when he finally gave himself permission to knock off.

Whelan found Mike Sullivan's work number through his LinkedIn profile.

"I was wondering if I'd hear from you again," Sullivan said. "After you left the other day, I put your question on my family's text chain.

My sister Courtney is five years older than me. I'd forgotten that she was pals with those girls at the pool too, especially these twins who were from Birmingham. Emily and Jessica. Courtney and Emily swapped email addresses and wrote each other for a while after summer was over."

"Great. By any chance, does she still have their contact information?"

"Nah. Courtney thinks those girls' last name was DeRosa, but she's not positive. My brother Brian was sixteen that year, and he had a summer job, so he only came down weekends while the rest of us were at the Saint for the whole month."

"Did he know the girls?"

"Not really. Brian was kind of a nerd, not into girls. But he was into cars. He says it was a totally sick red 'Vette. Let me put you on speakerphone and I'll read you what Brian says was the exact model."

A moment later, Sullivan was back. "Okay, he says it was a C4-ZR7, whatever that means. Probably a '99. He also said the guy who drove it was an a-hole. And just between us, I love my brother, but he can be an a-hole too. So for him to call a guy an a-hole? Well, trust."

Whelan was scribbling notes while Sullivan spoke. "Hey, man, this is great. Really helpful stuff. You've got my number now, right? So if you think of anything else, will you call?"

"Roger that. And now you've got me curious, so let me know if you find out anything else about poor old Hudson, will you?"

He scoured the internet for an Emily DeRosa who would have been fourteen in '02, which would have made her around thirty-five now, and he felt a flash of regret when the only online citation he found was an obituary in the *Birmingham News* for Emily DeRosa Palmieri, who'd died in 2019 of breast cancer.

Reading the obit, he noted that Emily's survivors, besides a husband and son, were two other siblings, including a twin sister, Jessica DeRosa Womble, of Coral Springs, Florida.

He easily found Jessica Womble. She owned a real estate franchise called Jess Sells ReMax. He called her number and got a recording telling him that it was a great day to buy or sell a house. He left a message with his name and number, saying he had some business to discuss, in hopes that she'd call back what might be a hot prospect.

Whelan got to thinking about obituaries, and the peculiar art and science of what they included and what was left unsaid.

Out of morbid curiosity, he typed Hudson's name into his phone's search engine. Seconds later, he was reading the paid funeral notice that had run in *The Atlanta Journal-Constitution* on July 31, 2002.

> Henry Hudson Moorehead, age eight; beloved son of Bradley H. and Kasey Ann Moorehead of Atlanta, died this week in Saint Cecelia, Georgia, after a tragic accident.
>
> Hudson was a bright, inquisitive third grader. He loved riding his bicycle, playing Nintendo, and cuddling with his cat, Boots.
>
> Survived by parents, paternal grandparents Henry and Sybil Moorehead of Highlands, N.C., and numerous aunts, uncles, and cousins. The family will receive close friends on Sunday at the Ansley Golf Club, from 5–7 p.m. In lieu of flowers, remembrances may be made to the American Red Cross.

Whelan's name wasn't included among the survivors.

His memory of Hudson's funeral was hazy. He'd stayed with a high school friend, because he knew, without asking, that Brad probably wouldn't welcome him at the Buckhead faux chateau.

Or, that's what he'd told himself at the time. Thinking back now, he forced himself to face facts. He hadn't stayed at the West Wesley house because of Brad, but rather because he couldn't face Kasey, her raw grief and despair. Her neediness.

The uncomfortable truth was, he'd been jealous of Hudson, of what Whelan felt was his mother's abandonment of her older son in favor of her new husband, new son, and affluent new lifestyle.

Whelan's face burned with shame now thinking about that day.

He'd arrived at the country club thirty minutes late, half-wasted on Jaeger shots, had stood awkwardly by his mother's side for a scant hour, then retreated to the patio, where he'd gotten so drunk that Brad had sent a cousin out to suggest that it was time for Whelan to leave.

Not a pretty scene. He hadn't seen Brad Moorehead since that day. The marriage to Kasey was over within a year, and by that time, Whelan had joined the marines and shipped out.

Whelan hadn't held any kind of service for his mother after she died, because she'd deliberately walled herself away from anyone who might have cared that she was gone. So what was the point?

Now that he was halfway down the rabbit hole of his unhappy family history, Whelan decided to dig deeper. He typed his stepfather's name into the search engine.

And that's how he found it—Bradley H. Moorehead, not of Atlanta. No. This Brad was a retired minister, who lived in Myrtle Beach, South Carolina, and helped run a street ministry for homeless veterans with addiction issues, called Fishers of Men.

Skeptical that this could be his late mother's husband, Whelan clicked on photos of the Myrtle Beach Brad. After all, his stepfather had been a big-time real estate developer, scratch golfer, indifferent and irregular churchgoer, and martini aficionado.

A newspaper photo showed him there was no doubt. It was Brad. He was nearly eighty now, his posture somewhat stooped, but there was the square lantern jaw, the chiseled cheekbones, a full head of white hair, and the piercing dark eyes. He'd traded in the hand-stitched Italian loafers and custom-tailored suits of his past for baggy dad jeans, no-name sneakers, and a T-shirt proclaiming him a Fisher of Men.

Whelan watched a two-year-old video clip from a Myrtle Beach television station, showing Brad soliciting blankets and warm socks for "his guys" for Christmas. The station ran a crawl across the bottom of the screen, listing a phone number viewers could call to make donations.

Without stopping to think, Whelan tapped the number into his phone.

Two rings. And then that voice. "Hello? This is Brother Brad."

He recognized the voice, that soft, cultivated Southern accent that spoke of prep schools and country clubs, not double-wides and honky-tonks.

Whelan found himself momentarily speechless.

"Hello?"

"Brad? This is Kasey's son. Whelan."

"Excuse me?"

"It's Scott Whelan. Kasey's son."

"Scotty?" Brad's voice cracked. "Scotty Whelan? Is that really you?"

"Yes, sir." Whelan was bemused that he'd automatically reverted to his youth, addressing the older man as if the years hadn't passed and Brad was still his stern, eternally disappointed stepfather.

"Praise Jesus!"

Was Brad crying?

"Oh, son, you don't know how often I've thought and prayed for you over these years. Are you still in the army? Your mom was so proud of you for enlisting."

"Actually, it was the marines. I've been out quite a few years now."

"Well, good for you," Brad said. "And I hope you're doing well? Got a family and settled down?"

"Doing well, thanks," Whelan said, neatly sidestepping the family question.

"And where are you living these days? I'd love to catch up with you and . . ." His voice cracked a little. ". . . make things right. I wasn't much of a dad to you when I had the chance, wasn't much of a husband to your mom, either, but, well, I'm a changed man these days. You could say I've seen the light."

Why was it, Whelan wondered, assholes only saw the light *after* the damage was done?

"I wasn't too eager to be parented back then," Whelan conceded, trying to be civil.

"You asked where I am. And that's actually why I've called you. I'm down at the Saint."

There was a long pause. When Brad spoke again, his voice seemed to have hardened. "The Saint Cecelia? What on earth?"

Whelan cut him off. "Kasey died, you know."

"Oh. No, I didn't know that. When?"

"Last summer."

"I wish I'd known. Your mother and I . . ." Brad sighed dramatically. "Well, another in my list of regrets."

"Mine too. Look, I don't want to take up a lot of your time, but all these years, I've had questions. About Hudson. And how and why he died."

"Water under the bridge now," Brad said, and Whelan could picture him, praising Jesus, or something like that. "You know how he died. In that pool, at the Saint."

"But why? He was a good swimmer. And I've looked into it. Talked to people who were there, including both the lifeguards. There were no other kids in the pool. One minute he was fine, then the next minute, gone. And there was no follow-up, no police investigation. The owners of the Saint saw to that."

"There was an investigation," Brad said.

"By who?"

"By me, well, a guy I hired. Your mother wouldn't rest, wouldn't leave it alone. She was sure there was some nefarious force at work. She couldn't sleep or eat. So without telling her, I hired my own investigator."

"Why is this the first time I'm hearing about this?" Whelan asked, stunned.

Brad laughed and for a moment Whelan recognized the pre-Rapture Brad.

"No offense, son, but you weren't really part of the equation back then, were you? You blew in and then out of your little brother's funeral in what, two hours? If that?"

"Probably less. And I'm not proud about that."

"There's enough shame to go around where that unfortunate chapter of our lives is concerned," Brad said.

"Did your investigator come up with anything?"

"Yes. And no. I had an autopsy performed, and that's when we learned that Hudson had eaten a lot of food before going into that pool that day. Cereal, which his mom had given him that morning, hot dogs and French fries from the snack bar at the pool, and then, the thing we couldn't account for, some kind of peanut candy."

"Are you saying Hudson, what? Got cramps or something? I thought that was an old wives' tale."

"No. It wasn't cramps. It turns out Hudson probably had an undiagnosed peanut allergy. He went into anaphylactic shock. Do you know what that is?"

"Yeah. A guy I work with down here got stung by a bunch of yellow jackets recently. Fortunately, he carries an EpiPen with him."

"My little boy didn't have that good fortune," Brad said. "Hudson's tongue and lips were swollen, and when they got him out of the pool, his lower abdomen was covered in red welts—hives. Any competent medical examiner would have seen the signs of an allergic reaction. But the Bonaventure County ME ignored those signs."

Whelan's mind immediately turned to what Mike Sullivan had told him about the man in the red Corvette handing Hudson a paper bag.

"You said Hudson got the hot dog and fries at the snack bar at the pool. What about the peanuts?"

"Peanut M&M's. At least a half-pound bag, probably. I never knew for sure, but I had my suspicions."

Whelan waited.

"My investigator turned up something else I wasn't expecting," Brad said reluctantly. "This is going to be hard for you to hear, son."

"I'm a big boy now, Brad," Whelan said impatiently.

"Your mother was having an affair that summer. From the reports I got, and what she later all but admitted to me, it was some young guy. All this while I was up in Atlanta, busting my butt to make a nice life for my family—for Kasey and my little boy. The investigator thought, but I could never confirm, Hudson saw something he shouldn't have."

"So what? You think this other man bribed Hudson? Who was it?"

"We never found out. I'd also hired an attorney. We put the Saint's owners on notice that I was thinking of suing for criminal negligence. After that, my investigator was never able to get access to the Saint to talk to folks who might have seen something. It would have meant getting a court order and things would have gotten . . . ugly."

Whelan's phone beeped to notify him that he had an incoming call. From Jess Sells ReMax.

Which was fine. He'd gotten what he needed out of his former stepfather.

"Hey, Brad. Sorry, I need to take another call."

He disconnected and picked up the incoming call.

"Hi!" A woman's perky voice greeted him. "Is this Whelan?"

"Yes. Thanks for calling me back."

"It's entirely my pleasure," Jessica Womble said. "Now, are you interested in listing or buying, or better yet, both?"

"Neither. I'm actually calling about something not related to real estate. I understand your family vacationed at the Saint Cecelia, back in the summer of 2002?"

The cheery tone was gone. "That's right, but how did you get my name?"

"It's a long story. Briefly, it was my little brother, Hudson, who drowned at the pool that summer."

"Ohhhh. I'm so sorry. I remember Hudson. He was a little cutie. But I wasn't at the pool that day. My sister and I were down at the beach."

"Doesn't matter. There's something else you could help me with. Do you remember a guy who was around a lot that summer? Drove a fancy red Corvette?"

"Oh yeah," Jessica said. "All the girls had the hots for that guy. He was a lifeguard down at the beach, which, now that I think about it, was why Emily and I spent so much time down there. Not that he ever gave us the time of day."

"What was his name? Do you remember?"

"How could I forget? His name was Ric. If I remember right, his family owned the whole place, or at least that's what he told all the girls. But you know how guys like that exaggerate, right?"

"Rrrright," Whelan said slowly. "Thanks, Jessica."

Whelan sat for a moment, letting it all sink in. Ric Eddings riding around in a flashy red Corvette. A stranger handing Hudson a bag of peanut M&M's. How easily his stepfather had accepted the fact that his wife had been having an affair with a younger man that summer.

He tapped the most recently dialed number on his phone and Brad picked up immediately.

"I'm glad you called back," his stepfather said. "If you wouldn't mind, I'd like to visit Kasey's gravesite. To pay my respects."

"There isn't a grave. She was cremated."

"Oh. Oh, son . . ."

"Just a couple more questions, Brad. Did you, by any chance, reach an out-of-court settlement with the Eddings family, after Hudson's death?"

"I don't see how that's relevant after all these—"

"Yes or no?"

"I did," Brad said finally. "To spare your mother the pain of a drawn-out lawsuit."

"And she never knew about the settlement, did she, Brad? You left her less than a year later, and the only thing she got out of her marriage to you was a lifetime of guilt and shame."

"Now, son—"

"Fuck off, Brad," Whelan said. "And don't call me son."

CHAPTER 48

∗ ∗ ∗

The bellman was pushing a luggage cart loaded down with suit-cases, a cooler, golf clubs, hanging garment bags, and a cat carrier containing a large cat who yowled its displeasure as the cart was wheeled past the guest relations desk and toward the front door.

Preceding it was Colonel McBee, and his long-suffering wife.

"Byeeeee," Livvy whispered.

She slipped out from behind the desk to witness the McBees' departure. A large champagne-colored Lincoln pulled beneath the porte cochere and the valet hopped out and ran around to help Mrs. McBee into the passenger seat. The bellman placed the cat carrier on the old woman's lap and closed the door.

In the meantime, Colonel McBee stood beside the open trunk, directing the loading and reloading of his luggage and loudly be-rating the bellman. Finally, when the task was completed, the Colo-nel made a show of peeling off some bills, which he handed to the younger men.

The attendants walked back into the lobby, shaking their heads.

"Big tipper, huh?" Livvy casually asked.

The bellman held up two singles. "Huuuuge. I can clock out now because I finally have enough money to buy a pack of gum."

Livvy looked at the time. It was after eleven. Checkout time was ten o'clock, but of course, the McBees regarded that more as a sug-gestion than a hard and fast hotel policy.

She stepped over to the reception desk where Carla, one of the clerks, was typing on her computer's keyboard.

"Has housekeeping been notified about the McBees?"

"Yeah, and now they've got to turn that room double time."

"Cool. Can you keep an eye on my desk? I've got a quick errand to run."

"Make it fast, okay? That bankers' conference starts today and the house is full."

Livvy raced to the room the McBees had just vacated and was relieved to see the door open, with the housekeeper's cart standing outside in the hallway.

She pushed the door open. "Hello? Sonja?"

The young housekeeper clutched her chest and gasped. "You almost gave me a heart attack. I was afraid they came back."

"Nope. I just watched them drive away. Good riddance!"

Sonja gestured around the room. "Look what they leave me with!"

The room looked like it had been trashed by an octogenarian heavy metal band. Damp towels were piled on the hardwood floor, the trash cans were overflowing, a lamp was knocked over in the corner, and the carpet was strewn with something.

Livvy gasped. "Is that what I think it is?"

"Kitty litter. So nasty."

"Pretty sure they didn't pay extra to have a cat in here," Livvy said, looking around.

"This isn't even the worst. You don't want to see the bathroom," Sonja warned.

"How did it get this bad?"

"They wouldn't let us in to clean for five days. We knock every day and they say just leave clean towels outside. Nothing we can do."

Sonja turned and started stripping the bed.

Livvy stepped over and lifted the edge of the pad to examine the mattress. It was obviously new.

"Does this mattress look like all the other mattresses in the rest of the rooms?"

"I guess. I don't really look except when we change out the mattress pad." Sonja yanked the pad off the bed and added it to the pile of bed linens on the floor.

Livvy whipped out her phone and took a photo of the mattress label.

"Is it hot in here to you?" she asked, fanning her face.

"Always hot in this wing," Sonja said, wiping her own dripping brow.

Livvy looked at the thermostat. It was set at sixty-eight degrees.

"Some of the guests complain to us, so we just tell them to pull the drapes shut and make sure the sliding glass doors are closed. But this room, the doors were closed already."

"What does engineering say?" Livvy asked.

Sonja made a face. "Nothing they can do. Old building, right?"

"Not really. I'm told this wing was built to match the way the hotel originally looked. I think it's only four years old."

"If you say so." Sonja bundled the soiled linens into a large laundry bag. "I gotta get this mess cleaned up. Big turn day and we already had one of our girls call in sick."

"You have a phone, right?"

Sonja patted the pocket of her uniform.

"Could you take a photo of the mattress labels for the rest of the rooms you clean today? Tell me your number and I'll give you mine so you can text the photos to me."

Livvy was leaving when she spotted a short stack of change on the dresser. She leaned in to get a closer look. Four quarters. "Don't forget your lavish tip," she told the housekeeper, who crossed her eyes and stuck out her tongue.

Charlie popped into Traci's office shortly after noon.

"I have some sad news to share," the general manager said.

"About Fred?"

"You heard already? I just got off the phone with Ric."

"I was there when he passed," Traci said.

"That must have been traumatic."

"It was peaceful, but sad. He got what he wanted. Died at home, no heroic rescue attempts."

Charlie sat back in the armchair opposite her desk. "It's the end of an era."

"How so?" Traci asked, annoyed. "Fred hadn't really been actively involved in managing the company for several years, but I'm still running the hotel and Ric is running the real estate side. It's still very much a family business."

"Sorry, that isn't what I meant. It's just, the old man was such a presence. He's always been synonymous with the Saint."

"I understand. You worked side by side with him for decades. By the way, sorry I didn't call you back earlier. I was sort of holding vigil at Fred's bedside."

"Ric wasn't there?"

"No. Alberta tried to call to let him know things had taken a turn for the worse, but his assistant said he was at a meeting up in Savannah."

"Probably for the best," Charlie said. "Poor guy. Lost his daughter and now his dad, all in a week."

"Uh-huh. So, about your call? What's up?"

Charlie frowned. "It's about that chef of yours, at the Verandah. I've been getting a lot of calls from our restaurant purveyors. She's burning down some longtime relationships."

"Like who?"

"Like Tommy Betz."

"The shrimper?"

"Seafood vendor. Like his dad before him. Tommy's been our seafood wholesaler for years and years. But this week, she up and fired him. Told him the Saint would take its business elsewhere."

"Did you speak to Felice? Ask her why?"

"I know why. It's this goddamn Gen Z. They think they know everything. She got a shipment of fish she deemed 'not excellent'—that's what she called it, and because maybe one fillet was off, she dumped the whole order and demanded that Tommy make good on it."

"What about the shrimp for the Beach Bash? You smelled it, Charlie. It was rank."

"It was one stinky piece of fish and she blew it all out of proportion, according to Tommy. And it's not just that. This girl . . ." Charlie fumed.

"Okay, boomer," Traci said, laughing. "She's a young woman, not a girl."

"Whatever. Now she's squawking about the rest of our purveyors. Doesn't like the quality of the beef, not happy with our produce wholesaler. Wants to use 'organic' veggies." Charlie used finger quotes to emphasize the word "organic." "Next thing you know, she'll demand we grow all our own vegetables."

"Lots of great restaurants already do that."

"Not on the scale we'd need to do it. We do grow a few things. Anyway, we're hoteliers, not goddamn dirt farmers. Buying produce the way we've always done it is much cheaper."

"Charlie, cheaper isn't always better. We didn't get to be a five-star resort by cutting corners."

He sat back in his chair and crossed and recrossed his legs again.

"It's called cost containment, Traci. You've been worrying about all the red ink we've bled since Covid and the remodel. This is what I do. I keep my eye on the bottom line."

Traci picked up her pen and scribbled notes in the margin of a printout she'd been reading.

"What's that?" He craned his neck to get a look.

"Nothing." She flipped the paper over. "Doodles. Charlie, do me a favor. Give Felice the benefit of the doubt. I know you want to do things the way we've always done them in the past . . ."

"It's called tradition," he said stiffly. "The Saint is about traditions. It's about relationships."

"But sometimes relationships and traditions no longer serve us in the ways they used to," Traci pointed out. "I really like Felice's cooking. It's fresh, it's inventive. The guests seem to like it too. I was looking at the Verandah transaction reports, and we've had a nice per-ticket bump, especially at lunch in the grill. That tells me it's working."

"It tells me it's summertime and people are hungry and thirsty."

Traci rolled her eyes. "Admit it. You don't like it because I went around your back and hired her myself."

"Hoke always let me handle all the hiring. That's the way it's always been done. Not only that, first you hired that waitress, that *girl,* and then you promoted her to guest relations, without even consulting me."

"Okay, maybe I could have handled that differently," Traci conceded. "But we were in a bind. And despite your misgivings about Olivia, who, by the way, is also not a 'girl,' I think she's really settling into the job. She's good at problem solving."

"Oh really?" Charlie stood and pointed toward the lobby. "Where's your problem solver right now? When I walked through the lobby just now, Carla, who is supposed to be working the front desk, was covering for Olivia."

Traci walked to the office door, poked her head out, and observed Carla engaged in conversation with a mother with two young children in tow, while a line of guests waited at the registration desk.

"I'll talk to her," Traci promised.

He threw up his hands in protest. "This is what I'm talking about. You've completely blurred the chain-of-command lines here. That girl thinks she's only accountable to you."

"Huh. And yet, I don't recall you getting your boxers in a bunch when Ric Eddings went around both of us and promised KJ's father you'd give him a summer job here."

"That was different. The Parkhursts are longtime members."

"Which was KJ's one and only qualification for getting that job," Traci pointed out.

Her cell phone rang. She glanced down at the caller ID and tapped a message telling the caller she was in a meeting and would call back.

"Tell you what, Charlie. Speak to Olivia. Just promise me you won't fire her."

"And what about the chef?"

"Do *not* fire her either. Just have a friendly conversation. Can you do that? Offer constructive criticism?"

"Of course."

"Thank you. Let me know how it goes."

As soon as the GM was gone, Traci tapped the call-back button. Whelan answered immediately.

"Hey. Sorry to bother you, but I've got some news to share. Are you available for dinner tonight?"

"I'm not sure. There's a lot going on today. My father-in-law died this morning, and we've got a big bankers' convention checking in, and my GM wants to fire my new chef . . ."

"I know about your father-in-law. I saw the ambulance this morning and followed it to the house on Golfview. I saw the EMTs bringing out the gurney with the body."

"Huh. You just missed me. That's how I spent the rest of my morning. Holding his hand and watching him slip away."

"I got the impression you didn't care for the old guy."

"It's complicated. I can't be a hypocrite and say I was fond of him, and he was awful to me, especially after Hoke died, but for better or worse, we're family."

"So. Dinner tonight?" Whelan asked.

She hesitated. "I don't think we should be seen together in public, especially here on the property."

"Why not?"

"Because you work for the Saint. Technically I'm your boss, and people could . . . misconstrue things. I'll tell you what. I won't have time to cook, but I'll order dinner for us from the restaurant. It'll have to be late, though. Can you come around eight?"

"See you then," Whelan said. "I'll bring the wine."

CHAPTER 49

* * *

"Young lady?"

Livvy had just finished booking sailing lessons for a pair of teen-aged brothers. She turned to see Charlie Burroughs bearing down on her with a malicious glint in his eyes.

She swallowed hard. "Yes, sir?"

"I'd like a word with you, please." He came behind the guest relations desk and showed her his cell phone.

"Do you see this? This is a one-star review posted on our website from a guest who just checked out this morning."

Butterflies took flight in her stomach as she read the review's headline:

THE SAINT HAS GONE TO HELL

The review was two paragraphs long. Phrases such as "terrible service" and "inedible meals" and "staff untrained, undisciplined, and unhelpful" stood out. And then there was this:

My wife and I have vacationed at the Saint for over thirty years, but this stay will most certainly be our last. The storied hotel's formerly high standards have sunk to the abysmal level of an interstate chain motel. Despite repeated complaints to the Saint's "guest relations" representatives, our room was poorly ventilated, the mattress of terrible quality, and we were subject to unbearable nuisance of ill-mannered, rude children. Add to that the horror of a murder happening on the hotel's property! Until this hotel's management solves these problems we will spend our time and money elsewhere.

She knew the author of the review without reading, but it was signed L.G.M., which she was positive was the work of Colonel McBee.

"Mr. Burroughs," Livvy said, "we did everything we could to try to make that guest happy. Engineering was sent up numerous times to check on the air-conditioning. We replaced the existing mattress with a new one. I spoke to one of the housekeepers a few minutes ago. Colonel McBee accused them of rifling through Mrs. McBee's jewelry, and after that, refused to give them entry to the room to clean it. As for the other complaints, I know he was unhappy about children, but we can't exactly tell families that their kids can't swim in the pool or walk past his room. Mrs. Eddings told him—"

"Mrs. Eddings doesn't need to be involved," Burroughs said. "You should have come to me. Now this same review is up on Yelp and Tripadvisor. It's done untold damage to our reputation. And it makes me seriously question your ability to do your job properly."

Livvy bit her quivering lower lip to keep from crying. "I'm sorry," she said.

"Do better," the general manager said, and he turned and walked away.

Traci was standing in the hallway just off the lobby, watching Charlie's heated interaction with Livvy. "Poor kid," she murmured.

Charlie was inches from Olivia's face, shaking a finger at her. Traci's first instinct was to speak to Olivia and try to smooth things over, but she didn't dare risk antagonizing her GM.

What, she wondered, had him so wound up? Colonel McBee was an irascible old crank. It was one bad review. The wording stung, but they'd had bad reviews before. They'd weathered other storms, and this one, it seemed to her, was little more than a squall. Or? Was Charlie right to be so sensitive to a bad review when the hotel's financial footing was in question?

There was no time to dwell on that. Her cell phone was buzzing in her pocket. She sighed when she saw that the caller was her brother-in-law.

"Hi," Traci said softly. "How are you?"

"As well as can be expected," he said, his tone flat. "Alberta told me you were there at the house, when he passed?"

"Purely by accident. I was just going to pop in to check on him this morning, and when I got there she told me he seemed to be failing. I'm so sorry, Ric, especially after . . ."

"I get it," he said, refusing to accept her sympathy. "Just letting you know I'm going to put off having any kind of a service for a while. It's too soon."

"I completely understand. Let me know if there's anything I can do to help out."

"Okay."

"Ric? Should we make some kind of announcement? To the Saint's members? So many of them knew your dad."

"Maybe later. I've got a lot on my plate right now."

He disconnected abruptly. "Who doesn't have a lot on their plate right now?" Traci wondered aloud.

Traci left a message on Andy Plankenhorn's voice mail, then decided to walk over to the Verandah for a late lunch—and some research. Her first impression was a good one: it was close to two, but every table in the dining room was occupied.

The hostess showed her to her usual table, and Garrett appeared immediately with water and menus.

"Mrs. E! Great to see you."

"Hi, Garrett. How's business?"

"Really good. A lot of folks from that bankers' conference came in early. We've been slammed this afternoon and I know we're fully booked over the weekend too."

She was about to order her usual, but changed her mind.

"What's the seafood special today?"

"We've got a great mahi sandwich. You can get it blackened or grilled. If you want something lighter, I know you usually like the lobster Cobb, but we've got a shrimp salad today, or grouper fingers."

"Is the fish locally caught?"

He shrugged. "I assume so."

"You know what? I'll try all three."

He laughed. "Really? All three?"

She patted her flat abdomen. "I'm starving, and you made everything sound too tempting to pass up."

He brought the mahi first. She looked around to make sure nobody was watching and took a small, delicate sniff. It smelled fine. The flesh was firm and it was perfectly cooked. The brioche bun, which she knew was baked in-house, was lightly toasted, and the "secret sauce" was both sweet and briny. A perfect one-two punch.

The shrimp salad was arrayed on top of a bed of microgreens, and Traci was dismayed that the greens were slightly wilted, perhaps a day older than they should have been. But the shrimp were sweet and plump and the aioli dressing was tangy with lemon zest and a great complement to the shrimp.

Garrett brought the grouper fingers last. He gestured to the other barely touched dishes. "Do you want me to clear these away, or should I bring the grouper back later?"

"You can box these up," she told him. He loaded the other dishes on his tray and placed the plate with the grouper in front of her.

The grouper fingers were lightly breaded and served with an Asian-inspired dipping sauce, with a side of juicy red tomatoes. The dish looked promising. She took a bite, chewed, and pushed the plate away. The fish had definitely been frozen.

When Garrett reappeared at the table with a large pink shopping bag with the Saint logo, she pointed at the plate with the grouper fingers. "Don't bother packing that one up."

"No? Everybody else was crazy about it. I think we only have two portions left."

"I didn't care for it," she said succinctly. "In fact, when you get back to the kitchen, would you please tell Felice I'd like the rest of the grouper eighty-sixed?"

"Ohh-kay. Was there a problem with it that I need to know about?"

"I'll discuss it with Felice later this afternoon. I'm going to come back and order takeout for dinner tonight."

Traci took the leftovers back to the cottage and stashed them in her fridge. She was still puzzling over Charlie's annoyance with Felice and Olivia, and decided more research was needed.

But she'd need to be incognito. She shed her work uniform; the skirt, blouse, blazer, and pumps. A more casual look was called for.

Back when she and Hoke were newlyweds, he'd tried to convince her that playing golf together would be "fun." He bought her clubs, cute golf outfits, shoes. She rode along on the golf cart with him for six months before finally confessing she found the game boring and pointless.

Now, she dug in the back of her closet and brought out a bin containing the long-abandoned outfits. She chose a white knit skort and pink-and-white-striped Saint golf shirt. Then she fastened her hair in a ponytail and donned a straw hat that would shade—and hopefully obstruct—her face. Spotless white tennis shoes and a pair of polarized sunglasses finished the ensemble.

Back in the hotel lobby she folded herself into a high-backed wing chair strategically placed within earshot of the guest relations desk. She pulled the brim of her hat low over her face and pretended to be absorbed in the latest issue of *Garden & Gun*, which, auspiciously, contained a favorable feature about the hotel.

Guests were checking in to the hotel in waves now, and Livvy was suddenly inundated with guests wanting to book their children into day camp at the last minute, guests wanting sailing lessons, tee times, and coaching from the Saint's tennis pro.

There was a family of four who were distraught that they hadn't been given adjoining rooms with their teenagers, and somehow, with a sold-out house, Livvy managed to move them into rooms across the hall from each other.

Then there was a middle-aged banker (he was still wearing his registration tag on a lanyard around his neck) who berated Livvy for her inability to secure a seven-thirty dinner reservation for his party of seven.

Traci peeked over the top of the magazine when his voice started causing heads to turn in the crowded lobby.

She was pleased that her young protégé managed to keep her composure while the banker launched a tirade of complaints.

"I'm so, so sorry," Livvy said. "With the conference here, the dining room has been sold out for weeks now. But I can manage to get you a table at the poolside restaurant. The dress is very casual, but the food is wonderful. And if that doesn't suit, there are several nice restaurants off-island, and if I call now, I think we can work something out."

As Traci watched, the banker's anger seemed to dissipate. Finally, he agreed that his party could "make do" with a table at the poolside café. Livvy picked up the house phone, spoke to the hostess, hung up, and smiled. "They're giving you the cabana table. It has a great sunset view, and here's a hint, order the Saintly Sinner cocktail. It's amazing."

With that, Traci stood and went back to her office, convinced that her instincts had been sound. Livvy was smiling, patient, flexible. She was everything Traci could want in a front-facing position at the Saint. Charlie would just have to get over his butt-hurt feelings.

CHAPTER 50

* * *

Andy Plankenhorn called back just as Traci was sitting down at her desk.

"Andy, hi."

"What can I do for you today, Traci?"

"I'm afraid I have some sad news. Fred passed away this morning, at home."

"Well," Plankenhorn said, his voice cracking. "That's a blessing. The last time I saw him, I prayed to the good Lord that Fred's time would come soon. Did Ric call you with the news?"

"No. I just happened to be at the house at the time. Alberta and I were with him. I was holding his hand. It was surprisingly peaceful."

"And where was Ric?"

"Coming back from a meeting in Savannah. He called me briefly, a little while ago, to tell me that he's postponing having a service for his dad because it's so soon after Parrish."

"Can't argue with that," Plankenhorn said.

"I hate to sound like a cold, calculating bitch, but, Andy, I have to tell you, I'm really anxious about what's going to happen with the estate. I mean, I'm obviously not expecting any kind of an inheritance. My main worry is that Ric, and that new lawyer of his, will have found a way, somehow, to wrest control of the hotel away from me. He can't do that, right?"

"I'd have to go back and examine your husband's will, and the legal arrangements Fred made before he fell ill, about the owner-ship of the parent company. But my memory is that Fred structured things so that he retained a majority, fifty-one percent interest in the Saint holding company, with the rest of the shares, forty-nine per-cent, divided evenly between the boys, er, that is, the brothers. Now, with your husband's untimely demise, you, of course, inherited his shares, per his will."

Traci sat, fiddling with a pen. She was silent so long, Planken-horn coughed gently.

"And you're worried . . ."

"That my scheming brother-in-law coerced his father to change his will so that Fred's will leaves me out in the cold. Why else would he have hired a new lawyer and dragged him over to the house, and even videotaped the encounter?"

"You don't know that."

"You've known Ric his whole life. What else could he be thinking?"

"I wouldn't want to speculate about Ric Eddings's motives, but I will say he was never the man your husband was. Now, Traci, before you assume the worst, I should tell you that there may be other is-sues at play in this whole affair. Issues that could possibly complicate Ric's ambitions."

"Like what?"

"I'm not at liberty to speak about that. At this time."

"God," Traci groaned. "I hate lawyers who are ethical and discreet."

"Until you need one yourself," Plankenhorn said, chuckling. "Now, try not to worry too much, my dear. I'll be in touch soon."

CHAPTER 51

* * *

Livvy was at the dorm, on her lunch hour, stretched out on the sofa in the lounge watching television, when the front door opened. She peeked over the back of the sofa and saw Madelyn Eddings enter, carrying a large suitcase.

Parrish's stepmother stood very still, looking around.

Livvy had seen Madelyn Eddings bustling around the hotel, fluffing pillows in the lobby, replacing faded flower arrangements, but she wasn't exactly sure what her job title was.

"Uh, hi," Livvy said, sitting up. "Mrs. Eddings? Is there something I can help you with?"

"What?" Madelyn, startled, dropped the suitcase. "Oh, Olivia. It's you."

"Yes, ma'am," Olivia said. "Did you need something?"

Madelyn picked up the suitcase and squared her shoulders. "My husband would like for me to gather together our daughter's belongings and bring them home."

Our daughter? Livvy thought.

She started walking down the hallway, her heels clicking on the vinyl floors, and Livvy jumped up to show her the way.

Madelyn pointed to the brass plaque with Parrish's name beside her bedroom door. "If you don't mind, I'd prefer privacy. This is . . . incredibly painful. For Ric and me."

"Okay, sure." Livvy turned and went back to the lounge, trying and failing to catch up with the show she'd been watching.

A moment later, Madelyn was back to the lounge. "Who's been rummaging around in that room?"

Livvy felt her face flush. "After the deputies searched the room, well, it kinda looked like a bomb went off in there. Felice and me figured it would be pretty upsetting for her family to come in and find her room like that, so we packed up her things . . ."

Madelyn let out a long sigh and dabbed at her eyes with a crumpled tissue. "I'm sorry, Olivia. I didn't mean to snap at you, or to imply that you did something wrong. That was very thoughtful of you two. I guess I'm still emotional about losing our girl. I know you and Felice were Parrish's good friends. And the boys too, of course."

"Yes, ma'am," Livvy said. "We all miss her, a lot."

"Thank you," Madelyn said. "Were there any other things of Parrish's, maybe things she'd left in your rooms, or in the common area, that didn't get packed up?"

Livvy's thoughts turned to the bitch book and she felt a twinge of guilt. "I don't think so. Parrish was way neater than me, or Felice. It was really just a matter of picking up the stuff the cops flung around her room. We folded her bedspreads and stuff and left them in there."

Madelyn glanced back into Parrish's room. "Olivia? We don't really have any twin-sized beds at our home. I was wondering—would you like to keep the comforter and pillows and the rest of the bedding? Maybe as a memory of Parrish?"

"Really?" Livvy was almost embarrassed at how readily she jumped at the offer. "If you don't need them, then yeah, I'd love to have them. That's so nice of you."

Madelyn gave her a knowing smile. "I'm really not the wicked stepmother Parrish considered me, you know."

"Uh, well, we didn't really talk a lot about family," Livvy lied.

"It was partly my fault. I'd never been able to have children of my own, so I desperately wanted Parrish to embrace me as a mother. Her own mother ran off when she was essentially a baby, so she had abandonment issues, and then, right when she's a teenager, along comes this rival for her daddy's affections. She resented me from the beginning, and I resented her for making things difficult in my marriage, for essentially forcing Ric to choose between us. It was always a power struggle, especially if we made the mistake of showing our affection to each other in front of her. She'd never had to consider her dad as a sexual being."

Eeeewwwww, Livvy thought. *Waaaayyy too much information.*

"Must have been tough," Livvy mumbled, anxious for the conversation to end.

Madelyn sighed. "I have so many regrets. And now it's too late." She studied Livvy intently. "You probably have a great relationship with your mom, right?"

"Yeah. She's awesome. Raised me all by herself. We're more like sisters than mother-daughter," Livvy lied again. It was getting to be a habit.

"Hold on to that," Madelyn advised.

Livvy texted Felice as soon as she got back to the hotel.

MEET ME IN BREAK ROOM,
STAT!

She watched the little bubbles on her phone, waiting for Felice's response.

CANT. LUNCH CRUSH. SEE
YOU AT 3.

Livvy fed quarters into one of the vending machines in the break room and was munching on a PayDay candy bar when Felice finally strolled in shortly after three.

The chef collapsed onto a chair and shook her head when she saw what her friend was eating. "How do you eat that crap and stay so skinny?"

"Never mind that. Parrish's stepmom showed up at the dorm while I was on lunch break."

"Madelyn? What did she want?"

"She said she was there to pack up Parrish's clothes and stuff. But she was definitely mad that we'd already packed everything up. Like, she tried to be all sweet and nice, but I didn't really buy it, you know?"

"Why do you think she was really there?" Felice brought out a plastic container of fruit and popped a grape into her mouth.

"Maybe she was looking for the bitch book? She didn't want me going into Parrish's room with her. Said she wanted privacy because she was so sad. And then she asked if maybe Parrish had left any stuff out, like, not in the room."

"How would she know about the bitch book? And why would she care?" Felice asked.

"I don't know. It was just a feeling I had. She kept looking at me this weird way. Like she knew I had a secret."

"You watch too much television," Felice said. "In the meantime, I got Charlie Burroughs all up in my grille. He's been raisin' hell with me because I fired our seafood wholesaler, which he then rehired. Which is crazy, because the guy's fish and shrimp are trash."

Livvy bit off a hunk of her candy bar and chewed. "He's gunning for me too. He went to Mrs. E and showed her the crappy review Colonel McBee left on the hotel's website."

"You know what I think? I think Burroughs must be getting kick-backs from these jokers. There's no other reason he'd insist we keep buying their shitty seafood and nasty produce."

"You really think that?"

"Happens all the time in the restaurant and hotel business," Felice assured her. "All kinds of sketchy deals go down."

"But why would he have it in for me? I'm just trying to do my job. Do you think it has to do with McBee?"

Livvy picked up a grape and stared at it. "I'll tell you, though, I do think there's something odd going on with the hotel mattresses.

"Today, I actually went up and photographed the label on the mattress in McBee's room after he checked out. And Sonja, the housekeeper, is supposed to send me pictures of the rest of the labels from the rooms on that wing."

"Wasn't there something about mattresses in Parrish's bitch book?" Felice asked.

"Yeah. I need to go back and see if I can figure out what Parrish wrote."

"We need to try to decipher her scribbles," Felice agreed.

"And in the meantime, what do we do about Mr. Burroughs? I can't afford to lose this job, and I can't stand the idea of having to move back home with my mom."

"I like it here too," Felice said. "I've got a free, safe place to live, a great kitchen to work in, high-class clientele. Finally getting to use some of the skills I learned in culinary school."

"And what about your new bestie?" Livvy teased. "Aren't I part of what you like about working at the Saint?"

"You'll do," Felice deadpanned. "I'll tell you what I'm thinking. Maybe we go see Mrs. E. She's the one who hired us in the first place."

"Don't you think that'll get us on Burroughs's shit list?"

"Like we weren't already?"

"Speaking of Mrs. E, here's another weird thing. I think she was sitting in the lobby today, wearing a disguise!"

"What? Like a wig and fake glasses?"

"More like a golfer girl getup, with a hat pulled down low over her face, and sunglasses. She acted like she was reading a magazine, but I think she was kinda spying on me."

"That *is* weird," Felice said. "Come to think of it, she had lunch at the Verandah today." She related how their boss had ordered three different seafood entrées and sent instructions through Garrett to take the grouper fingers off the menu.

Livvy looked at her phone and stood up. "I better go. If Mrs. E is running surveillance on me, I don't want her thinking I'm some kind of slacker."

Felice stood up too. "Oh, hey. I almost forgot. One of the servers heard some members talking about how Mrs. E's father-in-law died today. So, was he Parrish's grandfather?"

"Yeah. I think he'd been sick for a while." Livvy shrugged. "That'll make my mom happy. She's got some kind of major grudge against the whole family."

"Maybe you should call her and share the good news."

"I would, but I'm currently not speaking to her."

Felice rolled her eyes. "Talk about a grudge. Maybe you should get over being pissed at her. You don't know how lucky you are that your mom is still around to be pissed at."

Traci turned back to her computer. She checked the previous evening's report. They'd been at 70 percent capacity, which wasn't stellar, especially in what should be the Saint's high season, but this weekend was already a sell-through, which was a relief.

When she looked at their occupancy trends she saw that midweek bookings were lagging behind the previous year's data for the same time period.

The hotel's marketing team were urging her to start some down-pricing offers, but she'd resisted the idea, because Hoke had drummed it into her head that the Saint kept its exclusive status because the hotel *never* discounted.

But times had changed, and there'd been a widely publicized unsolved murder on the premises, which she knew had prompted a rash of cancellations.

Selena, the head of marketing, was a proponent of dynamic pricing, a sliding scale that offered last-minute deeper discounts on unsold rooms, which would be promoted across social media. According to her, it would bring the hotel younger guests who might never have been able to afford a stay at a hotel like the Saint, and more important, as Selena kept repeating, "Traci, an empty room does us no good. We need heads in beds."

Selena was right, she concluded, after studying long-range bookings for the summer. She clicked on her latest email and agreed to the new marketing plan, which Selena was calling "Come Summer at the Saint." The plan wasn't cheap—it included online advertising—but she remembered another of Hoke's aphorisms, one she knew was handed down from his father. "Ya gotta spend money to make money."

When she'd finally waded through as many memos and emails as she could stomach for one day, she looked up and it was nearly seven.

She called the Verandah and placed her dinner order. If she hurried, she'd have just enough time to pick up dinner, run home, shower, and change out of her golfing disguise.

CHAPTER 52

* * *

Felice met Traci at the employee entrance to the kitchen with the takeout order.

"Mrs. E . . ." Felice started. "I know Mr. Burroughs is pretty mad at me. And I just wondered if you'd put in a good word for me, because I really need this job. I love my work."

"Leave Charlie to me," Traci said. "The only opinion that matters is our guests', and they love your food. And so do I."

Felice's face nearly cracked open with her grin. "Oh, wow. Thanks!"

"We need a new seafood supplier," Traci said. "That grouper for today's special was frozen and not locally caught. And while you're at it, maybe we look into growing more of our own produce here at the Saint. We grow the annuals and perennials we use in landscaping, so why not put the hothouses to work with vegetables too?"

"That would be amazing. And I've already met with a local fisherman. He's a shrimper and his brother is a commercial fisherman. I can buy their stuff right off the dock."

"That sounds good, but you'll want to make sure they can provide the quantity we need," Traci reminded her. "In the meantime, what have you fixed me for dinner tonight?"

"You've got an appetizer of seared scallops with a pomegranate and Meyer lemon coulis, and I guarantee the scallops are fresh.

The salad is local tomatoes, peaches, basil, and burrata over arugula with a balsamic drizzle. Dessert is mini chocolate mousse
cheesecake."

"And the entrée?"

"A couple of little filets, for grilling, and two sauces . . ."

"That sounds sinful," Traci said, taking the takeout package from
the chef.

"Or Saintly," Felice said. "Let me know how you like the scallops."

"I will," Traci promised.

After she'd showered, Traci changed into a block-printed blue-
and-white caftan that was probably supposed to be a bathing suit
cover-up, but which she liked for its lightweight ease.

She twisted her hair into a messy French knot and was just about
to apply lipstick when the doorbell rang, setting Lola into a frenzy
of shrill barks, and her pulse racing.

"Lola, hush," she called, padding barefoot to the door.

Whelan stood in the doorway with a bottle of wine tucked under
each arm and a handful of daisies.

"Come in," she said, feeling her cheeks suddenly redden and
heat. Was this the first time she'd entertained a man, alone, since
Hoke? With a start, she realized it was.

Lola was still barking and now lunging at Whelan's ankles.

He leaned down to pet the dachshund, but Lola bared her teeth
and growled a warning.

"I'm sorry. She's not usually like this," Traci said, reaching for the
flowers. "For me?"

"For you, from you. I swiped them from the perennial beds near
the tennis courts. They were starting to get a little crowded, so I
pruned 'em. So to speak."

"Let's go into the kitchen and I'll get them in some water," Traci
said. He followed her through the house, taking in the gleaming
dark-stained hardwood floors, the creamy plaster walls, and arched,
vaguely Moorish-inspired doorways.

294 MARY KAY ANDREWS

The furniture tended toward dark, heavy antiques, stiff satin-covered sofas, and elaborately swagged and fringed brocade window treatments.

"The kitchen is right through here," Traci said as they passed through the dining room. Whelan paused to gaze at an enormous gold-framed portrait of a blond woman with one of those stiff '70s hairdos. She was dressed in a fancy hot-pink cocktail dress and seated in a fan-back rattan chair. Standing on either side of her were two little boys, dressed in fussy-looking smocked shirts, short pants, and high knee socks.

"Family?"

"My late mother-in-law, Helen. And that's Hoke, on the left, and Ric on the right."

Traci pretended not to notice Whelan's scowl when she mentioned her brother-in-law's name.

"The painting was hanging here when we moved into this house. Hoke wanted to take it down, but I didn't want to hurt his mother's feelings, and I guess I've just gotten used to seeing it there."

She gestured around at the living and dining room, which opened up through a series of arched doorways. "Helen hired a very famous Palm Beach designer to decorate this house."

"You don't mind living with another woman's taste?"

Traci shrugged. "I didn't grow up in a family with a lot of money or inherited things."

The kitchen was dated-looking and small, compared with the grand scale of the other rooms he'd seen. White cabinets, white appliances, yellow Formica countertops, and a small center island with a pair of yellow-vinyl-cushioned barstools.

She noticed Whelan's look of surprise. "My mother-in-law wasn't much of a cook. She used to say her favorite thing to make for dinner was reservations at the Verandah. We always intended to rip this out and enlarge it into the dining room to make it one larger, more casual space. Instead we bought a lot to build on. But . . ."

Whelan sniffed expectantly. "I take it you *do* cook?"

"When I have time, which I haven't lately. Tonight's dinner was catered by Felice, at the restaurant." She recited the menu as the chef had dictated it to her.

"Want me to open the wine?" He noticed a couple of wineglasses and a corkscrew on the counter. "What'll you have?"

"We could start with the white, or I've got a full bar over there." She pointed at a vintage rattan bar cart stocked with a dozen liquor bottles, mixers, a crystal ice bucket, and a bowl full of sliced lemons and limes.

"It's so hot out, how about a gin and tonic?" Whelan asked.

"Fine, I'll let you bartend while I get these appetizers plated up."

They sat at the kitchen island and sipped their drinks and devoured the scallops, filling the first few awkward minutes with idle chitchat about childhood pets, music, and anything that came to mind until the liquor had time to tamp down some of Traci's anxiety.

It took major effort not to stare at the man sitting across from her. He was probably a few years older than her, and his reddish-blond hair, which touched the collar of his pale blue polo shirt, was streaked with more than a little silver. His skin was weather-beaten and his hands bore the scrapes and calluses of someone who used them to make a living. His build was stocky, but muscular, and he wore faded jeans and Topsiders, with no socks.

He wore no jewelry except for a watch. And there was no telltale tan line on the ring finger of his left hand.

Not that Traci was interested. The man was an employee. That would be weird.

She busied herself ferrying the salad plates and wineglasses into the dining room.

"Here. Let me help." Whelan took the wineglasses and grabbed the bottles and the corkscrew.

She'd set their places at the end of the dark walnut table. Whelan set a glass at each place. He pointed at the salad. "Peaches and tomatoes, I get, but is that cottage cheese? I haven't had that since my grandma's house."

Traci laughed. "It's burrata, and it's very on trend. Sort of a soft, whipped mozzarella."

He tasted and nodded vigorously. "Damn, this is good."

"Are you a grilling kind of guy?" she asked, getting up to clear their plates.

"Always. It's the thing I miss most in my rat-hole of an apartment. No place to grill."

"You're in luck tonight," Traci told him. "We've got filet mignon and they're seasoned and ready to go, I just need someone to man my grill pan. I confess, I'm totally intimidated by it. Once that fat starts sizzling I panic and either take the steaks off too early or too late."

True to his promise, Whelan turned out to be a grilling ninja. Lola stationed herself under Traci's chair and whined and begged until Traci relented by tossing her the one tiny morsel she had left on her otherwise clean plate.

"Let's take dessert out to the screened porch," Traci said, pointing to the pair of French doors in the living room.

Traci sat on one of a pair of rattan pretzel chairs and Whelan seated himself opposite her with a glass of red wine and the chocolate dessert, which Traci pronounced herself too full to try.

The evening had cooled considerably, but a ceiling fan whirred overhead and the pinprick of fireflies flashed in the low-hanging branches of a gigantic live oak tree that shaded most of the backyard.

"This is nice," Whelan said. The backyard was smallish, but landscaped with colorful beds of ferns, caladiums, blue-and-pink blossoming hydrangeas, and the thickest, greenest grass he'd ever seen. "You take care of this yourself?"

"God, no. Junior, who is officially retired from the hotel now, does everything, including planting all the annuals and perennials. It's his baby, and he takes huge pride in his work."

"I've noticed that with quite a few of the folks who work at the Saint," Whelan said.

"Treat people right, and they'll do right by you, my dad always said."

"Are your parents still living?"

Her smile faded. "My mom is. They moved to Arizona twelve years ago after Dad retired, and Dad passed away a couple years later."

"And your mom stayed in Arizona?"

Traci picked up her wineglass and swirled the dark liquid before taking a drink. She knew what he was getting at. "They were living in one of those 'active adult communities.' Mom has her ladies she plays bridge with, her book club, and her church friends."

Whelan nodded, but she could see he still didn't quite understand.

"I love my mom, and I know she loves me, but we were never very close. She doesn't understand my life, what I do. After Hoke died, she couldn't believe I wouldn't just move away from here. From the memories."

"You never considered doing that?"

"Not really. We were finishing up the remodel of the hotel. I couldn't just walk away from the thing that had been his passion, and mine."

"Good marriage?" Whelan quirked one eyebrow.

Traci lifted her chin. "I think so. We were happy. We had so many plans . . ." Her voice drifted away. She was ready to close down this discussion.

"How about you?" she said. "Any family?"

Whelan stood abruptly. "Another glass of wine? It's Friday night, you know."

"Yeah, it is. No curfew for me, right?"

When he came back he set her glass carefully on the glass-topped table, but she noticed he hadn't refilled his own glass.

"I told you I had something to talk to you about, and I've been avoiding the topic all night," he said.

"Why is that?"

"Truth? I was enjoying the evening. A nice dinner, nice wine, especially nice company. I didn't want the nice part to end when I brought up the unpleasant stuff."

Now it was her turn to blush. "I've had a nice night too. As you might have guessed from Lola's reaction to you, I haven't had a lot of male company in recent years."

He laughed. "What about Junior?"

"Oh, Lola adores Junior, because he always arrives with a pocketful of doggie treats."

"I'll have to remember that for the next time."

Would there be a next time? Traci was surprised to realize she hoped there would be.

He took a deep breath. "Okay. You asked about family. I have some cousins on my dad's side, but we're not close. They're scattered all over the country, and I've led sort of a nomadic life myself. And then there's my stepfather."

His lips tightened. Traci gathered they were about to wade into the not-so-nice portion of the evening. She took another gulp of wine and waited.

Whelan gazed out at the backyard. A barred owl hooted from the darkness, and another hooted back. The thrum of cicadas nearly drowned out both.

"Your stepfather?" Traci prompted.

"Guess I should back up a little."

He told her about his follow-up phone call to Mike Sullivan.

"Sullivan told me that after my visit, he reached out to his older sister and brother, who'd also been at the Saint back then. The sister was fourteen, and she remembered the flashy car, but didn't know what kind it was. But the brother remembered. It was a very specific, very expensive Corvette."

Traci's mouth went dry. "A red Corvette?"

"Yeah. And then I tracked down another teenaged girl who hung out at the beach at the Saint that summer. And she remembered the Corvette's owner."

"Ric," Traci said, her hand shaking a little as she took another gulp of wine. "Ric Eddings. Hoke thought the 'Vette was a metaphor for his brother's obsession with the size of his dick. He called it Ric's little red dick."

Whelan rolled his eyes.

"I hadn't seen Brad, my stepfather, since the day of Hudson's funeral. So I looked him up online. He's living in Myrtle Beach, where he runs a program to help homeless veterans."

"Sounds like a very noble way to spend your retirement."

"Brad certainly thinks so. He's found Jesus. Refers to himself as 'Brother Brad.'"

"Did he tell you anything you didn't already know?"

"Yeah. After Hudson died, he was thinking of suing the Saint for negligence."

Traci's face went pale thinking back to that day. "Shannon and I, we did CPR, we did everything we were trained to do, but he was already—"

"It turns out there was nothing else you could have done, unless you had an EpiPen."

Her brow furrowed. "I don't understand."

"The county medical examiner attributed Hudson's death to drowning, but Brad was suspicious. He hired a private investigator, and then he had his own autopsy performed. The pathologist he hired discovered that Hudson died of anaphylactic shock."

"Like, from a bee sting? There were always yellow jackets around, because all the kids left Coke cans sitting around. We had to spray the pool area down with bug spray twice a day."

"It wasn't a bee sting. Hudson had an undiagnosed peanut allergy. And not long before he went to the pool that day, someone gave him a big bag of candy, most likely peanut M&M's, which he gorged on."

"The stranger in the red car, who handed Hudson a paper sack? You're saying that was Ric? Why? Why would he do that? And do you think he did it intentionally?"

"According to Brad, his investigator discovered that Kasey—my mom—was having an affair with a younger man who was around a lot that summer. They surmised that Hudson had probably seen something he shouldn't have. Maybe he let the boyfriend know what he'd seen, and maybe the boyfriend gave him the candy as a bribe—to keep his mouth shut."

Traci mulled it over, picturing Hudson, the pesky, skinny sunburnt kid, and Ric, tanned, bare-chested, cruising the island with the top down in his penile extension, flirting with any pretty girl that caught his eye. He'd even hit on Traci more than once, until Hoke, her placid, peace-loving Hoke, threatened to knock his brother's teeth down his throat.

"Brad claimed the PI couldn't find who Kasey's lover was because he couldn't get access to witnesses. Your father-in-law saw to it that he couldn't get past the front gates."

"But you don't believe Brad? Why would he lie about that detail now? Hudson's dead, your mom is gone."

"He didn't know my mom was gone until I told him this afternoon," Whelan said bitterly. "He divorced her within a year."

"Then, why?"

"Money. I'm positive once Brad found out Ric Eddings was sleeping with my mom, and that he was at least partially responsible for Hudson's death, he and his attorney went to Fred Eddings and threatened not just to sue, but to put the whole messy business, and the Saint, right in the public eye."

"Fred bought off your stepfather? Paid him to walk away? From his own son's death?" Traci shuddered. "Dear God. I don't know why I'm surprised, but that's so sordid. And unconscionable."

"Brad told me he never told Kasey about the PI, or what the second autopsy showed, because she was already despondent over Hudson's death. But I'm ninety-nine percent positive he kept it secret because as soon as he found out about the affair, he saw a payday coming. He never told Kasey he'd gotten a settlement. She never knew what had really happened. Brad made sure she paid for being 'an adulterer,' as he put it, and not just with the loss of her little boy's life. She left the marriage with nothing. She was broken."

Traci pushed the glass of wine away. "I feel sick."

Whelan nodded. "It's a lot."

"No. I mean physically sick." Traci jumped up, pushed the screen door open, and barely made it to the bottom of the steps before she was doubled over, vomiting into a bed of ferns.

Whelan waited a minute, then went to her. Her hair had come undone, so he gingerly reached over and held it off her face. She retched again and he waited. Finally, she straightened.

"Sorry." Her voice was wobbly and she was unsteady on her feet. He helped her back inside the house and she fled to the bathroom, where she washed her face, brushed her teeth, and attempted to fix her hair.

When she emerged from the bathroom she heard water running in the kitchen, which is where she found Whelan, at the sink, rinsing their dinner dishes and stacking them in the dishwasher.

"Well, I'm officially mortified, again," she declared.

"I shouldn't have sprung all that ugly stuff on you. It's a lot. Even for me. My only excuse is that I needed to unburden myself, and there's nobody around who'd understand. Except maybe you?"

Traci nodded. "I'm glad you told me. I'm not glad about what happened to Hudson and your poor mom, but selfishly, it's a relief to know it wasn't our fault—mine and Shannon's, I mean."

The teakettle whistled and she startled at the sound.

"Hope you don't mind. I thought some tea might settle your stomach."

She cocked her head and considered him while he poured boiling water into a mug with a teabag.

"You're a decent man, Whelan."

He slid the mug in front of her. "Please don't let that get out. It'll ruin my tough-guy reputation."

Traci dipped the teabag in and out of the steaming water, before placing the bag in the bowl of her spoon and wrapping the string around it to extract more of the tea.

"Honey?"

"What?" She startled again.

Whelan held up a plastic bear-shaped squeeze bottle, and chuckled.

She covered her face with both hands. "My humiliation is complete. There is nothing else I can do tonight to make a bigger fool of myself."

He slung a dish towel over his shoulder and began attacking the greasy grill pan with a steel wool pad. "I don't think you're a fool. I think you're sweet. Honey."

To cover her embarrassment she blew on her tea to cool it. "So what happens now? You got the answers you came here for. Where to next?"

CHAPTER 53

Whelan rinsed the grill pan and set it in the dish rack. "I guess that depends on you."

A strand of her damp hair had fallen across her forehead and he tucked it back behind her ear.

The tenderness of the gesture was not lost on Traci. She sat very still, trying to process how she felt about that, and about what he was telling her.

Whelan waited, until he realized she was not going to take the bait.

"I told you I'm good at finding things out, but I never explained how I got so good at it. After I got out of the marines, a buddy from my unit and I decided to go into business together. The plan was that we'd do background checks on businesses pursuing government contracts. My friend had some connections in the business. We'd vet their employees and potential employees and make sure they weren't felons or fraudsters."

She looked up from her tea, intrigued.

"My buddy was the data guy. He could find out anything online. We couldn't afford to hire investigators to canvass, so that's what I did. Call people, show up on their doorsteps, ask nosy questions about their neighbors or their nephew or their friend who'd applied for a civilian job on a military base."

"And?"

"It turned out we'd discovered a nice little niche market for ourselves. We hired some folks, all of whom I'd vetted first, of course. We started in California, because it has more military bases than any other state in the US—there are thirty-two, if you're counting. And the business grew from there."

Traci sipped her tea.

"We became crazy successful. Too successful. My buddy was married with three little kids and he never saw them because he was always on a flight to our next market, looking for that next deal. Two years ago, his wife gave him an ultimatum—sell out, or get out."

"And that's what you did?"

He grinned. "Yup. We made an indecent amount of money. My buddy and his family are living large in their dream house in Hawaii."

She gave him a questioning look. "And you're essentially a day laborer who makes, what? Fifteen dollars an hour? Doing backbreaking work in the broiling sun and driving an Uber in your spare time?"

"Living the dream," Whelan affirmed. "But for your information, I'm a crew chief, so I actually make eighteen fifty an hour."

"Why?"

"Why not? I'm easily bored. I'm single, don't need a lot. This is good, honest work. At the end of the day, I can lean on a shovel and see a flowerbed I helped plant or a tree I pruned, and it's something tangible."

"That's not really an answer," Traci said.

"Okay," he relented. "Your niece was murdered on this property, one week ago. I don't see much happening with that investigation. I'm not saying the local sheriff is incompetent, but I am saying I don't see much progress being made. My intention, unless you tell me to stop, is to poke around, ask questions quietly, and see what I can find out. I've got the perfect cover. I actually work on the property, and a day laborer in a work uniform can pretty much go anywhere, with maybe the exception of your fancy hotel, without raising suspicions."

"You really think you can find out who killed Parrish?"

"I can try."

Traci realized she'd been holding her breath, waiting for his answer. She exhaled now.

"There's one more reason for me to hang around," Whelan said. "I find myself endlessly fascinated with the potential to embarrass my beautiful boss."

* * *

The texts began landing in Olivia's inbox at eight on Saturday morning. A series of dings alerted her. She rolled over in bed and grabbed her phone. Six photos in all, from an unfamiliar phone number. She sat up in bed and squinted at the photos, which were fuzzy, but apparently some kind of label, a yellow diagonal slash on a shiny white background.

Suprema Comfort Rest 2000.

"Ahh." They were photos of the mattress labels from the new wing in the Saint. Sonja was an excellent housekeeper, but she was a lousy photographer.

Now what? She pulled Parrish's bitch book from its hiding place and flipped pages until she reached the one with the cryptic entry that she assumed was about the mattresses.

??? why beds bad, just bought all new? Ck w/ pch. Ask CB?

At least, that's how she translated the scribble. There was another line beneath that.

CB sez will tk w/ TE. Something not rite

Parrish's shorthand was a mystery. But she'd definitely been interested in the mattresses. Maybe it was time for Livvy to revisit the warehouse.

She scrolled through the Saint's phone directory until she found the name of the engineering guy who'd met her in the warehouse after her encounter with Colonel McBee, tapped the number, and was relieved when he picked up immediately.

"This is Ronnie. What do you need?"

"Hi, Ronnie. It's Olivia in guest relations. Are you working today?"

"According to my timesheet, yeah."

She laughed at his lame joke. "Is there any chance you could meet me at the warehouse this morning?"

"What's guest relations want in the warehouse?"

He had her stumped, but why did he care? "Something I need to check on."

"Whatever you need, I can check that for you," he said.

"Uh, is there a reason I can't go down to the warehouse like I did last time?"

"New rules. Mr. Burroughs thinks people have been pilfering. Anybody goes in there has to be supervised and sign in and out."

"Huh. Thanks anyway." She didn't want anyone to know what she was looking for.

Charlie Burroughs had instituted new rules. He'd tried to get her fired. Felice too. Could all of this have something to do with the bitch book?

She opened her door. The dorm was quiet, but predictably, the lounge area was a mess, littered with empty beer cans and a pizza box, not to mention the lingering scent of weed. The television was on, but muted.

"Typical," Livvy muttered as she paused outside Felice's bedroom door.

She knocked softly. "Felice?" she whispered. "You up?" She knocked again. "Felice!"

"Hell nah. Go away. It's my day to sleep in."

Livvy jiggled the door handle. Knocked again. "Let me in, Felice. This is important."

The door opened suddenly, and Livvy tumbled inside.

Felice stood with her hands on her hips, glaring at her. She was dressed in gym shorts and an oversized Miami Dolphins jersey.

"What's so important you had to wake me up on my one day to sleep in?"

"I think I might have an idea about what Parrish was writing about in the bitch book."

"That couldn't wait 'til later?"

Livvy showed Felice the page in the bitch book with the note about the beds. "These little chicken scratches? The common denominator is 'CB.'"

"And you think that's Burroughs?"

"Maybe. Here's the other thing. I wanted to get into the warehouse to compare the mattress labels on the beds in the new wing to the ones in storage. Because, maybe, they're not the same beds. I don't know. Maybe I'm grabbing at straws. But the guy I called in engineering says there's a new policy—instituted by Burroughs—that anybody who wants into the warehouse has to sign in and out, and be supervised."

Felice perched on the side of her bed, her pillow clutched across her abdomen.

"I don't like the guy, but why would he want to kill Parrish? Over some mattresses?"

Livvy tapped the bitch book with her fingertip. "What if he was ripping off the hotel? I don't know—substituting cheap mattresses for expensive ones? Parrish figured it out, after she saw the McBees' mattress, and what if she threatened to tell her aunt? Like, maybe this first line is questioning why the beds are bad, and she's making a note to check with purchasing? That's what 'pch' could be? And the second note, she's thinking she'll check with her aunt—'TE'?"

"Uh-huhhh," Felice said, leaning forward. "You're saying—maybe it wasn't just mattresses? Maybe there was other stuff going on?"

"Yeah. He could be skimming all kinds of ways. Kickbacks for vendors, bribes, embezzlement. Maybe he's cooking the books, ordering mattresses and TVs and stuff—there's a note in the bitch book about TVs, with just a question mark," Livvy said. "And submitting fake invoices or something? I don't know, I got a D in my only accounting class in college."

"But how do we connect all this to Parrish? Burroughs wasn't at the afterparty, right?"

"Maybe he had an accomplice," Livvy said.

"Or two?" Felice gestured toward the doorway.

"Remember, those guys were the ones who volunteered to go out looking for Parrish the morning after the party. And then they decided to clean up the mess. When have you ever known those two slackers to clean up after themselves?"

Livvy sank down onto the floor. "But why? Parrish was their friend. I know Garrett tried hitting on her, but he tried hitting on every woman with a pulse."

"Except me," Felice said drily. "Guess I give off a certain vibe to a certain type guy."

"And KJ? He's so sweet. I just can't picture him doing something like that."

"What if he didn't have a choice?" Felice asked. "What if Burroughs put him up to it? Like, maybe he threatened to fire KJ if he didn't play along."

"But KJ's family is loaded. His granddad's house is that gigantic white one with the columns on Ocean Drive. He doesn't really need to work here. It's just a summer job for him."

"I know that house," Felice said. "It looks just like the plantation house from *Gone with the Wind*. And not in a good way. What if Burroughs threatened to out KJ?"

Livvy stared, with her mouth open. "You really think he's gay?"

"Girl, my gaydar started blipping the minute he moved in here. But he's so deep in the closet, he probably found his grandma's Christmas presents."

Livvy shook her head slowly. "I still can't believe it."

"Does he ever leer at you when you're running around here in your little booty shorts and crop top with your titties hanging out?"

"Well . . . no . . ."

Livvy went to her room and came back with her phone. "Let's check KJ's social media."

She went to Instagram and typed in his name. "It's private," she reported.

"Uh-huh. Now check Garrett's," Felice said.

Garrett's account was public. He had 364 followers and it seemed that most of them were attractive women in their late teens through midthirties. His feed was a kaleidoscope of images of Garrett, surrounded with girls on the beach, surrounded with girls at a bar, at parties in the middle of a knot of girls.

"God, he's a total man-whore," Felice said.

Livvy was studying the photos. She enlarged one of Garrett, soul-kissing a girl with long, dark hair wearing a Saint T-shirt, ripped and altered to display a generous amount of cleavage.

"Hey, this is Chelsea. We worked together. She's a server at the Verandah."

"Not anymore," Felice said. "She's gone. As of last week."

"Did she quit, or get fired?"

"Fired, with a capital F. After lunch service, Garrett called security and they came and walked her ass off the property."

"Huh. Do you know Chelsea's last name?"

Felice scrunched up her face as she tried to recall the server's name. "Something with an S-H. Or maybe an S-C-H. Or S-W?"

Livvy was typing in the Instagram search bar. "Here we go. Chelsea Shalanian?"

"That's her," Felice confirmed.

Livvy pored over Chelsea Shalanian's Instagram feed. "Lot of pictures of her and Garrett for the last two months, but she hasn't posted about anything for the last ten days."

"Check her TikTok account. That girl Chelsea is not the type who goes away quietly."

A few seconds later the two of them were staring in wide-eyed wonderment at an elaborately choreographed TikTok video starring Chelsea and three of her friends, prancing around in their underwear, jumping on beds and screaming, "Fuck you, Garrett!" to a rap beat.

"Day-yummm," Felice murmured.

There were lyrics to the song, so obscene that they made both Livvy and Felice blush, but the repeating chorus was a toe-tapping "F-you, Garrett, you cheating piece of shit."

"There's dragging on the internet, and then there's dragging," Livvy observed. "I'd say the G-man has been well and truly dragged. I'll slide into her DMs and see if she'll talk to us."

"Go ahead," Felice said, yawning. "I'm going back to sleep."

Livvy barged back into Felice's room an hour later, dressed in shorts and a T-shirt. She shook her friend's shoulder, then pulled the covers from her head.

"Let's go. Chelsea's fired up and ready to spill her guts about Garrett, but she's gotta get to work by eleven, so we need to hurry."

Felice turned her back to Livvy. "I don't need to talk to that girl."

"I need backup on this," Livvy insisted. "Are you my wingman or not?"

"All right," Felice grumbled, crawling out from under the covers. "But why don't you just admit it. You're scared of the chick."

"Damn straight. I saw that video."

CHAPTER 55

* * *

Chelsea Shalanian was seated at a booth in the far back corner of the Koffee Kup in the village.

She scowled when she caught sight of Felice.

"What's she doing here?"

Felice raised both hands in a gesture of surrender. "Whoa! What did I ever do to you?"

"You mean, like, get me fired?" Chelsea shot back.

"Can we please all sit down?" Livvy asked, noticing the stares of diners at nearby tables.

Felice slid into the booth first and Livvy joined her.

"Girl, I swear, I had nothing to do with what happened to you. Don't try to put that on me," Felice said.

Their server was hovering nearby with a coffeepot. Livvy turned to her. "Two more coffees, please, and I'll have a maple bacon doughnut."

"Same," Felice said.

Chelsea sipped her coffee for a moment while she sized up the two women sitting across the table from her.

"Why do you care what happened between me and Garrett?"

"Confidentially? We're, uh, looking into some sketchy stuff going on at the hotel. And kinda wondering if Garrett's involved," Livvy said.

Chelsea picked at the toasted bagel on her plate while she considered the question.

"You mean like switching well liquor for call brands and charging customers for the more expensive booze? And then selling cases of the Saint's booze out the back door? And arranging for his buddies to get comped meals and rooms at the hotel? That kind of sketchy stuff?"

Livvy tried not to express her excitement at this revelation. "Is that true?"

"Shit, yeah. Garrett's got a lot of little side hustles. He's a shifty weasel, for sure."

"And he admitted to you that he was mixed up in this stuff?" Felice asked.

"Not at first. I had a few customers send their drinks back to the bar, complaining the scotch didn't taste like Johnnie Walker Blue, or whatever. After we started hanging out, Garrett told me the next time it happened to come to him and he'd take care of it."

"How did he handle it?" Felice asked.

"He'd tell the customer it was a mistake, apologize, and offer a free round for the table. Same thing with wine, subbing in the cheap stuff. Like, if a table was on their third round of drinks, they were definitely getting the cheap shit, because they were probably too drunk to notice. Him and Wally, the weekend bartender, have some kind of deal worked out."

"Who else knows about this?" Felice asked.

"Don't know. Some of the other servers might have figured it out, but I'm not sure they got tipped out accordingly."

"Did you get tipped out?" Livvy asked.

"In other ways," Chelsea said, smirking.

Livvy leaned across the table, her hands clasped around her coffee mug. "Did Mr. Burroughs know about Garrett's side hustles?"

"Hell yeah."

"No offense, but how do you know that for sure?" Felice asked.

"One night, Garrett was staying over at my place and he got a text, like at two in the morning. He jumped up, got dressed, and then took off like his pants were on fire. Two hours later, he came back, crawled in bed, and acted like nothing happened. But that morning, while he was in the shower, I looked at his phone. And yeah, I swiped his password, I'm a sneaky bitch when I wanna be. And the text was from CB, and it said 'Meet me at warehouse. Now.'"

"You think CB is Charlie Burroughs?" Livvy asked.

"Who else? There were a lot of other texts from him too. I didn't get to read 'em because I heard the shower stop running and I didn't want to get caught snooping."

"Do you know what other side hustles he had going?" Livvy asked.

Felice shot her an unspoken "calm down" look.

"He was getting clothes from the pro shop and reselling them," Chelsea said. "He gave me a silk blouse that cost three hundred dollars for my birthday. He kept all kinds of clothes at my place when we were together, all of it still with price tags, and then it would disappear."

"Did Garrett have anyone else helping him with all his side gigs?" Livvy asked.

"Not at first. But then, that cute rich guy, KJ, I think he valet parks and works at the boutique too? Him and Garrett got pretty tight when they moved into that dorm with y'all."

She pointed at Livvy. "I kinda thought maybe he was having a fling with you. Or Parrish. But he swore y'all were like sisters and brothers."

"More like distant cousins," Felice volunteered.

Chelsea glanced at her phone. She made a face. "Ugh. I gotta get to work."

"You got a new job?" Felice asked. "Where?"

"Whiskers and Wags. My mom's doggie day care place."

"Sorry," Felice said. "Hey, can I ask? Why did you and Garrett break up?"

Chelsea's bored expression got suddenly animated. "I shoulda known a guy who steals from his job and cheats at video games would cheat on me too." She looked over at Livvy.

"I figured out he was screwing around on me. All these texts signed 'M.' Gotta be that chick Misty. Works at the Saint's wellness spa? Calls herself an aesthetician? Gimme a break. She waxes people's coochies for a living. That's her actual job. But I fixed his little red wagon."

Felice grinned. "I can't wait to hear this."

"Yeah, I figured it out, but I didn't say anything for a day. Then, the last night he was at my place, I fixed him a beer with a little surprise in it. He staggered off to bed and passed out. And while he was sleeping, I did a little waxing myself.

"I took pictures." She picked up her phone and scrolled through her camera roll. "Wanna see?"

"Noooo," Felice and Livvy said in unison.

"Yeah, it's kinda hard to tell what it is. But if you know, you know." Chelsea winked, then stood abruptly. "Okay, ladies. It's been real."

Livvy and Felice stayed on at the diner after Chelsea left for work.

"Note to self," Livvy said, finishing her coffee. "Never, ever piss off Chelsea."

Felice nodded absent-mindedly, then looked up.

"She said she put something in Garrett's beer that knocked him out. Whoever killed Parrish did the same thing."

CHAPTER 56

* * *

Traci was filling Lola's food bowl on Sunday morning when she heard Ric's ringtone on her phone. She eyed the coffee mug she hadn't yet filled, sighed, and picked up.

"Hi, Ric. What's up?"

He cleared his throat. Traci dreaded what would come next. Throat clearing was Ric's tell, a sign that things were about to get ugly.

"With Dad gone now, I want to get something out in the open. The estate's lawyer is going to be contacting you, but I thought, what the hell, let's get this over with. I don't want any bad blood between us, you know?"

Traci's laugh was mirthless. "You mean, any more bad blood than already exists? Come on, Ric. Drop the act and go ahead and tell me what's going on. It's about the will, right?"

"Yeah, if you want to be crass, it is about Dad's estate. Anyway, a few weeks ago, when I was visiting with him, Dad indicated that he'd been rethinking how he wanted the businesses run long term, after he's gone. And he'd come to the conclusion that he wanted to hire a new lawyer to handle things. Andy Plankenhorn is getting up in years and he's definitely not as sharp as he needs to be. With all the new tax laws in effect for estate planning—"

"Let me stop you right there, Ric," Traci said. "We both know Dad hadn't been verbal in over a year and he could barely move at all. So spare me the song and dance. I know you brought in a new lawyer. I hear he's your frat brother? How convenient."

"Who told you that?" Ric demanded. "That goddamn Alberta—"

"It wasn't Alberta, not that it matters. I know you brought in your buddy and somehow got your dad to change his will. I heard you even videotaped it?"

Ric was getting heated. "This is exactly why I had it videotaped. So there could be no question about the clarity of Dad's mind. He was sick, yes, but Dad knew exactly what his intentions were, and as his only surviving heir, it was up to me to make that happen."

Traci put her phone on speaker and poured her coffee. She added half-and-half and sugar and sat down at the kitchen table.

"Skip to the important stuff, why don't you? You obviously can't wait to tell me how you've managed to screw me over."

At the other end of the line she heard the clinking of ice cubes and liquid being poured. She surmised Ric was having a Bloody Mary kind of morning. And now she wanted one too.

"I resent that," he said finally. "I've treated you as a member of the family since the day you and my brother got engaged, and for you to insinuate that I'm somehow involved in some kind of skulduggery as far as Dad is concerned, is way, way off base."

"Fine. Just tell me what you called to say."

He cleared his throat again, and she felt her gut clench.

"As you know, years ago, when Hoke and I were kids, Dad created Saint Holdings, our parent company. I was given control of the real estate and development piece of the business, and Hoke got the hotel and resort. When Dad set it up, he gave Hoke and me each twenty-four point five percent of the business. Dad retained the rest of the company stock."

"And when my husband, your brother, died, he left his holdings to me," Traci said, trying to sound bored, although her pulse was racing.

"Right." Ric paused and cleared his throat for the third time since the call began. It was, Traci thought, an ominous-sounding pretext.

"Long story short, as Dad's only living heir, I inherit most of his remaining stock in Saint Holdings, although as a gesture of his fondness for you, he left you a twenty percent interest, which I found to be a very touching act."

Traci was doing the math in her head as rapidly as she could. With his original 24.5 percent interest in the holding company, plus the 30 percent he'd inherited from his father, Ric was now the majority stockholder in the family firm.

"I actually am touched," she said cautiously. "But, of course, I retain ownership of the resort and the hotel, thanks to Hoke's careful planning, and not even you and your frat buddy can find a way to take that from me."

She took a sip of her coffee, but it had gotten cold.

"Despite what you think, I'm not some vindictive SOB. Just a savvy businessman who learned from the best. And my sole aim is to protect the long-term financial health of my family's legacy."

"What do you think I've been doing since the day Hoke died? I've not only protected the Saint's legacy, I've enhanced it."

"Come on, Traci, don't you think I'm keeping an eye on your bottom line? I happen to know your occupancy rates for May were down significantly from last year, while your operating costs are up. And last year's revenues were flat. Right?"

How the hell did Ric know so much about her bottom line?

She counter-punched. "How many of those egregiously overpriced building lots did you sell last year, Ric? What's the vacancy rate of your new retail shopping center? Seems like I'm seeing a lot of empty storefronts over there. Lots of unsold units in your fancy new townhouse development too."

"I don't even know why we're having this discussion, but I will say interest rates have been a challenge. I've hired a new sales director, and I'm confident that our long-term forecast is great."

"Yippee for you."

"Look, I didn't call you for some penny-ante debate. I just wanted to play fair and let you know that things are about to change."

It was warm in the kitchen with the morning light streaming in, but she felt a cold chill traverse her body.

"What are you talking about? I own the hotel and resort. There's nothing you can do to change that."

"True. But the real estate your failing hotel and resort are sitting on belongs to the holding company, of which I'm now the majority partner. In essence, I'm your landlord. When Dad formed the holding company, he set up a long-term leasing arrangement for Hoke for a largely symbolic one-dollar-a-year rent. That arrangement lapsed with Hoke's death, but Dad believed it would have been cruel to renegotiate the lease at that point."

Traci was quiet. She felt numb. Since the day her father-in-law died, she'd been essentially holding her breath, waiting for Ric to put his cards on the table. Now he'd done that, and his intentions were clear. One way or another, he would either push her out or buy her out of her hotel.

"So. It's been, what, four years? Given the current economic climate, which you just noted, Saint Holdings is going to have to renegotiate our lease agreement."

The coffee she'd drunk earlier burned in her stomach.

"Traci, are you there?" Ric couldn't disguise the glee he felt, delivering this bombshell.

"I'm here."

"Great. Well, if you look in your email inbox, you'll see I've sent you a copy of the will. Everything is set out in it. We'll be in touch soon with the terms of your new lease."

Traci poured a fresh cup of coffee and called Andy Plankenhorn.

"Andy? I'm sorry to call you on a Sunday morning, but it's kind of an emergency."

"Hello, Traci." She could hear him chewing. "It's all right. Forgive me for talking while I eat, but Georgia's biscuits just came out of the oven."

"I can call back later."

"Not at all. What's the emergency?"

"Ric just sent me a copy of Fred's new will. I've forwarded it to you."

"Oh dear. I don't like the sound of that."

"It's . . . I can't . . ." She had to pause to take a breath, willing herself not to dissolve in tears.

She recounted the conversation she'd just had with her brother-in-law.

Andy sucked in his breath sharply. "Ouch."

"He's going to gouge me, Andy. Raise the rent to an impossible rate. Somehow, he knows our profits are down and costs way up. He's been waiting all this time to pounce, and now, his moment has arrived."

The older man's voice was calm, even soothing. "Let's not panic yet. I'll read the will over, and then I'll call you with my thoughts."

"Okay," she said, taking a deep breath. "Please apologize to Georgia for my ruining your Sunday morning."

"Nonsense. She's babysitting the grandchildren. In fact, she's bringing them over to the Saint to go swimming in the pool this afternoon."

"Tell her to take the kids to lunch and have them put it on my account," Traci said.

"I'll do that. Now, try not to worry. Please?"

She paced the floor while she waited. She took Lola for a walk around the block, started a load of laundry, and tried to read, but concentration was impossible. She couldn't eat, and was afraid if she started to drink she wouldn't be able to stop.

Her phone rang while she was sitting on the screened porch, rocking back and forth in Helen Eddings's old wicker rocker and staring at the garden.

"Well?"

Plankenhorn chuckled. "You know, I can't believe Ric is capable of this kind of conspiratorial villainy." His deep Southern drawl drew out each syllable.

"I can."

The older man chuckled again. "Fortunately for you, he and his lawyer friend aren't nearly as clever as they think they are. Just on the face of what I know of Fred's medical condition from my last visit, it's impossible to believe that this new will could have been his idea, or that he actually had the capacity to execute it."

"Remember, Ric had it videotaped. To show that Fred knew what he was doing."

"The mere act of videotaping it could be construed as a form of coercion, in the eyes of some juries," Plankenhorn said.

"A jury? Oh God. I don't want to have to litigate this."

"I doubt it will come to that," he assured her. "In my opinion there is a major flaw in the way this will has been drawn. And ultimately this will be to your benefit."

"Please, please tell me about this hitch. I desperately need some good news."

"I don't mean to leave you on pins and needles, but I will need to go into the office and do some research. I promise I'll get back to you by this afternoon."

Traci let out a long, anguished sigh. "I'm losing my mind over here, Andy."

"Patience, my dear. Go for a walk on the beach. It's a beautiful morning out."

When she hung up the phone she looked over at Lola. "Wanna go for a walk again?"

Lola turned around, ran into the kitchen, and hid under the table.

"I take it that's a no?"

On an impulse, she picked up her phone, and before she chickened out, called Whelan.

He picked up on the second ring.

"You wouldn't want to go for a beach walk with me, would you?" she blurted.

"Sounds great. I've got nothing else going on. Where and when?"

"Now-ish?"

"Could you be more specific?"

"Meet me here at my place. I'll have the restaurant pack us a picnic lunch and then we can head over to the beach."

"See you in thirty minutes."

After she hung up, she gave Lola an accusing look. "See what you made me go and do? I called a boy and asked him out on a date. At least, I think it's a date."

CHAPTER 57

* * *

It was barely ten o'clock, but already the beach parking lot was rapidly filling and the raked-smooth sand was dotted with dozens of the Saint's pink-and-white-striped umbrellas and bright pink beach loungers.

"What happens if someone dares to bring an umbrella that's, say, yellow, or red, or God forbid, blue?" Whelan asked, surveying the scene from his seat beside her on the golf cart.

"Security would be alerted and the offenders would be dragged off in chains," Traci said. "But, as a practical matter, if you're a guest here, we provide you with an umbrella and lounge chairs, so why would you spoil the ambience by going rogue and bringing something else?"

The golf cart bumped along on a narrow, paved path that skirted the main beach, until the path ended abruptly in front of a large sign warning NO TRESPASSERS. DANGEROUS CURRENTS. NO LIFEGUARDS.

Traci steered around the sign and drove onto the hard-packed sand.

"Mind telling me where we're going?" Whelan asked.

"We call it Secret Beach," Traci said, skirting a bleached-out driftwood tree trunk. "Sometimes there's a wicked riptide. Which is why there's never anyone here."

He raised one eyebrow. "Should I be alarmed?"

"Not at all. Remember, I'm a certified lifeguard, or at least I was twenty years ago."

She slowed the cart again and skirted a long rock jetty that reached a couple hundred yards out into the surf. Two hundred yards from that, she stopped the cart and parked.

In a short time, Whelan had set up yet another pink-and-white umbrella and a pair of lounge chairs, while Traci unloaded the cooler and her beach bag.

Whelan produced the canvas tote bag he'd brought along. "Seems like a rosé kind of day," he said, handing her a chilled bottle.

"Perfect." She stashed it in the cooler, and after a moment of feeling weirdly shy and self-conscious, she pulled off her gauzy white cover-up to reveal a modest black tankini. She adjusted her sunglasses and pulled her hair off her shoulders into a plastic clip, then spritzed herself with sunscreen and handed the bottle to Whelan, who'd already peeled off his T-shirt.

He sniffed the bottle with exaggerated disdain, before applying it to himself. "So girly. Coconut and papaya."

"Sorry," Traci told him. "They were all out of the manly beer and butt-sweat scent."

He stretched out on the lounger with his arms over his head and Traci tried not to stare while appreciating his deeply tanned, slightly dad bod. His black sunglasses hid his eyes, and she hoped her own obscured hers.

"You haven't told me yet why you called," he said.

"Um, I called because it's a beautiful Sunday with low humidity and I was looking for some company, but Lola hates the beach."

He turned toward her and raised his sunglasses. "Try again."

She reached into the cooler and pulled out a couple of water bottles, handing him one and uncapping her own.

"You're stalling."

"How do you know me so well when we've only just met?" She gulped the cold water.

"I'm a professional investigator. I made a living by being observant."

Traci shrugged. "I told you that Ric was trying to screw me over somehow, right? Well, this morning he called to tell me exactly how he intends to do that."

"Something to do with your father-in-law's will?"

She gave Whelan a condensed version of her conversation with Ric Eddings.

"Of course, as soon as I got off the phone with Ric, I called Andy Plankenhorn. He was an old friend of Fred's, and the family lawyer until Ric replaced him with his frat brother. I forwarded Andy a copy of the new will that Ric emailed me."

"And? Is there anything your lawyer can do to stave off the big bad wolf at your door?"

"Maybe. He said he had to go into his office and 'check some things' and he promised to get back to me this afternoon with the details. In the meantime, to keep from going crazy with worry, he suggested I should go to the beach. To keep my mind off . . . things."

Whelan sat up in his chair, took off his sunglasses, and considered her for a moment. Then he leaned over and gently kissed her on the lips.

"So, that's all I am to you? A distraction?" He kissed her again before she could answer.

Traci found herself slowly leaning into Whelan, and the kiss. She wound her arms around his neck, savoring the unexpected tenderness of his embrace.

After a moment, she reluctantly pulled away.

"Is this a good idea?" Her voice was shaky. Hell, her whole body was shaking, vibrating with a combination of lust and apprehension.

"Depends on your point of view," he said. "It felt like a good idea to me, and I sorta got the general impression you were kinda into it too."

"I kinda was," she admitted, with a guilty smile.

She looked around. Their patch of beach was deserted, with the exception of a trio of seagulls who were pecking at something at the water's edge.

"Nobody is watching us," Whelan said, exasperation creeping into his voice. "Nobody cares. We're just two adults, stealing kisses on the beach. What could be better?"

"It's complicated."

"No. You're making it complicated. Here's the deal. I like you, and you don't seem to find me too repulsive . . ."

"Not repulsive. But you're an employee. And this is against company policy. It's right there in the employee handbook. Page four, paragraph seven."

"'The Saint discourages romantic relationships between employees and expressly forbids any expression of such relationships on company property,'" Whelan intoned.

"You looked it up?" Traci was impressed.

"And memorized it word for word."

"But did you see the next paragraph? The one that says—"

He cut her off. "Supervisors are expressly forbidden from pursuing relationships with subordinates. Infraction of this policy will be grounds for immediate severance."

Whelan flashed a wicked grin. "See, that's not a problem. My supervisor is a grizzled sixty-year-old with a beer belly and a mullet, named Manny. And I am in no way interested in pursuing a relationship with him, nor he with me. In fact, he's married."

"But, I mean, we're on company property," she said feebly.

He got up and jogged over to the NO TRESPASSING sign. A minute later, he was back. "According to that sign, this is Bonaventure County property."

"Technically, I guess that's true," she admitted.

He grabbed her hand and pulled her to her feet. "Come on, let's cut the nonsense and go for a swim—at the non-Saint-owned beach. If you're nice, I might let you demonstrate your lifesaving techniques on me."

Traci let herself be dragged toward the water, her hand still clutched in his as they ran into the surf and leapt into the waves.

The shock of the cool water was delicious on her sun-warmed skin.

Whelan released her hand and she dove under, did a scissor-kick, and emerged from the water a few yards away from him.

He swam toward her, doing a lazy crawl.

"You look happy," he said, when he reached her side.

She flung her arms around his shoulders and kissed him hard on the lips. "I am happy," she said, surprising herself. "It's crazy. My professional life is cratering, I might lose my hotel, but right now, in this moment, I feel happy. I've just kissed a hot guy, and I'm at the beach, in the ocean. I haven't swum in the ocean in years. It feels amazing, and right now, that's all I want to think about."

Whelan pointed at his chest. "Hot guy, huh?"

"Totally hot," she said, and kissed him again to prove her point.

While Whelan uncorked and poured the wine, Traci sorted out the contents of the picnic lunch that had been packed at the restaurant.

She opened a waxed paper packet and examined the sandwich, which was on a brioche bun. "Looks like turkey, Havarti, and fig jam. Also arugula." She looked over at Whelan. "Do you have strong feelings about arugula?"

"Nope. I'm arugula neutral." He took the sandwich and bit into it, nodding approval.

She doled out bags of chips and a container of crudités with hummus, then unwrapped another sandwich. "This one's chicken, Swiss, and avocado."

"All for you, my sweet," he said, handing her a plastic cup of wine.

She ate her sandwich and at one point he leaned over and dabbed a bit of mayonnaise from her lower lip, letting his fingertip trail down her neck until she shivered with pleasure.

"This is the classiest picnic I've ever been on," Whelan commented. "We should do this more often." He clicked his plastic wine cup against hers.

"And last, but not least, we have brownies," she said, lifting a box from the bottom of the cooler. "Felice makes the most decadent desserts ever."

He took a brownie, broke off half, and gave it to her. "I am a huge proponent of decadence. Desserts, and otherwise."

Traci was about to bite into her half of the brownie when she heard her cell phone ringing from within her beach bag.

"Oh God." She rummaged through the towels, cover-up, water bottles, lip balm, and sunscreen before unearthing it from the depths of the bag. "This should be my lawyer."

"Traci? I think I have some good news for you," Plankenhorn said.

"How? What?"

"It's too complicated to discuss on the phone. I'm actually headed your way."

"Right now? I'm at the beach, but I can be home and showered in about half an hour."

"No rush. I'm bringing someone with me, and I need to go pick them up first," Andy said.

Whelan was already standing, folding up his lounge chair. "I take it we're leaving?"

"Sorry. That was Andy Plankenhorn. He says he's got good news and he's on the way to my place, and he's bringing someone with him."

"We can have another picnic soon, to celebrate your good news," Whelan said. He leaned over and kissed her again, then began repacking the cooler.

CHAPTER 58

* * *

"Can you do me a favor?" Traci asked Whelan as she pulled the golf cart into her driveway. "I need to shower off really fast before my lawyer gets here."

"And you need me to scrub your back?"

"Not today," she said, laughing at the hopeful expression on his face. "But if you'll unload the golf cart and put everything in the garage, that would be great."

"Consider it done," Whelan said.

When she emerged from the shower dressed in jeans and a T-shirt with her hair still damp, she found him standing in the kitchen, still bare-chested, with a beach towel slung around his hips. He was unloading the remnants of their picnic from the cooler.

"Just take the rest of that home with you," she told him.

"Even the brownies?"

"Maybe leave me just one?"

"You got it. I hosed off the beach chairs and umbrella and stashed them in the garage. I also tried to bribe Lola with a treat, but I think she's still highly suspicious of me."

"I'll have a talk with her," she promised, walking him to the front door with cooler in hand.

"Thanks for today. It was everything I didn't know I needed."

"Any time. In fact . . ."

The doorbell rang, and through the glass sidelights she saw Andy Plankenhorn standing on her doorstep. He was dressed in baggy knee-length shorts, a golf shirt, black knee socks, and white tennis shoes. He was carrying a battered leather briefcase.

"Call me later, okay?" Whelan said. "I want to hear everything."

She opened the door. "Oh, Andy. Hi."

The older man looked her visitor up and down with a bemused expression. "Hello, there."

Traci felt herself blushing. "This is my friend Whelan. We're just back from the beach."

"I see that," Plankenhorn said, his eyes twinkling. He put out his hand to shake and Whelan took it. "Andy Plankenhorn. Attorney-at-law."

"Pleasure to meet you, sir."

Whelan leaned over, kissed Traci on the cheek, and strolled out of the house.

Andy turned to watch him go. "He seems like a nice young fella . . ."

"Come on in," Traci said, her blush deepening. "Can I get you something to drink?"

"Nothing, thanks."

She led him into the dining room and he placed the briefcase on the chair next to him, extracting a manila file folder, which he set on the table.

He removed his glasses and pinched the bridge of his nose, then wiped the smudged lenses on the hem of his shirt. "What I'm about to tell you could be construed, by some, as an ethical violation that could be grounds for my disbarment. However, after long consideration, and consultation this morning with a younger, sharper legal mind, I have concluded that your late father-in-law engaged in such an egregious criminal act that I can no longer remain silent."

"Andy?" Traci said, alarmed. "What are we talking about? I don't want you getting in trouble."

He smiled. "My dear, I am eighty-one years old. It is past time for me to do the right thing."

"I understand," Traci said. "I think."

He opened the file folder and handed her a printout of Fred's recently amended will.

Andy pointed at the front sheet. "You can see I've highlighted in yellow the most important paragraph in this document here."

"He leaves the bulk of his estate to his surviving heirs, right?"

"Correct. His home, investments, personal property, et cetera. Some of your mother-in-law's jewelry was to be left to Parrish, but sadly, with her death, that's a moot point."

"Okay," Traci said, waiting for Plankenhorn to get to the point.

He tapped the highlighted paragraph with his index finger. "This is where things get very interesting. This lawyer's work product contains some fatal flaws. In fact, this is such sloppy work that if I were this man's law school professor, I'd give him a big fat F in trusts and wills."

Get to the point, she wanted to scream, but instead she just smiled patiently.

"Fortunately for you, I believe that this will ultimately work in your favor."

"How so?"

"Two words. 'Surviving heirs.'"

"That's Ric, right? He gets the gold mine, and I get the shaft."

"No." The older man's gaze was fixed on hers. "There actually is another heir. Someone neither Ric nor this lawyer knew existed."

"What? Are you telling me Ric had another child?"

"Not Ric. His father. Fred Senior has another child. A daughter, in fact."

For a moment she was too stunned to speak. "Are you sure? I mean, how is this possible? And how do you know about this secret daughter?"

Andy stared down at his hands. When he looked up, his expression was somber. "Twenty-one years ago, Fred came to me and swore me to secrecy. Then he confessed that he'd fathered a child with a young woman. He claimed it was an accident, a one-time thing, and that the woman, whom he termed 'a little gold-digger,' deliberately got pregnant in order to trap him into making her a financial settlement."

"This is unbelievable," Traci said. "Where is this daughter now?"

"I'll get to that. Fred being Fred, he demanded the young woman provide proof that he was the father. The paternity tests confirmed her claim. Shortly after this daughter's birth, Fred had me draw up a legal document. He agreed to pay for the young woman's college education and to pay off the mortgage on the mother's home. In addition, there was a one-time fifty-thousand-dollar settlement, which was to be used for the child's maintenance. In return, the young woman had to sign a nondisclosure agreement."

"And he never saw his own daughter?"

"Not to my knowledge," Plankenhorn said. "I didn't meet the mother myself, until she came to my office to sign the paperwork, which is when she told me her side of the story. She was young and naïve. I've always felt badly that she didn't have adequate legal counsel, but I told myself that I had a fiduciary responsibility to my client. Going along with Fred, being a party to that shameful act, remains the biggest regret of my legal career."

Traci looked the older man squarely in the face. "And yet, you remained friends. And stayed on as the family's attorney."

"I kept doing business with him, yes. But the friendship ended. When I told Georgia what Fred had done, not naming names, of course, she was furious—gave me a tongue-lashing and said she never wanted to see him again. Helen was incredibly hurt. She and Georgia had been dear friends."

Traci got up and paced around the dining room. "Are you going to tell me who the young woman is? And the identity of her daughter?"

"I'm going to let her tell you herself. She's waiting, out in my car."

He picked up his phone and tapped a number on his contact list. "It's time," he said.

CHAPTER 59

* * *

The front door opened, and she heard the sound of footsteps in the hallway. Traci stopped dead in her tracks when she saw the woman standing there.

"Shannon?"

Her oldest friend was looking up at the high, wood-beamed ceiling, down at the black-and-white-checkerboard tile floor, running her hands across the rough-troweled plaster walls.

Finally, she turned to Traci. Her pale blue eyes were red-rimmed.

"Hey," she said.

"I can't believe this," Traci said, trying not to stare.

"It's true."

"Olivia? Fred was her father?"

"Afraid so."

"I don't know what to say. All these years. And you never, ever hinted."

Shannon bit her lower lip. "Now you know why. He made me sign that NDA."

Traci hesitated, then reached out and touched Shannon's hand. This time she didn't pull away. "Come in. Please?"

"Yeah. I guess it's time, huh?"

When they arrived in the dining room they found Andy Plankenhorn had packed up his briefcase. "I think I'll leave you two ladies now. I promised Georgia I'd meet her and the grandkids at the pool.

I'm sure you'll have more questions for me, but this is a start." He nodded at Shannon. "Call me when you're ready to leave, and I'll pick you up."

"No need," Traci said quickly. "I can give her a ride."

Shannon was staring at the Eddings family portrait, her expression one of pure poison.

"How can you stand to look at them, knowing who and what they are?"

"I didn't know then. The painting was hanging in the house when we moved in, and I didn't want to hurt Helen's feelings by taking it down."

Shannon gestured at the heavy furniture and ornate window treatments. "All this funeral-parlor-looking stuff? None of it looks like you. So, how come you kept all of it? Not like you couldn't afford to buy something else."

"Family heirlooms," Traci said, knowing how lame it sounded. "Helen picked out all this stuff."

"She's dead," Shannon said bluntly. "They're all dead now, except for that bastard Ric."

Traci tried to look at the painting, to see what Shannon was seeing, and her stomach turned. She took the portrait down and set it on the floor, facing the wall.

"Let's go into the kitchen. I've got some iced tea. Unless you want something stronger?"

"I don't drink. Remember?"

Traci didn't trust herself to drink now. She was afraid if she started, she might not stop. They sat at the table with their glasses of iced tea, each waiting for the other to speak first.

When she couldn't take another second of the silence, Traci blurted out the question that had been on her mind since Andy Plankenhorn's bombshell had landed. "Does Livvy know?"

"Not yet. I needed to see you first."

"It's a lot," Traci said. "Do you want to tell me about it?"

Shannon plucked the lemon slice from the rim of her glass and squeezed it into the tea.

"I wanted to tell you, you know. Not at first. I was still pissed at you. But later, after Livvy was born, I needed you to see how beautiful she was. And my mom, well, you know how she was. She loved Livvy instantly, but she was ashamed that her daughter was 'an unwed mother.' Can you believe people still talked like that?"

"Don't be too hard on your mom. She was a sweet lady. Just . . . old-fashioned."

"And set in her ways," Shannon agreed. "I warn you, I haven't talked about this to anyone since I met with Mr. Plankenhorn, twenty-one years ago. I might, kinda, choke up."

"I've got time. And plenty of tissues," Traci said.

"It was maybe a week before Hudson drowned. Mr. Eddings, that's what I thought of him as back then, left a note in my locker and asked me to meet with him, at his house. He hinted it was about a promotion. More money."

Shannon rolled her eyes. "Yes, I know now that it was a stupid thing to do, but at the time, it didn't occur to me to ask why at his house, and not at the office. I went straight there from work, on a Friday night. I was still wearing my lifeguard swimsuit, with just a pair of gym shorts over it. I was shocked when the old man answered the door. I guess I expected, like, a butler or something. He was in this sort of bathrobe thing. Said he'd just gotten out of the pool. He showed me into his office. I was kinda starstruck by the house, you know?"

"Yeah. That mansion was amazing. I had the same reaction the first time Hoke took me home to meet his parents," Traci said.

"So, we're in his office and he asks me if I want a drink. I was nineteen! I thought it was cool that I was day drinking with the boss. He actually fixed me a martini. I'd never had anything stronger than beer or the watered-down margaritas we got at Pour Willy's, and yeah, it went right to my head. I didn't realize, at first, how much he'd drunk before I got there."

"Oh God. I think I know where this is headed," Traci said.

"If only I had," Shannon said bitterly. "He tells me he's been watching me at the pool, thinks my personality would be great in convention sales. It'd mean a lot more money, travel. I was *so* broke. My car needed a new transmission. And travel? Hell yeah. The farthest I'd ever been from home was Disney World for our senior class trip. It sounded like a dream job.

"He's slamming back the martinis, and now I'm starting to get a little nervous," Shannon continued. "Especially after he insists I call him by his first name instead of 'Mr. Eddings.'"

She stopped and sipped her iced tea. "And he tells me that for this new job, I have to look the part. I'll need to wear really chic, classy clothes."

Her hands were shaking so badly the ice cubes rattled in the glass. "Oh God, oh God. This is the part . . ."

Shannon started to cry. Traci handed her a box of tissues. "You don't have to do this," she said, but Shannon shook her head violently, crying and hiccupping at the same time.

When she could catch her breath she resumed her narrative. "He had a dress he wanted me to try on. It was silk, and it still had the price tag on it, like, four hundred bucks. I'd never owned anything that nice. I went into the bathroom that was attached to his office, and as I was undressing, the door opens. It was him. I just froze."

Traci reached across and grabbed her friend's hands and squeezed.

"He was naked." Shannon put her head down on the kitchen table and sobbed.

"It's okay, Shan," Traci murmured, stroking her friend's shoulder. It wasn't until the tears were streaming down her own face that she realized she was crying too.

Shannon raised her head, grabbed some tissues, and blew her nose. "The worst part was, I wasn't really drunk. Tipsy maybe. And I wasn't drugged. I should have known better. As soon as I saw him in that bathrobe, I should have left. I wasn't some innocent virgin, Trace. I should have known what he wanted. I should have made him stop."

"No, Shan! None of this is your fault. He was an adult. A predator. He must have had it all planned out—the job offer, the dress . . ."

Shannon's face was red and blotchy from crying. "I told him to stop. I told him I'd scream and his wife would hear me. He laughed and said his wife was out of town."

She gulped and hiccupped. "He didn't use a condom, because he said he'd had a vasectomy, the lying bastard. When it was over, he gave me a hundred dollars. I threw it in his face. He said if I ever told anyone what we'd done—what *we'd* done!—he'd make sure I never got another job in Bonaventure County. I would have died of shame before I ever told anyone."

"Even me? Your best friend?"

"Especially you. Things were serious between you and Hoke. I was furious—and jealous."

"So what happened next?" Traci prompted.

"Hudson drowned, like, ten days later? It was the perfect excuse to get rid of me."

"I wish you could have told me," Traci said softly.

"Me too." Shannon sniffed. "I was so mixed up. I needed a friend."

"When did you find out . . . ?"

"Not until I was almost four months pregnant. My periods were never regular, if you remember. Plus, I was in denial. By then, it was too late. Not that I would have considered anything else. Telling Mama was the worst."

"I can't even imagine that. My mom used to say your mom was up at the church every time they opened the doors."

"Mama sure did love Jesus."

"Poor Jeannie. I bet she was devastated."

"At first she was. But then she said it was the Lord's will. After that, we were okay. I mean, she was still ashamed that I'd gotten knocked up . . ."

Traci's eyes widened. "You didn't tell her what Fred had done to you? It was rape, Shan. You were sexually assaulted, against your own will. What he did to you was a crime."

"I wouldn't allow myself to call it that. I just . . . blocked that day out of my mind. I would not be a victim. I told Mom that it was an older, married man from work. Anyway, she forgave me everything the first time she held Olivia."

"Can I ask? How did the whole settlement thing happen?"

"The minute I found out I was pregnant, I knew I had to grow the hell up. I couldn't be a kid having a kid. So I made a plan. I showed up at his house and rang the doorbell. There were two cars in the driveway, and one was a champagne-colored Cadillac, which I figured had to be his wife's."

"How'd you get past the security gates?"

"Remember that smoking-hot security guard, Omar?"

Traci laughed and fanned her face. "How could I forget Omar?"

"He was a sweetheart. The day I went back to the Saint, he was working the gate. I told him I needed to go clean out my locker and he waved me through."

"Damn, you're good," Traci said admiringly.

"The old man answered the door," Shannon went on. "He tried to close the door in my face, but I stuck my foot inside, and I leaned in and I whispered, 'I'm pregnant, you son of a bitch. And if you don't let me in and deal with this, I will find a way to tell your wife.'"

"Damn, Shan! I knew you were ballsy, but wow."

"I still don't know how I had the courage to confront him." Shannon stopped herself. "Actually, I do know. It was my baby. I'd felt her kick and I took that as a sign that I had to do something to take back control of my life. I owed it to her to make sure she'd be provided for."

Traci raised her iced tea glass and tapped it against Shannon's.

"He tried to deny everything," Shannon said. "But, like the kids say, I had the receipts. That night it happened, I went home, took off my bathing suit, stuffed it in my gym bag, and hid it in the back of my closet. Like, I never wanted to think about it again."

"Oh—kay."

"Remember what happened a few years earlier? Bill Clinton and Monica Lewinski and the blue Gap dress? Same. I took my bathing suit with me, and I waved it in his face. Told him I had proof. He called me every name in the book. When he finally quit yelling at me, I told him what I wanted."

"Badass," Traci murmured, shaking her head in admiration. "Total badass."

"Maybe. I was so dumb. All I asked for was money so that I could finish college, after the baby. And money to take care of her. And that was it. I told him I'd be in touch after the baby was born, and I walked out." She shook her head. "Too stupid to live."

"And then?" Traci prodded.

"And then Livvy was born. Mama knew a lawyer from church. He wasn't much of a lawyer, but we didn't know that. We trusted him. He contacted the old man. Sent him a photo of Olivia. And again, the piece of shit tried to deny being the father. He said he needed proof. So we did a paternity test. And there was no way he could wriggle out of it."

"Is that when Fred brought in Andy Plankenhorn?"

"Uh-huh. My lawyer said the old man should be on the hook for more than just my college and some money for the baby. Since the plan was for me to live with Mama, he said we should ask for her house to be paid off, and for a settlement to pay for Olivia's upkeep and education. Fifty thousand? I thought it was all the money in the world. I had no idea what day care or pediatricians or orthodontists cost. Or designer sneakers or cell phone plans . . ."

Shannon leaned back in the kitchen chair, staring up at the ceiling. "How's this for irony? Indirectly, I probably ended up pregnant because I was desperate not to live under the same roof with my strict mother. But if it hadn't been for her, Livvy and I would have been homeless. And now, Olivia goes to work for you here at the Saint, the absolute last place on earth I wanted her to be, because she was sick of living with *me*."

"I can do you one better," Traci said with a wry smile. "According to Andy Plankenhorn, when Ric got his dad to draw up a new will specifically designed to screw me over, he managed to screw himself over instead. Now, it looks like he gets to share his inheritance with Livvy."

Shannon drank the last of the iced tea. "That's what he told me when he called me this morning. I'll believe it when I see it."

"Andy knows what he's talking about, Shan. Livvy is going to own a sizable chunk of Saint Holdings. And there's nothing Ric Eddings can do to stop it."

"How's that make you feel? I mean, from what Mr. Plankenhorn said, she'll own a bigger share of the business than you. How is that even possible?"

"At first, I'll admit, I had mixed emotions. But maybe it's not such a bad thing."

"Huh?"

Traci smiled. "I know I've already told you this, but, Shan, Livvy is extraordinary in every way. You've done an awesome job of raising her by yourself." She sighed. "You're so lucky. I'd give anything to have a daughter like her."

Shannon tilted her head. "How come you and Hoke never had kids? You always used to talk about having five or six kids when we were growing up."

"We tried," Traci said wistfully. "We saw a fertility specialist down in Jacksonville. Turned out, Hoke had mumps when he was three, and it affected his sperm count. We were looking into adoption when he died."

"I'm sorry. I can't imagine what my life would have been like without Livvy."

"It's probably why Parrish and I were so close. She was the daughter I never had. It used to enrage Ric."

"And then you lost her too," Shannon said. "First your husband, then your niece. I'm sorry I've been such a bitch to you, Traci."

Traci waved her apology away. "Let's put it in the past. We were awesome together, back in the day, and we can be awesome together now, if you're okay with it."

"What's our next step?" Shannon asked.

"As soon as you tell Livvy about Fred and the will, we need to set up a meeting with Livvy and Andy and me."

"I'll talk to her as soon as I leave here," Shannon said, studying Traci's face. "This has gotta be weird for you, huh? Finding out that a twenty-year-old might be your future business partner?"

"Weird? Yes. But she's my best friend's kid. She's a natural, Shan. And let's be real—I need her on my side, because otherwise, Ric will squash me like a bug."

Shannon stood up from the table and stretched. "Hate to say it, but I better get home. I've got an early shift in the morning."

Traci dumped the remainder of her tea in the sink. "Then, let's roll."

They were passing through the Saint's security gate when Shannon turned to her. "Before I forget, was the hot dude I spied leaving here earlier Whelan? The guy who came to the hospital to ask me questions about Hudson?"

Traci blushed violently. "Yeah."

Shannon waggled her eyebrows. "A friend with benefits?"

Traci laughed despite herself. This was the old Shannon, the one she'd missed so deeply.

"We'll see."

"Come on! The dude is hot, single, and age-appropriate. I would definitely climb that."

"You can't tell me there isn't a man in your life, young lady," Traci countered.

"Well . . . there is a guy. He's a doctor at the hospital. Five years younger than me, which feels weird, but okay."

"A younger man? Me likey!"

Shannon gave her a friendly arm punch. "We were keeping things on the down-low while Livvy was still living at home with me, but now, well, things have gotten interesting."

"Oooh. So the two of you are playing doctor? And you're the naughty nurse?"

"I didn't say that."

"You don't have to."

They'd crossed the causeway and were on the edge of Bonaventure, listening to the radio, humming along, like the old days. Traci drove by instinct.

"Holy shit," she said, when she pulled the car up to her best friend's house. "I didn't even think to ask, and you didn't say any different. You still live here, right?"

"Yeah," Shannon said. "At least it's paid for."

"Do you still have that snack drawer in the kitchen that your mama kept stocked with Little Debbie cakes?"

Shannon laughed. "Now it's protein bars and kale chips."

"And that bathroom window we used to climb out of to go riding around after curfew?"

"As soon as Livvy hit fifteen, I replaced that window with glass block. And installed motion-activated lights. It didn't stop her from sneaking out, but at least it slowed her down."

Shannon opened the passenger-side door. "Gotta go. Been some kind of Sunday, huh?"

"Yeah. But mostly in a good way. Bye, Shan-a Banana."

CHAPTER 60

* * *

Olivia didn't answer the first time Shannon called her daughter that afternoon. So Shannon texted.

> *Please pick up. This is really,*
> *really important!*

A minute later the phone rang.

"Mom? What's going on?"

"It's complicated, and I need to talk to you in person. Can you come over to the house?"

"Now? No. I'm in the middle of stuff. I need to wash my clothes and pay some bills . . ."

"It won't take long. How about Riordan's then? In an hour?"

"Whatever."

Riordan's was in downtown Bonaventure, across the street from the municipal marina. It was surprisingly busy for a late Sunday afternoon, with boaters coming in hungry after a day on the water. She ordered two iced teas and two turkey club sandwiches, Livvy's favorite. Of course, Livvy kept her waiting for fifteen minutes. Shannon didn't care. It gave her more time to rehearse her spiel.

When Livvy did arrive, she slid onto the bench opposite hers, out of breath, dressed in a faded T-shirt, gym shorts, and flip-flops with her hair pulled back in an off-center ponytail and the sullen expression Shannon had come to expect. Livvy noted her mother assessing her appearance.

"I told you it's laundry day, and I have stuff to do, so don't give me that look, okay?"

Their server appeared at their table with their order. "I didn't know if you were hungry or what," Shannon said.

"Okay, spill," Livvy said, ignoring the food. "But I'm warning you, do *not* start on me about working at the Saint. I'm in a foul mood because I just had to write my college loan check. By the time I get done paying it every month, I've got almost nothing left."

"I don't think you're going to have to worry about that anymore," Shannon blurted.

"What? Did they pass a new law? Overrule an old one?"

"Please slow down and let me tell you this in my own way," Shannon said. She was jiggling her foot and tapping her fingertips on the tabletop, like she did when she was stressed or nervous.

Livvy reached across the table and stilled her mother's hands. "You're starting to freak me out. I promise, I'm listening. Just lay it on me."

"It's about your father. Your biological father. He died recently, and I just found out that he apparently included you in his will."

"The deadbeat left me some old hubcaps? A double-wide?"

"Don't joke about it, Liv, please. I talked to his lawyer this morning, or the man who used to be his lawyer. There's quite a large estate."

"Who is he?"

Shannon hesitated. "Fred Eddings."

"Are you shitting me?" Livvy shrieked. "That gross old man? Is this a sick joke?"

"Shhh." Shannon looked around nervously. People at nearby tables were staring. She'd seen two women who worked at the hospital come in to pick up a to-go order. They'd nodded politely to each other.

Livvy leaned across the table, her voice an angry whisper. "Mom? Talk to me."

"It was the last summer I worked at the Saint. As a lifeguard. He asked me to meet with him, about a new job. At his house. Like the little idiot I was, I went. He, um . . ." Shannon found herself tearing up again. She pushed her plate of food away and tossed money onto the table. "I can't do this in here. People are watching. It's a small town . . ."

"You're right. Let's get out of here." Livvy stood up. She stopped to speak to their server, and Shannon followed her out of the café. "Where did you park?"

Shannon pointed to her car, which was parked at the marina lot across the street.

They got in the car and Shannon rolled the windows down, gulping in the warm, humid air.

She turned in her seat, cupped Olivia's face between the palms of her hands. "I'm so sorry, baby. About all of it. Can you understand?"

"You're saying, what? He raped you?"

"I never allowed myself to call it that, because I didn't want to be a rape victim. I just blocked it all out, wouldn't let myself think about it. But yes, that's what it amounted to. I was only nineteen years old. He was in his sixties. His sons were older than me. And he was the owner of the resort. Afterward, he told me if I told anyone, he'd make sure I never got another job in Bonaventure County. So I didn't tell anyone. Not even Traci."

"And you never went to the police? My God, Mom."

"It was a different time. Somehow, I thought it was my fault. For being stupid enough to go to his house, for drinking the martini he offered me. I was so ashamed, Liv."

"Fucker," Livvy said fiercely, her eyes shining with unshed tears.

Shannon put a finger across her daughter's lips. "Hush. It was a long time ago. It's over and done with."

"I can't believe you never told me," Livvy said. "Did Granny know?"

"Nobody knew. When I found out I was pregnant, I went to him, and I told him he had to help me out, or I would tell his wife."

"Damn, Mom! You were, like, a blackmailer."

"No. I was a terrified, pregnant nineteen-year-old."

"You never thought of getting an abortion? I mean, it was legal then, right?"

"Yes, but I never even considered it. Anyway, the other reason I didn't tell anyone was that the cash settlement he gave me was conditional on my signing an NDA."

"It couldn't have been that much money," Livvy said bitterly. "It's not like we lived it up, buying secondhand cars and shopping for clothes at thrift stores."

"I didn't ask for much."

"How did the NDA happen?" Livvy asked.

"His lawyer was an old friend. He told the guy he'd had a one-time 'fling' with a girl who was now looking for a payday. I never saw the old man again. But when I met the lawyer, who actually seemed like a decent guy, I told him the real story, and I think he believed me."

Olivia turned that over in her mind for a minute. Shannon knew her daughter so well, she could almost see the wheels turning in her head.

"The lawyer you met with this morning who told you about my alleged inheritance—is this the same guy who made you sign that NDA way back when? Why would you trust him?"

"Who else was I going to trust?"

Shannon repeated what Andy Plankenhorn had told her about Fred Eddings's will, and how the new attorney Ric Eddings had hired to rewrite the original will had inadvertently used language that would divide the old man's estate between his living heirs—which would include the daughter nobody knew he'd fathered.

"Mr. Plankenhorn didn't have to reach out to me. The first thing he told me when he called today was how badly he'd always felt about the way the old man treated me. And I believe him. He's a decent man."

"Okay, I get that you trust him. But what exactly does any of this mean?" Livvy asked.

"He didn't go into a lot of details, but it looks like you might inherit a portion of your father's estate that would include—"

"Don't call him that," Livvy said sharply. "He was no father to me. He raped you, knocked you up, fired you, and abandoned both of us."

"Yes," Shannon said, her voice sounding calmer than she felt. It was hot out and her sweaty legs were sticking to the car's vinyl upholstery. She rolled up the windows and turned on the air conditioner.

"Yes, he did all that. For years, I wouldn't say his name out loud. And now you know why I was so panic-stricken when you took the job at the Saint. Ric Eddings is as bad as his old man. And this might sound crazy, but what if someone recognized a resemblance to Fred Eddings?"

"That's nuts," Livvy said. "There's a huge portrait of him hanging in the hotel lobby. Lit up like some kind of shrine. I see his face every day, and I look nothing like him. You hear me? Nothing!" Livvy's face was red and she was shouting again.

"You don't. You're right. You look like my people. Not his." Shannon managed a weak smile. "We have the same weird-looking toes, right?"

"Monkey toes," Livvy said with a nod. "That's what Granny used to call them."

"Same mole on your chin as me. Same annoying cowlick."

"And I got Granny's scary unibrow, which you didn't. Thanks for nothing, by the way."

"We won't call him your father," Shannon said, her voice low and soothing. "You don't ever have to say his name. We can refer to him as the sperm donor."

"Eeewww."

"Olivia," Shannon said, her tone serious. "You're nearly the same age now that I was when you were conceived. I had to grow up fast after that happened, because I had someone I was responsible for. But you're so much more mature and responsible than I was at that age."

"Thanks, I guess."

"And you're going to have a *lot* thrown at you in the coming weeks and months. Ric Eddings is not going to hand over half of his inheritance to you without a fight."

Livvy stared out the window at the boats coming and going in the marina, at sailboats and yachts and people unloading gear from dock boxes.

"Mom, what if I don't *want* their money? What if I don't want to fight? How many times did you tell me how awful the Eddingses were?"

Shannon had thought long and hard about this topic, ever since she'd gotten the phone call from Andy Plankenhorn.

"Because, Livvy, if you *don't* take the money, Ric Eddings wins. And the old man, even though he's dead now? He wins too. But if you do inherit, that money has the power to change your life, in a good way. Remember, I made the old man pay for my nursing school. That allowed me to have a career, a good one, helping other people. His money paid off Granny's house note, so you and I could have a safe place to live. Otherwise, I don't know where we'd have ended up. I don't have to tell you what a struggle it's been for us all these years, because you've lived it. You went out and got a job at the doughnut shop when you were only fifteen, drove the same kind of crappy cars I always drove. But now, if you want, you can pay off those school loans. You can go back to college, any college you want, and not worry about being buried under crippling debt."

Livvy was shaking her head with that oh-so-familiar stubborn set to her jaw.

"I know you claim to like that dorm you're living in," Shannon went on. "But maybe you could buy a house of your own. Think of it, Liv."

Her daughter's eyes widened. "You really think it might be that much money? For real?"

"Probably. And the big thing—the most important thing? People—and it's mostly the ones who've never had any—they say money can't buy happiness. But you know what it can buy? Choices.

The choice to be who and what you want. And maybe, if it's as much money as I think it will be, you can help out other people, and make a difference in their lives too."

Livvy did a little golf clap. "Nice speech, Mom. Did you practice that on the way over here?"

"Repeatedly. Will you think about it, please? Mr. Plankenhorn wants to have a meeting with you and Traci."

"Mrs. E? Why?"

"Because whatever happens with the old man's will directly affects her and the Saint. She's going to need you to be on her side."

"Are *you* on her side? I thought you guys were frenemies."

Shannon winced. "That was all on me. I've wasted half my life hating Traci for something she had nothing to do with. Another thing the old man took from me. My best friend. But we're good now."

Livvy tilted her head, and in the afternoon light, Shannon thought she saw a little of herself at that age. Stubborn, willful, and hopefully, brave.

She reached out her arms, and this time, Livvy allowed herself to be embraced.

CHAPTER 61

* * *

Livvy drove up to the Saint, parked in the employee lot, then walked into the lobby. She stood and stared at the portrait of Fred Eddings. His expression was haughty, imperious. She might have the old man's DNA, but that was the extent of the resemblance.

When she got back to the dorm, she opened her laptop and did a deep dive into her new "family" background.

She found a *Fortune* magazine story that talked about how the old man's father, F. A. Eddings, had moved south from Philadelphia to open a paper bag plant in Bonaventure more than a hundred years earlier, and then bought an undeveloped eight-mile-long island of pine trees and palmettos, and then built a luxury hotel and resort named after his youngest daughter, Cecelia.

"So that's where the name came from," she mused, as the realization slowly settled over her that Cecelia Eddings would be her great-great-aunt.

According to the six-year-old magazine article, the Eddings family's Georgia real estate holdings at the time were worth an estimated thirty million dollars.

"Thirty million?" she breathed. It didn't seem real.

When she emerged from her room, Garrett was in his usual position—sprawled across the sofa in the lounge area, wearing his headset and playing *Call of Duty*.

She gave him a curt nod, then went back into her room to fetch her basket of dirty clothes. In the laundry room, she dumped the clothes in the washer, tossed in a detergent pod, shut the door, and started it. When she turned around, Garrett was standing nearby, leaning against the kitchen counter, drinking from a carton of milk.

"Can you not do that?" she said sharply. "Use a glass like a normal person."

"Why? It's my milk, and I don't feel like having to wash a glass."

"Like you've ever washed a glass in your life," Livvy muttered. She reached around him, got a liter bottle of her favorite Diet Dr Pepper from the bottom shelf, and poured some into a glass, placing the half-full bottle back into the fridge.

"So," Garrett said. "Heard you been talking to Chelsea about me."

A cold prickle ran down her spine. *How the fuck????*

"We ran into each other in town," Livvy said.

"Don't believe that chick's bullshit," he said. "She's a lying whackjob. Did she tell you what she did to me?"

"She, uh, mentioned it."

"Yeah. I coulda had her arrested for sexual assault, you know that? One of my buddies is a sheriff's deputy. He coulda slapped the handcuffs on her, thrown her in the slammer."

"Why didn't you?"

"I got better things to do with my time. Anyway, I got her ass fired. And the word's out in this town. Who'll hire her now? Where's she gonna go?"

Livvy fixed him with a cool stare. "I wouldn't know. I try to stay out of other people's business and mind my own."

"Good plan," Garrett said. He looked around the lounge. "So, where's your sidekick today?"

"Sidekick?"

"You know. Chef Felice."

Garrett was getting on her last nerve. "How should I know? Maybe she's still at church."

"Praying for all us heathens," he said, wiping his mouth with the back of his hand.

"Some of us need prayer more than others," Livvy snapped. "Speaking of which, where's KJ? Haven't seen much of him this weekend."

"His grandparents are in town, so he's gotta suck up to Granddaddy."

She locked her bedroom door and texted Felice.

Where are you?

She waited while the little bubbles floated on her phone screen.

Church supper. About to leave.
What's up?

Livvy's fingers were trembling as she typed.

G just let me know he knows
we talked to Chelsea. Kinda
freaking me out. I think he
suspects something.

Another string of bubbles.

B cool. Leaving here now.

She put the phone down and picked up her laptop and went online to resume paying her bills, but after all the events of the day it was hard to concentrate.

"Okay, I'm outta here," Garrett called from the lounge. She heard the front door close, and a few moments later, heard his car start.

Livvy sprinted from her room to his. She tried the door, but it was locked.

As she was walking back to her room, her phone dinged to alert her to another incoming text. From Chelsea Shalanian.

CALL ME ASAP.

The front door opened. "Livvy?" Felice called. "I just saw Garrett leave. What's going on?"

Livvy met her in the lounge, holding up her phone. "I think the shit has officially hit the fan. Chelsea just texted me to call her."

"Wonder what she wants?"

"Guess we're gonna find out," Olivia said. She tapped the number embedded in the text and Chelsea picked up on the first ring. She put the phone on speaker.

"What the hell have you two gotten me into?" Chelsea demanded. "Garrett knows I talked to you."

Livvy and Felice exchanged worried glances.

"Did he say something?" Livvy asked.

"He didn't have to. When I got off work today all four of my car tires were slashed."

"How do you know it was him?"

"It was him. There was a little gift in my apartment too. A dead rat. In my bed."

"How could he know?" Felice asked. "We didn't say anything to anyone."

"Someone at the restaurant must have overheard us. Probably one of the waiters he drinks or plays darts with."

"Did you call the cops?" Felice asked.

"Hell no. His best friend is a sheriff's deputy. They're not gonna touch him."

Livvy swallowed hard. "He told me tonight he knows we talked to you. We're kinda freaking out over here."

"Yeah, me too. Anyway, I'm outta here. Soon as they finish putting new tires on my car."

"Where will you go?" Felice asked.

"My uncle owns a barbecue place in Tennessee. He'll give me a job."

"Damn, girl," Felice said. "You gonna let him run you out of town like that?"

"Yeah, Felice, I am," Chelsea said, her voice cracking. "I know what he's capable of now. You two better watch your backs. One more thing."

"What's that?" Livvy asked.

"You know how I told you Garrett was messing around with Misty? The chick at the spa? I got bad intel. Turns out Misty is engaged. To a massage therapist. A girl massage therapist."

"So . . . who's M?" Livvy asked.

"His side piece," Chelsea said. "That's all I know."

Livvy's hands were shaking by the time the call ended.

"Garrett spooked you that bad, huh?" Felice sat on the bed beside her. "You look like you've seen a ghost."

"It's not just him," Livvy said.

"What's going on? You wanna tell me about it?"

She needed to talk to someone, Livvy thought. And surprisingly, Felice felt like the only person who might understand.

"You know how I told you my whole life it's been this big dark secret about who my father was? Well, my mom just told me, and it's totally nuts. I'm shook."

"How nuts?" Felice asked.

Livvy leaned against the bed's headboard. "When I was a little kid, I'd make up stories about who my dad was. Sometimes he'd be a superhero, like Batman, or a really cool movie star, like Matthew McConaughey."

"I get that. I always knew who my father was, but I *wished* he was Denzel," Felice said.

"But what my mom told me today, it's mind-blowing, and from what she says, it's also potentially life-altering."

Felice grabbed her arm. "Are you gonna tell me who he is?"

Livvy took a deep breath. "Nobody else can know about this, okay?"

"I swear, I won't say a word. Would you please just tell me before I explode?"

"Fred Eddings is my biological . . . I can't call him a father. He was never that. Sperm donor. That's all he was."

"Whaaaat?" Felice grasped both her hands. "How?"

Livvy repeated an edited version of the revelation her mother had just shared.

"How awful. For your mom, and you," Felice said. "She never reported it to the cops?"

"She never told anyone. She was too ashamed. Like it was her fault she got raped."

"Damn, that's messed up," Felice said. "But, she didn't make him pay? At all?"

"He made her sign a nondisclosure agreement, and in return he paid off my granny's house and gave her money to finish school, and fifty thousand, to take care of my expenses."

"Only fifty thousand? Chump change! That family's gotta be worth millions and millions."

"I found a magazine story from six years ago that said the old man's real estate was worth thirty million," Livvy confided.

"How come your mom's finally telling you all this now?"

"Now that Fred Eddings is dead, there's a chance I might get an inheritance."

"You definitely should," Felice said. She snapped her fingers. "Damn! Pretty soon, you could be a millionaire. You definitely won't be slumming it with me here in this dorm."

Livvy looked around at her room. "This isn't slumming, and I actually kinda like living here with you. Anyway, I have to talk to Mrs. E's lawyer. There was some funny business with the old man's will, and my mom says Ric Eddings isn't going to give up any share of his inheritance without a fight."

Felice's eyes widened. "This means you and Parrish were secretly related, right? You'd be her aunt."

"I guess that's right. Another reason why we have to figure out who killed her. I got the name of a woman in the Saint's purchasing department. I'll reach out to her tomorrow and try to set up a face-to-face. And I'm gonna ask to meet with Mrs. E. What about you?"

"I went into the restaurant before we opened for brunch. Fortunately, one of the bartenders is pretty careless with his key card. He left it hanging from a nail in the kitchen, so I was able to get into the liquor storage area. Unfortunately, I didn't see anything suspicious."

"Doesn't mean there *isn't* anything going on," Livvy said. "Here's something. As soon as Garrett left a few minutes ago, I tried to get into his room. The door was locked."

"So? You always keep your door locked, and so do I."

"We lock our doors to keep *him* out. Wonder what he's hiding in there to keep *us* out?"

"Oh no," Felice said. "No way. Don't even think about it."

"All I'm saying is, let's get into his room and take a look around."

"You just told me the room is locked. I'm a chef, Liv, not a burglar. I don't know how to break into a locked room, and neither do you."

Livvy opened her laptop. "I bet there's a YouTube tutorial that can show us how."

"There is no 'us.' I'm not getting arrested for doing a B and E. Besides, what about KJ? What if he comes in and catches us in the act?"

"He won't. Garrett said his family's in town and he's at his grandparents' house."

"It's almost nine o'clock. He could be back here any minute. The answer is no."

But Livvy was already scrolling the pages of YouTube. She looked up and grinned. "Bingo. Check it out: How to unlock a door without a key."

"No no no no no," Felice chanted, heading for her own room. "I don't want to hear it."

Livvy watched the video, which made it look fairly simple. She didn't have what the tutorial called a Spam key—the kind that came on cans of processed meats or sardines—nor did she have a flattened paper clip or a bobby pin. But she did possess two items the You-Tube video suggested: a credit card and the tiny screwdriver that she'd bought to try to repair her favorite pair of sunglasses.

"Felice!" She banged on her friend's door. "C'mon. I need you."

"Go away. I'm sleeping." Felice's voice was muffled.

"Fine. I'll jimmy the lock by myself. All you have to do is be the lookout."

No answer. Livvy knocked again. "C'mon. I know you're not asleep. And if I get caught and go to jail, you'll be living here alone with those two jerks."

The door opened. Felice had changed into her pj's. "Let's get this over with."

Livvy stood in front of Garrett's door and took a deep breath. She tried to insert the miniature screwdriver into the keyhole, but her hands were shaking so badly she dropped the tool. She watched with horror as it slowly rolled under the doorjamb.

"Shit!"

Felice was standing in the open front door, gazing out into the darkness. "Hurry up, okay? The mosquitoes are already swarming me."

"I'm a little jumpy," Livvy reported. "Maybe I'll have a glass of wine to calm my nerves."

"Just don't get so calm you fall asleep on the job."

Livvy opened the fridge and uncorked the sauvignon blanc bottle. There was just over a glass left, a nice friendly pour, so, taking a cue from Garrett, she chugged the rest, then discarded the empty.

She rummaged around in the kitchen's utensil drawer until she came up with what she hoped would be a substitute for the now-missing screwdriver: the tiny stainless steel pick Felice used to extract meat from blue crab claws.

After the wine her hands seemed steady although her heart was thumping crazily. Following the YouTube tutorial, with her right hand she slowly inserted the pick into the keyhole, and somehow

managed to depress the tiny button hidden inside the doorknob. She
turned the knob with her left hand.

"I'm in!"

Livvy flipped the light switch. Felice stood behind, peering into
the room.

"What a pig! How does someone live in a garbage dump like
this?" She sniffed and made a gagging sound. "Nasty! Why am I not
surprised?"

Livvy stepped inside, avoiding a mound of clothing. The floor
was scattered with debris, empty beer bottles, and dirty dishes. The
bed was unmade. The closet was empty.

"That's weird." Livvy peeked under the bed and opened dresser
drawers, most of which were empty. "Felice, I think Garrett's moved
his stuff out of here. I think he's gone."

"Good," Felice said.

Livvy retrieved the screwdriver that had rolled under the door.
"Come on. Let's check KJ's room while we're at it."

Felice groaned but went back to her lookout post without an
argument.

Livvy used the pick again, with the same results. The door swung
open and she felt for the light switch.

KJ's room looked as pristine as it had on move-in day. The bed
was made with military precision, the floor swept clean. She opened
the closet. It was empty, with the exception of a couple of faded
polo shirts and a cluster of wire coat hangers.

"It looks like he's moved out too," she said. "Wonder what that
means?"

Livvy checked the lounge area, then came back to the kitchen to
find Felice standing in front of the open refrigerator. "Garrett's gaming console is gone," she reported. "He's definitely moved out. KJ
too. I don't like it. Something's going on with those two."

"Whatever it is, it can wait until morning," Felice said, setting her
jug of kombucha on the countertop. "Want some?"

"No thanks," Livvy said, yawning. "I've got a bad feeling about this, Felice."

"Drink some kombucha. It calms your nerves," Felice advised. She'd only poured a few ounces of the home brew before Livvy's phone rang, startling her so badly she knocked over the plastic jug.

"Shit!" Livvy grabbed for her phone, rescuing it from the rapidly spreading pool of liquid on the counter.

It was her mother. "Liv? Did you reach out to Traci? She's waiting to hear from you."

Livvy looked over at Felice, who was mopping up the kombucha mess and glaring at her.

"Not yet," she said, annoyed. "I'll call her in the morning."

"You're stalling. I know you. It's your favorite avoidance tactic."

"Mom! Quit nagging. I said I'd call, and I will."

"That's all I ask," Shannon said. "Good night, baby. I love you."

"Love you too."

Livvy hung up and grabbed a roll of paper towels. "I'm sorry," she told Felice as she swiped the paper towels across the counter.

"Never mind." Felice picked up her glass and took a few sips of kombucha.

"Back to the guys. When I see Traci tomorrow I think we need to tell her everything we know about those two."

"Now you're talking sense," Felice agreed. "Let's lock up and go to bed. I'm dead."

CHAPTER 62

* * *

It was after 9:00 P.M., and after thirty minutes of walking Lola around on the golf course, Traci was still urging her dog to take care of business when her cell phone rang.

"What are you doing?" Whelan asked.

"Me? Trying to keep Lola from eating fireflies."

"How did the meeting with your lawyer friend go today?"

She stopped by a clump of azaleas while Lola relieved herself. "Best way to describe it? Earth-shattering. Remember Shannon? My former best friend and the other lifeguard who got fired after Hudson drowned?"

"Sure. The nurse. Nice woman, although she didn't seem so keen on you, or your husband's family."

"That's because Fred Eddings raped her. When she was only nineteen. He lured Shannon to his house under the pretense of giving her a better job, liquored her up with a martini . . ."

"My God," Whelan breathed.

"She was too ashamed to tell me what had happened when she found out she was pregnant. No wonder she flipped her shit when Livvy told her she was coming to work at the Saint. It was her worst nightmare."

"And now, her kid owns a piece of the action, right?"

"It looks that way," Traci said. "Shannon was dreading giving Olivia the news. I can't imagine how she'll feel, knowing she was the product of a rape."

"Must have been a pretty emotional reunion," Whelan said.

"It was. Up until that summer, we'd been best friends for our whole lives, since the first day of first grade. Twenty-one years, I've wondered what I'd done to make her hate me. All these years she was keeping that secret bottled up inside. Not even her mother knew the truth. Until today, neither of us realized how much we missed and needed each other."

"Women's friendships," Whelan said, sounding baffled. "I don't get it. I couldn't tell you the name of anyone I went to high school with, let alone elementary school. I've got pals, yeah, marine buddies, guys I served with over the years. My former business partner? We haven't really talked since we sold the company. Every once in a while, he'll text me something, usually something about sports, but that's it."

"You mean to tell me you and your friends don't get mani-pedis together or meet up on Sunday mornings for a Target run?" Traci teased.

"Nope. But I could see myself doing a Target run with you, if the occasion arose."

"That's very sweet," Traci said. "By the way, Shannon spotted you leaving my house this morning and assumed we'd been . . . up to something. She thinks you have excellent boyfriend potential."

"I knew I liked her," Whelan said, chuckling. "Does she know about Ric? And his involvement in Hudson's death?"

"No. Today's news was enough of a shock—for both of us. I think it can wait."

"Maybe, she'd like, I don't know? Is closure a cliché?"

"It's a cliché because it's true," Traci said. "I know it gave me some peace, after all these years, knowing it wasn't our fault."

"I'm glad. Hey, the other reason I called is to fill you in on my visit to the sheriff's office after I left your place."

"He still won't let you see the investigative reports?" she guessed.

"Actually, I lucked out. The sheriff was out of town. But his chief deputy, guy's name is Shapley, happened to be in the office today and I might have bamboozled him a little. He let me read the file on your niece's death. He wouldn't let me copy it or photograph the pages, or even take notes. He sat me down in a conference room and watched while I read."

"Did you learn anything new?"

"A couple things. They were finally able to track down the members of that steel drum band that played your Beach Bash."

"Cedric and the Sunsetters?"

"Yeah. How'd you know?"

"They've played the Beach Bash for the last few years."

"That would have been good information for the sheriff's office to have before now, especially since the witness statements from the afterparty say they saw Cedric talking to Parrish shortly before she disappeared. Who hired those guys?"

Traci had to think for a minute. "Charlie Burroughs, our general manager, originally hired them, but I'm not sure about this year."

"But Burroughs would have had the band's contact info?"

"Probably."

"He told the sheriff he didn't know much about the band because Parrish hired them."

"Did the cops ever get in touch with anyone from the band?"

"They're back in Jamaica. The reports I read said repeated efforts to contact them failed."

"Sounds like maybe Cedric has something to hide. Or maybe he just doesn't like talking to cops," Traci said. "What else was of interest in that file?"

"Those two dudes who lived in your dorm with Traci."

"KJ and Garrett?"

"Yeah. Did you send them out to look for Parrish the morning she went missing?"

"My memory is that they volunteered to go, because I was so upset."

"While they were out there, they took it upon themselves to 'clean up' the area, hauling all the trash out, effectively destroying any evidence that might have been at the crime scene."

"You don't think they did that deliberately, do you?" Traci asked. "They were Parrish's friends. They were really upset after her body was found."

"Not sure what to think," Whelan said. "Let me ask you something else. How long has your general manager been at the Saint?"

"Charlie? He's been there for as long as I remember. He was the one who hired me as a lifeguard when I was nineteen. He's an institution."

"What do you know about his personal life?"

"Not much," Traci admitted. "He's divorced. No kids. He's kind of a workaholic."

"Would it surprise you to know that he filed for bankruptcy in 2018?"

"Are you sure you have the right Charlie Burroughs?"

"Very sure. He apparently got himself overextended trying to flip houses on the mainland for the rental market. The bank foreclosed on three of them. He managed to hang on to a house in Bonaventure. It's worth about six hundred grand."

"I had no idea he was having money problems," Traci said. "He's a pretty private guy. Quiet, steady. I honestly don't know what I would have done without him after Hoke died."

"Sometimes it's the quiet ones who surprise you," Whelan said.

Lola was doing what Traci thought of as the dance of the doggy doody, slowly rotating her compact body in tight circles, preparatory to her late-night potty stop.

"Come on, baby, drop it and let's go home," she urged.

"I beg your pardon?"

"Whoops. I was talking to Lola, not you," she said, laughing. "We've been walking for thirty minutes now, and I'm officially exhausted."

"When can I see you again?" Whelan asked.

"I'm not sure."

"Not sure you want to, or not sure you can?"

"It's not that I don't want to," she said reluctantly. "More like, should I?"

"No pressure, but you definitely should," he said.

"Let me sleep on it," she said. "Please?"

They'd arrived back at her house. Traci opened the kitchen door and Lola scampered inside. She walked around the house, locking doors and switching off lights as she went. She paused in the living room, seeing it with a new perspective.

Shannon had been right. The ornate Victorian furniture, overly elaborate window treatments, none of it held any real meaning for Traci. She wouldn't have chosen any of these Eddings family heirlooms for herself.

As a young newlywed, she'd been so eager to prove her worthiness of belonging to her husband's family that she hadn't stopped to consider the price of that acceptance. And Hoke, the younger son, had perhaps been an unwitting accomplice to his family's coolness toward her. Maybe because, deep down, he knew he'd always play second fiddle to Ric, his father's favorite.

Soon, she promised herself, she would jettison all this emotional and physical baggage. She would live the way she wanted. It was time. Past time.

CHAPTER 63

* * *

BOOM!

The explosion was so loud it rattled the windows in her room and woke Felice up from what felt like the deepest sleep she'd ever experienced. At first, she thought she'd dreamed it. She grabbed her glasses and struggled to sit up in bed, finally using both hands to push herself upright. She groped in the dark for the lamp on her nightstand, finally finding the switch, but nothing happened.

She smelled gas, and then, smoke. She walked unsteadily to the bedroom door, tried the wall switch, but nothing happened. The power was out. In her groggy state, she wondered if the sound had been a lightning strike, but would that shake the dorm?

Felice tried to open the door, but it wouldn't move. She turned the handle to unlock it, leaned against the door, and pushed hard. Nothing. The smoke smell was strong. Looking down, she saw wisps of it pluming from beneath the door.

Something deep in her lizard brain finally connected. Fire. The explosion was real. The power was out and something was blocking her door. She grabbed the bedspread from her bed and dropped to the floor, gagging and coughing, stuffing the spread under the door to block the smoke.

Her legs felt floppy, like uncooked spaghetti, but she went back to her bed, groped in the dark until she found the bottle of water she kept there, ripped the case off her pillow, soaked it in some of the water, and wrapped it around her nose and mouth.

Get out, her lizard brain said. *You've got to get out.*

She turned to the window and, after yanking the blind up, she pushed on the lower window sash. It didn't move.

Get out. Get out.

The lamp was the heaviest thing in the room. She picked it up, took a step backward, and swung as hard as she could. The glass shattered. Using the base of the lamp, she knocked the rest of the glass fragments out of the window frame. There was a screen too, but she battered it until it broke free.

She took a breath, looked around the darkened room. Her phone. She needed her phone. It wasn't on her nightstand. But she always left her phone right there. Her mind was muddled, she was panicking. What to do?

Just go. Get out.

Felice slung one leg over the windowsill, then the other, then dropped down onto the ground. Drifts of pine needles broke the fall, but she felt stabbing pains from the soles of her feet where she'd stepped barefoot on glass shards.

She was down on all fours, so she crawled away from the dorm, still gagging and coughing. When she was a hundred yards away she managed to stand upright.

Livvy! Where was Livvy? She looked around. The woods surrounding the dorm were quiet, the nearly full moon the only light breaking through the tree line. She smelled gas.

"Livvy!" Her throat was raw, her eyes burning.

"Livvy!"

Could Livvy have slept through the explosion? Felice wasn't sure. She had to find her friend's room, but she was so disoriented, her brain so muddled. She forced herself to look at the window she'd crawled out of, then spotted the next window down. Livvy's room.

She grabbed the lamp she'd thrown through the window, and made her way to the next window down, battering at it with the lamp base until the screen tore open and the glass shattered.

Smoke poured out of the window. "Livvvy!" she screamed. "Livvy!"

There was no answer. With a rush of adrenaline, Felice some-how managed to heave herself up and through the open window. She dropped to the floor, clutching the damp pillowcase to her face. Through the smoke she spotted Livvy, unmoving on her bed.

Flattening herself to the floor, Felice crawled hand over hand to the bed. "Liv!" she screamed, but her friend didn't move. She grabbed Livvy's hand, felt for a pulse. It was warm and there was a pulse. She also spotted her own phone on the nightstand, right beside Livvy's, and grabbed both phones and stuffed them into the pocket of her pajama pants.

"Liv! Wake up!" She shook her friend's shoulders. "Fire! We've gotta get out."

Livvy's head turned slightly in her direction. Her eyelids fluttered. She tried to speak, but was seized with a fit of coughing. "Huh?"

Could she still be this drunk, Felice wondered? How much wine had she had?

Giving up, Felice grabbed Livvy's arms at the elbow and yanked her off the bed. Once Liv was upright, Felice wrapped an arm around her waist. They were both gagging and coughing in the thick smoke. She took the pillowcase from her face and wrapped it around Livvy's. "Come on, girl. The dorm's on fire. We've got to get outta here. Can you walk?"

Livvy's knees buckled and Felice hauled her back upright. She half walked, half dragged her toward the open window. It was like hauling a living hundred-pound sack of potatoes.

"Liv!" Felice yelled. Her friend's face slowly swung around to give her a blank stare. "You have to jump out of this window. Can you do that? Can you jump?"

Without waiting for a response, she bodily picked Livvy up and shoved her headfirst through the window. As soon as Livvy's feet were clear, Felice jumped down too, falling with a soft thud atop her.

"Come on, we need to get away from here," Felice said, yanking Livvy to a seated position. "I think there's a broken gas line. The whole place could explode any minute."

Livvy slowly nodded. Her voice was as hoarse as Felice's. "Okay."

Felice stood and pulled Livvy to her feet. She wrapped her arm around her waist. "Away. We've got to get away from here. Can you walk now?"

Livvy mumbled something unintelligible.

Moving as fast as she could with the dead weight of her friend, Felice staggered away from the clearing where the dorm stood and toward the tree line, still gasping for air. Her legs and lungs gave out when they were about fifty yards away, and they both dropped to the ground at the base of a tall pine tree.

Felice pulled her phone from her pocket and tapped 911.

"Nine-one-one. What is your emergency?"

"Fire," Felice croaked. "At the Saint. I think there's a broken gas line. I heard an explosion, and then the lights went out."

"Ma'am, where at the Saint?"

Felice coughed. "Staff dorm. In the old golf cart barn. Send an ambulance. My friend . . . I think there's something wrong with her."

"Is she conscious?"

She glanced sideways at her friend. "Just barely. Please hurry."

"Ma'am? Is there anyone still inside the building?"

"What?" Felice's brain wasn't registering right. "What did you say?"

"Did everyone get out? Of the burning building?"

Oh God. KJ and Garrett? Had they come back last night? Her brain was foggy.

"I'm not sure," Felice said. "Hurry, please."

She turned to Livvy, whose eyes were open but unfocused. "Liv. I've got to go find KJ and Garrett. Will you be okay here?"

Livvy's head lolled back against the tree trunk. "Uh-huh." She coughed, bent forward at the waist, and vomited.

"Oh my God," Felice muttered. She pulled up the hem of her friend's T-shirt and gently dabbed the vomit away from her mouth and face.

"Stay here," she said.

She was dizzy and so unsteady on her feet. Slowly, she forced herself to move back toward the dorm. Smoke was pouring from the broken windows. She paused, trying to reorient herself, but the world seemed to be at a tilt, like she was walking in a carnival funhouse.

Felice tried to think. Where were KJ's and Garrett's rooms? Finally, she thought she'd regained her bearings. Their rooms were on the other side of the building.

She was so tired, she wanted to slump down to the ground and go back to sleep. But she picked up the lamp and forced herself to keep moving.

When she found what she thought was the right window she swung the lamp hard, repeating the action she'd used on her own window.

Smoke poured from the room, and the heat was intense.

"KJ!" she screamed. "Garrett!"

No answer, and she could see flames licking at the doorway. The heat drove her backward, away from the window.

Felice staggered on toward the next window. She paused, gulping for air, exhausted from her efforts, and in that moment, the window blew open, showering her chest and face with bits of glass. Smoke and flames shot out.

Her lizard brain kicked in again.

A hose. Hurry. Find a hose. Put out the fire.

There was a faucet on the exterior wall nearby, but no hose. The fire was spreading. If KJ and Garrett were in those rooms, there was no way they could be rescued. Not by her.

Get away.

She staggered away, maybe a hundred yards. She bent at the waist, her hands on her knees, and puked, the vomit splattering on her legs and her chest.

Her face was cut and bleeding. Her head was throbbing.

Her lizard brain had one more thought.

Your friend needs you.

CHAPTER 64

* * *

Half walking, half crawling, Felice made it back to where she'd left Livvy, who was now slumped sideways on the ground.

She pulled her back upright, leaning her against the tree, and not so gently slapped her cheeks. "Livvy! Come on, girl. Wake up!"

Livvy's eyelids fluttered open. "Hey," she said weakly.

"Can you walk? I think we need to get farther away from the fire."

Livvy coughed and her lips formed a goofy smile. "Where we goin'?"

Felice had no idea how much time had passed since she'd called 911. Time seemed like an abstraction. She closed her eyes. Rest. She needed rest.

The blare of sirens awakened her. She shielded her eyes with her hand. Red swirling lights and bright white blinking lights cut through the darkness. Two ambulances and two fire trucks. They pulled up beside the dorm and the firefighters swarmed out.

"Over here!" she called, trying but failing to stand. "We're over here!"

One of the firemen ran to her side. He looked down at Livvy. "Is she . . ."

"She's in and out," Felice said, coughing.

"Is there anyone else inside?"

"Don't know." Her throat was raw. "Maybe? Two other guys live here. I tried . . . broke the window . . . couldn't see inside. Smoke . . . and then something exploded."

"Where?" he said urgently. "Can you show me where they might be?"

Felice pointed toward the far side of the dorm. "Over there."

The firefighter spoke into the radio on his shoulder. "Unit two, could be two people, west side of building.

"Do you know how the fire started?"

"Sleeping. Loud boom. Maybe something exploded? Couldn't get out . . ."

An EMT ran up and knelt down beside Livvy. "Breathing is shallow. Erratic."

He looked over at Felice. "Your face is cut. Are you hurt anywhere else?"

"No. My friend. I don't know what's wrong with her. She's in and out."

"Okay. We're gonna take care of both of you. My name's Dave, by the way."

Her throat ached. "Felice," she managed to say. "And that's Livvy."

"You're bleeding," he said, gesturing to her feet, which were covered in blood.

"Oh. Glass. Broke window. Stepped on glass."

He touched her arm. "Your hands are burned."

She looked. The palms of her hands were red and blistering. And throbbing. Like her head, but different.

"Stu!" the EMT yelled at his partner. "Get the gurney. We've got a victim who's unconscious."

A moment later Stu ran up with a rolling gurney.

"What's wrong with that one?" he asked, pointing to Livvy. He knelt beside her, tried to pull Livvy's eyelids open.

"Any chance y'all were doing drugs?" he asked.

"No!" Felice coughed.

"You sure?" Dave asked. "No judgment, but your friend looks stoned."

Felice's head hurt so much. She tried to concentrate, to remember what had happened earlier in the night. An image flashed in her brain. Livvy, finishing off the wine from the bottle in the fridge. And herself, sipping half a glass of kombucha before the jug got knocked over.

"Maybe?" she croaked. She pointed at Livvy. "She had wine. I thought she was drunk, even though she didn't have that much, but after the fire I couldn't wake her up. She couldn't walk."

"What about you?" Dave asked. "Did you drink any wine?"

She shook her head and it felt like she'd been struck with a hammer. "No wine. Kombucha. My head hurts."

The two EMTs exchanged a look. "Sounds like they've been drugged," Dave said.

Stu was sliding Livvy onto the gurney.

"Help her," Felice managed.

"It's okay," Stu said. "We're gonna take care of both of you." He placed an oxygen mask over Livvy's face.

A man's voice cut through the darkness. "Is she dead? Oh my God. Is Livvy dead?"

Livvy and the EMTs looked up.

KJ emerged from a clump of bushes. His preppy shorts, embroidered with lobsters and sailboats, were filthy, his polo shirt torn. One eye was nearly swollen shut and his jaw was bruised and bleeding.

"I'm sorry," he cried. "I'm so sorry, Felice. We didn't mean to. I didn't want to hurt you. It was Garrett's idea."

Felice stared at him in disbelief. "You? You did this? You tried to kill us?"

"Not me. Garrett. It was supposed to be a little fire. That's what he told me."

"You drugged us?" Felice croaked. "The wine? My kombucha?"

Dave, the first EMT, stood up and grabbed KJ's arm. "What did you give them, you piece of shit? What was it?"

"Roofies. I didn't know Garrett was gonna do that."

"Felice? Livvy?"

KJ swung his head around. Traci Eddings was approaching in her golf cart, yelling their names.

"I'm sorry," KJ repeated, and then he fled back into the woods.

———

Traci jumped from the golf cart and ran toward the girls and the EMTs. "What happened? Are you all right?"

Felice found herself choking up, tears streaming down her face. She coughed, tried to speak, but couldn't find the words.

Dave spoke up. "They got out before the fire was totally involved. Some cuts and superficial burns."

Traci's voice rose. "What was KJ doing here? Why did he run off like that?"

"He and someone named Garrett apparently drugged their drinks, then set fire to that building where they were sleeping."

She turned and stared at the dorm, where a horde of firefighters had hoses trained on the building. Smoke poured into the humid night air. The roof collapsed, spewing showers of glowing orange cinders.

Traci's voice was anguished. "Why? Why would they do that?"

"Ma'am?" Stu had transferred Livvy to the gurney. "We need to get these ladies to the hospital. You can ask them questions later."

CHAPTER 65

* * *

When the phone rang, Shannon snapped instantly awake, sitting up and grabbing it. Working in hospitals for nearly two decades—morning shifts, night shifts, doubles—had wrecked her circadian rhythm. Combine that with raising a teenaged girl by herself, and she hadn't really had a sound night of sleep since bringing Livvy home from the hospital.

She glanced at the caller ID. It was Traci. And it was also 3:00 A.M.

"Shannon?"

"What is it? What's wrong?"

"Don't panic, okay? Promise me you won't panic."

"What's wrong, dammit? Nobody calls in the middle of the night with good news."

"You're right," Traci said. "First, Livvy is okay. She's gonna be fine."

"Traci Eddings, if you don't tell me what's happened to my kid, right now, I will—"

"There was a fire at the dorm. Felice woke up, smelled smoke, and got Livvy out safely."

"Why didn't Livvy wake up and get herself out?"

Traci hadn't been expecting that question. Shannon could almost hear the wheels turning in her old friend's head.

"They were drugged. Both of them, but Felice apparently didn't drink as much as Livvy."

"Jesus H!" Shannon leapt out of bed and began pulling on clothes. "Where's Livvy? Who drugged them?"

"They're both on their way to Bonaventure Memorial. I got to the dorm just as the EMTs were about to load them into the ambulance. From what I could see, Livvy just had some cuts on her feet from where Felice broke Livvy's window to get her out. They were giving her oxygen for smoke inhalation, but otherwise—"

"Who did this to them?" Shannon cut in.

"It looks like the other two guys who lived in the dorm. I'm on my way to the ER now."

"Me too," Shannon said, searching for her shoes. "I'll meet you there."

Traci was at a standoff with the emergency room admitting clerk.

"I need to see Felice Bonpierre," she said.

The clerk tapped some keys on her computer and looked up. "Nobody gets back there unless they're next of kin."

"I'm her mother," Traci said without hesitation.

The clerk didn't blink. "I saw them bring that girl in here a little while ago. If you're her mama, my mama is Beyoncé."

"Her father is Black."

"I bet he is. Anyway, there's a sheriff's deputy talking to her right now, so even if you were her mama, which you're not, I couldn't let you see her."

"Just tell me if she's okay," Traci pleaded.

"Looks like it to me. The doctor dressed her cuts and burns. She ain't on oxygen."

"Thank God," Traci murmured.

The sliding doors from the ambulance bay whooshed open and Shannon rushed inside, planting herself in front of the clerk.

"Where is she?"

"Who?"

"Myrna, do not fuck with me," Shannon said, her voice low and lethal. "My daughter Olivia was brought in here by ambulance. Now let me back there or I'll—"

"No point. She's still out of it. Dr. Ochoa saw her. She's in good hands. Now, why don't you just set over there in the waiting room and I'll let the nurse know you're out here."

"Let me see my baby girl," Shannon said with a hiss. "Right now."

The clerk shrugged, pushed a button, and a pair of automatic doors opened.

Shannon rushed through them and Traci followed close behind.

"Hey! You can't go back there—"

The doors closed, cutting off the clerk's objection. A nurses' station was directly in front of them, but was currently unmanned. Beyond that were four curtained-off examining rooms.

Shannon moved quickly ahead of her, pulling aside curtains until she reached the last cubicle. She peeked inside. "Here she is."

Traci heard her talking in low tones to a man, presumably Dr. Ochoa.

In the cubicle right next door she heard another man's voice, and then a young woman's voice, hoarse, but unmistakably her chef, Felice.

After a moment of hesitation, she stuck her head inside the curtain. "Felice?"

Felice was lying on a hospital bed. Her face was dotted with some kind of ointment and her hands, lying atop a sheet stretched up to her chin, were heavily bandaged. Sitting on a rolling stool beside the bed was a uniformed sheriff's deputy.

He had a graying crew cut and didn't bother to hide his annoyance at the interruption.

"Who are you? And how did you get back here?"

"It's okay," Felice told him. "This is Mrs. Eddings. My boss. At the Saint. She owns the dorm those guys tried to burn down."

The deputy paged back in his notebook. "That'd be KJ Parkhurst and Garrett Wycoff? They're your employees?"

"Formerly," Traci said. "As of right now." She gazed down at Felice, her fierce chef who looked so unexpectedly diminished and vulnerable in that hospital bed.

"How're you feeling?"

"Better. I think the drugs are wearing off." She held up her hands, which were swathed in gauze bandages. "But I don't think I'll be back in the kitchen for a few days."

"Never mind that. All I want is for you and Livvy to get better."

Traci glanced at the deputy. His name badge said he was Detective G. W. Shapley. "And I want you to arrest the men who did this to them."

"Yes, ma'am," Shapley said. "We actually have Parkhurst in custody. He didn't even make it off the island. We found him hiding out in the carriage house at his granddad's house."

"What about Garrett?" Felice rasped. "This was his idea. Him and Charlie Burroughs."

"Who's he?" the deputy asked, his pen poised above a small spiral-bound notebook.

"He's the general manager at the Saint," Traci said. She looked down at Felice. "But what do you know about Charlie's involvement?"

Shapley glared at her. "Ma'am? I'm asking the questions here."

He pointed at Felice. "What do you know about Burroughs's involvement in this matter?"

Felice shot her boss a sheepish look. "Livvy and me, we were friends with Parrish. So we decided we'd figure out who killed her, and why."

"And why would a couple of girls decide to play detective?" Shapley asked. "Talk about stupid. And dangerous. The two of you nearly got yourselves killed."

"Hey!" Felice croaked. "I don't appreciate being called stupid, or a girl."

"How?" Traci asked, ignoring the deputy. "What made you think Charlie was involved with what happened to Parrish?"

"Livvy found Parrish's notebook," Felice said. "She kept notes of all the complaints people had. She called it her bitch book." She shot the deputy a withering look. "We found it, hidden in her room, in her pillowcase, after the sheriff's office searched it."

"The blue notebook Livvy mentioned," Traci said.

Felice nodded. "She wrote about stuff she was suspicious about, at the hotel. There was funny business with mattresses and the televisions. And in the restaurant, they were switching cheap well-brand booze and wine for call brands. Garrett was involved. Burroughs too. One of Garrett's girlfriends, Chelsea Shalanian, told us all about it. She used to work at the Verandah, until Garrett got her fired."

She stopped speaking and fumbled for the cup of water on the tray next to the bed. Traci picked up the cup and held it so that Felice could sip.

"Thanks," the chef whispered.

"And when the two of you started sniffing around, that's when Charlie decided to try to get you fired," Traci said. She tapped the deputy on the shoulder. "Your people need to arrest Charlie Burroughs immediately."

"Back up," Shapley said. "We can't arrest someone just on your say-so."

"Bring him in for questioning then," Traci said. "Or does this young lady here have to continue to do your job for you?"

The deputy turned a page in his notebook. "What's his name again?"

"Charlie Burroughs. He lives here in town. On Blue Heron."

"Okay, we'll check it out."

"Felice," Traci said, "I'm so sorry you got mixed up in all this. I feel responsible. Is there someone in your family that I should notify that you've been hurt?"

"No! It's just an aunt down in Miami, but I don't want her to get upset. I'll be okay, Mrs. E." She held up her hands again. "Working in restaurants practically my whole life, I've had worse burns than this. My main thing is, when can I get back to work?"

"You want to come back? After what's just happened?" Traci shook her head. "Of course I want you back, more than anything."

"Okay, cool," Felice rasped.

"But we need to make sure you're healed properly," Traci added. "I have to say, right now, it hurts me to even look at you."

"Can you find out what's happened to all my stuff? In the fire? Everything I owned was in my room. My laptop with all my recipes. My knives, all my clothes. My whole life, really."

"Don't worry about that right now," Traci said. "The hotel is insured for any kind of loss you've incurred. And again, I don't know whether to be grateful or terrified that you and Olivia decided to try to solve Parrish's murder."

"Parrish was cool. What happened to her wasn't right. It was Livvy's idea to try to figure it out. Because she's really into all this true-crime stuff. At first, it was kind of like a little game we were playing. But then, after Burroughs tried to get us fired, we wanted to get back at him. Prove he was involved. Garrett too."

Just then, Detective Shapley pushed the examining room curtain aside.

"We sent an officer over to Burroughs's residence. He's gone."

"Gone?" Traci said blankly. "It's four thirty in the morning."

"He's in the wind," Shapley said. "And it looks like he left in a hurry. There's a couple expensive cars in his garage, a new Mercedes SEL and a brand-new Ford F-150, still got the dealer stickers on the windows."

"Livvy was right," Felice said.

The deputy just shook his head. "We've issued a lookout for Burroughs. And this Garrett kid. Ma'am," he said, addressing Traci, "any idea where Burroughs might head if he's on the run?"

She was still stunned that they were talking about the trusted GM who'd worked by her side these past four years. "Not really. He kept his private life private. Charlie actually gave me my first job at the Saint. Turns out I didn't know him as well as I thought I did."

She twisted the engagement band on her left hand. "He was a workaholic. Never talked much about his personal life. Except . . ."

The detective pounced. "Except what?"

"There was a cousin who used to come down here on her vacation in the spring. She'd stay at the hotel. Lorissa something. I don't remember her last name."

"That gives us a start," Shapley said. "Anything either of you can tell us about Garrett Wycoff?"

"He'd worked for us since high school. He was a favorite with our members and guests. And me," Traci said bitterly. "In May, when it looked like he might go work at another resort, I gave him a raise and promotion and promised him he could live in the new dorm."

"He'd been planning this," Felice said, staring down at her hands.

"How do you know?" the deputy asked.

"We, uh, kind of broke into their rooms, earlier tonight, I mean, last night. They'd basically packed up most of their crap. Even their gaming console. That's when we knew something was up. I think Garrett realized we were on to them."

Felice's face contorted and she suddenly started to weep. "We lived with these guys for a month. Ate pizza and drank beer and hung out with them. And they meant to kill us."

Felice was full-on sobbing now. She fumbled helplessly for the tissue box on the stand next to the bed with her thickly bandaged hands. Traci plucked some tissues and held one up to Felice's nose. "Blow," she commanded.

Felice did. Traci gently dabbed at the tears on the girl's face with another tissue.

"Thank you," Felice whispered.

"I was supposed to be the lookout at the front door—in case the guys came back. We didn't want to get caught snooping."

"What happened after that?" Shapley asked.

Felice sniffled. "We went to the kitchen. I got my jug of kombucha from the fridge. But then Liv's phone rang and she knocked over the whole jug. It spilled all over the counter and I figured maybe she was drunk, because she'd finished off the bottle of wine in the fridge. But really, I guess the roofies had already kicked in on her. Because she barely made it to bed. She couldn't even hardly walk."

Traci reached over and pressed the tissue to Felice's nose and she blew hard, then nodded to signal that she was done.

"I feel so guilty. About being pissed at her for knocking over my kombucha. She always made fun of me and called me a hippie and asked me how I could drink such nasty stuff."

Felice turned baleful eyes to Traci. "But her spilling most of it— so I only got to drink a little of it? Probably saved my life."

"But you risked your own life, to save hers," Traci pointed out. "So I think, when Livvy is herself again, she'll say it's all good."

"Maybe." Felice looked around the cubicle, at Shapley, who was assiduously scribbling notes. "When can I get out of here? I hate hospitals."

Her face sagged. "Except—I don't have any place to go to, and everything I own was in my room." She looked down at the hospital gown she was wearing. "I don't have anything at all, not even a pair of jeans."

"You can go home with me," Traci said firmly. "We'll figure out the rest later."

CHAPTER 66

* * *

Shannon sat in the world's most uncomfortable green vinyl chair, pulled close to the hospital bed.

Her daughter was sleeping. Just an hour earlier, a nurse she'd never met before had bustled into the cubicle and taken Livvy off the oxygen.

The nurse's name was Beth. "Your daughter's gonna be fine," Beth said, washing her hands at the sink. "I hear you work upstairs?"

"In ICU," Shannon said. "Did her drug screen come back yet?"

Beth hesitated.

"This is my kid we're talking about. And it's just between us," Shannon promised.

"Your kid is lucky. We see a lot of girls in here, some guy they meet at a bar dopes their drink, and . . . the worst happens."

"No lasting effects, right?" Shannon had worked the ER early in her nursing career, but that was well before roofies and date rape drugs were a thing.

"Shouldn't be," Beth said. "Her doctor will probably want to do follow-ups, make sure her liver function is good, but they'll tell you about that with all her discharge papers."

Shannon could have wept from relief.

"Your friend is still out in the waiting room. Why don't the two of you go get some coffee or something to eat? It's slow right now. I'll stay with Olivia. Give me your number, and I'll text you if she wakes up."

Shannon scribbled her cell number on a scrap of paper and handed it over. "Thanks. I guess some caffeine would be good."

Traci was dozing when she felt something tugging at her hair, which had come loose from her hair clip.

"Come on, spacy Traci, wake up. Let's go get a cup of joe."

She opened her eyes to see Shannon sitting next to her, wan and bleary-eyed.

Shannon led the way to the cafeteria. They each bought bad coffee and a stale muffin, then sat in the mostly empty room, their weary faces turned a ghoulish shade of yellow from the overhead fluorescent lighting.

"How's Liv?" Traci asked, taking a sip of the scalding brew.

"Still sleeping, but the nurse tells me all her blood work looks good and there shouldn't be any lasting after-effects. How's Felice?"

"Awake and eager to get cut loose of here," Traci said. "We just need the attending to sign her discharge papers."

"That's great. Really great. What'll she do now? Do you think she'll go back to work at the Saint? After everything that's happened to her?"

"The first thing she said when we were alone was that she can't wait to get back to work," Traci said.

"The dorm. Is anything left?"

"The fire chief called me a couple hours ago; it's still standing. They won't know more until daylight, but he expects there'll be a lot of smoke and water damage."

"Will you rebuild?"

"Probably. Our staff can't afford to live nearby. In fact, before the fire, and all the stuff that's gone on, I was thinking we need to come up with some other affordable housing solutions for our people."

Shannon blew on her coffee to cool it. "What happened tonight? The only thing I could get out of the deputy was that they already caught one of the guys."

Traci gave her a quick recap of the night's events. "That was KJ Parkhurst. His grandparents have had a house on the property for decades. Ric is friends with the kid's dad and promised to give KJ a summer job—without consulting me."

Shannon made a face. "Ugh. Ric Eddings raises his ugly head once more. I can't believe you've had to put up with his crap all these years."

"Unfortunately, it now looks like Livvy will have to put up with it too."

"If you think my kid is gonna let an asshole like Ric bully her, you really don't know her."

Traci guffawed. "You're right. Livvy is gonna be a total thorn in his side. And I'm gonna have a front-row seat."

She reached for Shannon's hand. "Do you think she'll have any interest in coming back to work for me at the hotel? I mean, I know she won't actually need a job, but selfishly, she's the best guest relations person I've ever had."

"If it was up to me, I'd say hell no," Shannon said. "I'm hoping she'll finish college and get a degree. But it's not my decision. And I guess what I've learned from all of this is that she's got a hell of a head on her shoulders."

"So you're gonna let her decide?" Traci looked dubious.

"I'm not saying I won't lobby for college, but I will promise to try not to be so controlling. And judgmental," Shannon added, with a wink.

She took in Traci's disheveled appearance and the dark circles under her eyes. "And what about you? Are you gonna be okay?"

"I think I'm still in shock. Especially about Charlie. I thought I knew him. The sheriff's deputy told me that when they went to talk to Charlie, he was gone. Apparently he'd been stealing from the hotel for quite a while. Whelan told me some stuff about what he'd found out about Charlie. I had no idea. At all."

"Whelan? You mean your new not-boyfriend? How's he involved in all this?"

"He used to own a big private security outfit. He sold it last year, I gather at a nice profit, and he decided it was finally time to find out the truth about his brother's death—and why his mother's life fell apart afterward. But you already know that part."

"Yeah, remember? He came to see me here at work. Asked me to go back over what happened that day at the pool, but I never did hear if he got any answers to his questions."

"He got his answers. And they're pretty ugly," Traci said. "Hudson had an undiagnosed peanut allergy. That day, right before he got to the pool, he ate a huge bag of peanut M&M's, given to him by a beach lifeguard who drove a flashy red Corvette and flirted with every girl on the island. And who was apparently having a secret fling that summer with Hudson's mom."

Shannon's eyes narrowed. "Are you talking about Ric? I'll never forget that car."

"Yeah. Me neither. Whelan tracked down his stepfather, Hudson's dad, whom he hadn't seen since the day of Hudson's funeral. The guy had hired a private pathologist, who did a thorough autopsy, which is when they discovered that Hudson drowned because he'd gone into anaphylactic shock. From the peanuts."

"What?" Shannon's voice echoed in the mostly empty cafeteria.

"It wasn't our fault, Shan. There was nothing we could have done to save him."

Shannon's pale face contorted with anger. "All these years. I blamed myself. I blamed you. But it was Ric. Whenever something bad happens, it's always Ric."

"Or the old man," Traci said. "Whelan's stepfather as much as admitted that Fred paid him off to avoid an ugly lawsuit, and the scandal."

Shannon started to say something, but her phone buzzed to signal an incoming text. She stood abruptly, still clutching the foam cup of coffee. "Livvy's awake. I gotta go."

CHAPTER 67

* * *

"Ma'am? Ma'am?"

Somehow, Traci had nodded off to sleep again in the waiting room. The admitting clerk was leaning across the counter, trying to get her attention.

"Yes?" Traci rubbed at her eyes.

"They just sent word that Dr. Ochoa finished your quote daughter's discharge papers."

She smirked when she said the word "daughter."

Traci nodded, then turned when the doors from the ambulance bay opened as Whelan rushed inside.

"Traci?" He was dressed in his work uniform, Carhartts, a Saint work shirt, and boots.

"Hey," she said, struggling to her feet. He wrapped his arms tightly around her, and pressed his lips to her ear. "You're okay, right? You weren't in the fire?"

"I'm fine. Really."

"Your hair smells like smoke. And ash."

"My new perfume."

"Not funny. You gave me a fright," he said, releasing his hold on her, but not before kissing her cheek.

"How did you hear about the fire?"

"I ran into one of the security guards when I stopped for coffee on the way to work. He'd just gotten off duty. I tried calling, but when you didn't answer your phone I panicked and checked your office."

Traci reached into the pocket of the windbreaker she'd thrown on hours ago. She brought out her cell phone and held it up. Dead.

"I heard the fire trucks and ambulance come racing past my house around three, so I got in the golf cart and followed the sirens. And ended up at the staff dorm," Traci said.

"Did everyone get out okay?"

"Felice and Livvy were the only ones there. They managed to climb out a window and escape before the fire spread too far."

"I saw the dorm. Or, what's left of it. There were sheriff's deputies and a fire marshal crawling all over it. I take it this was no accident?"

"No," Traci said, her expression somber. "KJ was there when I got there. He'd apparently been hiding in the woods, watching. He confessed. He and Garrett drugged some wine and kombucha in the fridge so the girls wouldn't wake up when the fire started."

She filled him in on what little she'd learned from Shapley, the sheriff's investigator. "KJ's in custody, but Garrett and Charlie are gone."

"Son of a bitch," Whelan said under his breath. He studied her face. "You're really okay, though, right?"

"Tired and worried beyond words, but physically I'm good."

"Ma'am?" the clerk called out.

Traci turned and walked to the admitting desk.

"You and your quote husband can take your quote daughter home now. An aide is bringing her out now."

"Huh?" Whelan asked.

"Don't ask. Just smile and nod."

She turned back to the clerk. "What about Olivia Grayson? Is she being discharged too?"

"They're just finishing up the paperwork," the clerk said.

The doors from the treatment area slid open and a nurse's aide wheeled Felice out. She was wearing a cotton hospital gown and clutching a plastic bag containing prescriptions and what was left of her clothes.

"Hi. They're sending me home. Wherever that is."

"My place," Traci said quickly. "Hope you like dogs, because Lola's there and eagerly awaiting the chance to jump up and greet you with a wildly inappropriate amount of crotch sniffing."

"Sounds fun," Felice said.

Whelan held out his hand. "Give me your keys and I'll pull your car up to the ambulance bay."

Traci handed them over.

"He's cute," Felice said. "Is he your . . ."

"Friend," Traci said, feeling herself blush.

The doors from the treatment area opened again and an aide wheeled Livvy out, with Shannon trailing close behind. The aide parked Livvy's wheelchair right beside Felice's, and Livvy reached over and gingerly touched her friend's arm.

"What happened to you?" she asked.

Felice shot a worried glance at Livvy's mother.

"It's the roofies," Shannon volunteered. "She doesn't remember most of what happened last night."

"Wish I didn't remember it," Felice said.

"Honey," Shannon said, addressing her daughter, "there was a fire at the dorm. Felice saved you. She got you out of the fire."

"For real?" Livvy laughed. "That's insane."

She looked over at Traci. "Hi, Mrs. E."

"No more Mrs. E. We're business partners now, so it's Traci. You too, Felice," she said. "If we're going to be roommates, you can just call me by my first name."

"Huh?" Livvy looked over at her mother.

"I'll explain later," Shannon said. "For now, I'm taking you home with me."

"No. I don't wanna go to your place. I want to go back to the dorm."

Shannon knelt down beside Livvy's wheelchair. "Listen to me, Liv. Last night there was a fire at the dorm. It was pretty bad, but like I said, Felice got you out."

"Oh," Livvy said. Her face crumpled. "KJ and Garrett? Are they okay?"

"They weren't there," Felice said. "It was just the two of us."

"My stuff?" Livvy asked, her lower lip trembling. "The pretty bedspread and comforter and pillows from Parrish?"

"I don't know anything about that, honey," Shannon said gently.

"Parrish's stepmother, Madelyn, came to get her other things. She gave me the bedspread and stuff."

"When was this?" Traci asked.

Livvy looked confused. "I'm not sure. Last week?"

"We'll get new bedding," Traci promised. "And we'll rebuild the dorm. Better than before."

Shannon touched her daughter's shoulder. "I'm gonna go get my car and bring it up here, and then we'll leave."

Traci followed her outside to the ambulance bay. "She doesn't remember any of it?"

"Like I said, it's the drugs. Dr. Ochoa said it's not uncommon. Doesn't matter."

Whelan pulled Traci's car up beneath the porte cochere, jumped out, and went back inside to get Felice.

"Call me later, okay?" Shannon called over her shoulder as she walked toward the parking lot.

A moment later, Whelan came back with Felice's wheelchair.

"I can walk," Felice insisted as she swung herself out of the chair and into the passenger seat of the car.

Whelan met Traci on the driver's side and squeezed her shoulder. "Plug in your phone, please. And, if it's okay, I'll come by after I get off work. In fact, I'll bring dinner."

"That'll be nice," she said.

Lola greeted the new houseguest with a marathon of tail-wagging, face-licking, and crotch-sniffing.

"Okay, girl, that's enough," Traci said, scooping her up and leading Felice to the guest bedroom. She opened the door and Felice slumped down onto the bed.

"You've got to be pretty beat," Traci said, leaning against the doorjamb. She checked her watch. "It's nearly noon. Did they give you anything to eat back in the ER?"

"Some Jell-O. And a couple cartons of Ensure. Bleahh." A tear slowly rolled down her cheek, and she gestured at the bag of clothes she'd brought home from the hospital. "It just hit me again. That's everything I own right now. Everything else is gone; my laptop, my notebooks with my recipes. My knives . . ."

Traci sat down on the edge of the bed. "I can't imagine how you feel right now. But I promise, things will get better. Did you happen to upload your recipes to the cloud?"

Felice's face brightened. "Yeah. Dropbox. I put everything there."

"Great," Traci said briskly. "Anything else you need, including a new laptop, we'll order online."

Felice nodded, but she still looked troubled.

"What else are you worried about?" Traci asked.

"I can't just stay here with you," Felice said. "It's nice of you to invite me, but I need a place to stay. So I can get back to work." She held up her gauze-wrapped hands. "As soon as I get these bandages off."

"I was thinking about that while I was sitting out in that waiting room. It's not a permanent solution, but it occurred to me, we have an executive suite at the hotel. Charlie used it sometimes, and I even stayed there for a few weeks, after my husband was killed and I couldn't face coming back here."

"Executive suite?"

"Like an apartment. There's a bedroom, bathroom, living room, even a small kitchen. I was thinking you could move in there. And you can stay until we get the dorm rebuilt, or whatever you decide."

"Really?" Felice's expression brightened. "Why would you do that for me?"

"Because you're the best chef we've ever had," Traci said. "My husband's mantra was hire the best and treat 'em right." She laughed. "Okay, so maybe that doesn't apply to KJ and Garrett, but it absolutely applies to you and Livvy. I'm going to do everything in my power to keep you working right here at the Saint."

Felice yawned.

"Rest now," Traci said.

She closed the guest room door and went into her own bedroom. She dropped her clothes on the floor, walked into the bathroom, and ran a hot shower. She sniffed a strand of her damp hair. Whelan was right. She smelled like smoke and ash.

After she'd dressed she went out to the kitchen and brewed herself a cup of tea. She'd intended to make a list of phone calls. There was so much to do. She glanced over at the phone she'd plugged into a charger, then resisted the urge to start making calls, start the search for a new general manager and new headwaiter. And probably, she sensed, she'd also have to look for a new guest relations manager.

Instead, when she pulled a pad of paper and a pen from a kitchen drawer, she started making a list of things to be grateful for. It was a coping mechanism she'd learned in therapy, after Hoke's death, when every day seemed bleak and pointless.

Number one on the list was that Livvy and Felice were alive.

Two was that Shannon was back in her life again.

And number three? Easy. Whelan was number three, with a bullet. He was a good man.

Everything else in her life, and her work, she concluded, would take care of itself.

CHAPTER 68

* * *

The county fire marshal was waiting when Traci arrived at the dorm. She gasped and felt physically ill when she saw the burnt-out wreckage of the former golf cart barn. The concrete-block walls were smoke-blackened, but still standing, and the roof had caved in. It was a miracle that Felice and Livvy had escaped death.

The fire marshal was a woman named Dahlia Diaz. In her forties, she wore a long braid down her back and was outfitted in a Bonaventure Fire Department baseball cap, polo shirt, jeans, and knee-high rubber boots.

Traci introduced herself. "I know this is probably a dumb question, but I did promise I'd ask. Was there anything salvageable in there? Like laptop computers, for instance?"

"No, ma'am," Dahlia said sadly in her thick Southern accent. "It's all a total loss. If you want, I'll walk you around and tell you what we found."

The fire marshal led her around to the rear of the dorm, the area where the kitchen and laundry room had been. She pointed at a hole in the block wall near the back door, which was resting on the ground nearby. "The fire started here. You can see the washer and that gas dryer. See how the door was blown off?" She pointed at the jagged hole in the concrete block. "It looks like your arsonists put some articles soaked in an accelerant in the dryer. Likely kerosene. It was also sprinkled throughout the kitchen and the rest of the building. Then they set the dryer on high. When it got hot enough with the built-up pressure, it blew the door off and ripped the gas line here open."

Traci's mouth went dry, thinking of the narrowly avoided potential of that explosion. "Smart," she murmured.

"Not that smart," Dahlia said. "We can trace the fire's route. We know accelerants were used, from the burn patterns on the floor. I will say your employees were fortunate they got out when they did."

"What's the next step?" Traci asked.

"Up to the sheriff's office," Dahlia said. "I'll file my report with them. No question it's arson, though."

She was almost back to her cottage when her phone rang. Someone from the Bonaventure sheriff's office was calling.

"Mrs. Eddings? This is Deputy Shapley. We met earlier today at the ER?"

"Yes. What can I do for you?"

"We could use your assistance. We've been trying to interview KJ Parkhurst, but he insists you're the only one he'll talk to."

"Me?" Traci was stunned.

"He wants to get some stuff off his chest. We believe it's only a matter of time before his rich daddy figures out what all kind of trouble sonny boy is in. When that happens, he'll bring in some high-dollar Atlanta criminal attorney and KJ won't say another word to us. So if you could come down here and talk to him that'd be real helpful."

Shapley met her in the lobby of the sheriff's headquarters.

"What exactly do you want me to say to KJ?" she asked as they walked down a long hallway lined with stern-faced portraits of past sheriffs.

"Let him do the talking. Try to stay friendly. Neutral. If you can get him to tell us about the fire, and how it started, great. But the bigger issue is the murder of your niece. We'd really like to get him talking about that."

They stopped at a desk where a female deputy was seated, typing at a computer monitor. "This is Deputy Gruver."

The deputy was a dumpling-shaped woman with a pleasant smile. She took Traci behind a screen, patted her every which way possible, then nodded and returned her to Shapley.

He gestured at a door with a window in the middle. "He's waiting for you. We'll be watching through a one-way mirror on the other side, and recording the interview. We don't believe Parkhurst is violent, so he's not handcuffed. But if you feel uncomfortable or threatened, just tell him the interview's over, and we'll come in immediately."

"No handcuffs?" Traci frowned. "What if he . . ."

"He won't," Shapley said. He pointed at the window into the room. "Look at him. He hasn't slept, won't touch the food he's been given. He's a whipped dog."

Shapley's description was apt. KJ was dressed in an ill-fitting orange jumpsuit with BONAVENTURE COUNTY JAIL stenciled across the front. It was probably the cheapest logoed clothing item he'd ever worn. He was unshaven, his hair greasy and stuck to his head. There were deep shadows under his eyes, and the black eye he'd sported last night, plus the bruised jaw, were turning purplish green.

"Ready?" Shapley asked.

Traci took a deep breath. "I guess."

KJ had been slumped down in the chair with his eyes closed, but when she entered the room, he sat up straight.

"Hi, KJ," Traci said. She was so nervous her palms were sweating, her pulse racing. Her voice came out high and squeaky, like a cartoon mouse.

"Mrs. E. You came."

She sat in the chair across from him at the table and waited.

KJ stared down at his lap. "I, uh, I wanted to tell you I'm sorry. For everything that happened. You were nice to me. Treated me right. I feel real bad about all of it."

"All of what?" she said impassively.

"You know." He raked his fingers through his hair, looking every-where except at her.

"You mean the fire? At the dorm?"

"Yeah. That and all the other stuff. I'm not like that. Really, I'm not. I've never been in any trouble before. Well, no serious trouble."

Because you're a Saint—a rich white kid who never had to take respon-sibility for his actions, Traci thought.

"Then how did you get mixed up with Garrett and Charlie Burroughs?"

He looked up, surprised. "You know about Charlie?"

"Some of it, but I was hoping you'd tell me."

His cheeks bloomed crimson. "They were blackmailing me. I didn't have a choice."

"They figured out you were gay?"

Now he looked right at her. "You knew?"

"I guessed."

"That bitch Marcie figured it out. She saw me leaving the Back Porch."

"The gay club in town?"

"Yeah. It was Wild West night. I was just having a little fun. But she spotted me and let Burroughs know. Pretty sure she's sleep-ing with him. One day I was working in the boutique, and pricing some really expensive sweaters. The count was way off. When I told her, she said I better mind my own business. That's when she told me she'd seen me at the Back Porch and I should keep my mouth shut unless I wanted my granddad to know I was a friggin' faggot."

The words sent a chill down Traci's spine. Marcie Meadows had worked at the Saint for at least five years. She was hardworking and efficient, great at merchandising the shop, and fabulous as a sales-woman, and also as a thief, apparently.

"So, it started with the thefts. Clothing from the boutique? What else?"

"Everywhere, really. Garrett sold cases of booze out of the trunk of his car, to people in town. And he'd let his buddies drink free at the Saint, or get them comped rooms at the hotel, so he could eat and drink free at bars and restaurants in town."

"And Charlie? What was his department?"

KJ made an expansive gesture with both hands. "He took a cut of everything. I was the noob—you know, the new guy—so I wasn't in on everything. But I heard he made a lot of money when the hotel was being renovated. Garrett said anybody who did business with the Saint had to do business with Charlie first."

"That included the seafood and meat wholesalers in the restaurant?"

He shrugged. "Yeah."

"Whose idea was it to burn down the dorm?" she asked.

He grimaced. "That was Garrett. Livvy, she thought she was some kind of detective. She used to watch all those true-crime shows and listen to murder podcasts. Her and Felice kept poking around, asking questions."

"He figured Felice and Livvy knew about his operation?"

"Yeah. He found out they'd talked to one of his old girlfriends and she told them a bunch of stuff. Garrett said if we didn't do something, right away, we'd go to prison."

Traci leaned forward, trying to get him to look her in the face, but he still averted his eyes. "Tell me about the fire. How did you do it?"

KJ looked down at his hands again, clenching and unclenching them. "Sunday, after the girls left, we went in and put the roofies in everything in the fridge. Felice's kombucha, Livvy's open bottle of wine, a bottle of Dr Pepper, all of it. We waited until we figured the girls were zonked out, then we snuck back into the dorm. There was a load of towels already in the dryer. We soaked them in kerosene, then set the dryer on high. Because it was a gas dryer, it was supposed to blow up, once it got hot enough inside."

KJ gingerly touched his bruised jaw.

"How'd you get those bruises?" she asked.

"Garrett was really pissed because he saw Livvy searched his room. He had one of those little hidden camera things, and he watched her on his phone. We were supposed to leave after we did the dryer thing, but he dragged out some more towels and clothes and put 'em around the dorm and outside their rooms, and sprinkled kerosene there too. I didn't know it, but he'd brought along these little spike things, and he stuck them in the locks on their doors, so they couldn't get out."

"You mean, so they'd be burned alive?" Traci's stomach churned as she pictured what could have happened.

"I told him that was taking it too far. He threw some punches, called me a fruity little titty-baby." KJ rubbed his bruised jaw.

"Then we went out to the woods to wait. By then, Garrett had cooled down. We smoked some weed 'cuz we were both pretty amped up."

"Was Charlie there?" she asked.

"He told us he'd meet up with us and give us some money to get away. But he ghosted us."

"How long did you wait?"

"Dunno. I fell asleep. I woke up when the dryer exploded. Flames were shooting out of the kitchen windows. Garrett took off on the golf cart. He left me behind."

No honor among thieves, Traci thought.

"Where did Garrett go?"

KJ ran his fingers through his greasy hair again. He looked nothing like the puppy-eyed frat boy who'd reported to work at the Saint in his pop-collared polo shirt and boat shoes only a month earlier.

"Not sure. To his girlfriend's, maybe?"

"The one who works at the Saint's spa?" she asked.

KJ laughed bitterly. "Who knows? He was boning a lot of chicks in town."

"Why didn't you leave when Garrett did?"

He put his head down on the conference table, cradling it in both hands.

"Don't know." His voice was muffled.

"Come on," Traci said, making an effort not to lose her temper. She glanced toward the one-way mirror, knowing Shapley was on the other side, silently willing her to get to the most urgent issue at hand.

"You know what I think?" she said softly. "I think maybe you're not like Charlie or Garrett. You're a decent person who made some bad decisions."

Slowly, he raised his head. Now he looked right at her, his eyes red-rimmed and full of self-pity. "I'm not anything like them," he said.

"KJ. Could you tell me about what happened at the afterparty? With Parrish?"

He buried his head again. "I can't talk about that."

She waited. Looked up at the large clock on the wall. Heard it ticking, heard her own breath, in and out, in and out, synced to the second hand of the clock. KJ's shoulders shuddered. And still she waited.

Minutes passed. He sniffled and wiped his nose on the sleeve of his jumpsuit.

"It was a mistake," he said, tears running down his cheeks. "A huge mistake."

"Whose idea was it to drug Parrish?"

He shook his head again, tears streaming down his face. "I can't . . . I mean, I need to call my dad. I don't want to say anything else. Call my dad, please."

He gave her the puppy-dog eyes again. "I'm so sorry. I never thought any of this would really happen. I was stoned. So was Garrett."

There it was. The confession. She'd done what she'd been asked to do. But she had more questions.

"The next day, you went back out to the Shack, pretending to look for Parrish, even though you knew she was dead. And then you and Garrett got rid of any evidence. Cleaned things up nice and neat, didn't you?"

His face had turned to stone. He pointed toward the window. "Call my dad. I want a lawyer!"

"Where did Charlie and Garrett go?" Traci persisted. "Where are they now?"

He shrugged and looked at the ceiling.

"I think you know, KJ," she said. "Why protect them? They ran off and left you behind. Probably the two of them are splitting the money you three stole from me."

KJ sniffled again and wiped his nose on the other shoulder of his jumpsuit.

She pointed at the mirror. "There's a detective behind that glass. He's recorded everything you just told me, including your confession to theft, arson, attempted arson, and a bunch of other stuff. I'm no lawyer, KJ, but I do know that Georgia is a death penalty state. You might want to think about that."

He stiffened. "I didn't kill anybody. I want a lawyer."

Traci exhaled. She'd done what she'd come here to do.

The door opened and Shapley stepped inside. He gave her a curt nod, then directed himself to KJ. "Does Garrett know where you are? How about Burroughs, the boss-man?"

"Lawyer," KJ repeated. He put his head down on the table.

"I'll walk you out," Shapley said as they left the interrogation room. "I wouldn't worry too much about Burroughs and Wycoff. I've had deputies posted outside the gates to your property since I spoke to your witnesses at the hospital. If he's on that island of yours, we'll find him."

"They could be anywhere by now," Traci said.

"We'll catch them," Shapley repeated. "Go home now."

CHAPTER 69

* * *

The house was too quiet. Livvy had been asleep since they'd gotten home from the hospital. Shannon opened her daughter's bedroom door and peeked inside.

She found her daughter sitting up in bed, scrolling on her phone. "Moooom," Livvy groaned. "I'm alive, okay?" She held out her wrist. "Here. Take my pulse if you don't believe me."

"Can you blame me? You scared the living daylights out of me today. You could have been burned alive in that damn dorm."

"But I'm okay. Can you please just chill?"

"Rude!" Shannon said, and she slammed the door and stomped out to the kitchen. The next thing she knew, she was calling Traci.

"Hey!" Traci said. "So weird. I was about to call you. How's Livvy?"

"Rude and annoying. Why don't you come by and see for yourself?"

"I'm just leaving the jail. I can be there in fifteen, if that works."

"The jail?"

"I'll fill you in when I get there."

Shannon sped around the house, looking for something to dust or neaten up, but the place was already spotless. She chewed on her lower lip, thinking of what Traci's reaction would be to her modest-at-best residence.

She vacuumed the living room rug anyway, and was in the process of using the Swiffer on the terrazzo floors in the entryway when Livvy emerged from her room.

"What the heck are you doing? Are you on meth or something?"

"Is it a crime for me to want my house to look nice? As it happens, Traci is going to drop by. I don't want her to think we're some kind of poor white trash."

"Poor white trash? Who says that anymore?" Livvy shook her head and started to say something, but the doorbell rang.

"Act nice," Shannon warned.

She ushered Traci out to the kitchen and they sat at the dinette. Shannon sat opposite her, and Livvy slid into the chair beside her mother's.

"Oh, Shan," Traci said, running her hand over the green Formica tabletop. "How many times did we sit at this table, doing homework?"

"A million times, give or take," Shannon said. "You want some coffee or something?"

"I'm good, thanks. How are you feeling, Livvy?" Traci asked.

"Fine! Except I wish you'd tell my mom to stop hovering over me." Livvy pried one of her own eyeballs open with her fingers. "See? Awake, alert, and healthy as shit."

"She slept the whole afternoon," Shannon said.

Livvy rolled her eyes. "How's Felice? Is she feeling okay?"

"Amazingly, yes. She was resting when I left the house."

"What were you doing at the jail?" Shannon asked.

"I went because KJ refused to talk to the cops. He insisted that he'd only talk to me."

"What, did he expect you to wave your wand and forgive him?" Shannon asked.

"He confessed to helping Garrett start the fire," Traci said. She repeated KJ's account of that night, how they'd put roofies in the girls' drinks and waited until they'd both passed out before reentering the house to turn the clothes dryer into a firebomb.

"Garrett probably got the hookup for the fentanyl," Livvy said. "He always had drugs."

Shannon wrapped a protective arm around her daughter as they listened to Traci's narrative. Her face paled and then twisted in fury as she heard how the two roommates had waited in the woods, getting stoned while waiting for the fire to start.

"But what about Parrish? Did he admit they killed her?" Livvy asked.

"KJ said he and Garrett were stealing from the hotel, and that Charlie was the boss. He refused to talk about Parrish. Insisted it was a mistake, and he wanted his dad. And a lawyer."

"Sweet Jesus," Shannon said.

"I knew it!" Livvy exclaimed. "She'd made notes about all that stuff in the bitch book."

"Oh!" Livvy clapped a hand over her mouth and she looked sheepishly at Traci. "I found the bitch book hidden in a pillow, in Parrish's room. I should have given it to you, but I had this stupid idea that we could prove what those guys were up to."

Her face fell. "But maybe it burned up in the fire?"

"Felice told me about how you two found Parrish's notebook," Traci said.

"I miss Parrish," Livvy said, her lower lip trembling. "And I can't believe they'd kill her over some stinking mattresses and televisions. We were having so much fun that night. Until, you know . . ." She pulled her cell phone from her pocket and scrolled through her camera roll.

"Look," she said, holding up the phone. "That's us, in the golf cart, on the way to the afterparty. Parrish didn't even want to go, but I talked her into it . . ."

Shannon studied the photo. "Geez, side by side, the two of you in those same Hawaiian dresses, same goofy smiles . . ."

"Let me see that," Traci said, taking the phone. "You look almost like twins," she murmured.

"Not really," Livvy said. "Parrish was taller and so much prettier."

"A mistake," Traci said slowly. "KJ said it was all a big mistake."

"Of course he'd claim that," Shannon said impatiently.

"What if it really was a mistake?" Traci said, her eyes riveted to the photo. "Whelan saw some of the investigator's notes. More than one person at the party said that the last time they saw Parrish she was talking to Cedric, the lead singer from the band."

"I saw them together too," Livvy said. "He handed her a Solo cup of the punch. And a joint."

"Which was probably what killed her," Traci said. "But what if they didn't mean to kill Parrish at all? What if . . ."

She stood abruptly. "Text me that picture, please, Livvy. I've gotta go."

"Go where?" Shannon asked.

"Back to the island."

CHAPTER 70

* * *

On the drive back to the Saint, Traci kept replaying the interview with KJ over and over in her mind. She couldn't get over his casual tone as he told how he and Garrett had hidden in the woods outside the dorm, getting stoned, waiting for the fire to start while Livvy and Felice, their friends, were locked inside, unconscious and helpless.

"Then Garrett took off on the golf cart," KJ said. He'd sounded so bitter at his coconspirator's betrayal.

Where had Garrett gone after he left the scene of the fire, she wondered. How far had he gotten on the golf cart? She only remembered seeing two cars in the parking lot at the dorm following the fire.

She picked up her phone and called Livvy.

"Hey, Mrs. E."

"Liv, what kind of car does Garrett drive?"

"Huh?"

"Car? What make and model does Garrett drive?"

"Lemme think. Okay, yeah, he drives, like, a crappy old Nissan. Black, with a lot of rust. Why do you want to know?"

"Just wondering."

What if, Traci thought, she'd been wrong? What if one or both of the men were still on the island? Where would they be?

Her phone rang as she was pondering the possibilities. It was Whelan.

"Hey. I thought we were having dinner together. I'm here with Felice. Where are you?"

Damn. She'd completely forgotten.

"Just getting ready to cross the causeway. See you soon."

She found Whelan and Felice in the kitchen, unloading the takeout cartons he'd brought. Felice was still dressed in the scrubs she'd been given at the hospital.

Whelan lifted the lid on one of the containers, handing it to Felice. "Shrimp fried rice?"

"Love it," Felice said.

"From the Chinese place across the street from my apartment in the village," Whelan said. "Not a ton of choices in this town that might suit a chef like yourself; we've got pizza, barbecue, Mexican, Chinese, and Southern fried."

"I miss decent Chinese food," Felice said. "We had our pick back in Miami."

"I don't know that you'd call this decent," Whelan said. "More like sub-mediocre. But I brought some egg rolls, potstickers, some crab Rangoon, and beef and broccoli. Hopefully, something for everyone."

Traci placed dishes, napkins, and cutlery on the table and they served themselves buffet style, with Felice awkwardly using a spoon to feed herself.

Afterward, Felice picked up a paper bag and spilled half a dozen fortune cookies onto the tabletop.

Whelan took one and opened it. He read it aloud: "*Make yourself necessary to someone.* Deep, huh?"

Felice handed her cookie to Traci. "Can you open that for me, please? These mitts aren't good for much right now."

Traci pulled the paper slip from the cookie and read. "*Courage is not the absence of fear; it is the conquest of it.* I'd say that's pretty apt in the light of the last twenty-four hours."

Whelan handed Traci a fortune cookie. "Let's see what yours says."

She opened the cracker, read it, blushed, and crumpled the paper in her fingertips.

"What's it say?" Felice asked. "Come on now, we read ours."

"It's silly and meaningless," Traci said, but before she could discard it, Whelan reached over and pried it from her fingertips.

"Fair is fair." He cleared his throat and roared with laughter as he read Traci's fortune out loud. *"The one you love is closer than you think."*

"Oooh, Mrs. E," Felice said, waggling her eyebrows. "Looks like you made a love connection. Wonder who that could be."

Traci started to clear the dishes in an attempt to distract her dinner companions.

"What did the fire marshal say when you met with him?" Whelan asked.

"The fire marshal is a woman. Named Dahlia Diaz. The fire was started in the gas dryer. KJ and Garrett loaded it with towels, sprinkled it with kerosene, and then set the dryer on high, creating, essentially, a firebomb. Then they sprinkled more towels with kerosene and put them outside the girls' bedrooms. Then Garrett put some kind of pick in the doorknobs to keep the girls locked in."

"The fire marshal told you all that?" Whelan asked.

"No, she told me that it was arson. KJ Parkhurst told me the rest."

"How did that come about?" Whelan asked, startled.

"That sheriff's deputy, Shapley, called me. They apprehended KJ, hiding out in the carriage house behind his grandparents' place here. He refused to give them a statement, said the only one he'd talk to was me. So I went to the jail this afternoon and met with him."

"You believe anything that fool tells you?" Felice asked.

"He freely admitted most of what I just told you. He also copped to the thefts from the hotel, but of course, he said it was all Charlie's idea, and that Garrett was the one who did the dirty work. KJ claimed the two of them blackmailed him into going along with everything by threatening to out him to his family."

"Whose idea was it to kill Parrish?" Felice asked. "Satan?"

"KJ wouldn't talk about Parrish's murder. At all. Just kept saying it was a big mistake."

"A mistake? What do you think he meant by that?" Whelan asked, leaning forward with his elbows on the table.

She dumped the dishes in the sink and sat back down at the table.

"After I left the jail I dropped by Shannon's to check on Livvy, who, by the way, seems to be relatively unscathed. Of course, she's still processing everything that's happened, and still mourning Parrish. She showed me a selfie she snapped of the two of them, when they were on the way to the afterparty. Both dressed in their Hawaiian-print dresses, their faces pressed close together with these goofy smiles . . ."

"Parrish wasn't goofy very often. She must have been having a good time that night," Felice said wistfully.

"Both Shannon and I were suddenly struck by how much they looked alike in that picture," Traci said. "And it started me thinking . . ."

"You think maybe the murderer didn't intend to kill Parrish? That it literally *was* an accident? But why would someone target Livvy?" Whelan asked.

"Livvy saw Cedric, the guy from the band, chatting Parrish up, handing her a Solo cup, presumably of punch, and a joint. The guy didn't know Parrish, or Livvy. Maybe someone just told him—"

"Paid him, probably," Felice put in.

"Hired him to hit on the pretty girl in the flowered dress," Traci continued.

"But why?" Felice asked.

"This is a long shot, but what if someone found out that Livvy stood to inherit a big chunk of Fred Eddings's money? And they wanted to stop that from happening—at any cost."

"I was under the impression that nobody knew that Livvy was Fred's child, or that the will had been changed," Whelan said.

"Me too," Traci said. "But what if someone else knew about the NDA Shannon was forced to sign? What if they found out right after Ric got his dad to change the will?"

Felice shook her head. "Livvy told me it was a big dark secret who her daddy was."

"Who else knew that Fred was Livvy's father?" Whelan asked.

"Andy Plankenhorn, obviously, and Shannon's lawyer, but he died years ago."

"If Livvy's out of the way, Ric Eddings gets to inherit the whole enchilada, right?"

"In theory. But what if someone else *did* know about the NDA?" Traci said.

"Like who?" Felice asked. She'd been watching the back-and-forth like a spectator at a Ping-Pong match with rules she didn't quite understand.

"Madelyn Eddings. After Fred was too frail to live alone in the big house, she personally took charge of moving everything out of that oceanfront house, and then moving him into Gardenia. Maybe she found a copy of that NDA when she was cleaning out his office?"

"So helpful," Whelan quipped.

"Ugh. I never did like that lady," Felice said. "Sticking her nose in our business at the restaurant, coming around all the time, having special lunches with Garrett."

"You saw her with Garrett?" Traci asked.

"Yeah. A lot. She had *opinions* about the dining room. This one time, I went into the storage room, and they were just coming out, looking kinda sex-drunk, and I remember thinking if it was anyone else, I'd think they were back in there doing the nasty. But she's waaay older than him, got a rich husband. Why would she be messing with some little waiter?"

"Maybe she wanted revenge on Ric. Everybody in town knows he was running around on Madelyn."

"Maybe." Whelan looked dubious.

Felice stood up, yawning. "Mrs. E, if you don't mind, I'm going to take my pain meds and go to bed now." She turned to Whelan. "And thank you, Mr. Whelan, for the dinner. When I get these bandages off, I'll play around with some recipes, come up with a menu for an Asian-themed dinner, later in the summer."

"Please invite me, when you do that," Whelan said.

"Good night, Felice," Traci said. "Get some rest."

Whelan pointed to the wine bottle he'd set on the counter. "The guy at the liquor store promised me that this is an excellent pairing with subpar Chinese food. Wanna give it a try?"

They took the wine out onto the screened porch, and Lola trotted out to find a place on the wicker sofa between Whelan and her mistress.

"I think she's starting to like me," Whelan said, scratching the dog's long, silky ears. He kissed Traci lightly. "Obviously, she believes your fortune cookie, even if you don't."

Traci glanced over her shoulder, toward the kitchen door. "I've got one of my employees staying here, Whelan. This doesn't seem . . . appropriate."

"Come on, Traci. You heard Felice, she's taking her pain meds and going to bed. She's not going to be peeping out the window at us. And even if she did, who would she report us to? Her supervisor, which is you?"

"Technically, her direct supervisor is Charlie Burroughs. Who, as of today, is no longer an employee of the Saint."

"You're deliberately changing the subject again," Whelan said.

She took his hand in hers. "Just give me a little time, please? To deal with all of this?"

Whelan shook his head. "You, of all people, should know tomorrow isn't guaranteed, to any of us. I'm attracted to you, and I think the feeling is mutual. Why shouldn't we act on that? Why should we wait? Why should we have regrets?"

"You're right," Traci admitted. "You're absolutely right. I want this." She grabbed the collar of his shirt and pulled his face closer, resting her forehead against his. "I want you, Whelan, in the world's worst way." She kissed him, to demonstrate just how much she wanted to take things to the next level.

Pressed tightly between the two bodies, Lola wriggled and barked in protest.

"Shut up, please," Whelan whispered, his lips tickling her ear.

She drew back. "Excuse me?"

"I meant the dog, not you."

Whelan wrapped his arms around Traci's neck and pulled her closer. "We'll be very quiet. Very discreet."

"The guest bedroom is right next to my room," Traci pointed out.

He was kissing her neck, running his hands up under her shirt. "If only you knew someone who owned a hotel, quite nearby."

Traci gasped as his thumb traced lazy circles around her nipple. "God no," she gasped.

"'God no, don't touch me like this'?" he asked, lowering his head to her breast.

"God no, we are not checking into a room at the Saint. Can you imagine if word got out that Mrs. E was shacked up there with . . . a man?"

"Who cares?" He pushed her blouse off one shoulder and started unbuttoning it.

She heard her phone ringing from within the kitchen and pushed his hand away.

"Let it go to voice mail," Whelan urged. "We're busy here."

"Wait," she said, cocking her head. "Let me see who's calling."

"Bonaventure County sheriff's office," the caller ID voice intoned.

She jumped up. "I have to take this."

"Mrs. Eddings? This is Wynnton Coyle over in Bonaventure. Thought you'd like to know that your general manager, Charlie Burroughs, was in an accident tonight over in Wayne County."

"What happened?"

"He tried to outrun a state trooper. Was going nearly a hundred miles an hour when his car left the road and hit a utility pole. The trooper says your man sustained some pretty serious head injuries.

He's being life-flighted to the emergency room down in Jackson-ville. The woman who was in the vehicle with him, Marcie some-thing, has some fractured ribs and a broken femur. They're treating her at the hospital in Jesup."

"Is he . . . going to make it?"

"Don't know," Coyle said. "I'll keep you posted."

She disconnected and looked up to see Whelan walking back into the kitchen with the half-full wineglasses in hand. Lola trotted close behind.

He sighed and poured the dregs of his wineglass into the sink.

"The sheriff told me Charlie Burroughs tried to outrun a state trooper earlier tonight. He hit a telephone pole going nearly a hun-dred miles an hour. His head injuries were so bad they're air-lifting him down to the trauma hospital in Jacksonville. Marcie was with him, but not injured as severely."

Whelan winced. "Will he live?"

"They don't know yet."

"Do you hope he does?"

"Charlie was like an uncle to me. I trusted him completely, but now that I know the level of betrayal, what he was capable of? I honestly don't know how I feel about him. I don't want him to die. I want him to live, so I can look him in the face and ask him why."

"I understand," Whelan said, but clearly, by the look on his face, he didn't. "I'll let myself out."

"Whelan?" Traci called, but he didn't turn around as he walked out the front door.

* * *

Traci sank down onto one of the barstools drawn up to the kitchen table. She regarded her own half-full glass of wine and dumped it out.

Lola sat at her feet, looking up, her expression unreadable.

"Men, huh?" Traci said. "They want what they want when they want it."

Lola scampered to the back door and began scratching at it.

"Again?" Traci grabbed the retractable leash and clipped it to Lola's collar.

The golf course grass was thick and damp beneath her feet. Lola trotted along in front of her, stopping to sniff every tree trunk and clump of flowers. Once, she stopped to bark a warning to a green tree frog whose hysterical peeping made Traci chuckle.

Lola trotted over to a bed of asparagus ferns and caladiums planted in the shade of one of the live oaks, and took care of business.

"Good girl," Traci said, taking out the plastic poop bag she'd stuffed in her back pocket, along with her phone.

As she was stooping, her phone pinged with a notification from the Ring camera at her front door.

She opened the app and stared in horror at the grainy image of a man in a hoodie standing on her front porch, peering into the house through the sidelights on either side of the door. He was dressed in baggy gym shorts, with the hood pulled low over his forehead, but she recognized him. Garrett Wycoff. Had she locked the front door after Whelan left?

She turned and began sprinting back toward the house as fast as she could. She stopped twenty yards short of the house, crouching down behind a tree. Hands shaking, she scrolled through her contact list and tapped Ray Bierbower's number. It rang three, then four times. "This is Ray," his voice mail said. "Leave me a message."

"Ray," she whispered. "This is Traci. I just got a Ring notification. There's a man standing on the front porch of my house. I think he's trying to break in. I'm out on the golf course with my dog, but Felice is in the house alone. Please send a patrol car ASAP."

Her next call was to Whelan. As pissed as he was with her, would he even pick up?

"Hey," he said, his voice holding lingering traces of his annoyance.

"Whelan, I'm out on the golf course, walking Lola. I just saw Garrett on my Ring camera. He's at the house, and Felice is there, alone."

"Jesus," Whelan said. "Did you call nine-one-one?"

"It'll take forever for them to get here from the mainland," Traci said. "I left a message for Ray Bierbower. Can you come back here? Please?"

"I'm just across the causeway. I'll turn around. But you stay away from the house, okay? In the meantime, call nine-one-one and stay put until Bierbower or the cops or me get to your place. Understand?"

"Felice is there by herself," Traci said. "What if he—"

"He won't."

She called 911, and then the sheriff's number, repeating the request for help.

"We'll have a unit out there within fifteen minutes," the dispatcher said.

"Hurry," Traci whispered.

She peered around the trunk of the tree in time to see a light snap on in the kitchen. To her horror, she spotted Garrett through the glass storm door, shoving Felice into the room at gunpoint. Felice was in her scrubs, her hair bound up in a wrap. Even from this distance, Traci could see the terrified look on her face. Garrett was shouting something at her, but Felice was shaking her head.

Lola let out a low, guttural growl. She was standing at alert, her ears set back and quivering, body rigid, tail tucked, teeth bared.

"No," Traci whispered. "Easy, girl. Easy."

She bent down to scoop her up, but it was too late. Lola rocketed forward, her barking sharp and frenzied, trailing the leash and handle behind as Traci raced to try to intercept the dog, who was faster and focused on her rescue mission.

Garrett froze, uncertain of what was happening, then turned toward the door, gun in hand.

In that moment, Felice leaped forward and kicked Garrett squarely in the groin.

He screamed and fell to his knees and Felice, emboldened, kicked him again, with a ferocity that frightened and impressed Traci, who yanked the kitchen door open. Somehow, Garrett was still clutching the gun in one hand, while protectively cupping his genitals with the other. Lola was on him now, snarling and snapping.

"Get the gun," Felice cried, raising her bandaged hands above her head while raining blow after blow on the downed man with her bare feet. She stood, looking down at Garrett, who was writhing in agony on the floor.

"How you like that, motherfucker? You gonna point a motherfuckin' gun in my face? You gonna drug me and my bestie and try to burn us alive?"

She planted her foot hard in the middle of his face. His nose burst open, spurting blood.

Traci stomped hard on Garrett's gun hand. He yowled, and Traci kicked the gun, sending it skittering across the kitchen floor. She picked it up and pointed it at Garrett. "Don't move."

———

Whelan was the first to arrive on the scene. When he burst through the kitchen door the first thing he saw was Traci, sitting on a barstool, pointing a gun at the intruder. The second thing he saw was Felice, seated at the kitchen table with Lola in her lap, glowering down at the intruder.

The third thing he saw was Garrett Wycoff on the floor, trussed up like a Thanksgiving turkey with what looked like the cord from Lola's retractable leash. His face was swollen, his nose a bloody, pulpy mess.

"What happened here?" he asked Traci.

"Lola doesn't like it when criminals break into our house," she said wearily. "Plus, he pulled a motherfuckin' gun on Felice. He got what he had coming."

CHAPTER 72

* * *

"This was all Madelyn," Garrett said. He was sitting in the interview room at the Bonaventure County sheriff's office, pressing an ice bag to his ruined nose.

Traci and Whelan sat on the other side of the one-way window, listening in.

"How's that?" Coyle asked, his tone neutral.

"It was her idea, all of it. The fire at the dorm, trying to get rid of Livvy, that was all Madelyn. I'm telling ya, man. That is one stone-cold bitch.

"Me and Charlie were happy with the way things were going, but then, during the remodel, she said we should step it up. She said Mrs. E didn't know her ass from a hole in the ground, because, you know, she was walking around like a zombie after her husband got killed."

Traci winced and Whelan rubbed her shoulders.

"Back up," Coyle said. "What kind of 'things' are we talking about here? And be specific."

Traci listened while her former favorite waiter tonelessly laid out his crimes against her and her business, laying most of the blame at Madelyn's feet.

"Once Madelyn got her claws into us, she wanted more. The old man gave her the job as design director, which was like letting a drunk run a liquor store, so she upped the ante, buying cheaper TVs, mattresses, furniture, like that, then dummying up purchase orders for more expensive shit. She put the squeeze to contractors doing the demo and build-out on the new wing. It was a lot of money, not that I saw that much of it."

"How did Madelyn become a partner in your crimes?"

"How do you think?"

"Are you saying you and Madelyn Eddings had a sexual relationship?"

"Oh yeah."

"And during the course of that relationship, you revealed the illegal activities you and Charlie Burroughs were engaged in?"

"Not revealed. She figured it out. I never did know how, but once she did, she was all in."

"How did that sit with you and Charlie?"

"What could we do? We knew she'd go to the cops if we didn't cut her in."

"Right," Coyle said. He'd been scratching notes on a yellow legal pad. "Tell me about the night of the Beach Bash, when Parrish Eddings was killed."

"Jesus, what a clusterfuck," Garrett said. "It wasn't supposed to be Parrish. It was supposed to be Livvy. That fucker Cedric was so stoned, he could barely walk."

"Livvy? Do you mean Olivia Grayson?"

"Yeah. Madelyn said Ric had gotten his old man's will changed, so he would inherit most of the family company, but in the meantime she found out Livvy's father was Ric's father. How messed up is that?"

"How exactly did Madelyn Eddings discover this information?" Coyle asked.

"Last year, when the old man got too crippled up to live alone, Madelyn moved him into a smaller house. She was going through his files and found an NDA that Fred made Livvy's mom sign."

"By NDA you mean a nondisclosure agreement?"

"Right. Livvy's mom couldn't tell anyone who the baby's daddy was, and in return, she got some money."

"Did Madelyn tell Ric Eddings about that document?"

Garrett's laugh was mirthless. "Hell no. She hated his guts. He always had a side piece."

"Why didn't she divorce him?"

"Two words. Pre. Nup. If she left, she'd get nothing."

Coyle kept scribbling on the legal pad. "Take me through the night of the murder. Where did the fentanyl come from?"

"I can't remember. Maybe Cedric?"

The sheriff looked up. "Try again."

"A guy I know in town. Strictly small-time. And I'm not telling you his name."

"We'll get back to that. What happened next?"

"I knew Cedric from the other years his band played at the Beach Bash. I gave him the stuff, and told him to give it to Livvy."

"What was KJ Parkhurst's role in this project?"

"All he had to do was get Livvy to the party. But at the last minute Parrish decided to come too. And that's how the fuckup happened. We pointed Livvy out to Cedric. But he was blasted on weed and coke. All he saw was a white girl in a flowered dress."

"Parrish Eddings."

"Like I said, it was a clusterfuck. Me and KJ got kinda wasted too. We didn't figure out 'til the next morning, when Mrs. E came to the dorm looking for Parrish, what happened."

"After that, you went out to the Shack, under the pretense of looking for Parrish, but really, you wanted to clean up the crime scene," Coyle said.

"Madelyn was having a shit fit. I'm telling you, everything that happened was her idea."

Coyle looked down at a phone, which he'd placed on the table between them, and rubbed his eyes.

"Let's cut to the chase here. Why didn't you leave the island, after the fire?"

"I couldn't. My piece-of-shit car was dead," Garrett said. "I texted Madelyn, to tell her what happened, and she said I should just go hide out somewhere, until it was safe to leave."

"Back up. Did you know Livvy and Felice got out of the dorm alive?"

"I left as soon as the dryer blew. But KJ texted me they'd gotten out."

"We have KJ in custody, by the way," Coyle said, watching Garrett's face.

Garrett rolled his eyes. "I told Charlie it was a mistake, bringing him in. Guy's a lightweight."

"You said Madelyn suggested you hide out. Where were you up until tonight?"

"A cottage that Madelyn knew about. A snowbird owns it, only stays there from Christmas through Easter. It was our hookup house."

Coyle pushed his chair away from the table and crossed his legs. "Why did you show up at Traci Eddings's house tonight?"

"Madelyn fucked me over," Garrett said. "Totally ghosted me. I needed a car, and money to get off the island, and I figured Mrs. E had both. I was gonna make her go over to the hotel, get some cash out of the safe. I was never gonna hurt her. The gun was just to persuade her."

Coyle pointed to the phone. "Are there texts on your phone? From Madelyn?"

"Hell yeah. She'd text whenever she wanted to get with me."

"And you saved those texts? Didn't delete them?"

Garrett smirked. "Insurance."

Traci's fingers itched to slap the smile off his face.

"Text her now," Coyle said.

"She won't answer. I've called, like, a dozen times."

"It's different now. Tell her KJ is in custody, and Charlie's in custody, and the two of you need to talk. Tonight. Or you'll go to the police with what you know."

"Fuuuccck," Garrett said, hanging his head. "You got Charlie?"

"And his girlfriend," Coyle said. He tapped the back of the phone. "Text her. Tell her you need to meet up at that house you told us about."

CHAPTER 73

* * *

Traci intercepted the sheriff in the hallway outside the interview room. "I want to be at that house when Madelyn gets there."

"Nope." Coyle looked over her shoulder, and she turned to see Deputy Shapley escort a handcuffed Garrett out of the room.

"Get that nose doctored," Coyle called out. "And clean him up so it doesn't look like he was mugged by a girl gang."

Garrett looked over his shoulder at Traci and Whelan. "Madelyn ain't coming to that house. She's super smart and crafty."

"Not crafty enough to make sure you deleted all those text messages between the two of you," Traci sniped.

Shapley gave Garrett a shove. "You better hope she does show up. Or you're going down for murder, while she walks. This better be the performance of your life."

Traci waited until Garrett was out of earshot. "Sheriff? Those two conspired to murder a member of my family, a young woman who was very dear to me. They stole hundreds of thousands of dollars from my business, attempted to kill two more of my employees, and burned down one of my buildings in the process. I intend to be there when you arrest Madelyn Eddings."

"No, ma'am," Coyle said. "You're here strictly as a courtesy. Now, you go on home, and we'll call you when and if we have Madelyn Eddings in custody." He gave her a curt nod.

"Screw that," Traci muttered, watching him walk away. "I wasn't asking for permission."

Whelan had been standing behind her, observing the exchange. She turned to him now.

"Are you in?"

"All the way."

"I know which house Garrett calls the hookup house," Traci told Whelan, on the way back to the island. "It backs up to the seventh hole. Owned by Joe and Anita Deibel. We manage the house through the Saint's rental program."

They were halfway across the causeway. "What makes you so sure?"

"His car is broken down, so he must have walked over from there to my house tonight. Plus, I know Madelyn helped Anita Deibel order new furniture and window treatments for their cottage this past spring. Makes sense she would still have the key. It's Oleander Cottage."

"Aren't oleanders poisonous?"

"Like Madelyn," she said.

They walked across the golf course from Traci's house, keeping to the shadows. She pointed to the small stucco cottage. "That's it."

Oleander was one of the original 1920s cottages Hoke's grandfather, F. A. Eddings, built when he developed the resort. She knew it had the same floor plan as Gardenia Cottage, where, ironically, Fred Eddings had drawn his last breath only days before.

The house was dark, with a screen porch that ran across the back.

"How do you propose we get in?" Whelan asked.

Just then a light blinked on from within the house, and a couple of silhouetted figures were visible moving about.

"We're gonna walk up and tell the sheriff we're here."

"And if the sheriff doesn't like that plan?"

"He'll have to arrest me. But I'm betting he doesn't have the will, or the time, to do that before Madelyn arrives."

"You really think she'll show up?"

"She can't afford not to. That prenup? She's got to convince Garrett to keep his mouth shut, or she'll lose everything."

The door to the screened porch was unlocked. They stepped inside, then walked over to the French doors leading inside, where they saw the sheriff and Shapley, who was taping something to Garrett's bare chest.

She tapped lightly on the glass. The sheriff whirled around, his hand on his holstered service weapon.

"Judas Priest!" he exclaimed, opening the door. "You're lucky I didn't just put a bullet in you. What the hell are you two doing here? I don't want you spooking our suspect."

Traci stepped past him. Whelan hesitated for a moment, then followed.

"We won't spook anyone." She pointed to a doorway on the far wall of the living room. "That's the powder room. We can hang out in there."

"This is so fucked up," Garrett moaned. His nose was bandaged, but already bruises bloomed beneath both eyes. "As soon as she sees me like this, she's gonna figure it out."

"Tell her you got in a fistfight with KJ," Whelan suggested.

"Did you text her yet?" Traci asked, looking around the living room, wondering if Madelyn had ripped off Anita Deibel the way she'd ripped off the Saint. She touched the drapery stretching across the front window, which was some kind of cheap, synthetic fabric. Yup, Madelyn had been here. She pointed at Garrett, who'd pulled his shirt down. "Is he miked up?"

"Never mind that," Coyle said. "You two need to leave. Now."

Shapley walked to the front of the house. "Too late," he called softly. "She just pulled into the driveway."

"Judas Priest!" Coyle pointed to the powder room. "Get in there and don't make a goddamn sound."

———

The powder room in Oleander Cottage was much smaller than the one in Fred Eddings's house. Traci sat on the closed lid of the commode and Whelan leaned against the sink.

They heard the front door open, and the sound of footsteps crossing the tile floor.

"Hey." Garrett's voice was muffled, but audible.

"Oh my God, baby. What happened to your face?"

"Last night I got up to pee and in the dark I tripped over the chair in the bedroom."

"Let me see," Madelyn cooed.

The sound of her sister-in-law's voice made Traci want to puke.

"I'm okay. Just . . . I really need to get the hell out of Dodge. Did you bring the money?"

"I only had a couple hundred. Tomorrow, when I can get to the bank—"

Garrett's voice was shrill. "Jesus, Madelyn. I did everything you told me to. I put my life, my job on the line. A couple hundred?"

"I shouldn't even give you that," Madelyn said. There was a hard edge in her normally breathy little-girl voice. "You had one job. Get rid of Olivia Grayson. Instead you killed Parrish, screwed up the fire at the dorm, and that girl is *still* alive. You could fuck up a one-car funeral."

"None of that was my fault," Garrett protested. "I need money— more than a lousy two hundred bucks—and a car, so I can get off this island. I can't stay here another night, Madelyn."

"Where am I supposed to get a car? Ric's gonna notice if his Porsche goes missing."

"I don't care. Gimme the keys to the Lexus. You can tell him it got stolen."

There was a long pause.

What the fuck? Traci turned to Whelan and mouthed the words.

"Jesus, Madelyn!"

There was a scuffle, and then muffled thuds, and finally, a loud bang, unmistakably a gunshot, followed by a bone-chilling scream, and then more scuffling, and a door banging open.

Whelan reached past her and burst out of the powder room with Traci close behind, at the same time the sheriff and his deputy ran from the nearby master bedroom and tackled Madelyn.

Garrett Wycoff was sprawled on the floor, cradling his right elbow, in a spreading pool of blood, moaning and cursing. The sheriff hauled Madelyn, dressed in her stylish pastel Lululemon workout gear, to her feet. She squirmed as Coyle pinned her arms behind her back and snapped handcuffs on her wrists.

Shapley pulled a radio from his utility belt and called for an ambulance.

Madelyn's eyes narrowed when she noticed her sister-in-law. "What the hell are you doing here?"

"I came to watch you get your ass arrested," Traci said. She whipped her phone from the pocket of her jeans and clicked off a few frames. "Smile, please."

Traci looked over at Shapley, who was kneeling beside Garrett, wrapping a towel around his arm. "She shot me," Garrett whimpered. He looked over at Traci. "You believe she shot me?"

"You needed shooting," Traci said. "So does she."

CHAPTER 74

* * *

"Long night," Whelan said as they crept into Traci's kitchen at two in the morning. Lola, asleep in her bed beneath the kitchen table, picked up her head, wagged her tail, and promptly went back to sleep.

"The longest," she agreed.

He picked up the car keys he'd left on the counter, brushing a chaste kiss on her forehead before heading for the front door.

"You're leaving?" She caught his hand with hers.

He stood very still. "You want me to stay?"

"Yeah. I, uh, I do."

He pointed to the hall and the guest bedroom. "What about Felice? And the very clear, completely unambiguous company policy about romantic interactions between supervisors and employees?"

"I think maybe I had a moment of clarity tonight."

"Really? When did that happen? In between rushing to save Felice from a gun-wielding assailant and watching your sister-in-law get handcuffed and shoved into the back of a police cruiser?"

"I can't pinpoint the exact moment. But hiding out in that tiny little bathroom with you, and then walking back here with you, it struck me that things could have gone sideways a couple of times tonight. What if we hadn't gotten that gun away from Garrett? What if the bullet from Madelyn's gun—I don't know, what if it had ricocheted, and hit one of us? I don't want to watch you drive away tonight, Whelan, and wonder what if? What you said earlier, about wanting to be with me, and wanting more? You were right. I do want more. I *deserve* more. And I don't want to waste any more time thinking about the what-ifs."

He wrapped his arms around her waist and kissed her. "Well, since you put it like that, I don't think the company policy is going to be a problem anymore. Because I quit."

Traci frowned. "You can't quit."

"Why not?"

"Because you're fired. I'll file the paperwork first thing in the morning."

"Me? Why?"

She started to unbuckle his belt, but thought better of it. Instead, she took his hand in hers and began to lead him in the direction of her bedroom.

"Sexual harassment," she said.

He stopped and pulled her toward him. "Sounds promising."

CHAPTER 75

* * *

Six Weeks Later

Traci was loading groceries into her car when she glanced across the street and spotted the black Porsche. It was parked in a handicapped parking space. Typical.

She was waiting, leaning against the hood of his car, when Ric Eddings emerged from the liquor store with what she assumed was a handle of scotch wrapped in a brown paper sack.

He clicked the remote to unlock the Porsche, ignoring her presence. He tried to step past her, but she didn't budge, deliberately blocking access in the narrow slot.

"Do you mind?" He was looking up the street, shifting from one foot to the other, impatient to get away, either from the parking services officer, whose light utility vehicle was paused up the street a block away, or from Traci.

"Actually, I do. I've been calling and texting for the past six weeks. We need to talk, Ric."

He scowled. "I've got nothing to say to you. Or your little protégé."

"Are you referring to Olivia? Your half sister?"

"Get away from me," Ric said, deliberately hip-checking her. She bumped him back hard, apparently catching him off guard, because he went sprawling onto the asphalt road.

He scrambled to his feet, his face flushed with a mixture of rage and embarrassment. "You fucking bitch. I'll see you and your scammer friend in court. I don't care how long it takes. She's not getting a dime of the old man's money."

Traci cocked her head to get a good look at him. His nose was bulbous, the veins enlarged, and the whites of his eyes were yellowish. He'd lost weight and his expensive golf clothes hung off his formerly stocky frame. His hair needed cutting, and he'd started growing a patchy beard, which was coming in gray. He was aging before her eyes.

"Hope you hired a better lawyer than that hack you got to draw up that last will of Fred's," she taunted.

"You're the worst thing that ever happened to my family," Ric said, turning back to the Porsche. "Now get the fuck out of my way."

She was unmoved by her brother-in-law's hostility. "You'd like to blame everything that's happened on me, wouldn't you? But here's the thing, Ric."

She tapped his chest with her forefinger, and he slapped her hand away, but she was undeterred.

"You are the architect of all your own misfortune. You screwed around on Madelyn, so she screwed around on you with Garrett as payback because she knew that prenup meant she'd get nothing if she left the marriage. You tried to screw me over by having your father's will rewritten, but all you managed to do was screw yourself—because you didn't know you had a secret half sister."

"Don't!" Ric said, his voice sharp.

"You can deny it all you want, but there's a paternity test that says otherwise. Madelyn found it, and the NDA that Fred forced Shannon to sign, when she was packing up to move him out of the big house. So she came up with a plan to erase Livvy from the Eddings family picture. Instead, she managed to kill the only thing you ever truly loved. Parrish."

At the mention of his daughter's name, Ric reached past Traci and grabbed the Porsche's door handle. But Traci stood her ground.

"You can't scare me off, and you can't screw me over anymore, Ric. I'm going to see to it that your old man and you finally do right by Olivia. You want to drag things out in a long court battle, have at it. You'll end up just like Fred. Rich, yeah. But sick and bitter. And alone."

He was facing Traci now, his back to the street, so he didn't see the meter maid, who'd alighted from her vehicle and was approaching with a gleam in her eye and a ticket book in her hand.

"I'll never stop missing Hoke or Parrish. They'll always be a part of my life. But they're the past, and I'm choosing to move ahead." She turned to go back to her car, and Ric started to say something.

"Sir?"

He turned to see the meter maid, scribbling something on her pad.

"I was just leaving," he protested.

She ripped the ticket from the pad and handed it over. "Take this with you. Five-hundred-dollar fine for parking in a handicapped space."

EPILOGUE

* * *

One Year Later

"Almost ready?" Traci glanced over at her unlikely business partner, who'd dashed into the Saint lobby with only minutes to spare.

The sun was low on the horizon and the drinks had been flowing since the hotel doors were thrown open an hour earlier.

Livvy took a deep breath and nervously adjusted the wide silk sash of her deep-rose-pink ankle-length gown. A wildly expensive selection from the hotel's new designer boutique, the silk dress and even the sandals, metallic bronze with a wedge heel, had been a "coming out gift," from Traci, who'd insisted that Olivia had to look the part if she was going to play the part.

"I don't know if I can do this," Livvy whispered. At least a couple hundred people, members and hotel guests, were gathered on the Riverside patio outside, waiting expectantly.

"Nobody knows if they can do something until they do it," Traci said, her face glowing with a newfound serenity. Her hands rested protectively on her abdomen, at the barely discernible bump beneath her own flowing pink caftan.

"Ain't that the truth," Whelan quipped as he reached out for her hand and gave it a gentle squeeze.

"No, seriously, I feel like I might barf," Livvy said. "There were six television vans with their crews set up outside the front gates when I drove down from Savannah just now, including one from CNN.

There was a story in this week's *People* magazine." Livvy shuddered as she repeated the headline. "'Sins of the Fathers: Money, Murder and Mayhem Among the Magnolias.' A producer from *Dateline* has been texting and calling me. They want to interview me for the story they're doing on Madelyn. They've already done a jailhouse interview with that scumbag Garrett."

"What does Andy say? About the *Dateline* story?"

"Mr. Plankenhorn thinks I should wait, at least until the trial is over. And I agree. This whole thing is majorly cringe."

Livvy wasn't exaggerating. Madelyn Eddings's arrest for the murder of Parrish, combined with the attempted murder of Livvy and Felice, had touched off a national media melee. The press couldn't get enough of the salacious details—how Ric Eddings's wife seduced a waiter fifteen years her junior to enlist him in a plan to eliminate a newly found rival for the Eddings family fortune, and how the plan had backfired when a stoned musician named Cedric had bungled the delivery of the fentanyl-spiked joint, serving it instead to Madelyn's stepdaughter Parrish with lethal consequences.

The tangled web of extortion, blackmail, arson, and theft that Madelyn and her partners in crime spun was still generating ripples of scandal, even a year later. KJ Parkhurst had cut a deal to testify against his co-defendants, and was serving a five-year prison term, but Charlie Burroughs hadn't survived the injuries he'd sustained while fleeing from the state patrol.

"I feel like everyone is looking at me. Just waiting for Fred Eddings's bastard kid to screw up," Livvy said.

Traci tucked her arm through Livvy's. "Get used to it, kiddo. They used to look at me the same way, after I married Hoke. Everyone, including his family, wondered how an Ain't like me managed to snag a prize like Hoke. After he died, when I had to step in to run the hotel on my own, people, especially Fred and Ric, were always watching, waiting for me to screw up. Spoiler alert, Liv. You're gonna screw up. Hopefully your screwups won't be as massive as mine were, but it's gonna happen. The difference is, I'll be here to help you when it does."

"I'll be here too," Whelan reminded her. It had taken both women months to convince him, but Whelan had finally, reluctantly agreed to take on the role of the Saint's general manager.

"I don't know a damn thing about running a hotel," he'd protested when Livvy broached the subject.

"Neither do I. But you know how to run a business, and Traci knows hotels, and I'm learning. So we'll learn together."

"At the very least you won't try to steal us blind, right?" Livvy joked.

A server in a white jacket paused in front of them with a silver tray laden with flutes of prosecco. Livvy took a glass and sipped while the waiter looked expectantly at Whelan. "Sir? Bourbon rocks?"

"And a club soda for Mrs. Whelan, when you get a minute."

"Is your mom coming tonight?" Traci asked Livvy. "I left a pass at the gate for her."

"We called when the plane landed in Savannah, and she said she wasn't sure. You know how she is about this place. Still thinks there's a bogeyman hiding behind every oak tree."

The waiter was back with their drinks. Whelan handed the club soda to Traci and took a sip of his bourbon. "We?" he said, quirking an eyebrow. "Who's 'we'?"

"Whelan!" Livvy and Traci groaned in unison.

"She's told you all about Nick," Traci said. "Multiple times."

"You actually met him when we were here over Christmas," Livvy added. "You took him out fishing on the *Little Miss Magic*."

"Oh yeah. Now I remember. He's the character who can't tell a flounder from a redfish."

"Stop," Traci said, elbowing him. "You told me you liked Nick a lot."

"I believe what I said was that he's okay. For a Yankee."

"He is *not* a Yankee. He's from Baltimore," Livvy said.

"An Orioles fan? Surely you can do better than that," Whelan said.

"Could you just be nice to him? Please? I really like him, and I think he likes me. His family is great. I invited them down for Beach Bash next weekend, but they already had plans. They want me to come stay at their cabin in Maine later this summer."

"Sounds like it's getting kind of serious," Traci said. "What's Shannon say about that?"

"Weirdly, I think she's okay with it. Anyway, she's much too busy having her own little fling to worry about my love life. I call him Dr. BoyToy just to mess with her," Livvy confessed. "But I think it's awesome that she's finally allowing herself to cut loose and have some fun. I was kind of worried she'd be all weird and lonely with me away at school at Georgetown."

"Shannon is doing just fine. We saw her out with the doctor last month, at the Community Chest fundraiser. She looked fabulous . . ."

"Heyyyyy, y'all." Felice approached with an enormous silver platter of appetizers. She slung an arm around Livvy's shoulder. "When did you get in? I didn't see your car over at Gardenia."

"Felice!" Livvy hugged her former roommate, who was dressed in head-to-toe pink, from her pink-and-white houndstooth-check pants to her monogrammed chef's coat to the towering pink toque. Livvy looked her up and down. "Gurl! Where's the rest of you?"

"I'm thirty pounds lighter," Felice said, beaming. "I took up running."

"And Pilates," Traci added. "She's a beast."

Livvy helped herself to a tiny canapé. "Ohmygawd! It's divine. What is this?"

"Shrimp Louis bites in puff pastry. I just added them to the summer menu. You like?"

"Looovve," Livvy said. "How's the new apartment?"

"Haven't moved in yet," Felice said. "The kitchen countertops are back-ordered."

"She's still camping out in Whelan's old place in the village," Traci said. "But Javi swears the first six staff housing units will be done by Memorial Day."

"Sweetheart?" Whelan said, nudging her. "Hate to interrupt, but I think it's almost go time." He pointed out at the lowering sky, which had turned a deep purple, shot through with streaks of gold and orange.

"I better get back to my kitchen," Felice said. "Training a new sous-chef."

"You're coming by the cottage later, right?" Livvy asked.

Felice ducked her head. "I would, but I've kinda got a date."

"Bring him over tonight," Livvy begged. "Nick and I want to meet him."

"You already did. Remember Dave? The EMT from that night at the dorm?"

"Fortunately, I still have large memory gaps from that night," Livvy said ruefully. "But a hot EMT is always a good idea, right?"

"He's not usually a late-night guy, but maybe he'll make an exception for you. And me."

"Would you look at that sunset?" Traci asked. She took Livvy's hand in hers as Leo opened the double doors to the patio. The two of them strolled out onto the flagstones, while Whelan lingered a few steps behind, content to sip his bourbon and watch the two women step into the spotlight.

"Don't be nervous," Traci murmured, smiling and nodding her head at familiar faces in the crowd. But she was surprised to feel the butterflies in her own stomach: the uncertainty, the self-doubt, the vulnerability, the fear. But then she remembered a piece of advice Hoke had given her so many years ago. "If what you're doing doesn't terrify you, you're not doing it right."

The Saint's members, the old-guard regulars, and some of the repeat hotel guests greeted the resort's new co-owner with enthusiastic applause, and some whistles from a sandy-haired young man near the bar whom Traci assumed was Livvy's beau Nick.

A trumpeter stepped down to the water's edge, and as the sun melted into the river's mirror-like gray-green surface he played the opening notes of "Retreat," startling a lone egret who squawked indignantly before taking flight, silhouetted against the final blaze of sunlight.

Livvy raised her glass and turned to face the assembled members. "Here's to another beautiful summer at the Saint," she called, in a clear, loud voice. Glasses were clinked and prosecco was drunk. A jazz quartet, Livvy's idea, struck up "Summertime," and servers circulated with trays of appetizers.

Livvy was quickly surrounded by well-wishers, congratulating her on her new role at the hotel. She circulated among her guests, laughing and chatting like the seasoned hospitality professional she was—baptized, as Traci reflected, by fire.

After an hour or so, Traci leaned her head on her husband's shoulder. "Take me home?"

"Always," Whelan said, the smile lines at the corners of his eyes crinkling as he kissed the top of her head.

He helped her into the front seat of the golf cart and they set off on their now routine circuit of the property, down the winding cart paths cut through deep green swaths of grass. Twilight had descended, and with it, the thrum of cicadas, which Traci thought of as summer's perpetual soundtrack.

The path wound past Gardenia Cottage, which had been deeded over to Livvy following the bruising court fight with Ric Eddings, who'd filed for divorce from Madelyn within hours of her arrest for the murder of her stepdaughter.

Fred Eddings's wheelchair ramp had been removed. Livvy had slowly begun decorating the place to her own taste, and Traci had spent hours over the previous weeks making sure the cottage would be ready when its new owner returned home for summer break.

"Let's go past the villas," she said, trying to suppress a yawn. "I want to see how much progress the guys made today."

"You're driving poor Javi crazy, you know," Whelan said, veering off the path and onto the road that would take them to the site of the former dorm.

"I just need them to feel more of a sense of urgency to finish the units," Traci said as they approached the site.

Whelan braked the cart to a stop. "Look!" he whispered, pointing to the right side of the road. A doe nibbled at something in the grass, while two wobbly legged fawns stayed close by.

"Ohhh," Traci breathed. "So beautiful." Just then, the doe looked up, twitched her tail, and bounded away into the woods, followed by her babies.

He started the cart again and soon they'd arrived at the cluster of cottages Traci had christened the Little Saint. Built in the same Spanish revival style as the hotel, with exteriors of pale pink stucco, the villas were arranged in a horseshoe shape around a central greenspace courtyard that would provide a place for residents to gather for barbecuing, games, socializing, and relaxing.

"It's going to be nice, right?" Traci asked, snuggling up next to her husband on the bench seat.

"Very nice," Whelan agreed. "Let's go home now, okay, boss-lady?"

Traci sighed contentedly. "Home sounds perfect. I was thinking you could start assembling the baby's crib tonight."

He pulled her closer. "Maybe later." He whispered his plans for the evening in her ear and she blushed.

"Home it is."

ACKNOWLEDGMENTS

* * *

Dear Readers:

My list of acknowledgments must start with you—all of you who consider my latest book an "auto-buy," who preorder, show up at book events, request that your library purchase my books, comment on my social media posts, leave five-star online reviews, and otherwise continue to support me as a writer. Thank you, thank you!

Booksellers, bookstore owners, librarians, I salute and thank you for putting my books into the hands of readers.

For research for *Summers at the Saint*, I am grateful to Chris May, Christina York, Connie Lassiter, Mary Balent Long, Esq., and G. M. Lloyd.

My Friends and Fiction cofounders and coconspirators: Patti Callahan Henry, Kristy Woodson Harvey, and Kristin Harmel; plus librarian Ron Block and Meg Walker of Tandem Literary, (the Swiss Army Knife of book marketers) have been with me every step of the way on this book's journey to publication, from the first glimmering of the idea through seven a.m. writing sprints, through the agony of revision and the ecstasy of (finally) typing THE END. I can't think of a better crew to have had with me in the trenches. Also, thanks to AV nerd Shaun Hettinger, for literally pushing the buttons and making sure we actually go LIVE week after week.

Those of you in our more than 225,000-strong Friends and Fiction community have my everlasting gratitude for hanging out with us on Wednesday nights for the past four years. (And buying our books!)

As always, I am so thankful for the wisdom, guidance, humor, and saintly patience of Stuart Krichevsky, my agent of more than two decades, and his gang at SKLA. Ditto to Meg Walker, for her advice, marketing expertise, and willingness to be my book tour roadie. To Team MKA at St. Martin's Press, led by my genius editor and publisher Jennifer Enderlin, there are not enough words to express my thanks and admiration. Huge thanks to the entire SMP team, but especially Jessica Zimmerman and Erica Martirano.

Never last and never least, my family: Tom, Andy and Meg, Mark, Molly and Griffin, and Sarah sustain me with their endless love and support.

ABOUT THE AUTHOR

* * *

Credit: Bill Miles

Mary Kay Andrews is the *New York Times* bestselling author of *Bright Lights, Big Christmas; The Homewreckers; The Santa Suit; The Newcomer; Hello, Summer; Sunset Beach; The High Tide Club; The Beach House Cookbook; The Weekenders; Beach Town; Save the Date; Ladies' Night; Christmas Bliss; Spring Fever; Summer Rental; The Fixer Upper; Deep Dish; Blue Christmas; Savannah Breeze; Hissy Fit; Little Bitty Lies;* and *Savannah Blues*. A former journalist for *The Atlanta Journal-Constitution*, she lives in Atlanta, Georgia.